Redemption

WHAT READERS ARE SAYING

"This is the first book I have ever read by this author and I have to say I couldn't put it down till I finished it. What a ride I got! Love, action, excitement, crime families—heck, what more could you ask??"
—Amazon reader "cedarblue," 5 stars (on *Malavita*)

"This story truly exceeded my expectations. *Revenge* is action-packed, and when the pace picks up, it does not slow down.... I cannot wait to read the next book."
—*The Romance Reviews (TRR)* site, 5 stars, Top Pick (on *Revenge*)

"Here is to a WHOOPING 5 stars. If I had to describe this book in about four words, it would be action-packed, sexy, romantic, and adrenaline-rushing.... This would make a kick-butt movie! There were times when I was fanning myself, sitting on the edge of my seat, and so mad I had to put it down. The steamy scenes were oh so delicious!"
—*Reading on the Wild Side* blog, 5 stars (on *Revenge*)

"The suspense keeps the pages moving quickly in book two of the Blood and Honor series. A fast pace, credible characters and a complex plot guarantee hours of entertainment."
—*RT Book Reviews* magazine, 4 stars (on *Retribution*)

"*Redemption* knocks it out of the PARK!!! This is the novel I was waiting for!!! ...I was blown out of the water on this one."
—*Steph's Book Retreat* blog, 5 stars (on *Redemption*)

"This series is awesome!!! If this series was ever made into a movie, it would put *The Godfather* to shame! I am always pulled into the lives that Dana creates in her books, heart beating so fast it is like I am part of the story line!!! If you are looking for fantastic writing style and being pulled into a story, this is it!! I VERY HIGHLY RECOMMEND THIS BOOK. I WANT TO GIVE IT MORE THAN 5 STARS."
—*Julie's Book Reviews* blog, 5 stars (on *Redemption*)

"When I compare the quality of the writing, the complexity of the plot, and the development of the characters in this series to other books I have awarded 4 or even 4.5 stars to, this one is clearly worthy of a much higher rating than many of them. Not only do I look forward to reading more in the series, I am also really excited and can hardly wait."
—*Lindsay and Jane's Views and Reviews* blog, 5 stars (on *Redemption*)

ALSO BY DANA DELAMAR

Blood and Honor Series: Mafia Romance

Malavita (Prequel)
Revenge (Book One)
Retribution (Book Two)
Redemption (Book Three)
Reckoning (Book Four)

Writing with Kristine Cayne

Total Indulgence Series: MMF Ménage Romance

Her Two Men in London (Book One)
Her Two Men in Tahiti (Book Two)
Her Two Men in Sonoma (Book Three) – coming 2018

Redemption

BLOOD AND HONOR
BOOK 3

DANA DELAMAR

ISBN (print): 0984931163
ISBN-13 (print): 978-0-9849311-6-3
ISBN (ebook): 0984931171
ISBN-13 (ebook): 978-0-9849311-7-0

Publisher's Note: This is a work of fiction. Names, characters, places, and incidents either are the product of the author's imagination or are used fictitiously, and any resemblance to actual persons, living or dead, business establishments, events, or locales is entirely coincidental.

Book cover design by Dana Delamar © 2018

Cover photo: © Depositphotos.com/tverdohlib.com

Title page logo design by Scarlett Rugers © 2012

Author image courtesy of LGImages

Ebook formatting: LK Ebook Formatting

Editing, proofreading, and print formatting:
By Your Side Self-Publishing
www.ByYourSideSelfPub.com

ACKNOWLEDGMENTS

Many people contributed to the creation of this book. No writer goes it alone, and I am certainly no exception.

As always, I can never adequately thank my wonderful critique partner, Kristine Cayne. She devoted many, many hours of her time and attention to this book, and it is vastly improved as a result. Thank you, thank you, thank you!

I'd also like to thank my beta readers, Kim, Stephanie, and Trish, for their insights, comments, and catches. You made this book better than it was!

Many thanks to Luigia Tella for promptly and thoroughly answering my questions about Italy. Any errors are my own.

I owe a great debt to Romance Writers of America® and specifically my hometown RWA® chapters, Eastside RWA and Greater Seattle RWA, for providing inspiration, support, guidance, friendship, real-world craft advice, industry contacts, and knowledge that proved invaluable. Thank you all.

Last but not least, I'd like to thank my family, my friends, and most of all, my ever-patient husband, James Davis, for bearing with my craziness. You will always be my honey bunny.

CAST OF CHARACTERS

The Lucchesis

Enrico Lucchesi (LOO kay zee) – *capo* (head) of the Lucchesi *cosca* (crime family)

Kate Lucchesi – wife of Enrico Lucchesi

Antonio Legato – *capo di società* (second in command) of the Lucchesi *cosca*

Bianca Lucchesi – daughter of Domenico Lucchesi, Enrico Lucchesi's first cousin

Fedele (feh DAY lay) **Lucchesi** (deceased), **Alessandro (Sandro) Lucchesi, Matteo Lucchesi** – brothers of Bianca Lucchesi and sons of Domenico Lucchesi

Francesca Lucchesi – mother to Bianca, Sandro, and Matteo Lucchesi; widow of Domenico Lucchesi

Ruggero (rooj JAIR oh) **Vela** – bodyguard to Enrico Lucchesi

Nick Clarkston – illegitimate son of Enrico Lucchesi; Interpol agent

Delfina Clarkston (née Andretti) – daughter of Dario Andretti; married to Nick Clarkston

Rinaldo Lucchesi – deceased; Enrico Lucchesi's father; former *capo*

Domenico (Dom) Lucchesi – deceased; first cousin to Enrico Lucchesi and former *capo di società* of the Lucchesi *cosca*

Antonella (Toni) Lucchesi (née Andretti) – deceased; Enrico's first wife; daughter to Carlo Andretti and sister to Dario Andretti

CAST OF CHARACTERS (cont.)

The Andrettis

Dario Andretti – *capo* of the Andretti *cosca* (Milan branch)

Ilaria (ee LAR ee ah) **Andretti** – wife to Dario Andretti

Lorenzo Andretti – grandfather of Dario Andretti; *capo* of the Andretti *cosca* (Calabrian branch); head of La Provincia (ruling commission of the 'Ndrangheta, the Calabrian Mafia)

Cristoforo (Cris) Andretti – son of Dario Andretti and *capo di società* of the Andretti *cosca* (Milan branch)

Benedetto Andretti – deceased; son of Lorenzo Andretti; former *capo di società* of the Andretti *cosca* (Calabrian branch) and head of La Provincia

Carlo Andretti – deceased; son of Lorenzo Andretti; former *capo* of the Andretti *cosca* (Milan branch)

Salvatore (Sal) Ruscino – brother-in-law to Benedetto Andretti; *capo di società* of the Andretti *cosca* (Calabrian branch)

Other Characters

Giovanna (joh VAN ah) **(Gio)** (Joh) **d'Imperio** – daughter of Gianluca d'Imperio

Gianluca (jon LOO kah) **d'Imperio** – *capo* of the d'Imperio *cosca*

Leandro (lay AHN droh) **d'Imperio** – *capo di società* of the d'Imperio *cosca*

Orlando Farnese – nephew of Ruggero Vela

Violetta Legato – sister of Antonio Legato

Vittorio Battista – godfather to Enrico Lucchesi and *capo* of the Battista *cosca*

Silvio Fuente – officer of the *carabinieri*

GLOSSARY OF TERMS

bambina/bambino (bam BEE nah/bam BEE noh) – baby, child

basta (BAHS tah) – enough (as in "I've had enough!" or "Stop!")

bella/bello, bellissima (BEHL lah/BEHL loh, behl LEE see mah) – beautiful

bene (BEN ay) – good

bisnonno (beez NOH noh) – great-grandfather

buon Natale (BWOHN nah TAH lay) – Merry Christmas

buongiorno (bwohn JOR noh) – good morning/afternoon; hello

capisci (KAH pee shee) – you see, you understand

capo (KAH poh) – head (don) of a crime family (*cosca*); plural *capi* (KAH pee)

capo di società (KAH poh DEE so cheh TAH) – second in command of a *cosca*

Capodanno (kah poh DAHN noh) – New Year's Day

cara (CAR ah), *caro* (CAR oh) – dear, sweetheart

carabinieri (car ah bin YAIR ee) – Italy's national police force; a single member of this force is a *carabiniere* (car ah bin YAIR ay)

ciao (CHOW) – informal hello and goodbye

comparaggio (cohm pah RAH joe) – the Southern Italian institution of co-parenthood, whereby the person making this vow swears to be as a parent to the child. A co-father is referred to as *compare*; the "parent" and "child" are *compari*. The vow is thought of as indissoluble and incorruptible. Within the Mafia, *compari* will not betray each other.

contabile (cone TAH bee lay) – accountant; treasurer for a *cosca*

cosca (KOHS kah) – a crime family; plural is *cosche* (KOHS kay)

Cristo (KREES toe) – Christ

davvero (dahv VAIR oh) – really, seriously

Dio mio (DEE oh MEE oh) – my God

dottore (dote TOR ay) – doctor; the "e" is dropped when used with a last name

fidanzato (fee dahn TZA toh) – fiancé

figlio (FEEL yoh) – son

grazie (GRAHTZ yeh) – thanks. *Mille* (MEE lay) *grazie* means "Many thanks."

idiota (ee dee OH tah) – idiot

Madonna (ma DOEN nah) – the Virgin Mary; Mother of God

malavita (mah lah VEE tah) – the criminal underworld, the criminal life

mandamento (MAHN de men toh) – district, region; plural is *mandamenti*

merda (MARE dah) – shit

mi dispiace (MEE dees pee YAH chay) – I'm sorry

minchia (MEEN kee ah) – holy shit, fuck

molto (MOLE toe) – very, a great deal, a lot

Natale (nah TAH lay) – Christmas

'Ndrangheta (en DRAHNG eh tah) – the Calabrian Mafia, or "The Honored Society." Members are *'Ndranghetisti* (en DRAHNG eh tees tee), or "men of honor." A single member is an *'Ndranghetista*.

nonna (NOHN nah), *nonnina* (nohn NEE nah) – grandmother, granny

nonno (NOHN noh) – grandfather

padrino (pah DREE noh) – godfather

panettone (pah net TOH nay) – traditional (Christmas) cake from Milan

papà (pah PAH) – dad

pasticceria (pah stee chah REE ah) – pastry shop, bakery

per favore (PAIR fah VOR ay) – please

perfetto (pair FEHT toe) – perfect

polizia (poh leet TZEE ah) – Italian police

pollo alla cacciatora (POH loh AH lah catch a TOR ay) – chicken Cacciatore

porco Dio (POR koh DEE oh) – literally "pig God"; *very* vulgar religious curse

porca miseria (POR kah mee ZAIR ee ah) – literally "pig misery"; means "damn" or "bloody hell"

prego (PRAY go) – welcome

principessa, principe (prin chee PESS ah, PRIN chee pay) – princess, prince

puttana (poot TAH nah) – whore, prostitute

GLOSSARY OF TERMS (cont.)

ragazza, ragazzo (rah GAHTZ ah, rah GAHTZ oh) – girlfriend, boyfriend

sì (CEE) – yes

signore, signora, signorina (seen YOR ay, seen YOR ah, seen yor REEN ah) – sir, madam, miss; the "e" is dropped from *signore* when used with a last name

Sottotenente (soh toh teh NEN tay) – Second Lieutenant

stronzo (STRON tzoh) – shit, turd, bastard

tesoro (tay ZOR oh) – darling, honey (literally "treasure")

ti amo tanto (TEE AH moe TAHN toh) – I love you so much

troia (TROY ah) – slut; plural is *troie*

vacca (VAHK kah) – cow, whore

vaffanculo (vahf fahn COO loh) – go fuck yourself

vai con Dio (VEYE COHN DEE oh) – go with God

zio (TZEE oh) – uncle

PROLOGUE

Eleven years ago
Rome, Italy

On a day like this, the sun shouldn't be shining. Not when his parents were dead, his older brother dead. The sky should be weeping, like Antonio's little sister, Violetta, who clutched his hand in the hospital waiting room. "Hush," he whispered to her, stroking her hair, making his voice gentle, steady, even though he shivered inside. She was only six, not ten and a half like he was. She was still a baby.

"I want Mamma," Violetta said.

So do I. But he couldn't say that aloud. "Zio Gino is coming for us."

Her wailing increased, and the nurse behind the counter looked over at them. Antonio pulled his sister onto his lap, letting her wrap her skinny arms around his chest, her damp face burrowing into his shirt, despite the blood covering it. Blood from their parents, blood from their brother Aldo. He hadn't been able to do anything for them. All he'd been able to do was pull Violetta from the car wreck. Somehow, the two of them had escaped with only bruises and scrapes.

"Violetta." Their uncle crouched down in front of them and placed a hand on her knee. Relief swept through Antonio, and the shaking in his belly moved up into his chest, the sob that had been building for hours trying to escape. He wanted to let it out, but something in his uncle's face stopped him. He was looking anywhere but at Antonio.

"Zio!" Violetta launched herself from Antonio's grasp and into Uncle Gino's arms. "What's happened to Mamma and Papà and Aldo?"

"They're gone, *cara*. To heaven. With Nonna Clara and Nonno Ugo."

A fresh wail burst from Violetta's lips. "No!"

Frozen, Antonio watched his uncle comfort her. "Shh, *bambina*, it'll be all right." He was staring at Antonio as he said this, but his eyes flicked away again. What was wrong?

Antonio finally forced himself to speak. "Zio?"

1

A slight shake of his uncle's head, his frown stern, his gaze fixed on the floor. "We can afford only one child."

Antonio's stomach clenched into a ball. Only one of them? But there was no decision to make. "Take Violetta."

His uncle nodded. "That is what I thought to do."

"Will Nonna Agnese and Nonno Vitale take me?" Antonio asked.

Again, another slight shake. "They are too old, Tonio. They have to live with us now."

Tears blurred Antonio's vision, but he blinked them back. "Where will I go then?"

"The government will take care of you. They will find a home for you. Another family."

But I don't want another family. I don't want anyone else but you. He kept the words stuffed inside, lodged in his throat. At least Violetta would be taken care of. That much he could be thankful for.

He wanted to cry, to beg his uncle to take him too. But he had to be a man, not a boy. He had to be strong for his sister. Violetta leaned toward him, grabbing his hand, her big brown eyes wet with tears. "Tonio, I don't want you to go."

"It's just for a while." Focusing on his uncle, he asked, "You'll visit, yes?"

"Yes." But again he didn't meet Antonio's gaze.

Oh. Antonio swallowed hard, understanding in an instant. This was goodbye. Forever. They wouldn't come, wouldn't keep track of him. Maybe Violetta would try, but she was only six. In time she'd forget him. He would be just a dim memory to her, little more than a ghost, like his parents and Aldo.

"Be good and brave," Antonio said to her, giving her a quick hug.

"I will." She clutched his shirt and burst into tears again. "I'll miss you, Tonio," she choked out, her breath catching and hitching.

"I'll miss you too, Vee." His voice was so thick he wasn't sure she could understand him. "Take good care of her," he said to his uncle.

Zio Gino gently detached Violetta's hand from Antonio's shirt. "We'd best leave now."

Antonio nodded, unable to make a sound. When the social worker came for him a short time later, he still couldn't speak. He pretended to listen when she spoke, her words washing over him, none of them what he wanted to hear. Something about an orphanage in Rome. Something about how someday he'd have a new family.

None of it mattered anyway. The only people who mattered, the only things that mattered, were gone.

He was alone. A boy with no family. A boy with no home.

CHAPTER 1

Present day
Milan, Italy

Something was wrong, but figuring it out seemed beyond him at the moment. Slowly stretching his injured left shoulder, Antonio Legato slumped down in his office chair and closed his eyes, shutting out the spreadsheets he'd been staring at. His first day back at work at the Banca di Falcone, and he felt utterly lost. Not to mention more tired than usual. He'd never had to recover from a gunshot wound before—much less two of them—despite having worked for Don Enrico Lucchesi for coming up on two years. Although Antonio had been shot at several times, he'd never been seriously hurt. Up until the engagement party for the don's son, six weeks ago.

Pushing back from the desk, Antonio rose and paced over to the window, looking out at the beautiful park across the street. Leave it to Don Lucchesi to pick such a scenic spot for his bank.

With a sigh, Antonio pressed his forehead to the window. He really ought to try to make sense of the figures in La Provincia's account. Right now they didn't, and considering that the account was the repository of all the funds the various families in the 'Ndrangheta, the Calabrian Mafia, were contributing to the war effort against the Russian *Mafiya*, many powerful men had a keen interest in what happened to that money. The most powerful of those men being Don Lorenzo Andretti, the head of La Provincia—the quasi-ruling body of the 'Ndrangheta— and head of the Andretti family, until recently the bitter enemies of the Lucchesis.

Supposedly, with the marriage of Don Lucchesi's son Nick to Delfina Andretti, all that enmity was over. Supposedly the two families were united. Supposedly now they'd have peace and common cause against the same enemy: the Russians.

Antonio wasn't so sure though. If the figures he was seeing were any indication, Lorenzo Andretti was up to something. Something bad.

And as Lorenzo Andretti's banker, the Lucchesis were stuck in the middle of the mess—whatever it was. Tomorrow Antonio and Don Lucchesi were flying to Calabria for a meeting of La Provincia, and in case anyone asked, he needed to understand what had happened with the account.

He needed to talk to Don Lucchesi. Surely he'd be able to make sense of all this. Antonio printed out a copy of the last twenty transactions and headed to see the don, his footsteps echoing on the marble floors.

By the time Antonio reached the don's office at the end of the corridor, he had to stretch his shoulder again. The doctors said he'd been damn lucky. He could have been paralyzed or killed.

He hadn't felt lucky at first. He'd lain face down for weeks, too exhausted to move, too drugged up to care, his only bright points in each day the frequent appearances by Kate, Don Lucchesi's wife. She wasn't Antonio's—never would be Antonio's—but he'd caught himself repeatedly fantasizing about what could have been, had she not been in love with the don. The fact that she'd made a fuss over him on his twenty-second birthday, which he'd had to celebrate in bed, had only made it more difficult for him to stop his wayward desires.

Kate's pregnancy agreed with her—her auburn hair seemed thicker, lusher than ever, her creamy white skin aglow whenever she smiled at him and smoothed his unruly hair back. The fact that she was only twenty-nine, so close to him in age, didn't help matters.

When he'd first awakened to Kate's touch in the hospital, Antonio had flashed back to a horrible bout of the flu he'd had at age nine. The year before his parents had been killed. His mother had done the same thing then—brushed his hair out of his face, pressed the cool back of her hand to his cheek. Was it really so much that he desired Kate, or was it more that he enjoyed her loving touch?

He'd had his share of women, but after the first one had cut him to the bone, he'd never allowed any of them in, never given any of the rest the chance to reject him, to size him up and find him wanting. Kate was the first woman in a long, long time he'd let himself care for.

And he shouldn't have. It had been a mistake, and he wasn't sure how to fix it.

Taking a deep breath, he knocked on the don's door, waiting for the summons to enter. When he heard it, he pushed the door open. "Tonio," Don Lucchesi said, greeting him with a smile. "How does it feel to be back?"

Disorienting is what he wanted to say. "Wonderful" is what he said.

"*Bene*. What do you have there?"

"Something I wanted to ask you about."

The don motioned him to one of the chairs in front of his gleaming mahogany desk. "Before we talk about that, there's something we need to discuss."

A tingle started in Antonio's gut. Had he done something wrong? But that was foolish—he'd just come back today. If something was wrong, it couldn't be his fault. "What?" he asked.

Leaning back in his chair, Don Lucchesi crossed his arms. "I'm not quite sure how to say this, but it can't wait any longer." The don shifted in his chair, making the leather creak. He cleared his throat, then said, "I've bought you an apartment in Cernobbio. You'll have Raffaele and anyone else you care to choose as a guard. It's my present to you. For Natale." A chill swept across Antonio's back. If the apartment was a Christmas gift, why was the don's voice so flat?

"I don't understand. You want me to move out?"

"It's time. I need to start treating you like my second in command, not my bodyguard." The don wiped at a bit of dust on his desk, not meeting Antonio's gaze. "We need to strengthen our alliances, and you're going to need a wife and a home of your own. I'm thinking about Giovanna d'Imperio."

Where was all this coming from? This was the first time the don had mentioned Antonio marrying. And then it hit him. "Is this about Kate?"

The don said nothing, but the muscles in his jaw worked. When he spoke, his tone was clipped. "You used to call her *la signora*."

"She insisted on Kate."

The don waved his words away. "You have five days to move your things. The men will take care of it, of course. I want the move completed before Sandro and Matteo's *comparaggio* ceremony, which will be two days before Natale."

Antonio felt like he'd swallowed a stone. A big jagged one. "So you want me out of the way. Do you want me out of the *cosca* too?"

"Of course not. The situation is just tense at the moment."

That was a complete understatement. Ever since Don Lucchesi had been forced to kill Domenico Lucchesi, his first cousin and former *capo di società*, they'd done their damnedest to keep the secret of Don Domenico's treason from his family, from his remaining sons, Sandro and Matteo. Because Don Lucchesi didn't want to have to take their lives too. But the fact that he'd given Antonio the position that Sandro felt rightly belonged to him hadn't gone down well, and relations between the two branches of the family were still rocky, even after the don had taken Sandro into the bank. The *comparaggio* ceremony—whereby the don would recognize Sandro and Matteo as sons—was supposed to mend the rift.

"Should I leave my position here, then? So far today, I've avoided Sandro, and maybe he's been avoiding me too, but that isn't going to last."

"It's not that, Tonio, and you know it. If I'm to keep Sandro and Matteo in this family, if I'm to take them on as sons, I have to make some concessions. And one of them is treating you—"

"Like an employee?"

Don Lucchesi sighed. "'Differently' is what I was going to say."

"So this is just about Sandro and Matteo? Kate has nothing to do with it?"

"It's safer not to have the two of us in the same home."

"Is it? Is that what you would say to Nick if he were here? If he were your *capo di società*?"

Another sigh. "There has been enough strife already. The last thing I want, or need, is to throw more wood on the fire. Dario Andretti has those recordings of Dom somewhere, and if he leaks them, if Sandro and Matteo hear them, they'll know what really happened that night."

The night two and a half months ago when Antonio had urged the don to put a bullet in his cousin Domenico's brain for his betrayal of the family. The night Antonio had learned that sometimes you couldn't trust your own blood.

But then again, he'd already known that, hadn't he? Zio Gino had proved it when he'd taken Violetta and left Antonio behind. Left him to fend for himself.

Left him even after he'd known how horrible life was for Antonio in the orphanage.

What did he keep doing wrong? Zio Gino was only the first person to find Antonio wanting. He hadn't been the last. And now Don Lucchesi was turning his back on Antonio too.

"Tonio, I'm sorry," the don started to say when his secretary opened the door.

"Signorina Lucchesi to see you. Shall I send her in?"

A strange mixture of excitement and dread swirled through Antonio's belly. Had he heard correctly? Bianca was here? He barely had time to wipe the surprise off his face before she walked in. There was no mistaking her—the same rich flowing caramel brown hair, the same flashing green eyes, the same delicate face.

But Bianca was no longer fifteen. She'd filled out into lush curves, and he flashed back to their one and only night together—how she'd arched beneath him and called his name, her nails digging into his shoulders, her breathing ragged in his ears, her scent swirling in his nostrils, driving him to bury his face in her neck, her hair, as he'd groaned his release. She'd been his first. The one he'd given his heart to. The one he'd never forgotten. But she'd forgotten him all too easily, hadn't she?

He met her gaze head-on, hoping his face didn't betray his memories or the emotions they aroused. Alarm registered on her features for just the barest moment before she focused on Don Lucchesi instead.

What the *hell* was she doing here?

———— ◆ ————

Her heart pounding, Bianca Lucchesi smiled at the man she'd come to see while doing her best to ignore the one she'd never wanted to see again. Antonio Legato. She'd arranged to meet her uncle at the bank instead of at his home because she'd hoped to avoid Antonio. And here he was anyway.

Dio mio, would her heart never slow down? One glimpse of him had been enough to bring everything back. Everything she'd tried so damn hard to suppress. To forget.

She widened her smile. "Zio Enrico," she said as he came around the desk and embraced her, kissing her on both cheeks. Marriage had agreed with her godfather. He was still lean, still handsome as sin, with that black hair and those chocolate eyes. He looked happy again—not stricken, the way he'd been at the funerals for her father and her brother Fedele.

"*Prego*," he said, motioning to the chair beside Antonio. "I don't believe you've met my *capo di società*, Antonio Legato."

Would Antonio say something about their past? She stuck out her hand and tried to appear mildly interested. Anything but infuriated. Or hurt. "Don Legato," she said.

Antonio rose and took her hand in his large one. *Cristo*, he'd grown. He was a man now—at least six feet, with the broad shoulders and slim hips of a male in his prime.

His blue eyes met hers, a shock of unruly blond hair falling just over them. Though he seemed a little pale, a wave of heat rolled through her. How many nights had she dreamed of him? How many times had she relived those moments they'd spent together?

He flashed her a casual smile, as if he were completely unaffected by her, and pressed a kiss to her knuckles, the light brush of his lips reminding her of other places he'd kissed.

"Signorina Lucchesi. It's a pleasure. I haven't seen you since secondary school."

"I wasn't aware you knew each other," Enrico said.

"We had a class together," Antonio said. "Chemistry, I believe."

Bianca wanted to kick him in the shin. Was he trying to *flirt* with her? Chemistry! Yes, they'd had it. But outside of class.

"You're mistaken, *signore*. It was biology, not chemistry."

"My error." He was still grinning at her—the arrogant bastard. Did he think she still wanted him? Well, if he did, he was wrong.

Antonio released her hand, and they retook their seats. Bianca's skin tingled where he had touched her, and she resisted the urge to press her hand to her mouth, to feel that tingling against her lips. *Damn him.* Antonio Legato was a hundred different kinds of infuriating.

And he knew it.

"What brings you here today?" Enrico asked her.

She took another breath, then delivered the lie she'd carefully rehearsed. "I'm a bit at loose ends, and I thought perhaps I could help out at the orphanage."

"Of course. I'm sure Dottor Laurio could find something for you to do."

"Perhaps your wife needs help with the records?"

"Perhaps." He smiled. "You'll have to ask her." He leaned forward. "Is that truly what brought you all the way to Milan?"

She'd been prepared for this too. This time she could tell the truth. "I'm concerned about Sandro." She shifted in her seat, all too aware of Antonio beside her. She hadn't counted on having this conversation in front of him. Especially since he was wrapped up in all of it. "Sandro's very upset." She glanced at Antonio. "He feels disrespected." And that was putting it mildly. Don Lucchesi had given Sandro's birthright to Antonio. And with absolutely no explanation.

Enrico's smile vanished. "I thought that might be the reason."

"You must address this soon," she said, then hastened to add, "Don Lucchesi."

"He is not happy about the *comparaggio*? He hasn't said anything to me about it."

Bianca shook her head. "He says you are toying with him. That the ceremony means nothing. That bringing him into the bank was nothing. Not when you also brought in Dario Andretti's son. He's almost as angry about that as he is about your picking Don Legato to be *capo di società*."

Enrico's face darkened, and the hand on his desk clenched into a fist. She risked a glance at Antonio and saw him stiffen. A look flashed between the two of them. Were they considering—

No, not yet. Not unless Sandro persisted. Not unless he made a move against the don.

Her belly tight with fear, she leaned forward, placing a hand on the edge of the desk. "Mamma is trying to get him to see reason. But he's got Papà's temper." She tried to smile, but it disappeared, and she wasn't going to force it. If only Papà hadn't been killed, if only Don Lucchesi hadn't put Antonio in her father's place, things would be different. They'd still be one big happy family, Uncle Enrico and his wife visiting for leisurely suppers.

Except that was a lie. Her family hadn't been happy since Bianca's mistake. Her shame. At least *she* hadn't been. *Dio* knew what had happened during the six years since her father had sent her away.

At least Don Lucchesi didn't know of her shame. Only two people outside her immediate family knew. One of them was Giovanna d'Imperio, but Gio would never breathe a word. She'd sworn it.

The other was Antonio. Bianca's face heated. How could he sit there, how could he flirt with her, how could he act as if they didn't have a *child* together? He truly was as callous as Papà had said. He'd told Antonio about the baby, had given him a choice, and Antonio had said to get rid of the child. As if she could ever do that. Giving up their son for adoption had nearly killed her. But the alternative—what a cold *figlio di puttana*. That made him well-suited to the 'Ndrangheta, didn't it? She shouldn't have been surprised to hear that he'd joined, but she'd fallen for his act when they'd been in school. She should've known better. Antonio was an orphan, a tough streetwise boy. Not the gentle soul that she'd thought. Not that boy at all.

Her uncle spoke, pulling her out of her reverie. "Bianca, I'm at a bit of a loss with your brother. I don't want to remind him of what he owes me, but perhaps I must." She swallowed hard. Yes, Sandro needed to remember what he owed the don. His loyalty, his fealty. Utter and complete. Anything less was mutiny, betrayal. Treason.

Her brother walked a tightrope. The don would give him a touch more tolerance, because he was family, because he was blood, because he was his godson. But even blood went only so far.

If Sandro didn't come back into the fold, if he didn't stop railing against his *capo*, he'd end up dead.

"Mamma and I are trying. Perhaps if you offer him something—"

"*He* does not make demands of me. He is my blood, yes, but he needs to remember his place."

"Which should be at your side," she said, keeping her voice soft. Antonio shifted in the seat beside her, but said nothing.

"I have my reasons. It is not your place *or* his to question them."

She lowered her gaze. "Have we displeased you in some way? I thought you and Papà—"

"We were close. I miss him very much."

"Then why?"

"Bianca, do not push me." His tone was a warning. One she'd heed. She nodded, but still she wondered, her eyes sliding to Antonio. His face was carefully blank. Just what role had he played in all this dissension in her family? Once again, her family was at odds, and once again, Antonio Legato was at the heart of the conflict.

———— ◆ ————

Bianca Lucchesi. She'd come and gone, and Antonio had reeled back to his office, thoroughly undone. The last time he'd seen her, a few weeks before she'd left for boarding school, she'd told him, with absolutely no sugar to coat it, that her family would never accept an orphan, that he should put any notion of them as a couple entirely out of his head. That he was nothing. Worthless. That their time together had been a lark for her. "A nice memory," that's what she'd said.

He slammed his fist onto his desk. "Nice" is not how he would have ever described their time together. Amazing. Hot. Overwhelming. Those were the words he would've used. But not "nice."

He thought he'd gotten over her. But he hadn't. He'd even made up an excuse to avoid the funerals for her father and her brother. He'd told Don Lucchesi that her brothers were likely to be upset, that he hadn't wanted to cause any additional drama at a time when the focus should have been on Don Domenico's and Fedele's deaths. And while that was true, the real reason had been *her*. He'd hoped to avoid Bianca. Preferably forever.

Damn. He'd reacted just the way he'd hoped he wouldn't. He'd even—*Dio* help him—he'd even *flirted* with her! Why? Why on earth couldn't he have just ignored her? Been as chilly, as polite, as she had?

Because she'd always been special to him. Apparently much more so than he'd been to her. Until Kate, Bianca had been the only person outside his family that he'd ever felt connected to. She'd cared about him when he'd been so alone.

And if he was honest, she'd hurt his pride. Bianca had been a challenge. She'd been asked out many times, but she'd never dated a single boy in their school. Until him. He'd persisted to the point where she'd jokingly called him "mosquito," but she'd finally agreed to see him, though she'd said they had to keep it quiet. Her father didn't want her dating anyone.

Turned out, her father didn't want her dating *him*.

A sharp rap on his office door shook him out of his thoughts. He'd been so rattled, he hadn't even asked Don Lucchesi about La Provincia's account. Perhaps the don had remembered. "Come in," Antonio called.

But it wasn't his *capo*. Sandro Lucchesi, eyes blazing, charged in and right up to Antonio's desk. Placing two meaty hands on the polished mahogany, Sandro leaned forward, his black curls falling over his forehead. "You think you're so clever, but I've caught you."

Adrenaline rocketed Antonio to his feet and he balled his fists. "*You* don't address me that way," he barked. Sandro was a few centimeters shorter, but very nearly matched him in weight. And he had the Lucchesi name. But Antonio was *capo di società*, and Sandro had to respect that.

"I've been checking around, *capo*"—Sandro put as much sarcasm into the title as he could—"and I've just finished talking to Cesare Palumbo. He saw you with my father. About four hours before Papà's body was found. Cesare said that you both were acting strangely. Really tense."

Fuck, fuck, and double fuck. Had Cesare seen the gun Antonio had been pressing into Don Domenico's back? Probably not, or he'd have done something about it. Antonio had thought they'd been unobserved. How the hell had Cesare seen them? Fuck! He needed to talk to Don Lucchesi. If the truth got out—if Sandro learned how his father had truly died—there'd be no hope for the Lucchesi family. Sandro and Matteo—maybe even Francesca and Bianca—would have to die like their traitorous patriarch. Like Don Domenico.

Those were the rules they lived by. A traitor's family died along with him.

But Don Lucchesi hadn't had the heart to condemn them along with Don Domenico. They were all the family he had left. The last of the Lucchesis.

Antonio took a breath. He needed to stay calm. To think. "Of course we were tense. Carlo Andretti had kidnapped Don Lucchesi's wife. I was sent to guard your father."

"Then why is he dead?"

Antonio groaned inwardly. He'd said too much. "He refused the escort. Said he could get home by himself."

The look on Sandro's face couldn't have been more skeptical. "My father refused a guard? On *that* night, of all nights?"

Antonio shrugged. It was all he could do. "He didn't explain himself to me."

"Of course not. He didn't have to explain himself to a mere *guard*."

"I'm no longer a guard." He tried to keep his voice as even as possible.

"I am well aware of that. So just how did a *guard* become *capo di società*?"

Again, Antonio shrugged. "Don Lucchesi has his reasons."

"And what reasons are those?"

"You'll have to ask him."

Sandro leaned closer to Antonio. "I will. I will get to the bottom of this. And I will have what is mine." Sandro rapped his knuckles on Antonio's desk, then he jabbed a finger at Antonio. "You'd best watch your back, Legato. When I prove that you killed my father, I won't hesitate to cut you down. In fact, I'll relish the opportunity."

"You cannot threaten your *capo di società* and not expect to answer for it."

Sandro laughed. "Do your worst. You think my *padrino* will make me lick your boots? I'm like a son to him. And soon I will *be* his son. And you? You will still be street trash."

Antonio didn't even think. He just threw the punch, his fist connecting with Sandro's jaw in a quick uppercut that threw Sandro off-balance. Antonio followed with a blow from his left. Agony seared across his upper back as the shot connected.

Not. A. Good. Idea.

Sandro staggered back and Antonio inhaled against the pain, rounding his desk in an instant, shoving his body into Sandro's. They were so close he could smell the espresso on Sandro's breath. "Insult me again, and I will discipline you in front of the *cosca*. Don Lucchesi doesn't like to take fingers. But the idea doesn't bother me."

Sandro wiped at the blood trickling from his nose and sniffed. "Peasants do fight with their fists, don't they?"

"I was going to start with one finger. Would you like it to be two?" Part of him hoped Sandro would keep pushing. He'd love to show Sandro a thing or two he'd learned on the streets.

The door banged back on its hinges and Cris Andretti walked in. He took in Sandro's bloody nose, then addressed Antonio. "I heard you out in the hall. Need help?"

"Fuck you, Andretti," Sandro said. "Like you could even touch me."

Cris crossed his arms, and the movement made his broad chest and shoulders even more impressive. "Try it."

Sandro looked from Cris to Antonio. "Well, now I *know* you killed my father. Your friend here is a fucking Andretti, if you haven't noticed."

"They're our allies."

"*Your* allies, maybe." After a pause, Sandro shook his head and smirked. "You don't get it. Cesare Palumbo is only *one* of the men who doesn't trust you or my uncle. He's willing to follow me. There are others. I wonder how many?"

Antonio's stomach turned to stone. Sandro was talking about an out-and-out mutiny. A catastrophe for the *cosca*, and annihilation for the Lucchesi family. "You're bluffing."

"Maybe you bluff, Legato. I never do." With that, Sandro stomped out and Cris followed him. Which left Antonio to contemplate the huge hole he'd dug for himself.

What was he going to tell Don Lucchesi? He'd let his temper get away from him, and instead of defusing tensions with Sandro, he'd inflamed them. He'd even stupidly threatened to take two of Sandro's fingers! The don would never stand for that.

Antonio plopped onto the top of the desk with a thump and rubbed his left shoulder. When he shifted his weight, papers crunched beneath him, and he stood up and discovered what he'd sat on. The statement for La Provincia's account. On top of everything else he'd fucked up, was he going to tell the don he couldn't figure this out either? Was he going to give Don Lucchesi another reason to question his choice of Antonio as *capo di società*? No. No he wasn't. He was going to solve that problem himself.

And somehow, he'd figure out how to bring Sandro Lucchesi to heel.

Preferably without a bullet.

CHAPTER 2

Calabria, San Luca

Anticipating his anointment as the most powerful man in the 'Ndrangheta, Lorenzo Andretti descended the well-worn stone stairs to the crypt beneath the sanctuary of Our Lady of Polsi Church in the heart of the Aspromonte mountains. A murmur of male voices drifted up the stairway. His left knee cracked, and he inhaled against the sudden pain. The doctor had advised him to start using a cane, but canes were for men older than he. Men who were ready to shuffle off into history, into oblivion. Lorenzo was not one of those men. He had years left to him yet.

But even he had to admit that his eighty-four years weighed on him. His eyesight was dimming, his hearing failing, his joints aching. But his appetite—in all things—remained undiminished. He'd been hungry since his youth, and that hunger had never died, never ebbed, no matter his success, his comfort. The man who didn't hunger was no longer a man. He was a shell. A worm. A bug, to be crushed beneath the feet of true men.

As long as he drew breath, Lorenzo would be the one doing the crushing.

So many men had died by his hand or at his order, he no longer could give an accurate count. Hundreds, perhaps? The only ones who'd mattered, the only ones who'd counted, were long in the past, however. Martino Monetti, the *capo* Lorenzo had killed to gain his first *cosca*, he was one of those who'd counted. The first man Lorenzo had outsmarted, though far from the last.

He rounded a corner and paused, letting his knee rest before descending the final dozen steps. The voices were louder. He could pick out Gianluca d'Imperio's deep bass, the softer baritone of Vittorio Battista. But the voices that *weren't* there— He frowned. He'd never been one for sentiment. Sentiment got a man killed, more often than not.

Still, he had to admit to missing Benedetto. He'd been his last remaining son, the one Lorenzo had counted on to carry the Andretti legacy forward. But now

Benedetto was gone. His betrayal still stung, but perhaps it shouldn't. Benedetto, despite his mistakes, despite his lies, despite his perfidy, had delivered the perfect situation into Lorenzo's lap. The chance at last to unify the families under one umbrella, to put them under the aegis of one family, one man.

And Lorenzo was that man. He'd show the others that today.

Taking a deep breath, he pushed off from the stone wall and descended the remaining steps as briskly as he could, steeling his features so they didn't betray the cost. He detested painkillers—they dulled the senses, took a man off his game. Pain was useful; it focused the mind.

And pain could be ignored. Pain could be locked in a compartment and buried.

Not even his wife, his lovely Serafina, not even she knew the extent of his aches. She'd been a good partner to him, she'd kept her word and supported him, she'd borne him three strong sons, she'd done her part to repay him for freeing her from Martino Monetti.

But Lorenzo trusted no one. Not anymore. Not since Benedetto. And Lorenzo never made the same mistake twice.

He stepped into the low-ceilinged room and saw the roughly one hundred and fifty family heads and their *capi di società* standing or sitting in clusters throughout the long space. Candles flickered in sconces and candelabras around the perimeter. Over the years, they'd talked of running electricity into the crypt, but Lorenzo preferred to keep things as they were. Stark. Primitive. The way they needed to be. The way the 'Ndrangheta needed to be. Enrico Lucchesi and Vittorio Battista could talk all they wanted about the need to modernize, the need to educate their children, the need to learn how to prosper in the modern technological world of the twenty-first century.

Though there was some truth to what they said, at its brutal, bloody heart, the world belonged to men who weren't afraid to kill, who weren't afraid to reduce situations to their bare bones. The mighty ruled the meek. Always.

Lorenzo crossed the length of the room, his footsteps and the men's voices echoing around him, their chairs scraping as they started to take their seats. Lorenzo reached the front of the room and took a seat in an elaborately carved high-backed wooden chair that sat upon a dais, along with a small table and another matching chair. It wasn't quite a throne fit for a king, but it would do. He took his seat and folded his hands together, resting them lightly in his lap.

He looked at his companion on the dais: Don Vittorio Battista, who had long been the second in charge at meetings of La Provincia. He got Vittorio's attention and inclined his head slightly, the signal to start. Vittorio tapped a knife against his water glass and cleared his throat.

The rows of *capi* fell silent, all eyes turned to Lorenzo. He'd been the one to call them there. It was time to inform them of his plans. It was time to reveal the future.

Lorenzo scanned up and down both sides of the room, waiting a few beats too long to speak. The more time a man had to think, the more his anxiety rose. And he wanted these men anxious.

Finally he leaned forward. "As you know, a great tragedy has befallen us. A few weeks ago, the Andretti and Lucchesi families—our united houses—were viciously

13

attacked by those blond-haired dogs, the Russians." He paused, his gaze resting on Antonio Legato, Enrico Lucchesi's blond-haired blue-eyed *capo di società*. No need to say anything directly. Let the others draw their own conclusions. Let them remember that Lucchesi had brought a northerner, an orphan, an outsider, into their midst.

Shifting his focus to his grandson, Dario, then to his great-grandson, Cristoforo, Lorenzo continued. "And now my last remaining son, Benedetto, is dead. Though some say he'd allied with the Russians, I know in my heart"—he tapped his chest— "I know Benedetto would never betray me. He loved me too much, he allowed his love for his father to guide him, to keep him from resisting them during the attack." When Enrico Lucchesi snorted, Lorenzo's gaze snapped to his, daring Lucchesi to contradict him. His heart beat a little faster. Just how big were Lucchesi's balls?

Lucchesi met his stare and leaned forward from his seat in the front row. "With respect, Don Andretti, that is not how it appeared to me."

"You are certain my son was a traitor?"

Lucchesi folded his arms across his chest. "No."

"Then let us agree that appearances can be deceiving."

"You will get no argument from me on that."

Lorenzo inclined his head slightly and allowed a hint of a smile to touch his lips. Lucchesi would be trouble, as he'd expected. But Lucchesi could be managed.

"Good. We should be friends, Don Lucchesi. Our families are joined again, and soon a new generation will spring from that union. Let us not be adversaries in this room, or any other."

Lucchesi nodded, but his stance remained the same—eyes hard, body stiff, unyielding. But no matter. He'd bend in time. Or die.

Turning away, Lorenzo addressed the others. "Now is not the time for petty disagreements. Now is not the time for squabbles between us. Those days are past. We must act as one unit, as one whole, if we are to repel our enemies. A Russian attack on Italian soil—this insult cannot stand, lest we encourage them to attack us again."

"What are you saying, Don Andretti?" Gianluca d'Imperio asked.

"I am saying that we must take the next step in our evolution. We must recognize the need for cohesion. We must recognize that the past is the past, that our days as independent units are over. We are one family, one *cosca*. We are the 'Ndrangheta."

A swell of voices broke out, some gruff, some protesting, some merely questioning. "And who will lead us?" Gianluca asked, his booming voice cutting through the noise. "You?"

Lorenzo suppressed a smile and sat back. "I have given it some thought, and I am willing to pave the way."

Enrico Lucchesi rose. "No." His voice wasn't particularly loud, but in it was a challenge every man recognized, and the room fell silent.

Lorenzo raised a brow. "No?" He held Lucchesi's gaze. "Did we not already discuss this, Don Lucchesi? Did you not already agree to run Lombardy?"

"Well, I'll be fucked," Gianluca d'Imperio said.

Ignoring d'Imperio, Lucchesi spoke again. "I never agreed to you running things, Don Andretti."

Lorenzo swallowed down his irritation. If he could risk having them all at his throat, he'd dispense with the pleasantries and impose his will. But he wanted, at a minimum, the semblance of agreement, cooperation. He hated having to "discuss" this issue, he hated having to "ask" for their agreement. But this battle couldn't be won by sheer force alone. They were too many, should they unite against him. And unfortunately, he needed Lucchesi and his bank. For now.

"Who then, do you propose?" Lorenzo asked. "Yourself?"

"No. Don Battista."

"Don Battista is a worthy choice." Except that Vittorio Battista was likely to oppose everything Lorenzo wanted. "I had thought, however, that Don Battista would enjoy another role in the organization."

Vittorio laughed, but it ended in a smoker's hack. "And what role is that, Lorenzo?"

"Head of the Tyrrhenian side of Calabria. You'd be busy, but not so much that you couldn't continue to enjoy your life on Capri."

The Tyrrhenian side was a huge concession, but as long as Lorenzo got the rest of what he wanted, it wouldn't matter for the moment. There'd always be time to deal with that issue later. And from the sound of Vittorio's lungs, nature might take care of that particular problem before long.

"You'd give me the Tyrrhenian side?" Battista said and whistled. "You must be getting generous at last."

Lorenzo allowed himself to smile. "Not generous. Just practical. I know I have angered some in this room, and I realize that given my son's behavior, I may be suspect myself." *How* suspect, they'd never know. "But I also know that I am the one man here who wants vengeance against the Russians more than any other. I know that *I* will be vigilant against our enemies. I know that *I* will keep us strong. I know that *I* will keep us safe."

"Would any of us do less?" Lucchesi asked.

"I will excuse the question due to your relative youth, Don Lucchesi." He caught the eyes of some of the older *capi*. "You are too young to remember the first time the Russians tried to attack us. I pushed them back to Siberia, where they belong."

"And murdered your own son in the process," Lucchesi said.

"Of course. Remo had allied with the Russians."

"That's the second time one of your sons has done so. Who would have thought that Carlo would have been the one with any honor?"

Lorenzo's blood caught on fire, scorching his veins. This fucking brat Lucchesi, how dare he throw Remo in his face? After the sacrifice he'd made—

Not now. Lorenzo inhaled deeply through his nose and smoothed down his tie. "Need I remind you that I have overlooked the transgressions your family has made against mine? Carlo and Benedetto didn't kill themselves."

"My son did you a favor. He put Benedetto down before you could yourself— or are you saying you'd have let him live?"

Fucking Lucchesi. The man was clever with words. "Of course not. But I still should have made the decision."

"Even for a clear case of treason?"

15

Lucchesi had just given him an opening. "Even then. Does a *capo* not run his own family?"

"Not if you get your way."

"You misunderstand, Don Lucchesi. I am not proposing taking those rights away. I am proposing that we evolve. At least a little. I think all of you can agree that La Provincia has made your lives easier, yes? We have fewer disputes settled in the streets, we have more peace, and we have more prosperity, because we aren't fighting petty wars between our families. I am merely proposing an extension of La Provincia into a military and organizational branch above all the families. La Provincia would wage campaigns against our enemies and coordinate our efforts to break into new markets and exploit new business opportunities. And of course, continue to mediate between families. But never would La Provincia interfere in the internal affairs of a family. That power remains with the family head. It is sacrosanct. Is it not?"

Lucchesi reddened slightly, recognizing the subtle threat in Lorenzo's words. Good. So the man wasn't a fool. Brave, yes, but not a fool. Lucchesi knew his son was at risk, that Lorenzo could insist on taking his vengeance for the unsanctioned execution of Benedetto.

"On that, we agree," Lucchesi said and sat back down.

Lorenzo folded his hands together again and laid them in his lap, relaxing back into the chair. "For Calabria, there will be three divisions, or *mandamenti*: the first, the Ionic side, meaning the Aspromonte mountains and Locride; the second, the Tyrrhenian side, meaning the coast facing Capri, and all of the Gioia Tauro region; and the third, the central city of Reggio Calabria. Outside Calabria, we will have a *mandamento* in Lombardy and may later add others as our operations evolve. For now, we will focus on the areas where we have the most power and the greatest concentration of financial interest. Each *mandamento* will have a *capo*."

"And who will run Reggio Calabria?" Gianluca asked.

"I had thought to."

"Of course," Gianluca said with a snort. "And who will have the Ionic side?"

Lorenzo's eyes shifted to Salvatore Ruscino, his *capo di società*. Normally, he'd have never chosen a man who wasn't an Andretti, but Sal's family had married into the Andretti line, and Sal had proved himself loyal. Five years of hard prison time, and the man hadn't cracked. "Salvatore will have it."

A round of protest erupted, led by d'Imperio and Lucchesi. "You expect us to let you control two-thirds of Calabria?" Lucchesi asked.

"I had thought with you in charge in the north and your *padrino* in charge of the Tyrrhenian side, that you, of all people, would be content."

Don Battista broke in, rising to his feet. "While I too am concerned with the concentration of power in Andretti hands, we will get nowhere arguing. I suggest we vote on Don Andretti's proposals. First, on the expansion of La Provincia's role. Second, on the heads of La Provincia and the four *mandamenti*."

"Before we do so, I would like to clarify one thing," Lucchesi said. "The head of La Provincia should be an elected position with terms of office. Not a lifelong role. Nor a hereditary one. Just as the heads of the *mandamenti* should rotate."

Lorenzo gritted his teeth. Of course Lucchesi would try to curb him. The bastard. "A reasonable proposal, Don Lucchesi. What do you say to four-year terms?"

"Agreed." A chorus of murmurs and nodding heads backed Lucchesi up. Gianluca d'Imperio didn't look happy, but after a moment, he too nodded.

There was one more thing, and best to mention it while they seemed agreeable. "To fund the expanded operations, each family agrees to tithe an additional ten percent." Some grumbling broke out. A reminder was due. "It's not only the Russians. The Albanians want in. So do the North Africans."

Lorenzo stared down the men closest to him. "Agreed?" Lucchesi glanced briefly up at the low ceiling, as if asking *Dio* for advice, then he nodded. After that, the rest fell in line. When the murmurs ceased, Lorenzo signaled Don Battista to start the vote. Battista moved to the back of the crypt and returned moments later with a large ceramic vase and two smaller bowls of stones—one bowl of white, another of black. White meant yes, black, the opposite.

The small bowls were passed around and each man selected one stone of each color. Then Don Battista took up his two stones in one hand and dropped one in the vase, keeping his choice concealed by placing the remaining stone in his pocket. The men remained seated during voting, while Don Battista carried the vase around the rows, each man casting his stone in the same manner.

Lorenzo watched the voting avidly, his pulse quickening. If the vote to expand the powers of La Provincia didn't go his way, he'd have a raft of new headaches to handle. Chief among them, Alexei Vilanovich, brother to Ilya Vilanovich, who'd been killed during the Russians' botched assault on the engagement party for Enrico Lucchesi's son and Dario's daughter. Lorenzo had paid Alexei an enormous sum to delay his revenge on the Lucchesis. And to make up for the spectacular blunderings of Benedetto, who'd assisted Ilya in his ill-fated attack largely because he'd racked up an enormous debt to the Vilanovich clan.

Lorenzo cast his stone and smiled, projecting a confidence he didn't quite feel. He'd never doubted himself, not even after Remo. But now that he'd failed with all three of his sons, questions plagued him. How had he managed to raise two sons—Remo and Carlo—who'd been little more than rampaging lions, all ego, impatience, and bite? And another, Benedetto, who'd proved to be an inveterate gambler and the most clever liar Lorenzo had ever known? All three had turned on him. All three were disappointments at best. And his grandsons were no better—in fact, they were worse. Dario aside, they weren't even clever. And Dario was just as disloyal as his father Carlo.

But somehow, somehow, Dario had raised a son, Cristoforo, who had the family loyalty his father lacked. The boy was reasonably bright, and certainly fearless. Almost to the point of foolhardiness. But that behavior could be curbed. Lorenzo watched his great-grandson cast his vote, the boy meeting his eyes as he did so. Good. Had Cristoforo voted against him, he'd no doubt have looked away.

Don Battista finished the rounds and confirmed that each man had cast a stone. Then he counted them out, making two piles on the sarcophagus of some long-forgotten personage.

The seconds ticked by, Lorenzo restraining the impulse to ask for the results and keeping his hands folded in his lap lest they betray him by fidgeting. At last, Don

Battista finished his counting. "It is close," he said. "I ask for someone to verify the count."

Gianluca volunteered, and Lorenzo suppressed a sigh. It was maddening having his future depend on the votes of these men. Years and years of planning had gone into this moment. A pat on the back here, a snarl there, the payoff or the punch delivered as needed, until he felt he had enough men either in his pocket or too terrified of him to object. Winning this election would be his greatest triumph. But had he miscalculated? The vote should not have been close. Perhaps he should have allowed Vilanovich to attack again, to kill Lucchesi's son or perhaps Dario. Perhaps the *capi* weren't yet worried enough about the Russian menace.

D'Imperio muttered to himself as he counted, dropping each stone from the vase into a bowl of black or white, the stones ringing against the ceramic. *Hurry, you fool!*

At last Gianluca whispered something to Don Battista, who nodded and turned to address the assembly. "It is decided. La Provincia shall be expanded."

Lorenzo allowed himself a small smile only. Best not to gloat before the final votes were cast.

Gianluca retook his seat, but he locked eyes with Lucchesi for a moment as he did so. Then he spoke. "Before we vote on the *capi* of the *mandamenti*, I propose we *capi*, we family heads, have a choice. More of a choice than we've been currently presented." He gazed around him, and various men nodded in agreement.

Vaffanculo, Don d'Imperio. Lorenzo tried to make his question mild. "You would have us here all night?"

"If need be. If I must subject myself to not one, but two, additional layers, by *Dio*, I will not do so without more say."

"You do not like the proposed candidates?"

"I do not like realizing that I should have been running for office months ago."

He'd thought the fact that the man's own daughter had been one of those attacked would have made d'Imperio more tractable. But a man with big coffers—and Gianluca's were overflowing—wasn't used to obeisance. Gianluca had grown rich and full of himself in the north. He didn't have the daily reminders of how lean life could be like the *capi* in Calabria did. And that was a problem.

"Fine then. Let the candidates for *capi di mandamenti* step forward."

"And for head of La Provincia," Gianluca said.

Lorenzo almost laughed aloud. Gianluca had balls, he did. But he'd rubbed many the wrong way with his ostentatious displays of wealth. From his Rolex to his tailored Armani suit, to his thousand-dollar loafers and the diamond-encrusted rings on his fingers, d'Imperio screamed wealth and privilege. The *capi* of Calabria were a plain lot by comparison. Even Enrico Lucchesi, as rich as he was, kept his wealth understated. Yes, Lucchesi wore a fine suit and a nice watch, but remained unadorned other than a plain gold wedding band and the ring with his family's crest. His ownership of the bank they all laundered funds through gave him a position of power and trust he'd never abused. If Lucchesi were to step forward, there could be trouble.

"Who then are the challengers?" Lorenzo asked, putting an edge on the last word as a reminder. He could be a friend—or a deadly foe. It behooved these men to remember that.

"I am," Gianluca said. "For head of La Provincia and head of Lombardy."

"Anyone else?"

Dario cleared his throat. "Me. For head of Lombardy."

So the Lucchesi-Andretti alliance in the north was weak. What a fool Dario was. "Anyone else?" Lorenzo asked.

Lucchesi spoke. "Me. For head of La Provincia, as well as Lombardy."

Damn the man. "Very well," Lorenzo said, fighting not to betray his anger. He'd known it was a risk. But he couldn't put expanded powers in place without a vote. And there were always ways to get rid of problems. Bullets, knives, or bombs. Any one of these would suffice to eliminate Lucchesi and anyone else who proved troublesome. The problem was, he'd have to act with discretion. Or let loose Alexei Vilanovich.

But none of that could happen until Lorenzo had control of the Lucchesi bank. And that could take a year or more.

The votes proceeded. First for the *mandamenti* heads. Lorenzo handily won his position, as did Sal and Don Battista. Even though they'd all run unopposed, the family heads could have cast enough "no" votes to force other candidates to run.

The vote for Lombardy took two rounds. Dario was knocked out in the first, but Lucchesi and d'Imperio were close going into the second round. Just before the vote started, Gianluca spoke, loudly enough to draw everyone's attention. "Would you like to place a wager, Enrico?"

"What wager?"

"A million that I win."

Lucchesi gave a wry smile. "Too rich for my blood."

Lorenzo felt a great easing in his belly. Gianluca's hubris had just ruined his chances.

Moments later, the votes were cast. Lucchesi by a landslide. Now if only Lorenzo could get Lucchesi to make a similar blunder. He had just moments.

"Are you sure, Don Lucchesi, that you will be able to manage not only Lombardy and the bank, but also being head of La Provincia? That is a heavy burden for one man's shoulders."

"I'm up to the task."

"And have you solved the problems in your own *cosca*?" Lorenzo asked, his eyes coming to rest on Antonio Legato again. Antonio fidgeted and looked away, and Lorenzo repressed a chuckle. The boy was an open fucking book.

"Yes," Lucchesi said.

"Your *capo di società* seems less certain."

The boy reddened and his hands curled into fists. "If Don Lucchesi says a problem is solved, the problem is solved," the boy said, his voice thick with emotion.

He was far too easily riled. Why on earth had Lucchesi chosen him over his own blood? There was a story there, one it might benefit him to uncover. "As you say," Lorenzo said with a polite nod, as if the upcoming vote didn't trouble him in the least.

And as it happened, it didn't. He won handily.

The first step to his ultimate victory. Lorenzo smiled with contentment. The dominos were falling into place.

CHAPTER 3

Antonio burned with shame. He'd cost Don Lucchesi the election. The don said nothing as the men gathered into groups and chatted, breaking out the cigars and the grappa and the limoncello to celebrate. It was nearly one in the morning.

When was he ever going to learn to hide his feelings? How many times had his mentor Ruggero yelled at him when he was training to be a guard? According to Ruggero, Antonio telegraphed everything—every thought, every emotion, every move he was going to make. And that made him vulnerable. And a liability as well.

He'd gotten better at governing himself, but he was still too likely to let his temper best him. As he had today. He'd walked right into Lorenzo's trap.

But two could play that game. Antonio had studied La Provincia's account thoroughly last night, and the numbers didn't add up. Nor did the payees.

Many of the dubious transactions had taken place during Benedetto's reign. But a series of recent wire transfers—all terminating in Liechtenstein—raised Antonio's brows. Yes, they were to different accounts. But all the accounts were at the same bank. Taken individually, there was nothing remarkable about the transactions. Except that they'd drained nearly every cent from La Provincia's holdings. And here Lorenzo was, with his hand out, asking for another ten-percent tithe. What was he up to?

Taking a deep breath, Antonio approached Lorenzo Andretti. The old man was enjoying a cigar and a plate of mixed cheeses, meats, and olives that the monks had brought in. Antonio's stomach rumbled. He hadn't eaten in hours. But this couldn't wait.

"Don Andretti, may I have a word?" Antonio asked, pulling up a chair and sitting down beside the fearsome don.

Lorenzo took another drag on his cigar, then exhaled through his nose and mouth, not making any effort to keep the smoke away from Antonio's face. *Stay calm. He's trying to upset you.* Finally the old don spoke. "Still smarting?" he said with a smile.

Antonio ignored the jab. "It's about La Provincia's account. I'm in charge of it now, and I noticed something unusual."

The don rolled the cigar in his fingers, not taking his eyes from Antonio's. "What are you talking about?"

"You are the only person authorized to make withdrawals, yes?"

"Now that Benedetto is dead."

Antonio fumbled about for a moment, not sure how to phrase his question without it sounding like an accusation. "Has the cat stolen your tongue, *signore?*" Lorenzo asked.

"No. I just—" He paused, then started again. "There seem to be a large number of withdrawals lately. The account is nearly empty."

"It will soon be full again, once the tithes are made."

"Yes, but I may be asked to account for the funds—"

"By whom?"

"Don Lucchesi, among others."

"What business is it of his?"

Antonio furrowed his brow. Was he serious? "Questions may be asked."

"*Who* will ask these questions?" Lorenzo's eyes narrowed. He leaned forward, jabbing the lit end of the cigar at Antonio. "Are you accusing me of something?"

"I'm just trying to determine what happened to the funds."

"It isn't your place to question me." Lorenzo waved the cigar in the air. "These men trust me. The elections made that clear."

"These men are afraid," Antonio said, keeping his voice pitched so that only he and Lorenzo could hear it.

"And you aren't?"

"Ilya Vilanovich tried to kill me. He didn't succeed. So let the Russians come. Let them do their worst. I can take it."

Lorenzo waved away Antonio's statement. "The words of a fool."

"You haven't answered my question."

"You haven't asked one."

"Where did the money go?" Antonio asked, the words leaving his lips in a rush, his guts in a knot.

"You already know the answer."

"I know which bank it went to, yes. I don't know why. And I don't know if it is still there."

"And *that* is all you need to know. Get out of my face, boy."

Antonio rose. He'd certainly pissed Don Andretti off, but he couldn't tell if it was just the don's characteristic arrogance or if he'd rattled the man. "When the questions come, I'll be back."

———— ◆ ————

Lorenzo bit down on his cigar as Legato walked away. Impudent little fuck. Who did he think he was?

But the boy was right. Questions would eventually be asked. Questions Lorenzo didn't want to answer. The truth was that Benedetto's gambling had left the Andretti *cosca*'s finances in a shambles, and Benedetto had borrowed heavily from La Provincia without anyone noticing. And now—damn him—Lorenzo had been forced to do the same. Getting Alexei Vilanovich and his clan to cooperate had cost more than a little—much more. And then there had been the multimillion euro payoff to Italo Baldassare, the prime minister of Italy. Lorenzo needed Baldassare's cooperation and influence; anti-Mafia forces in the legislature, the judiciary, and among the populace were starting to gain ground. All thanks to the outright bully tactics of the Neapolitan Camorra and the Sicilian Cosa Nostra. The Sicilians had killed judges and set off bombs in public places, while the Camorra openly sold drugs on the streets and had turned Naples into a cesspool. Such visibility jeopardized Lorenzo's plans.

If Benedetto hadn't left him alarmingly close to penniless, he wouldn't have had to take the risk of using La Provincia's funds. He could have—he *should* have—been able to handle everything with his own money. He should have been able to keep his dealings private. And now this fucking little *orphan* threatened everything.

Lorenzo took a calming drag on his cigar. There had to be a way out. Then he grinned. *Of course.* All he needed to do was turn the problem back on Legato, back on Lucchesi. Accuse *them* of wrongdoing, of draining the account.

But he needed backup. Lucchesi was well-trusted, well-respected. Lorenzo needed unequivocal proof, and he needed someone influential in his court. His eyes swept the half-light of the crypt, coming to rest on Gianluca d'Imperio. D'Imperio had already challenged Lucchesi once. No doubt he wasn't happy about Lucchesi's growing power in the north and his alliance with Dario. It wouldn't take much to tip d'Imperio into further suspicion. Gianluca trusted Lucchesi with his fortune—for now. But what if Gianluca discovered that his money wasn't so safe? What if there were proof that Legato—and by extension, Lucchesi—had been mismanaging it, if not outright stealing from Gianluca? Lorenzo drew greedily on his cigar. There'd be hell to pay, that's what. And if Lorenzo had the right players in place, he could swoop in and take over the bank.

His great-grandson could be one of those players, if unknowingly, at least to start. By the time Cristoforo realized he'd been used, it wouldn't matter. He'd be firmly in Lorenzo's pocket.

But he needed someone else to do the actual dirty work—to make bad trades, to make unauthorized withdrawals—and best of all, pin it on Legato.

It was time to travel north. Time to call on Sandro Lucchesi. The boy couldn't possibly be happy about being passed over.

No. Most likely, Sandro was primed for vengeance.

———◆———

It had been two days since she'd seen Antonio at the bank, but Bianca had thought about little else since. Again and again, she'd turned over his callous behavior in her mind.

How could Antonio have been so cold? Had she truly meant nothing to him? When they'd met at school, she'd been so lonely, the only girl in a family of boys, the one her parents—especially her father—rarely had time for or took little notice of. Her brothers had practically demanded attention with their brash, boisterous ways and tendency to get into trouble. She'd been the "good girl," the one her parents hadn't had to worry about. The one they'd ignored. So when Antonio had chased her, when he'd lavished so much time and attention on her, was it any wonder she'd eventually given in? Was it any wonder she'd craved such closeness with him? That she'd broken every rule she'd been raised by—keep to your kind, stay a virgin until marriage, and mind your father?

She'd thought she'd meant something to Antonio, that they'd shared a bond that went far beyond an adolescent crush. And yet, the evidence stared her in the face: She mattered to him no more than any other conquest.

Despite her family having sat down to dinner, a time usually held as sacred in their household, her mother and her brother Sandro were arguing, their voices an angry buzz in the background. That buzz turned into a blare when Sandro smacked the table and said the rudest, most foolhardy thing a man could say.

Bianca almost choked on her *pollo alla cacciatora*, and her mother's fork dropped on her china plate with a clank. "What did you just say?" Mamma asked, her gaze boring into Sandro.

Sandro pushed back from the dining room table and wiped his mouth with a napkin. "You heard me, Mamma. Don Lucchesi can go fuck himself. I won't be taking part in the *comparaggio* ceremony. And neither will Matteo." He looked at his younger brother, who nodded, but kept his eyes fixed on his food.

Bianca swallowed her mouthful of chicken and took a sip of wine to wash it down. She glanced at her mother, who was red in the face, her hands trembling beside her plate. Before Bianca could speak, her mother sprang up and stalked around the table to Sandro, grabbing him by the back of his shirt collar and forcing him to focus on her.

"You listen to me, Alessandro Lucchesi, and you listen good. I've already lost your father and your brother. I'm not going to lose you too."

Sandro reached up and carefully removed his mother's hand from his collar. His tone was firm, but soft. "Mamma, I'm not stupid. This whole business stinks, and you know it. Zio Enrico picks an orphan, a fucking *guard*, over me? And then Fedele is killed by Zio Enrico's son? A son who's married to a goddamn Andretti?"

"Fedele's death wasn't Enrico's or his son's doing. That was Dario Andretti."

Sandro took her hand in both of his. "Listen to me, Mamma. Zio Enrico is cutting us out. Not just me. All of us."

"He's kept a roof over our heads. We still get your father's share."

"But he hasn't given me or Matteo a place in the *cosca*. I should be by his side, not that damn outsider!"

"You will get your due, Sandro," she said and stroked a hand through his coal-black curls.

"I won't get my due until that orphan is gone."

"You don't get anything if you continue to defy your *capo*. He wants to take the vow toward you and your brother. If you spit in his face, what do you think will happen?"

Sandro said nothing, and the room grew silent except for the ticking of the hall clock. Finally he sighed and nodded. Mamma visibly relaxed, and Bianca took a breath. She'd been ready to jump in, but if Sandro wouldn't listen to Mamma, he was even less likely to listen to her.

She eyed her brother carefully, but he appeared relaxed. He even rose and kissed their mother on both cheeks, framing her face in his hands. "You're right, Mamma," he whispered. "I will get what I'm due."

A cold fist clenched Bianca's heart. Sandro meant what he said. He wouldn't be content until he had what he thought was his.

And he'd die in the attempt.

She needed to talk to him in private, to make one last effort to persuade him to turn away from this course. This horrible, disastrous, course.

———— • ————

Sandro sipped at his steaming cup of espresso and contemplated the gorgeous view before him. Lake Como, tranquil in the moonlight, so unlike the volcano that raged inside him. He huddled deeper in his jacket, warming his bare hands on the cup as he raised it to his lips again.

The door behind him opened, and he turned, seeing Bianca step out onto the rear terrace of their home. Like him, she was bundled up in a thick coat and scarf against the December chill. But she wore gloves and carried two heavy blankets. "I thought you could use this," she said, handing one over.

He set the cup down on the ceramic table and accepted the blanket, laying it across his lap. The chair next to him scraped across the flagstones as Bianca sat down.

"What do you want?" he asked.

"You have to stop this."

"I agreed, didn't I?"

She shook her head. "I've been gone a long time, but I still know you. You'll go to the ceremony, you'll say the words, but you won't mean them."

He almost laughed. So she did still know him. "This isn't your problem."

She leaned toward him and gripped his forearm, her fingers digging in. "It *is* my problem. How much more do you think Mamma can take? I've never seen her so upset. You can't do this to her."

"And I can't sit by and watch my birthright go to another. To a fucking outsider. Not even another Lucchesi. I could understand if Zio Enrico had chosen his own son as *capo di società*—even if the bastard did kill Fedele. I could still understand it. I don't like Niccolò, but he's blood, at least. And I blame Dario Andretti for what happened to Fedele."

"It doesn't matter whether you like it or whether you understand it. You just have to accept it." She squeezed his arm again, and he placed a hand over hers, the cold leather of her glove soft under his palm.

Maybe if she understood, she could help him. "I didn't want to tell Mamma this, but I think Legato killed Papà."

Her eyes widened and her mouth opened in distress. "What?" she asked, the word little more than a whisper.

"He was the last one seen with Papà. He claims Papà refused a guard that night. That doesn't make sense."

She sat back in the chair, pressing a gloved hand to her lips. "I don't believe it," she said, her head shaking slightly.

He leaned forward. "Do you see now? I can't let him get away with it."

"But why would he kill Papà?"

"Maybe they had a fight. I don't know. All I can think is that he somehow discredited Papà. I'm not sure if Zio Enrico gave the order, but there's got to be a reason our *padrino* chose Legato to take my place."

"But if Zio Enrico thought Papà was a traitor, we'd all be dead."

"I know. But think about it. He doesn't have a lot of family. Maybe he felt merciful."

"Maybe," she said. Then she leaned closer. "I asked him whether we'd displeased him, and he got upset and told me to stop pushing for an answer."

So he was right. Legato had discredited their father somehow. And now Sandro was paying the price. But he would get what was his. Even if he did have to work with Lorenzo Andretti.

"You see, then?" He held his sister's gaze, waiting for her to nod. When she did, he continued, keeping his voice low. "I have a plan, and you could make it a lot easier."

She bit at her bottom lip. "What plan?"

"I'm going to do to Legato what he did to Papà."

"You're going to kill him?" The shock on her face didn't bode well.

He shrugged. "I don't think I'll have to. I'm going to show Zio Enrico that he can't trust Legato."

"And how could I help with that?"

"You can get close to Legato in ways I can't. His guard will be up around me. But everyone knows he can't resist a pretty girl."

Her brow crinkled. "Are you suggesting I *sleep* with him?" she asked, her tone aghast.

Well, at least his sister hadn't fallen for Legato's charm, unlike every other female on the planet. "I know it's a lot to ask, but you want to help me avenge Papà, yes?"

She sat back in her chair and crossed her arms over her chest. "I can't, Sandro." Her voice cracked.

"Come on, Bee. It's not like you're still a virgin or something."

Her eyes flashed at him, her features stiff with fury. "Don't you throw that in my face."

"I'm sorry." He waited a second, then said, "All I need you to do is get the password to his work computer. How you do it is up to you."

"That's all?" she asked. He couldn't miss her sarcasm.

He spread his hands and shrugged. "I think you owe Papà. Don't you?" He hated to twist the knife, but it was a small price to pay if he won in the end.

She swiped at the tears spilling down her cheeks. "I made a mistake, Sandro. I trusted someone I shouldn't have."

"You shouldn't have put yourself in that position."

"I was just a girl."

"Papà was devastated."

"And you think I wasn't? I lost my child. He's somewhere out there, and I can't find him!"

She covered her face with her hands, and he almost took the words back. But if he wanted to be *capo* someday, he couldn't be soft. Her shoulders shook as she let out a sob. "I hate myself so much, Sandro. You don't know how much."

"Papà's watching us. If you help me claim what's mine, I'm sure he'll forgive you." He rose and stepped around the back of her chair, wrapping her in his arms. "Help me, Bee," he whispered in her hair.

She was quiet for a long time. Was he going to have to dangle the carrot of finding her boy as well? He had a hunch how to find the kid, and in case she had second thoughts, having that information would provide him some insurance.

"Okay," she finally said and took a shuddering breath.

Sandro smoothed a hand over her hair and smiled to himself. It was only a matter of time before his knife was buried in Legato's chest.

CHAPTER 4

Although Antonio had finished moving his things out of Don Lucchesi's villa only the day before, it already felt strange to be back in this house that was no longer his home. He'd lived here for the past two years, he'd walked its halls day and night, he'd roamed every bit of the surrounding property.

But now he no longer felt welcome. Don Lucchesi had kicked him out. And on top of that, the don was welcoming Sandro and Matteo into his family in the tightest way possible—as his sons.

Antonio crossed the heavily decorated foyer. Kate was celebrating her first Christmas in Italy, and throughout the villa, the piney scent of fresh evergreens and the soft glow of tiny white lights, shiny ornaments, and fine fabrics were blunt reminders that he was going to be alone for the holiday. He headed out to the terrace in back, where a huge table, groaning with food, had been set up in an enormous tent with heaters to keep everyone comfortable. All the underbosses of the Lucchesi *cosca* were there, along with their families, and of course Don Battista, Don Lucchesi's *padrino* and his own *compare*. Sandro, Matteo, Bianca, and their mother were standing off to one side, conferring with Don Lucchesi and his wife, Kate.

He hardly knew where to look. Normally he'd greet Kate and stand with her and Don Lucchesi, but now that seemed unwise. And he certainly wanted to stay as far from Sandro and Bianca as possible. All of these people he had ties to, yet he'd never felt so alone.

Someone nudged him in the side. Ruggero Vela, Don Lucchesi's personal bodyguard and Antonio's former mentor. "How do you like the flat?" Ruggero asked.

Antonio shrugged. "It's very big."

"You hate it," Ruggero said with a chuckle.

"I don't hate it, it's just…" He let the words trail off. A lump rose in his throat. It was lonely with Raffaele as his only company. And while Raffaele was a good sport and close to him in age, Antonio barely knew him.

Ruggero gripped his shoulder. "It'll feel like home soon."

Antonio studied Ruggero's profile, but the guard's face gave nothing away. Had he imagined the empathy in Ruggero's voice? They'd been friends of a sort once, though after Antonio's promotion, Ruggero had put some distance between them. Whether out of respect or jealousy, Antonio didn't know.

He wished he could tell Ruggero that Don Lucchesi had done Antonio no favors by giving him this job, but he didn't want to sound ungrateful. He risked a glance at Bianca and her brothers. Sandro gave him a look that was the very definition of "the evil eye," while Bianca seemed not to notice that he was even there. He should have been happy about that, but he wasn't. Had she been rocked—for even a second—by their meeting? Or was he the only one knocked off-kilter?

Don Battista called them all to order. Rubbing a hand over his mostly bald head, he made a slight bow to the crowd. "Today, we are gathered here, friends and family, to witness the most solemn of vows, a vow that unlike some others"— he twirled his wedding band, to the laughter of the crowd—"cannot be broken by any act. Not even the oath so many of us took"—he winked at the reference to the 'Ndrangheta initiation—"can boast that. That vow can be broken by death or infamy. This one, the vow of *comparaggio*, is cast in stone."

He motioned Sandro and Matteo forward, then Don Lucchesi, his own godson. He put an arm around Enrico and hugged him close to his side. "Many years ago, I pledged such an oath to Enrico and became his *compare*—not just his *padrino*. I swore that I would take Enrico as my flesh and blood, as my child, that I would protect and shelter him as a parent would. That I would never betray him." Here Don Battista smiled. "I have kept my promise, yes?"

Enrico nodded. Don Battista released him and clapped his hands together with a grin before producing a knife from his jacket pocket. "Give me your hand." Enrico placed his left hand, palm up, in Don Battista's left. With the point of the knife, Don Battista drew blood from Enrico's palm. Then he motioned Sandro and Matteo forward, likewise pricking their palms. Don Battista dabbed a finger in all of their blood, then drew a red cross on each of their palms. "This cross represents the intersection of your lives, as well as your devotion to each other. This vow, parent to child, child to parent, is sacred. It cannot be breached. Your blood flows in each other's veins. Once done, this vow cannot be undone. If you do not wish to engage in this vow, speak at this moment, or consider the matter decided for all time."

Enrico looked at Sandro first, then Matteo. They both met his gaze steadily. Antonio had half-expected Sandro to balk, but apparently he'd gotten over his anger at his *padrino*. At that moment, Sandro glanced up, meeting Antonio's stare, then he smiled. It was not a happy grin. It was a triumphant one.

Clearing his throat, Antonio looked away. "I don't trust him," Ruggero muttered, motioning with his chin to Sandro. Startled, Antonio asked why. "He's too pleased with himself."

"He thinks I killed Don Domenico."

Ruggero whistled softly. "And why does he think that?"

"Cesare Palumbo saw me with Don Domenico that night. Sandro knows I was the last one to see his father alive."

"He knows shit."

"Right now. But what if he discovers the truth?"

"He won't. If Cesare knew anything, you'd already be dead."

"Thanks for the vote of confidence."

"Never underestimate a man out to avenge his family. Carlo Andretti made that mistake, and look where he is now."

"You really know how to cheer someone up." Antonio tried to keep his tone light, but the severity on Ruggero's face bled the levity out of his words.

"Don't follow in Carlo's footsteps."

"Just what am I supposed to do?" Antonio observed Enrico embracing his two new sons, kissing them each on both cheeks.

"Keep your eyes and ears open. If it looks like Sandro intends to act against you, don't hesitate."

"But Don Lucchesi—"

"You still call him that?" Ruggero asked. "He should be 'Don Enrico' or 'Enrico' to you. You're not his guard anymore."

Was that resentment in Ruggero's voice, or had he slipped back into the mentor role? "It's just difficult for me to make the switch."

"And that's part of the problem. You're *capo di società*. Act like it. Or men like Sandro Lucchesi will run right over you."

"As I was saying before you cut me off"—Antonio gave Ruggero a severe look, which Ruggero answered with an approving grin—"Don Lu- Don Enrico is taking Sandro as his son. Right this minute. If I act against Sandro on a suspicion, if I act before I have proof, what is Don Enrico supposed to do?"

Ruggero sighed. "You're fucked, I'll give you that. But still, I'd rather be alive and asking forgiveness. Yes?"

Ruggero was right, and yet Antonio had to tread carefully. Don Enrico seemed on edge with him. Upset about something. Well, not just anything.

Kate. Antonio's eyes found her. He missed her. That was the thing he missed most about not living at the house. Talking to Kate. They'd spent a lot of time together these last few months, and he'd grown so close to her. Yes, he still found her attractive, but it was so much more than that. She'd become a friend, family, almost like a sister. His chest tightened a little. He wondered what Violetta was doing at this very moment. Did she ever think of him?

He hadn't seen Violetta in years, not since their last disastrous reunion when he'd been fourteen. Her reaction to seeing him had been worse than ever, her hysteria at their parting so pronounced he'd not known how to handle it, other than to stay away and out of her life. Which was what his uncle Gino had always wanted. He'd made that abundantly clear each time Antonio had run away from the orphanage in Rome. Each time Zio Gino had sent Antonio back, his ears deaf to Antonio's pleas. Antonio should have known to stay gone, to stay up north, after Don Enrico had come and taken Antonio out of that orphanage.

Had Zio Gino had a hand in that? Had he cared enough to arrange a spot for Antonio at the Lucchesi Home for Children? It was a nice thought, but he was probably fooling himself. His uncle had wanted him gone, and if he'd done anything for Antonio, it had been for that reason alone. Not because he cared about Antonio. And that was all that mattered.

Even Don Lucchesi—Don Enrico—even he had never quite been willing to take Antonio in. Antonio had just been a substitute for the son Enrico had left back in England. Nick. And now, Enrico had Sandro and Matteo too.

There was no room for Antonio in Don Enrico's heart. Just as there hadn't been in Zio Gino's.

Or Bianca Lucchesi's. There she was, a smile on her face, content as a cat. She'd used him, she'd had her fun, and then she'd told him he wasn't good enough for her family.

He looked away from Bianca and tried to swallow down his bitterness, but it bubbled back up. He was fucked, as Ruggero had said. And in more ways than one.

That's how it was always going to be, wasn't it? Him on the outside, nose pressed to the glass, looking in. And no one else giving a damn.

"If you're feeling sorry for yourself, stop." Ruggero's low rumble interrupted his thoughts. "Everyone has it hard. And there is always someone who's had it harder than you."

"You don't know—"

"I don't? Both my parents died because of me."

"What?" This was news to him.

"My mother died having me. And my father—" Ruggero abruptly stopped speaking.

"I'm sorry. I—"

With a flick of his hand, Ruggero cut him off. "It doesn't matter. What's done is done. The question is whether you're going to let it define you."

"I'm not."

"You sure about that?"

Antonio jammed his hands into the pockets of his suit jacket so no one could see the fists he couldn't help making. "I think I've had enough lectures to last me a while."

"As you say, *Don* Legato." It still surprised Antonio to hear that title. Especially from Ruggero. "Have you chosen your second guard?"

"No. I'll be fine with one." *Since it's so much "safer" for me to be on my own.*

"I noticed Raffaele isn't with you."

"I'm letting him rest."

"You need a guard with you at all times, now that you're *capo di società*."

Antonio patted the Glock in the holster under his left armpit. "I'll be fine. It wasn't so long ago that I was a guard myself."

"You've never been the target before."

"You applying for the job? Is that why you're insisting?"

Ruggero shook his head. "My place is here. With the don. But you should have a second guard."

"Like I said, I don't need one."

"You should reconsider." When Antonio didn't respond, Ruggero said, "I'm headed to Calabria right after this. The don has agreed to try my nephew Orlando as *contabile*."

"*Bene.*" It was about time they had a new treasurer for the *cosca*. Perhaps Antonio could sit down with Orlando and go over La Provincia's account. Orlando might be able to help him trace the transactions. "Finally taking that vacation? It'll be nice to be with your family for Natale."

"I'll be here for Natale. Early afternoon."

"You're kidding me. You'll be turning around and coming back almost as soon as you get there."

"I'll be gone for two full days, and part of a third."

"That's not a vacation. That's a weekend."

"My sister won't like it, but I don't trust Sandro being in Don Lucchesi's house. Even if it is Natale."

"I'm sure it'll be fine. Take at least a week. Or else I don't see why you're going at all."

Ruggero huffed with laughter. "Had to. Orders."

"And you couldn't think of a good excuse this time."

"He's still in danger, but he won't hear it."

Antonio's grin faded. "Who from?"

"Just a feeling." Ruggero shrugged.

"The Andrettis?"

"They're allies now." But Ruggero's words dripped with sarcasm.

Antonio sighed. "Never a moment's rest."

"No. But we knew that going in. Listen, I'd better get on the road."

"Taking the Maserati?"

"Of course. Haven't had a chance to open her up yet."

"Try not to get any tickets."

Ruggero laughed. "Don't count on it." Ruggero left Antonio and headed over to the receiving line that had formed to congratulate Don Enrico, Sandro, and Matteo. Kate, Bianca, and Signora Lucchesi were in that line as well. Antonio was going to have to face all of them at some point. The only one who wouldn't be a problem for him in some way was Signora Lucchesi. He'd start with her then.

Francesca greeted him warmly, her mouth curving into a wide smile, her hands clasping both of his. "Don Antonio. It's so nice of you to come."

"I couldn't miss such a happy day."

"Of course not." She motioned him to one side. "I've heard from Don Enrico that you're looking for a wife." Antonio suppressed his surprise and managed a nod. Signora Lucchesi smiled again and squeezed his forearm. "Perhaps you'd consider my Bianca?"

What was she thinking? Could there possibly be a worse match, given the situation? "I..." He hesitated. "I'll consider it." Not the truth, but a lie was easier. If only Signora Lucchesi knew how her daughter felt about him.

The next in line was Bianca. She held a hand out to him and offered a tentative smile. He took it, his stomach dropping to the flagstones. He couldn't do this. He couldn't pretend anymore. Couldn't pretend he didn't hurt.

He dropped her hand without saying anything and strode away. He hadn't gone far when he heard Kate behind him. "Tonio!" she said, catching hold of his arm just as he reached the doors leading into the house.

"Let me go." He bit off the words in an attempt to discourage her.

"Look at me."

He turned and met her gaze, her familiar green eyes comforting and disturbing at the same time. He wanted to throw his arms around her and hug her close, but he couldn't do that. Everyone was staring at them. Including Don Enrico. The set of his jaw told Antonio that the don wasn't pleased.

"*Signora*, it would be best if you returned to your husband's side."

Her brow creased. "What are you talking about?"

"He didn't tell you why he asked me to move out?"

Now she seemed even more perplexed. "He said you wanted to go."

Antonio almost wanted to laugh, though it wasn't funny. "My mistake."

"He kicked you out? Why?"

"You truly don't know, *signora*?" He glanced down at her hand still on his arm. She released him. "But he knows it's not like that."

"I don't think he does."

She turned and scanned for her husband, catching his eyes and motioning him over.

Antonio didn't like the cold expression on the don's face. When he reached them, Kate took her husband's hand and motioned him and Antonio inside. "We need to talk," she said. "All three of us."

Don Enrico didn't look happy. But then none of them were. They spread out in the don's study, Antonio taking a position by the windows that overlooked the garden and the assembled guests. Kate sat on the sofa, Enrico in the chair next to her. So the don was more upset than Antonio had thought. Normally he'd have been as close to her as possible.

Kate crossed her arms and shot her husband a look that could have frozen the lake outside. "What is going on in that head of yours?" she asked.

Enrico sighed and ran a hand over his face. Then he glanced at Antonio before focusing on her again. "Must I say it?"

"Yes." Her voice sounded a little thick. Antonio studied her closely. Were those tears in her eyes? *Cristo.* He didn't want to cause problems between them.

"You are too close to him."

She shook her head. "You trust me so little? After everything?"

"It's not that."

"Then what is it?"

Enrico glanced at Antonio again, an intensely uncomfortable expression on his face. "I would rather not have this discussion right now."

She shook a finger at him. "No. You may be the *capo* of the family, but you don't get to move us around like dolls. And you certainly don't get to do things that affect us without giving an explanation." Antonio's mouth practically dropped open. He'd never have spoken to the don that way. And he was quite sure Enrico didn't like the fact that Antonio was witness to Kate's behavior. The don rose from his chair and paced off to the desk at the far end of the room. He gripped the back of the chair behind it, but didn't sit. "Kate, this is a conversation we should have in private."

"Not when it affects Antonio. You kicked him out. Why?"

"I told you."

"Are you jealous?"

The word hung in the air between the three of them, and Antonio wished he could fade into the woodwork. The don's hands were biting into the leather of his desk chair. Enrico took a breath, then spoke. "The two of you are so much closer in age. There is a…" His words trailed off, then he resumed speaking. "There is a bond between you. It's always been there, and it's grown stronger since the time you spent together at the Villa d'Este. When you and I were apart." He paused again, and when he looked at Kate, Antonio winced at the naked anguish on the don's face. "It strengthened again, during Antonio's convalescence."

Kate rose and went to Enrico. "Antonio and I are friends. But that is all. Antonio *is* special to me, I can't deny that. Aside from you, he's the one friend I have here."

Antonio's throat tightened at her words. So she felt just as alone as he did. No wonder they understood each other so well.

She stroked a hand along her husband's jaw. "You own my heart, *caro*. But a small piece belongs to Antonio. And of course to my family. There is room enough for me to love all of you."

"I'm sorry, *cara*. I just—" He stared at his desk. "I grew concerned."

"There is nothing to worry about. Nothing." She stroked the don's hair and Antonio had to look away. He turned to the window and caught Bianca staring at him. Their gazes locked for a moment, then she broke the contact.

A painful longing filled him, almost suffocating him with the pressure that formed in his chest. He wanted what Enrico and Kate had. Did he want it with Bianca?

He wasn't sure. Even if he did, even if she wanted him, her brothers would never agree to it. Despite anything Signora Lucchesi wanted.

Maybe he should just… walk away. Step down from *capo di società*, go back to being a guard. Maybe an underboss. Something other than this. At least he wouldn't be causing problems every time he turned around.

"So then we can stop this foolishness, and Antonio can move back in," Kate said. "He should be with us at Christmas."

Enrico didn't respond right away. After a moment, he said, "There is still Sandro to think of."

"He can swallow his pride," Kate said.

It was time to put an end to this. Antonio broke in before Enrico could reply. "No. I should stay on my own." He took a deep breath before continuing. "And I think I should step down so you can give Sandro *capo di società*."

Kate inhaled sharply and Enrico rose. "Absolutely not. Sandro may be my son now, but that changes nothing."

"It doesn't?" Antonio spread his hands, the longing in him turning to anger. "You have three sons as of today, and two of them are older than me. Nick may have given up his claim, but Sandro hasn't. Choosing me for this position was a mistake."

"You seem to forget why I selected you," Enrico said.

"Sandro doesn't know anything. He thinks I killed his father. And I don't think he knows anything about what happened between Don Domenico and Carlo Andretti."

"Perhaps. But I can't trust him. If he does find out, what then? I can't have a *capo di società* who blames me for his father's death. I could never turn my back on him."

"Then pick someone else. Someone they can't argue with."

"How would I explain that?" Enrico tapped his own head. "Think about it, Tonio."

"I have. There's really only one solution." His heart beat fast. But could he actually say it? "Make me your son."

A shutter closed over Don Enrico's face. "I cannot. Not at this time."

Disappointment ravaged him, tore away the last vestiges of his self-control. Antonio smacked a fist down on the windowsill. "Not ever, you mean." He took a ragged breath, but it didn't help. "You've put me in a terrible position, you've put *yourself* in a terrible position, all because you're concerned about offending Sandro. And the worst of it is that now I know where I fall in your affections. Dead last."

"That is not true."

Raising a hand, Antonio started ticking off points on it. "It's not? Let's see. You never took me in because it turns out you have a real son out there." He put down a finger. "Then you chose to take in Sandro and Matteo and make them your sons." He put down two more fingers. "All because you made a promise to Don Domenico, who betrayed you!" He put down another finger. "And then you kicked me out of your home because of my friendship with Kate and because having me here makes Sandro unhappy." He put down the last finger, his hand clenching into a fist. He wanted to punch something, anything.

The don approached. "There is some truth to what you've said."

Antonio felt like he'd swallowed a rock. "All I ever wanted—" He forced himself to stop before he said the rest. He had some pride after all. "Never mind."

"What were you going to say?"

"There is no point." He held the don's gaze, making his face a mask of stone. "What's done is done."

"Tonio, I will make it up to you. When things with Sandro settle down—"

"And what if they don't?"

"They will. In time."

Antonio snorted. "And so I must wait. As usual. Why do I even listen to you?" He swallowed hard. "You kept a son hidden from everyone all of these years. How can I believe what you say?"

"You *will* have what you are due in time, Tonio. Trust me."

"I am at the end of my patience, Don Lucchesi." His voice shook as he said the words. For a moment, he wished he could take them back.

The don looked hurt. "You doubt my word?"

Antonio almost said that he couldn't believe in fairy tales, but he pulled himself back from the brink. "I need some time alone. To think. I will see you at the office on Monday."

"Tonio—" Kate said, and she moved to stop him.

He brushed her off. "It's best, *signora*, if we don't speak."

Those were all the words he had left in him. The last civil words he could muster. The rest of him was nothing but fury.

———————◆———————

After Antonio had stalked out of the study, Kate rounded on her husband. "Can't you see what this is doing to him?"

"I'll make sure he gets what he deserves."

"How?"

"It's not a decision I can make lightly. Or without your consent."

A prickle of unease rippled across her back. "What are you talking about?"

"I'd like to make Antonio my son. Legally."

"An adoption?"

He nodded. "I would have him take the Lucchesi name. He would be my heir, after Nico. And since Nico wants nothing to do with the 'Ndrangheta and Antonio does, Antonio would inherit. Before any of our children."

As usual, her husband was full of surprises. "You've been thinking about this for a while."

"I've told you before. I never wanted this for myself or my children. And I know you didn't want this life either."

"What are you saying?"

"I want out. I want both of us and our children out."

"But how?"

"I have a plan. I'm not sure it will work yet."

"Tell me."

He shook his head. "When I'm sure."

She thought about arguing, but the stubborn set of his face told her to wait. She'd pushed her husband far enough today; no doubt he was mortified that she'd aired their dirty laundry in front of Antonio. "Are you going to tell Antonio, at least? He should know what you're thinking."

"You saw how upset he is with me already. If something goes wrong, I'd rather not have him know."

"What do you mean, if something goes wrong?"

"Sandro and Matteo. If I can't satisfy them some other way, I'll have to make Sandro *capo di società*."

Her stomach tightened. "I see."

He turned miserable eyes to her. "And the view is wretched."

CHAPTER 5

Bianca read the letter again, her eyes filling with tears. She rolled over on her bed, clutching the wrinkled paper to her chest. The Lucchesi Home for Children refused to open any adoption records without a court order. They hadn't even confirmed if they *had* the records for her son.

As far as her family was concerned, the past should remain buried. They'd never help her with her quest.

But she'd already lost Papà and Fedele. She couldn't lose her baby too. Though he wasn't a baby anymore. He was just a day shy of six years old.

Her beautiful little boy, whom she hadn't seen since the night he'd been born. She didn't even know what color his eyes were. Had he taken after her or Antonio? Or was he a blend of them both? Did he like sports? Did he like vegetables? Was he a bold child or a cautious one? Was he happy?

Her chest and throat grew so tight she could hardly breathe. She had to find her boy. The boy she'd named Luca. She had to know how he was. *Who* he was.

What if he was with a family who didn't love him? What if he was miserable?

What if he knew he was adopted, and he missed her?

She stifled a sob, crushing the letter to her mouth, hot tears coursing down her cheeks. She had to convince Kate to let her help with the records at the orphanage. Somehow she had to get access to them.

Tomorrow she'd talk to Kate. Tomorrow she'd start getting answers. But tonight—tonight she'd pray. *Dio* had to take mercy on her. He had to.

Her mobile phone buzzed on her nightstand, making her jump. She sniffed hard and wiped at her tears before answering. Sandro's glee-filled voice greeted her. "Lover boy's on the loose. He's at Barfly. As usual."

"What?"

"I had him followed. I figured the way he ran off today that he was upset and would fall back on old habits. And I was right."

Her stomach sank when she realized why he'd called. "You want me to go after Antonio tonight? I feel like hell."

"As long as you don't look it, it doesn't matter."

"Sandro, I can't. Not tonight."

"What's so special about tonight?"

Six years ago, she'd gone into labor. A day later, on Christmas Eve, her boy had been born. But Sandro didn't care about that.

"Bianca?"

"I just can't."

"It's that time of the month?"

"*Dio*, you are rude!"

"Well, is it?"

"No."

"Then get yourself together and go. He's probably getting drunk. It's the perfect opportunity."

No doubt he was right. But how could she possibly—

"Bee, think about Papà and Fedele."

She sighed, guilt eating at her. She couldn't do anything to find Luca right now. And besides, didn't Antonio deserve some comeuppance after how he'd treated her? After how he'd treated Luca? How he could have just walked away... she'd never understand it.

Yes, Antonio deserved a little taste of the bitter dish he'd served.

——— • ———

The music pounded hard and fast, reverberating in Antonio's chest as he threw back another drink. He glanced around Barfly, the strobe lights and garish décor feeling a little alien to him tonight, even though he'd been there many times before. Maybe it was all the decorations for Natale.

Someone slapped him on the back. "There you are!" Cristoforo Andretti shouted in his ear. Giovanna d'Imperio had come with Cris. Wonderful. He'd wanted Cris's company, not Gio's. Hopefully she'd keep her hands to herself. Despite what Don Enrico had said, he had no intention of pursuing Gio. First, Cris wanted her. And second, Gio's father would never accept him.

None of them ever would.

"Tonio." Gio placed a hand on his cheek. "You look miserable. What's wrong?"

Everything. Every fucking thing. He took a breath and stared into his empty glass. "Don Enrico took the vows today."

"The *comparaggio*?" Cris asked. Antonio could barely bring himself to nod. "Fuck," Cris said.

"Exactly."

"Have things gotten any easier with Sandro and Matteo?" Gio asked.

"I almost broke Sandro's nose last week. That's how good things are."

"Well, you have to understand how he feels," Cris said.

"How he feels is irrelevant. Don Enrico chose me. That's all that matters."

Cris looked away and focused on signaling the bartender. The bunched muscles in Cris's jaw told Antonio everything he needed to know. Cris was taking their side. Which was ironic, considering that Sandro and Matteo hated the

Andrettis. But Cris had inherited his role, had expected to be *capo di società* since birth. So of course he'd think Sandro was the wronged party.

Antonio had had his fill of entitled *principi della Mafia*. He jerked away from the bar, swaying when he stood. *Whoa.* All at once the alcohol slammed through his system. He hadn't eaten anything at the *comparaggio* party, and he'd downed several drinks since he'd arrived at Barfly. Maybe that hadn't been such a good idea.

Cris snagged his sleeve. "Listen, I can't help how I feel. I'm just trying to make you see the other side."

"You're supposed to be my friend. At least that's what I thought."

"What kind of friend would I be if I agreed with everything that came out of your mouth?"

Gio placed a hand over Cris's. "*Tesoro*, I think Tonio needs our sympathy, not arguments."

"This is business, Gio. There's no sympathy in this life. You should know that."

With well-manicured fingers, she flicked a strand of honey-streaked brown hair out of her eyes and glared at Cris. "Remember when you were trying to console Delfi because she thought Nick had betrayed her?" He nodded. "Well, you still suck at it."

Antonio took a deep breath. The last thing he wanted was to cause friction between Cris and Gio. Especially since Don Enrico's plan for Antonio and Gio could reach their ears. "I'm sorry. I think I'd better work off some of this alcohol." Before they could stop him, he wove through the crowd to the dance floor, his steps a little unsteady. Maybe he should just go home.

He was about to head for the exit when he spotted a short, dark-haired girl with a gorgeous rack. Hmm. He'd been celibate for months now. Maybe a fuck was in order. He headed her way, and she gave him a coy smile. He returned it and raked her up and down, making sure she saw his appraisal.

A fuck would be just the thing to get the Lucchesis off his mind. All of them. Including Bianca.

Especially Bianca.

———— ◆ ————

Bianca winced when she stepped inside Barfly. Between the deafening music and the lights sweeping over the crowd, she'd be lucky if she didn't develop a migraine.

Tugging at her too-short skirt and pulling her low-cut blouse up a little, she scanned the crowd for Antonio, but didn't see him. Could he have left? Only if *Dio* was taking mercy on her. She felt like a whore in this outfit, but Sandro had insisted. He'd told her that Antonio went for *troie*—the trampier, the better.

A tall muscular man bumped into her, and she stumbled. "Sorry," he said and steadied her.

The petite brunette at his elbow squealed just as Bianca recognized her. "Bee! It's you!" Giovanna d'Imperio opened her arms and launched herself at Bianca, folding her into a tight hug. "You haven't returned a single one of my calls!" Gio stepped back and shook a finger at her.

Bianca grinned at Gio. It had been far too long since she'd spoken to the girl who'd been her best friend before Bianca had left for Switzerland. A rush of affection welled up in her. Why had she been avoiding Gio?

Because there were so many things she didn't want to discuss. Even with Gio.

"I'm sorry, Gio. I really am. It's been so difficult, between Papà and Fedele—" Her voice grew too thick to continue, and tears blurred her vision.

"Oh sweetie." Gio hugged her again.

Bianca closed her eyes, the tears on the verge of spilling. This complete forgiveness was just so Gio. She should have been angry, she should have hated Bianca for the way she'd cut Gio out of her life, the way she'd stopped taking Gio's calls and answering her letters.

But here Gio was, just happy to see her friend and ever ready with a hug. Like nothing had ever happened.

Bianca embraced Gio tightly, then stepped back, wiping at her tears. Gio sniffed too and wiped her own, her long hot-pink nails making the task harder than it should have been. She blinked at Bianca. "Am I a mess?"

Bianca laughed. Gio hadn't changed a bit. "No. You look great."

The young man who'd bumped into Bianca took Gio's elbow and smiled. "Aren't you going to introduce me?" he said to Gio.

There was something familiar about him, but Bianca couldn't quite place him. Gio's eyes widened and she clapped a hand over her mouth. "Oh, where are my manners? Bee, this is Cristoforo Andretti. Cris, this is Bianca Lucchesi."

He stuck out a hand. She took it, then let go mid-shake. His father had engineered Fedele's death, and his grandfather had ordered her father's murder. Cris reddened slightly, seeming to realize the awkwardness at the same time. His mouth opened, then shut, then opened again. "I'm sorry about your brother. And your father."

Anger boiled up in her. "So easy for you to say."

He raised his hands in surrender. "I understand how you feel. But those were not my decisions." He paused. "And now there is peace between our families."

She stared hard at him. "There is peace between the Andrettis and Don Lucchesi."

Gio slipped an arm through hers and patted her hand. "Sweetie, Cris isn't the enemy."

"Is he your *ragazzo*? Your *fidanzato*?"

Gio tilted her head and eyed Cris Andretti up and down. "Not officially."

"Good. Then I don't have to talk to him." What was wrong with her? She was losing control of her emotions.

She took a breath and let her gaze sweep over the packed dance floor. A couple a few feet away were plastered together, the man's big hands cupping the girl's rear through her skin-tight dress as his hips ground against hers. Disgusting. They were practically having sex right there in front of everyone, the man's blond head pressed against hers, his mouth working at the girl's neck. A flash of heat—utterly unexpected—shimmied through Bianca. Antonio had done that to her, his tongue and lips on her neck had made her quiver, made her melt—

The blond looked up, his eyes meeting hers, and a shock rolled through her. Antonio.

It was just like her father had said. Like Sandro had said. Antonio was a dog, sniffing after anything female.

He hadn't changed, and he never would.

Gio nudged her, apparently putting two and two together. "Sweetie, we need to talk."

"Yes, we do."

Antonio went back to kissing the girl's neck, his gaze still on Bianca. So he was rubbing it in. *Figlio di puttana.*

Bianca turned away. Now she was face to face with Cris Andretti again. She should just leave. Surely Sandro would understand—

Cris placed a hand on her shoulder. "Bianca, I can never erase the wrongs my family has done to yours. But I would hope you could see past my name. If not for my sake, then for Gio's. Someday"—he gave Gio a smile so sweet it was almost heartbreaking—"I hope to be her *fidanzato*, and eventually her husband."

Bianca inhaled deeply. He seemed sincere. And Gio wouldn't lie to her. She never had. Except perhaps about how she'd lost Bianca's favorite blouse when they were fourteen. "Okay. I'll try."

"*Mille grazie.* That is very generous of you."

"So," Bianca asked, motioning over her shoulder with her thumb. "How many girls has Antonio humped tonight?"

"First one this evening, as far as I know," Cris said.

"Usually it's five or six," Gio added. She frowned. "I used to be one of them. But not anymore."

Cris wrapped an arm around Gio's waist and pulled her into his side. "He knows I'd kill him if he touched you."

Gio laughed and nudged Cris. "He knows my *father* would kill him."

Cris smiled and pressed a light kiss to Gio's lips. Jealousy swamped Bianca. She wanted that. She wanted a *ragazzo*. She wanted to feel that carefree. That happy.

That young again.

Cris spotted an empty table along the wall and ushered Gio and Bianca over to it before it was scooped up. When they took their seats, he leaned over to Bianca. "Antonio told us about the *comparaggio*. Your brothers must be happy."

"My brothers—" She was cut off by a familiar voice.

"Are they here?" Antonio asked, looking around. He plopped into the chair next to her.

"No. I came by myself." Remembering why she was there, she leaned toward him, giving him an eyeful of her cleavage. His gaze traveled right where she wanted it to go, and she laid her fingers on his wrist. When he flexed his hand, she felt the shift of the muscles in his forearm. A thrill shot through her. What would it feel like now, to have him lying atop her? He was so much broader, bigger, than he'd been back then.

His eyes shifted to where she was touching him. Her first instinct was to withdraw her fingers, but she resisted it, and instead lightly caressed his skin. He felt warm, his skin soft. "You left today without saying anything," she said.

He moved closer, bringing his other hand up and laying it over hers, stilling her fingers, trapping them. "And what was I supposed to say?"

She had no answer. The fire in his gaze, the anger, took her aback. Though of course he'd be angry. His position was threatened. But he deserved it. If Sandro was right—if Antonio had killed Papà—he deserved a lot worse.

Without question, he deserved what he was going to get for abandoning her and their child.

She motioned him forward and put her lips to his ear. "You liked me once, Tonio. I'd think you'd have plenty to say to me."

He drew back and stared at her, his face unreadable. Time to give him a moment to think. She rose, clutching her handbag, and tapped Gio on the shoulder. "I need to powder my nose," Bianca said.

"Oh! Me too." Gio apparently recognized that Bianca wanted to talk.

They pushed their way through the crowd to the women's restroom. Inside, the thumping of the music sounded like a giant's frenetic heartbeat, but at least they no longer had to shout.

"What are you up to?" Gio asked. "I thought you were angry with him."

"Maybe I've changed my mind." Bianca ran a brush through her hair, which fell in perfect waves around her face and down to her shoulders. She'd always been proud of it. Gio reached behind Bianca and pulled her hair back, revealing her ears and jawline.

"You should wear it up," Gio said. "And I know you haven't changed your mind. So tell me, what's going on?"

Bianca stared at herself in the mirror. With her hair up, she looked more vulnerable. Delicate. She couldn't be that way. Not with Antonio. She shook her head, freeing her hair from Gio's hands, then turned to face her friend and leaned on the edge of the sink. "What do you know about the night my father was killed? Has Cris told you anything?"

Gio shrugged. "I only know what I've heard through my family. Cris and I don't talk about business."

"Do you think Antonio could have had anything to do with it?"

Gio's eyes widened. "Why would you say that?"

"Sandro said—" She stopped herself. Perhaps it was best to keep Sandro's theories private.

When she didn't continue, Gio crossed her arms. "Your brother talks a lot of shit, you know."

She did know. Still, he wouldn't have made that up. Would he?

"You didn't answer my question," Gio said. "What are you doing with Antonio?"

Bianca turned away and rummaged in her bag, not sure what to say. Her hand closed on the tube she was searching for. She applied a fresh coat of lip gloss, loving how it smelled. Like vanilla. Finally she settled on an explanation that might satisfy Gio. "Maybe I'm not done with him yet."

Gio gave her a wide grin and smacked her on the arm. "*Davvero?*"

Bianca smiled into the mirror and winked at Gio. "You'll know soon enough."

———◆———

Antonio switched seats so he could speak to Cris without shouting. "What did Bianca talk to you about?"

"She made sure to let me know I come from a family of snakes." Cris rolled his eyes.

Smothering his impatience, Antonio tried again. "Did she say anything about me?"

Cris grinned. "She wanted to know how many girls you'd danced with. If you can call what you were doing dancing."

A thrill rippled through Antonio's belly. Was she jealous? If so, maybe he had another shot at her.

Of course, that would only make matters worse with her brothers. But at this point, how much worse could they get? Sandro had already said Antonio would be eating a bullet if Sandro had his way. And since Signora Andretti approved the idea of Antonio and Bianca together, perhaps she could convince Sandro to accept it.

Cristo, he was being stupid, getting ahead of himself. He didn't even know what Bianca was thinking. Though she seemed friendlier tonight. That *was* a good sign, yes?

He surveyed the jammed space, looking for the two girls, the wait making him tense. What if Bianca had just been teasing him? What if he'd misread her—

He shook his head and chuckled to himself. She'd touched him—only on the arm—and here he was, fifteen all over again, nervous as hell and half-hard already, just from thinking about the possibility of having another chance with her. Of having her in his arms, pressed groin to groin, her heavenly little mound grinding into him...

Two small hands covered his eyes from behind. "Guess who?" a female voice asked.

Merda. That girl he'd been dancing with. What was her name? It started with an "E" or an "I"—"Iliana?" he said aloud.

Her hands left his eyes and tweaked his ears. "Elena," she said emphatically. "I thought you were getting us drinks."

"I ran into a friend."

Elena turned to Cris and scanned him up and down, then smiled wickedly. She leaned over and whispered in Antonio's ear. "I've always wondered what two guys at once would be like. Do you think your friend would be interested?"

Antonio suppressed a groan. How did he get himself into these situations? Because he let his *cazzo* do the thinking. He was about to explain that he had no desire to share his bed with another guy—even if there was a girl in the mix—when Gio and Bianca returned. Bianca looked annoyed. *Fuck*. Though Gio seemed mildly amused. Until Elena put a hand on Cris's shoulder.

Gio bustled around Bianca and over to Cris. "Hooves off, *vacca*," she hissed at Elena.

Bianca crossed her arms and glared at Antonio. "Elena, this is the friend I ran into," he said, motioning to Bianca.

Elena gave him a look that could have withered rock. "I see. I was only good enough for you to grind on when your *ragazza* wasn't around."

"She's not my—" he started to say, but Elena was already out of earshot. With a sinking stomach, he turned back to Bianca. She stared at him a moment longer, arms crossed beneath her ample chest, and then to his complete surprise, she uncrossed them and sat down beside him. She leaned in. "I think you and I should talk," she said. "Some place quieter." A coy smile toyed with her lips.

Minchia! Was she giving him another chance?

———•———

Her heart fluttering in her throat and her hand engulfed in Antonio's, Bianca followed him as he towed her through the teeming mass of tightly packed bodies and then out Barfly's back door. They exited onto an alley. The door clanged behind them, shutting out most of the sound in the crowded club, though the low thumping of the bass followed them even outside.

Apparently this was the smoking area. Couples and groups were clumped around a cluster of rickety tables dotted with ashtrays. A large doorman guarded the rear entrance to Barfly. Antonio pulled her a few meters down the alley toward a dimly lit alcove. It was quieter there, and nicer without the high-intensity glare of the lights behind the club. He tugged her into the alcove and positioned her so her back was against one of the stone walls that enclosed a doorway. He could see the others behind the club if he wished. All she could see was him.

He was standing too close to her, crowding her really, but somehow she didn't mind. The image of him kissing that girl's neck rose unbidden in her mind, a sudden bolt of desire and irritation mixed blasting through her. How could she possibly still want him? How could she possibly be jealous?

Antonio pressed a step closer, his large body in his open black leather coat radiating heat. Her hands and face were cold already in the late December air, and her jacket was still in the coat check. He lifted his hands, settling them on her shoulders, cradling her neck between them, their heat making her want to nestle into him. But she held her ground and tried to ignore the shivers that ran through her. It was the cold, damn it. The cold. Not him. Not Antonio.

"You wanted to talk?" he murmured, his eyes drifting down to her lips, then back up to meet her gaze. His mouth curved into a sexy, lazy grin that she recognized from the one time they'd slept together, the grin he'd given her after they'd made love. When he'd known she was his.

How dare he assume he had her again? She wanted to slap that grin away, to grab his hands and push them off her. But she couldn't give in to that impulse. Not if she wanted to help Sandro. Not if she wanted to know the truth.

Not if she wanted to punish Antonio and give him a taste of what he'd done to her.

She settled her hands over his and snuggled up against his hard, hot body. "I can't think of anything to say," she whispered.

His grin widened. "I can." His hands slid up and cupped her cheeks, then

43

Antonio slanted his mouth over hers, the press of his lips firm, insistent. Confident. So different from when they'd been teenagers. He was a man now, and he kissed like one. Not that she had any experience kissing other men. She just knew.

His tongue slid against her lips and she opened to him, not successful in suppressing the moan this invasion tore from her. Antonio was the first man—the *only* man—who'd held her in the last six years, quick hugs from her father and brothers aside. Those short, affectionate embraces were nothing like this. They didn't threaten her control. They didn't make her quiver, didn't make her weak. Didn't make her lose track of why she'd come here. Of why she was kissing him. But at the moment, she didn't care about any of that. She just wanted to feel. To lose herself.

Bianca molded herself to Antonio, her hands slipping under his jacket and splaying across his well-muscled back. He felt like granite beneath her fingers. One of his hands slid down to her bottom and cupped it, pressing her into him so she could feel the steely length of his *cazzo* against her belly.

Dio, she wanted him, she burned for him. An ache pulsed between her legs. She was wet, so wet, already. All he had to do was touch her there. All he had to do was ask, and she'd be his—

No. It was one thing to seduce him. It was another to be seduced *by* him. Especially tonight.

She placed her hands on his chest and pushed him back. Antonio was dangerous; he was the lit match to her powder keg. One touch, and she was ready to blow.

And she couldn't have that. She had to stay in control at all costs.

He stared at her, panting as fast as she was. "What?" he asked and stepped closer to her again. "What is it, Bee?" His voice, so husky, so soft, was almost her undoing. He'd called her "Bee" back then. He'd called her "Bee" and told her he loved her.

And she'd taken that love and crushed it in the harshest way possible.

Was that why he'd walked away from her and the baby? Was that why he'd shot her father—if Sandro was right?

She needed to think. She needed to get her wits about her. She needed to get as far away from Antonio as possible.

"I think this is enough for one evening," she said.

He smiled. "Does that mean there will be more?"

Dio help her. "Yes." She stepped back from him and rubbed her arms, and he quickly slipped off his jacket and draped it over her shoulders. She pulled it closed, getting a whiff of his scent—the light citrus of his cologne and an undercurrent that was purely him.

Her throat tightened as they walked back to the club. Why must everything be so complicated?

She wished she'd never heard of Antonio Legato. She wished she'd never kissed him.

She wished she didn't want to kiss him again.

CHAPTER 6

Bianca tightened her grip on the steering wheel and turned up the gravel drive to the Lucchesi Home for Children. Kate hadn't been at home when she'd called. Zio Enrico had told her that Kate was already at the orphanage, but only for a half day, since it was Christmas Eve.

She parked next to a sleek black Maserati with a burly man behind the wheel. He gave her a once-over when she got out, and she realized it was Tommaso, one of Zio Enrico's guards. So he must be there to watch over Kate's car. Bianca nodded to him, and he smiled and waved. Tommaso had been one of the few guards who'd survived the attack by the Russians the day of Nico and Delfina's engagement. *Grazie a Dio* that Zio Enrico hadn't invited her family. Of course, after her brother Fedele had tried to plot with Dario Andretti against Enrico—and had paid the price—the Lucchesis hadn't exactly been one big happy family. And Zio Enrico had apparently had some inkling that there would be trouble at the party, so he'd invited almost no one in any case. Someday she'd learn the details about what had happened.

But today she hoped to learn something else—where her little boy was.

She walked up the front steps and noted another guard leaning up against the wall by the door. He was smoking and trying to look bored, but he thoroughly assessed her, his gaze clinical at first, then shifting to something else. He gave her a half-smile that she returned with a flirty little wink before stepping inside.

Antonio Legato did *not* own her.

She started down the hall, her pulse thrumming in her ears. What if Kate said no?

Bianca was about to knock on the door to Dottor Laurio's office when she noticed another hulking guard lurking in the corridor. He stood next to another office door, but kept his eyes roving between her, the main entrance, and the exit at the far end of the hallway. Apparently her uncle was taking no chances, truce with the Andrettis or no. She approached the guard and saw that her instincts were correct. The brass plaque on the office door read "Kate Lucchesi."

She addressed the guard. "Bianca Lucchesi to see *la signora*."

He nodded, then stepped inside and closed the door behind him. She heard the murmur of voices, then he came back out. "*Prego*," he said, opening the door wide and motioning for her to enter.

Taking a deep breath, Bianca entered Kate's domain. The office appeared to have been freshly painted and redecorated, with a new desk and chairs. Several lush plants sat atop the filing cabinets and a large poinsettia dominated a corner of Kate's crowded desk.

The woman in question looked up from her laptop and greeted Bianca with a warm smile. Kate came around the desk and embraced her, giving her quick kisses on both cheeks. "You wanted to see me?"

"Yes," Bianca answered, reminding herself to speak in English. Kate's Italian wasn't bad, but she spoke slowly and her pronunciation was a little off. "I thought I could help with the records." She surveyed the cramped office. "It appears to be a great deal of work, yes?"

Kate smiled again. "Your English is very good."

"I went to an excellent school, and all our classes were taught in English."

For a moment, Kate studied her, but her eyes dropped to the desk before she spoke. "It must have been hard being away from your family for so long. And then to lose your father."

Bianca swallowed against the lump in her throat. "It was." She stared at her joined hands in her lap. "And then Fedele—" She stopped before she choked on the rest and wiped away a tear that clung to her lashes. Would this *never* get any easier?

Kate handed her a box of tissues. Bianca blushed and waved them away. "Don't be embarrassed," Kate said. "Now that I'm pregnant, I cry at anything. Yesterday it was because I saw a TV commercial with a lost kitten. A kitten!" Kate groaned and sat back in her chair. "I'm driving Enrico crazy. He's always asking me what's wrong."

"I am sure he does not mind."

Kate brushed a few strands of auburn hair off her face and smiled. "He's pretty patient. But I'm not." She motioned around her office. "I'd love some help with this mess."

Bianca let out a breath. *Grazie a Dio.*

An hour later, Bianca was set up with a laptop and a pile of files to transcribe. Kate showed her the forms to fill out and which folders to save them in on the network. Bianca didn't have her own account, so Kate gave her limited guest access to the network. She could save into a folder that Kate had designated, but she couldn't browse the existing folders for the records that had already been computerized. And she saw when she opened her first manila folder that the case was that of a girl whose last name started with *N*. Had Kate already finished the "L" names?

"Do I shred the paper records after I finish?"

"Not yet. To be sure the information is accurate, I have Gina, the secretary, read through them and compare the paper to the computerized record."

"Has she caught up to you then?"

Kate shook her head. "She's still somewhere around *G*."

Bianca's pulse quickened. So perhaps her paper file was still here—*if* her father had brought the baby to this orphanage. "Where do I put the folders when I am finished?"

Kate pointed at the cabinets behind her. "In there. The red cardboard marks where to start."

They worked for close to three hours, Bianca occasionally asking a question, waiting for the moment when Kate would leave her alone with the files. Finally Kate rose and stretched her back. The pregnancy was just starting to show. "Hungry?" Kate asked. "I know we're supposed to be fasting today for Christmas Eve, but with the pregnancy, the doctor recommended I eat. The cook is making me *trofie* with pesto and chicken. Want some?"

Bianca shook her head and somehow kept her eyes from darting to the file cabinet with the drawer marked "L—M." "Mamma is making a big dinner."

"I thought you were eating with us."

Averting her gaze, Bianca shrugged. "I think we've had a change of plans. Sandro is still not in the best of moods."

Kate sighed. "Okay, then. Will it bother you if I eat in here?"

"Not at all." As soon as the door closed behind Kate, Bianca was out of her seat and at the filing cabinet. She eased the drawer open and started scanning the tabs. Her fingers skimmed through the files until she reached the names starting with "Lu." Heart pounding, she reached the end of the names starting with "Lub." "Luc" names were next. She reached "Luca," then "Lucc." She found a file for "Lucchese," then one for "Luciano." No file for "Lucchesi."

Disappointment flooded her. Had her father not brought the baby here? Had he taken her son to some place in Switzerland? If so, she had no hope of ever finding her child. Where would she even start? The hospital had been no help, beyond confirming they'd released a child to her father and a doctor. She was sure she'd heard her father say something to her mother about a Dottor Laurio. Once she'd learned that was the name of the director for the Lucchesi Home for Children, she was sure she'd been on the right path.

She'd been wrong.

Her throat closed up. She'd failed. She'd failed herself and her baby.

The door to the office opened, and Bianca shoved the heavy file drawer shut. It screeched as Kate came in bearing two plates and said, "I brought you a little in case you changed your mind." Bianca froze in front of the drawer, hoping Kate wouldn't notice which one it was.

Kate set the plates on the desk, then traded places with Bianca. They took their seats, Bianca's hands trembling from nerves. She stared at the hand-twisted *trofie*, a pasta she'd always enjoyed. But there was no way she'd be able to swallow even a single bite. Kate picked up her fork and looked at Bianca. "You won't find that file in the cabinets."

A spark of hope lit in Bianca's chest. Kate knew! But then her words sank in. She wasn't going to help.

"*Per favore*," Bianca said, the words tumbling out, sounding desperate even to her own ears. "*Per favore*. I have to know where he is."

"I wish I could tell you. I truly do. Unfortunately, those records are sealed."

"But I am his *mamma!*"

"I know. You'll still need a court order to open the records."

Tears spilled down Bianca's cheeks. *"Per favore."*

Kate started to cry too, and she rounded the desk and crouched down by Bianca's chair. When she put her arms around Bianca and stroked her hair, that only made Bianca cry harder.

"Why will you not help me?" Bianca asked.

"I can't. Not this way. But if you petition the court—"

"How? With what money? My family wants me forget about him. But I cannot."

"I'll speak to Enrico. We will help you."

"You could just show me. No one has to know."

"And what happens when you try to see him and the family finds out? The orphanage would get shut down. Confidentiality is crucial."

Bianca didn't want anything to happen to the orphanage, but could she trust Kate? "You *will* help me?"

Kate nodded. "Even if Enrico won't, I will." She patted Bianca's hair and kissed her cheek. "Now eat your *trofie*, before I do. I'm starving!"

Bianca gave her a tentative grin and hoped Kate was telling the truth. She wasn't sure she could stand another disappointment.

———— ◆ ————

Antonio paced around his new flat. Should he call Bianca? Ever since they'd kissed last night, he'd thought of nothing but her. That kiss had burned him up inside, made him think of how good they could be together, instead of the disaster they'd been.

He was being an idiot though. Her brothers—no matter how much he might wish otherwise—would never accept him. If Sandro knew about the kiss, he'd probably shoot Antonio now and worry about the fallout later.

And what about Bianca herself? She'd been so hot and cold with him—her behavior hardly made sense. Unless...

Unless she was fighting being with him for the same reasons.

His mobile phone rang, startling him. He didn't recognize the number on the display, so he answered with caution.

"Antonio?" Bianca. His stomach gave a nervous flip, something that hadn't happened with a girl since he'd been a teenager. Since he'd approached Bianca the first time.

"Sì. How did you get this number?"

"Kate gave it to me."

"When did you talk to Kate?"

"I'm helping at the orphanage." Her words seemed flat, and she abruptly fell silent.

"Is everything okay?" he asked.

"I'm a little distracted." Again, that little flip in his gut.

"Please tell me I'm not the only one thinking about last night." He almost slapped himself. *Play it cool, idiota.*

"You're not," she finally said. But she didn't sound happy about it.

"Bee, what's wrong?"

Again, she hesitated, and his pulse sped up. Had her brothers somehow found out about the kiss?

Finally she spoke. "Can we meet somewhere?"

He named a café near his flat and they agreed to meet in an hour. After they ended the call, he released a breath he hadn't realized he'd been holding. What if it wasn't her brothers? What if she'd been playing him again?

And here he'd gone and given her ammunition. What a sap.

———◆———

Antonio hadn't seen her yet, and Bianca observed him for a moment undetected. He was sitting outside at the café he'd suggested in downtown Cernobbio, tapping one foot and fiddling with a cup of espresso. Good. He was nervous. Maybe she'd get something close to the truth from him.

She approached from behind and set her hand on his shoulder as a test. He jerked violently, twisting to meet her, his face a hostile mask that fled the moment he recognized her. He was definitely on edge and prepared to fight.

Settling into the seat opposite him, she took her time ordering an espresso from the waiter who'd been hovering nearby. After the man left, Antonio leaned forward. "What's going on, Bianca?"

"Why were you hanging out with Cris Andretti?"

"He's my friend."

"*Is* he?" she asked, her tone accusing.

"*Sì.*"

"You'd choose the Andrettis over the family you've pledged yourself to?"

"I haven't chosen the Andrettis over the Lucchesis."

"*Davvero?*"

"Bianca, what are you really asking?"

"The Andrettis killed my brother and my father. And here you are, so cozy with them."

"I'm comfortable with *Cris.* But that's as far as it goes."

Her anger jumped from simmer to boil. "Sandro tells me otherwise."

Antonio's eyes narrowed and hostility veiled his features again. "He knows nothing."

He didn't deny it. Something twisted in her gut. "You hated my father."

"Not true."

She ignored what he said and leaned across the table so he'd hear her whisper. "You hated him and you killed him. Just like you wanted me to—" She cut herself off, unable to say the words.

Confusion etched his brow. "I didn't kill him. And what was the rest of that? What do you think I wanted you to do?"

She hesitated. He sounded sincere. When she said nothing, he continued. "Yesterday you were all over me, and today you want to bite my head off. What's wrong with you? Why are you asking me about Cris *now*? Why not last night?"

Her gut quivering, her hands shaking, Bianca took a deep breath. How did he do this to her? She was every kind of mixed up—enraged, disappointed, confused. She clenched her trembling hands together in her lap.

His gaze roamed her face and his expression softened. "Tell me, *per favore*. What's wrong?"

Tears blurred her vision. Of course he had no idea. For all he knew, she'd killed their baby. "Do you—" she started, then stopped when her voice grew too thick.

"Do I what?" he asked, his question so soft, so tender, her tears spilled over.

"Do you know what day it is?"

"December twenty-fourth. Why?"

"Our son was born six years ago today."

His eyes widened. "Our son?"

Anger filled her. He hadn't agonized like she had. He hadn't suffered like she had. And he never would, would he? "Yes. I couldn't go through with your orders to kill our baby."

"What the hell are you talking about? What game is this?"

"Game? It might be one to you. But it's *never* been a game to me."

The waiter interrupted with her espresso, and she wrapped her cold hands around it gratefully, inhaling the familiar aroma, though caffeine was probably the last thing she needed on top of all the adrenaline.

Antonio said nothing for a moment, then he rapped the table with his knuckles, making her jump. "Bianca, tell me straight out: What the hell are you talking about? Are you saying I got you pregnant?"

The incredulity in his tone gave her pause. Did he truly not know? Papà had told him, Papà had given him a choice... hadn't he?

She stared at Antonio and nodded. "*Sì.*"

"Why the hell didn't you tell me?" Before she could answer, he continued. "Oh wait. That's right. You wanted nothing to do with an orphan." He shook his head. "No wonder your father always gave me a hard time. It's a wonder he didn't put a bullet in me."

"You honestly didn't know?"

"What makes you think otherwise?"

"Papà told you. *You* wanted nothing to do with *us*. He said you wanted me to get rid of it."

"I would never say that."

"I might have believed that if you hadn't joined the 'Ndrangheta."

"What does that have to do with anything?"

"You're a killer now."

He leaned forward and stabbed the white linen tablecloth with a long finger. "I may be many things, but I wouldn't kill my own child. And I would never ask you to do so." He stabbed the table again, his blue eyes piercing her. "*Never*, Bianca. I am not a monster." He sat back and ran a hand through his hair. "Where's our son?"

She shrugged, her vision once again blurring with tears, her stomach contracting with shame. "I don't know."

"What do you mean? How could you not know?"

"He was adopted."

"What?" The blade of his voice cut into her. "How?"

"My father arranged it."

"It's illegal. I never signed my rights away."

She shrank back into her chair. "You're not listed on the birth certificate."

"Who was then?"

She shook her head. "No one. I said I didn't know your name."

"*Dio mio.* You didn't tell them you'd been raped."

"No," she whispered. "I just said I'd been drunk. I never accused you or anyone else of taking advantage of me."

He let out a puff of air. "At least you were honest about that much."

"I didn't know what else to do. Papà was so angry."

"You didn't even have the good taste to pick a boy with a *name.*"

"Tonio—"

"No." He slapped the table with the flat of his hand. "No. You told me your family didn't want you with an orphan. The truth was, *you* didn't want an orphan. If you'd wanted to be with me, you would have told me."

"We were fifteen. What were you going to do? You didn't have any family, any money. And if I'd gone against Papà—"

He slapped the table again. "Fuck!" The word exploded from his lips. "How could you keep this from me? How could you let me think, all these years, that you hated me?"

"It was the right thing to do. We would never have been able to be together. You weren't part of the 'Ndrangheta then."

He was silent for so long, his face immobile with anger, that she feared for what he'd do next. Finally he spoke. "Where was the adoption handled?"

"At the Lucchesi Home. But I can't get access to the records."

"I can."

"Kate said I needed a court order—"

"Fuck that. I'll get those records."

"But she said—"

"*Basta!*" He leveled her with a stare. "*I* will get them. No child of mine will grow up without me."

He rose from the table and stalked away, his boots thudding on the stone walkway.

A sob rose in her throat. He hadn't known.

And Papà had betrayed her.

———— ◆ ————

Luckily, when Bianca arrived home, she found her mother alone in the kitchen. She was making *cannoli*, the rich dessert that Sandro loved.

"We need to talk," Bianca said.

"About what, *cara*?" Her mother wiped her hands on her apron and took a seat at the kitchen table.

"The baby." Bianca sat opposite her mother, her heart beating fast.

Her mother's face softened and she reached out and took Bianca's hands. "Oh, sweetie. I'd forgotten. It was today, wasn't it?"

She nodded stiffly, determined not to weaken. "Papà lied to me."

"About what?" Her mother's consternation seemed genuine.

"He never told the father."

"How could he? He didn't know who that was."

"No. *You* didn't know. Papà forced me to tell him. He said he'd talk to him, give him the chance to do the right thing. But he never did."

Her mother sat back in her chair, letting go of Bianca's hands. "Are you sure?"

"I'm sure. The father didn't know. He does now." She twined her fingers together. "I'm so furious with Papà. How could he lie to me like that?"

Her mother looked away. "I'm sure he did what he thought was best."

"He ruined my life!"

"Who's the father?" her mother asked.

"That's not important."

Her mother leaned forward. "It's *everything*, Bianca, and you know it. Now, who?"

"Antonio."

Her mother's brows popped up. "Legato?"

Bianca nodded and searched her mother's face, but didn't see the disappointment she'd expected. Why?

"I understand what your father did and why he did it. Antonio had nothing to offer you then."

"Papà could've helped us—"

"Yes, he could have. But he chose not to. Your father wanted more for you."

"He wanted more for the *family*, you mean."

"There is nothing wrong with ambition."

Bianca crossed her arms. "Do you agree with what he did?"

"I said I *understood* it. Understanding and agreeing are not the same thing."

"But had you known, you wouldn't have fought him."

Her mother teared up then, her nose reddening, her face crumpling. "I wouldn't have. But not because I didn't love you. Because I *do*."

"How can you say that? I have this hole right here." Bianca tapped her chest with a closed fist. "I ache. I think about him every day. My baby is out there somewhere and I don't know where he is, or who he's with, or if he's happy. What if they're awful to him? What if he's miserable?"

"I'm sure his parents love him as much as you do."

"*I'm* his parent! I'm his *mother*. He should be with me!" A sob ripped from her throat. "I let him go. What kind of mother does that?"

"You wanted what was best for him." Her mother reached for her hand again, but Bianca snatched it away. "If you'd kept him, if you'd stayed here, what future would you have had? You were still half a child yourself. You and Antonio were not ready to be parents."

"We could have managed."

"Maybe. But what prospects did Antonio have?" Her mother softened her voice. "He wasn't one of us. He was an outsider. An outsider with no family. Who could have predicted that your uncle would take him into the *cosca*? I can't think of another *capo* who would."

"We could have survived—"

"And what if Antonio had turned against us? What if he hadn't joined the 'Ndrangheta? You would've had your father risk our lives over a boy no one knew?"

"*I* knew him."

"Did you? Did you really? Had you predicted who he'd become? Did you know he'd willingly embrace the *malavita*?"

She hadn't. Few things could have surprised her more. He hadn't seemed the sort. He hadn't seemed the sort at all.

Oh, there was a toughness about him, and at his height and weight, he cut an imposing figure. But there was something—something soft about his eyes. Something that told her he wasn't a hard man. Not inside.

Not yet.

But if Sandro's plan succeeded, what kind of man might Antonio be then? Particularly if he learned her part in it.

She needed to talk to Sandro. It was time to end this stupid game.

She owed Antonio that much.

CHAPTER 7

Antonio slammed the car into park outside Don Enrico's villa. He took a deep breath, fighting for some semblance of control. How could Bianca have done this? How could she have stripped him of his child?

The answer stared him in the face—she truly didn't care for him. She never had. When she'd dismissed him the first time, he should have believed her. He'd almost fallen for her act all over again.

He shook his head and scrubbed a hand over his face. She was a good actress. A damn good one.

But what else should he have expected from a daughter of Domenico Lucchesi? He'd been a good actor too, and he'd stabbed Don Enrico in the back. At least now Don Domenico's enmity toward Antonio made sense. The man had considered him the lowest of the low.

But he'd have married Bianca. If he'd been given the chance. He would never have abandoned her. He would never have abandoned his child.

And he wasn't about to now. He left the car and bolted up the front stairs, his feet eating up the distance before he even quite knew what he wanted to say to Kate.

Maddalena answered the door. "Signora Lucchesi," he said.

"She's in the solarium," the maid said and stepped aside to let him in the house.

He strode down the hall, his boots echoing on the marble. His path took him past Don Enrico's study. Mercifully the door was closed, so he was spared from making up some excuse for being here. For wanting to see Kate.

His teeth ground together. This had been his home. And now he was a fucking guest. He'd been exiled, and for what? Nothing. Not a damn thing.

So he cared about Kate. So what? He could care about her and be her friend. It would never be more than that between them. Never.

It would never be even that much between him and Bianca. They'd never be friends, much less lovers, much less in a relationship. None of that would come to pass.

Was this his payment, some kind of karmic retribution, for how he'd conducted himself with women?

At the end of the hall, he turned into a large airy space full of plants and floor-to-ceiling windows. A second Christmas tree, smaller than the one in the sitting room, was in the corner, its gleaming lights reflected in the glass of all those windows, backed by the darkness of early evening. Kate was curled up in her favorite chair, a book in hand, as usual.

She looked up, concern written all over her features when she saw him, and he felt a little pang. "What is it?" she asked. "Did something happen?" Her eyes shifted in the direction of her husband's study, and she started to rise. "Is he—" she began, but he shook his head.

"It has nothing to do with the business. It's personal."

The crease between her brows deepened. "You look like you want to kill someone."

He ran a hand through his hair and nodded. "I do. But the bastard is already dead."

"Who?"

"Don Domenico."

He could see her working it out for herself, but she wouldn't be that easy. "Why?" she asked.

"No games, Kate. You know why I'm here."

She closed her book on her thumb and sat up straighter. "No, I don't."

"But you can guess."

Her frosty stare was a surprise. "I could. But I won't."

"Bianca's baby. I'm the father."

"She just told you?"

"Yes. And I'm not waiting a minute longer to see him."

"I'm sorry, Tonio, but I'm afraid you are." The severity of her expression put a deep crease between her brows.

Was she truly going to deny him? "Kate, you have to tell me."

She shook her head. "I can't."

"Why not?"

"First off, it's a closed adoption. Second, your name's not on the birth certificate. Third—and most important—if I did tell you without a court order, the Lucchesi Home would lose its license. As much as I care about you, I will not jeopardize the lives of all those children."

"No one has to know."

She laughed. "So you aren't intending to charge out to see the child? Maybe even take him?"

His cheeks heated. Both ideas had crossed his mind. "This can't wait, damn it." He tapped his fingers along the seams of his trousers.

She crossed her arms. "Yelling at me and making demands will not bully me into helping you."

"I'm not trying to bully you." He touched her shoulder and let his hand slide down her arm to take her hand. "*Per favore.*" He brushed his lips across her knuckles. "*Mi dispiace.*"

"You're sorry for what?" A crisp voice asked from the doorway. Don Enrico.

Antonio dropped Kate's hand and stepped away from her.

The don advanced, his face hard and still as carved marble. "What is going on here?"

"It's a private matter," Antonio said.

"Involving my wife?"

"Indirectly."

The don planted his fists on his hips and stared Antonio down. "There should be no secrets between us. Especially not ones that you share with my wife."

Kate broke in. "I *do* have a name. I'm not a possession."

The don focused on her, his face softening slightly. "*Cara*, you know I don't mean it that way."

"I suppose I should consider myself lucky you haven't pissed on me to mark your territory," Kate said.

The don's mouth dropped open and a smile tugged at his lips. "You are, as always, direct."

"I hate game playing. And I hate being fought over by cavemen."

Antonio dropped his eyes to the floor tiles and blushed. He was guilty of trying to play on her emotions—that hint of flirtation when he'd kissed her hand—but it felt so normal, so easy. So... right somehow.

Maybe the don had a point about Kate. Antonio had yet to meet a woman he hadn't wanted to charm, and here he was, doing it again.

Don Enrico looked hard at Antonio, then at Kate. "One of you needs to tell me what's going on. *Now.*"

Kate glanced at Antonio, making plain that she felt it was his decision to say anything. He sighed. He didn't have another choice. "I just found out I fathered a child when I was fifteen. He was adopted out through the Lucchesi Home. Without my knowledge or consent. I want to find him."

Enrico raised his brows, then directed a question to Kate. "And you know where the child is?" She nodded and explained why she couldn't tell Antonio. "What about the mother?" he asked Antonio. "Will she tell you?"

Antonio gazed at the tiles. "She doesn't know either."

"Well then, you need to go to court with her. It sounds like she may be willing to acknowledge your status."

"She is. But we can't go to court."

"Why not?"

Meeting Kate's eyes, Antonio wondered how much he should say. She slowly shook her head. So the don didn't know about Bianca. "She can't. Her family wants to keep it buried." He hesitated. "Plus, they don't approve of me."

The don's gaze shifted from Antonio to Kate, then back again. "Who is this girl?"

"I can't tell you."

"I may be able to help with her family. There may be some connection to the *cosca*, the business, especially if they're from here."

Antonio suppressed a groan. The don would despise him once he knew. There'd be no calming down Sandro, no rapprochement, once the past between Antonio and Bianca came into the light.

The don studied him, a frown on his face. "What's the problem? Who *is* she?"

Kate broke in. "Tonio, perhaps you should consult with her, let her decide whether to involve Enrico?"

He'd have to call Bianca. He'd hoped to avoid her for the rest of their lives. But his luck couldn't be that good, could it? "Fine." He whipped out his phone. He told Bianca where he was and the situation.

"I'll be there in ten minutes," she said, not an ounce of fight in her tone.

He wasn't sure it was even that long before Bianca walked into the solarium, her green eyes red-rimmed and swollen, her light brown hair falling into her face. She looked thoroughly miserable, and some tiny part of him wanted to pull her into his arms. But she'd lied to him about something monumental. How could he ever forgive her?

The don glanced from Bianca to Antonio. "*Davvero?*" he asked.

"*Sì,*" Antonio said with a curt nod of his head.

The don appeared flummoxed. "But when? How?" And then understanding dawned on his face. "Switzerland."

Bianca nodded and twisted her hands together. "Papà didn't want anyone to know. He was... ashamed of me." Her voice broke on "ashamed," and again that tender impulse rose in Antonio. *No.* No, he wasn't going to forgive her. Not now. Not ever. She'd given his child away. Discarded him like trash. And why not? She obviously thought the same of Antonio. She'd told him as much.

"Does Sandro know about Antonio?" the don asked.

"No."

"Good. We need to keep it that way." He crossed his arms and focused on Antonio. "You didn't tell me the situation was this complicated."

"How could I?"

The don let out a long sigh. "Now I know why Dom didn't like you."

"So what do we do?" Bianca asked. "Will you help us?"

"That is not possible."

"*Per favore,*" Bianca whispered, unshed tears making the words almost indecipherable.

"I cannot trust the two of you to stay away from the child. And without the possibility of a legal solution, I do not see what else I can do. I will not risk the orphanage, no matter how much I care about you."

Kate placed a hand on her husband's shoulder. "What if you checked up on the child? At least to reassure them that he is well cared for?"

"What pretext would I use?"

"Perhaps you and Dottor Laurio could say that you're following up on the adoptions? To make sure that everything is satisfactory?"

"Too flimsy. And I'd rather not involve the director."

"Okay then. What if you pose as a lawyer? On behalf of Bianca. Asking if they'd consider changing the adoption to be open?"

The don took a deep breath. "Maybe that could work."

Bianca wiped her tears, and Antonio relaxed his clenched jaw. Perhaps there was some hope. But it was far from what he'd hoped for.

"I wish I could hold him," Bianca said. "I wish I could see him."

As bad as he felt for her, Antonio couldn't help his bitterness. "At least you got to see him once. I never have."

"I can help with that," Kate said. "I have the file with me. There's a picture. Wait here."

She left the room and returned a few minutes later, a Polaroid in hand. She held it out to them, and he and Bianca each took one side, drawing together as they gazed down on their son. The newborn in the photo was red and wrinkled. Antonio saw nothing of himself in the child, but still his throat sealed up, his eyes growing hot. *His* son. *His* child.

Bianca started to shake beside him, and she let out a strangled sob. Before he could stop himself, he put an arm around her and she sagged against him, her arm stealing around his waist. "*Mi dispiace*," she whispered. "I'm so, so, sorry, Tonio."

"I know, Bee. I know." He couldn't quite bring himself to forgive her. Not yet.

He wanted to hate her, he wanted to hurt her, he wanted to despise her. Yet he couldn't. She was suffering like he was. *More* than he was. How much worse had it been for her, knowing all this time, but being unable to do anything about it? How difficult must it have been for her to place her child in the arms of strangers?

When she finally stopped crying, Bianca looked too wrung out to drive, so Antonio offered to take her home. She accepted his offer with a nod, saying nothing until they got in the car. "Can we just drive around for a while? I'd like to see the lights for Natale."

"Fine." If it made her happy… though why would it? With no family anymore, Natale had been tough on him, and it was a holiday he didn't look forward to. For her, after giving up a child on Christmas Eve, it had to be brutal. He thought about saying so, about asking, but he didn't think he could talk about it without getting emotional. It had been a long, long day. Too long.

They were driving past a church when she put a hand on his arm. "Stop." He pulled off onto the side of the road and she got out, not waiting for him, and headed to the beautifully lit nativity scene. He followed behind, not sure why she wanted to see it.

She stopped in front of the manger and wrapped her arms around her torso, as if she were giving herself a hug. It took him a moment to notice that her shoulders were shaking. He put an arm across them. "What is it?"

She motioned to the manger with the baby in it. "He looks so alone."

"But he's not."

Her tears came harder. Apparently that was the wrong thing to say. He had no idea how to comfort her. No idea what to do.

And he had no idea if he could forgive her. Anger still simmered inside him. He hated seeing her like this, but it was her fault, wasn't it? She'd chosen to push him away. She'd chosen to be alone.

She'd chosen to give up their child.

They didn't speak for the rest of the drive. When they finally pulled up in front of her house, he glanced over at her, huddled against the door. Dark circles ringed her eyes, but they weren't only from smudged mascara. "You look exhausted, Bee."

"His birthday always hits me hard."

He stifled the impulse to apologize for her having to go through that alone. If she'd told him, he would have done something. But what? What would he have been able to do? "I should have known."

"Well, now you do," she snapped. "Do you feel any happier?"

He had no answer for that. She was getting out of the car when the front door opened and her mother came down the stairs. "Is everything all right?" she asked when she saw Bianca's face.

"Not really, Mamma," Bianca said, her voice breaking. Signora Lucchesi folded Bianca into her arms, rocking her back and forth.

Should he leave? There really was nothing more for him to do, but Bianca had left the car door open. He slipped out of the Alfa and came around the side. As he passed by them, Francesca snagged his sleeve. "Stay to dinner."

"I can't intrude on your Christmas Eve," he said, offering her a false smile. He didn't have anywhere else to be, but she didn't know that. Kate had invited him over, and he'd turned her down too.

"I insist, unless you're going to Enrico's." When he hesitated, unsure whether to lie, she added, "Sandro isn't here. We had a fight earlier about going to Enrico's—he thought you were going to be there—and I have no idea where he is. So I've decided to make us something here." She waited a beat, then added, "And I know all about the child now. Including your part in it."

Oh. In that case... "*Grazie.*"

He shut off the car and followed them inside. Their home was more modest than Don Enrico's, but still a far cry from the one Antonio had lived in as a child.

They didn't eat in the dining room, instead settling around an old wooden table in the spacious kitchen. Matteo joined them, not commenting on Antonio's presence. Signora Lucchesi dished up their meals herself—a delicious seafood stew—and poured them each a big glass of Sangiovese.

Antonio was ravenous, since he'd observed the traditional fast during Christmas Eve day. He'd allowed himself nothing but numerous cups of espresso.

He shoveled in the stew like a starving man, and Signora Lucchesi smiled in approval. "More?" she asked when he finished. He readily agreed.

In contrast, Bianca had hardly touched her stew. "Eat, Bee," he gently urged her.

Tears slid down her cheek, and he reached over and took her hand. "I can't," she said. "We're never going to see him, are we?"

"I'm sure Don Enrico will figure something out." He tried to project a confidence he didn't quite feel.

"See who?" Matteo asked.

When Bianca didn't say anything, Signora Lucchesi supplied the answer. "Her baby."

Matteo looked from his mother to Bianca to Antonio. "*Merda.*"

Antonio waited for a stronger reaction, but when none was forthcoming, he nodded. "You've got that right."

"So you don't know where he is?" Signora Lucchesi asked.

Antonio shook his head. "The don's wife knows. But there are laws. They don't want to risk the orphanage. And I don't want them to either. I grew up there."

"That must've been difficult," Signora Lucchesi said.

He laughed. "The Lucchesi Home was a palace compared to the first place I landed in."

"I meant losing your parents." The *signora*'s voice was so very soft.

A lump in his throat threatened to strangle him. "It was."

"And now you have no one?"

"My sister Violetta is with my Uncle Gino's family."

A frown creased her brow. "But they didn't take you?"

"He said they couldn't afford it. We were never rich."

"But surely someone else?"

"We were never a large family either."

She sighed. "But you must see them sometimes?"

With a shake of his head, he acknowledged the bitter truth. "I haven't seen them in almost eight years. Not since the last time Don Enrico took me there."

"Not even your sister?"

"My uncle strongly suggested I leave her alone. He said it was too upsetting for her, hearing that I was unhappy."

Signora Lucchesi crossed her arms beneath her ample bosom. "I do not like your uncle very much."

He couldn't suppress a smile. Then he had to ask. "Did you know I was the father?"

"No. I had no idea until Bianca told me earlier today." She gazed down at the table. "I let Domenico handle all that. I wish…" She let out another sigh. "I wish I could have done something different." She gave him a tight smile. "I would like to know my grandson. He's the only one I have."

"Kate gave me his picture," Bianca said. She reached into the handbag she'd slung over the back of her chair and pulled out the photo. She studied it for a moment before passing it to her mother.

Signora Lucchesi stared at the picture, then she traced the baby's features with a trembling finger. "He's beautiful." She smiled. "He looks just like you, Bianca."

Bianca sniffed back tears. "What if we don't get him back?"

"*Dolcezza*, let's not worry about that now," her mother said.

"It's *all* I worry about!"

Antonio rose. He leaned over the back of Bianca's chair and put his arms around her shoulders from behind. "Let's trust that Don Enrico will think of something."

And in the meantime, he'd follow the don and find out where their son was himself. He was not leaving matters to fate. If necessary, he'd break any law he had to.

He was getting back his son. No matter the consequences.

————◆————

Sandro couldn't believe his ears. He paused in the doorway to the kitchen.

60

Legato was the father of his sister's baby? *Figlio di puttana!* And the don *knew*, and he was trying to help them?

He stalked into the kitchen, surprising Legato and his sister in a close embrace. "Get your hands off her!" Sandro roared. He grabbed Legato by the shoulder and hauled him away from Bianca.

"Sandro! Stop it!" Mamma yelled. But she had no right to say anything. She'd known. And still she'd invited this trash into their home. Into their *lives*.

He drilled a fist into Legato's gut and followed it with a quick uppercut to the jaw. Legato reeled back, his boots scraping on the tiles. But quicker than Sandro had anticipated, the blond bastard shook off the blows and tackled him to the floor, pinning him. Legato grabbed Sandro's shirtfront and yanked him up, then slammed him back down. Sandro's skull smacked the tiles, hard. Pain lanced through his head, and he saw murder in Legato's eyes. Had Papà seen the same thing during his last moments?

"Antonio! You'll kill him!" Bianca screamed and grabbed at Legato's arms.

The bastard shook her off and rose. "I'm done."

Sandro rubbed the back of his skull and winced. He already had a large lump. "You fuck my sister, you get her pregnant, and then you abandon her? I'd say you're done," Sandro said. "I'll make sure of it."

"I'd like to see you try," Legato sneered. "You touch me again, and you're dead. I'm your *capo*. Don't forget it."

"*Vaffanculo!*" The expletive exploded from Sandro's lips as he got to his feet.

"You're out of chances. I'm taking that finger now," Legato said.

"Antonio, *per favore*," Bianca said.

Legato gave her a dark look. "Only because *you* asked." Then he addressed Sandro. "We aren't finished."

"Hardly," Sandro said, his eyes following Legato's back as the bastard left the house.

It was time to call Lorenzo Andretti. Time to fill his partner in. Time to bring their plans to fruition.

———— ◆ ————

Her hands still shaking, Bianca waited until Antonio left before seeking Sandro out. She needed to talk him down. He was in his bedroom, holding a bag of ice to the back of his head. "Are you all right?" she asked.

"Does it look that way?"

"I meant, do you need to go to the hospital?"

"No." He tossed the bag on the table beside his bed. "I want that bastard out of our lives. Get that password."

"Sandro, he's not who you think he is. I never told him. I pushed him away. He never knew about the baby."

"He's a fucking liar. Think about it. Legato had to know about the baby. That's why he killed Papà. He saw an opportunity to get back at him, and he took it. And then he set it up so the Andrettis would take the blame. It all fits."

"But it doesn't explain why he became *capo di società*."

"Like I said, he discredited Papà somehow. I don't know how. But I can feel it."

Bianca didn't know what to think. She'd swear that Antonio had been sincere. His reactions, everything he'd done since she'd told him, were consistent with him not having known. But there was still that niggling detail: Why had the don picked him over Sandro? Why Antonio, of all people?

Sandro shook his head. "You're thinking of reasons to defend him."

"I'm just trying to make sense of all this."

"You can't. Nothing that's happened since Papà died has made sense. Look at our *padrino's* behavior since then. He married his son into the Andretti family. Even though the Andrettis supposedly killed Papà and arranged for Nico to kill Fedele—if you can accept that story. Why would our *padrino* continue to seek peace with the Andrettis after all that? Zio Enrico avenged *his* part of the family. But ours?" Sandro threw his hands up in the air and hissed in frustration. "He doesn't fucking care. Something is wrong, Bee. He's gone over to the enemy. And we're supposed to meekly go along for the ride. Well, *fuck* that. I refuse. And you should too."

"I agree that something's not right. But I'm not sure what we should do without knowing more."

"You should do what I ask. Out of love for me. Out of loyalty to this family."

"I refuse to ruin Antonio and Zio Enrico without concrete proof that they've done something wrong."

Sandro's face darkened and his eyes went flat and cold. "If you don't get that password, I'll pay a visit to Legato's bastard myself, and then you'll be sorry."

Alarm lanced through her. "You can't possibly know where he is."

"I do." He didn't seem to be bluffing. Her stomach compacted into a ball.

"How could you possibly know where to find him?"

The grin he gave her chilled her to the marrow. "Getting that information was dead simple, once I thought it through."

"Tell me."

He shook his head. "That would take all the fun out of it."

"Sandro, you wouldn't hurt him. He's just a child."

"You have two days. You want to protect your brat? Get me that password."

"*Per favore.* Have mercy on me, on my boy."

"Did Legato show Papà any mercy?" When she didn't say anything, he drove the point home. "He didn't. And I'm the same way. Help me, or suffer."

Sandro had never backed away from any threat or any promise he'd made during the entire time they'd grown up. Not once. He had to have figured out some way to access that file, something she hadn't thought of. "You'll need to take me back to Zio Enrico's. I left my car there, and I'll need it." She couldn't believe the words that had come out of her mouth. But what other choice did she have?

CHAPTER 8

How long had she been standing outside the door to Antonio's building? Why couldn't she just raise a hand to press the buzzer? Why couldn't she do such a simple thing?

Taking a deep breath, Bianca tried to focus. She had to save her son. And if Sandro was right—if Antonio *had* killed their father—he deserved what was coming.

But if Sandro was wrong, if Antonio was innocent... She couldn't worry about that. Her son was in danger. One thing at a time.

Before she could stop herself, she jabbed at the intercom button beside Antonio's name on the list of tenants and waited, her heart drumming in her chest. A man whose voice she didn't recognize answered the buzzer but didn't ask any questions once he heard her last name. Must be a guard.

The outer door unlocked with a buzz, and she entered, pausing at the base of a wide marble staircase. All she had to do was put one foot in front of the other. That's all she had to do.

The journey up the stairs was too short, and soon she stood outside Antonio's door, her heart in her throat. She had to get a grip on herself, or he'd know something was wrong. She tapped on the door and when it opened, she tried to compose her features, to look anything but panicked.

The young man who answered couldn't have been any older than Antonio. Thick black hair framed his face and nearly fell into his hazel eyes. He gave her a quick up-and-down before breaking into a beautiful grin that must have dazzled a million hearts already. "*Ciao, bella.*" He opened the door wider and ushered her in. "I'm Raffaele. Antonio's guard. He's on the balcony."

She hadn't counted on a guard being there, but of course he'd have at least one. That was going to complicate things. One thing at a time, yes?

She dropped her handbag on the occasional table and crossed the great room to the double doors that led outside. The flat was richly furnished—though sadly there wasn't a single Christmas decoration in sight—and every surface gleamed.

Somehow she doubted Antonio had done the decorating. Or the cleaning. Nothing about the place reflected the man she knew.

Then again, she didn't know him all that well, did she? Maybe *this* was who he was. Maybe he'd turned into a man who cared about money, about appearances. About his position. Did he care enough to kill for all this? Was he just a clever con man, as her brother had implied? Had her memories of Antonio as a boy clouded her judgment?

She opened the glazed doors and stepped outside onto a wide stone balcony that overlooked a garden courtyard. A lighted fountain splashed below. The cloak of night gave the scene a certain allure, and normally she'd have relaxed and breathed deeply of the cool air. But she could hardly take a breath. Antonio was there, at the far end of the balcony, his back to her.

When he turned to face her, her pulse leapt and she nearly jumped out of her skin. He was bathed mostly in shadow, but the lights in the living room clearly revealed her to him. "What are you doing here?" he asked, his voice low, cautious.

She shook her head, all at once so overwhelmed she couldn't speak. Tears started to form. She hated herself. She hated him. She hated everything that had happened to them. And yet there was nothing she could do to fix it. She could only make it worse. *Was* going to make it worse.

He came toward her. "Bee? What's wrong?"

She shook her head again and reached for the door. She couldn't do this. Shouldn't do this.

He placed a hand against the door and held it shut, then touched her cheek with the other hand, his fingers skimming her skin. "What is it?" he asked, his eyes searching hers. She opened her mouth to say something and instead a sob poured out, and the next thing she knew, his arms were around her and he was holding her close. "Tell me."

She wanted to, but how could she? Sandro would make good on his promise— she had no doubt of that. "It's been a tough day," she whispered.

He laughed. "You are the queen of understatement."

She hugged him tighter, nuzzling her face against his chest. She felt so safe with him. If only it weren't an illusion. If only she could be honest with him. If only she knew the truth about what had happened the night her father had died.

If only her boy weren't in danger.

They held each other in silence for what seemed like a very long time. Gradually she became aware that he was rocking her gently back and forth, his hands making soothing circles on her shoulders. He hummed something under his breath.

She didn't deserve his mercy, his kindness. Releasing him, she tried to step away, but he didn't let go. "Relax. Let me hold you."

Did he really mean that? Had he forgiven her? She melted into him, and when he shifted his weight, she felt his erection pressing against her belly. Well, his already being aroused would make things so much easier.

She reached down between them and caressed him through his jeans. He arched into her hand, then stepped back with a little hiss. He rubbed a hand across his face and shook his head. "I can't believe I'm going to say this, but we shouldn't.

I'm not sure this is what you really want."

Bianca stared at him, openmouthed. He genuinely cared about how she felt? She smiled then, and the lump in her throat had nothing to do with sadness.

"You look happy for once." He stepped forward, tracing her upturned lips with a long finger.

"You never cease to surprise me."

"I have grown up a bit since we were last together."

Her grin widened, and unable to resist the pull of his eyes, she moved closer and ran a hand down his well-muscled chest. "I can see that," she said, a husky note entering her voice. The memory of his kissing her outside Barfly sent a frisson of pleasure rippling through her. She wanted that again. She wanted that closeness, that bliss. Anything to wipe away the sadness that lurked in her heart, the threat that lurked in her family. Anything for a few moments of escape.

His hand slid down to her bottom and pulled her flush to him. "I like seeing you smile. It's been too long."

"Haven't had much to smile about."

"Let's see if I can change that," he murmured, before touching his lips to hers. She opened to him immediately, no hesitation this time, and he deepened the kiss, his wicked tongue sending jolts of electricity through her. Desire pooled in her belly.

How she'd yearned for this, all those long and lonely years. Despite everything. The chemistry between them—there was nothing false or faked about it. She'd been attracted to him since they'd first met, when he'd been a boy. Now that he was a man, she found him appealing in a way that was nearly overwhelming.

He released her mouth, leaving her gasping, and started to kiss and nip at her neck, making her breath catch and her knees go weak. She let out a little cry and bared her neck to his teeth, his lips. Clutching at his shoulders, so broad and strong beneath his jacket, she inhaled the scent of leather and his cologne, their perfume sending her higher, making her dizzy with need, with want.

The scrape of his teeth along her skin, the way he mouthed her throat, sucking and biting at her like she was a feast he couldn't devour quickly enough, made her wet. She wanted him inside her. She wanted him this instant.

She reached down between them again and caressed him. This time he pressed against her hand greedily, and he didn't object when she unfastened his jeans and plunged her hand inside.

He felt like velvet over steel beneath her fingers. She encircled him with a fist and pumped up and down, then ran her fingers across the head. He groaned and placed a hand over hers. "You're killing me," he whispered.

"I know." She grinned, thrilled to see him so turned on, so at her mercy. Just as she was at his. "Let's take this inside," she said.

"We don't have to." He steered her out of the light into the darkness at the far end of the balcony.

A thrill raced through her. Here? Outside? "Tonio, someone will see us."

"It's dark. Very dark." He snaked a hand up under her skirt and ran his fingers teasingly over her mound, then pressed her thong into her cleft, his fingers caressing the nub of her *grilletto* through the fabric. The sensation made her gasp.

"Tonio—"

"Shh." He shifted his fingers, slipping them under the scrap of cloth that covered her and in between the slippery lips of her sex. "You're so wet," he said as he stroked her, making her shiver and moan. "So wet for me. For this."

She was, she couldn't deny it. He'd know she was a liar if she tried to. "*Per favore*," she whispered against his neck, not sure what she was asking. For him to stop or to keep going.

"Turn around and grab the railing." His voice had roughened, and the urgency behind it further ramped up her arousal. In a daze, she complied. It was better if she couldn't see him; it'd give her more chance of keeping some emotional distance from him, from what he was doing. What *they* were doing.

Bunching her skirt up at her waist, he bared her backside to the cold air. He ran his hands appreciatively over her bottom, then slid his fingers back down to her greedy sex. "I wish I could see you," he whispered, as he pressed a kiss to her cheek.

She started to answer, to pretend to agree, when he slid his thumb inside her and made her cry out in pleasure. She arched her back and pressed into his hand. Two of his fingers found her *grilletto* again, sliding against either side of it, their touch a tease, not quite giving her what she wanted. "*Per favore*," she moaned again.

"Not yet," he whispered, his breath hot in her ear, his breathing fast like hers, his cock straining at her hip.

His fingers continued to slip and slide in her wetness and she arched farther, trying to wiggle her *grilletto* beneath them, but he laughed and continued to tease her. When she finally said, "I beg you," he gave her what she wanted, his fingers caressing her aching nub, their pressure firm and fast, strumming her until her pleasure spiraled and she let out a groan.

Before she could come down, he pushed into her, his thick *cazzo* stretching her, the fullness shocking and welcome after so many years of longing. "Tonio," she whimpered and backed up against him.

"*Dio*, you're tight," he said, his voice hoarse, awestruck. His fingers dug into her hips as he thrust into her. One of his hands found her mound again, and he stroked her as he plunged into her, hard and fast, his hips slapping into hers. "You're mine, Bee," he panted. "You're mine."

"Yes," she answered, her mind a blank except for him, except for what he was doing to her. With her. For her.

She bit down on her lower lip to suppress a cry of pleasure as she peaked again. With a quick jerk, he pulled out of her. *Grazie a Dio*. She hadn't even given a thought to contraception.

Just like last time.

But obviously he had grown up. He sagged against her, his breathing fast. "Sorry about that. Almost forgot. I meant to use a condom, but—"

She touched a finger to his lips. "It's okay. I forgot too." *And I shouldn't have*, she almost added.

He kissed her lightly and tugged her skirt down, then tucked his still-erect *cazzo* back in his jeans. "Let's take this inside. I want to see you."

"But Raffaele—"

Antonio pressed a finger to her lips. "Do you think I never heard Don Enrico and his wife?"

A flush rose to her cheeks. "I'm not used to this."

"Well, get used to it." He kissed the tip of her nose, then took her hand in his and tugged her inside.

What exactly did he mean by that? The memory of what he'd said to her— "You're mine, Bee. You're mine"—flooded her brain. She'd agreed at the time because it had felt so right. A knot of worry formed in her stomach. Maybe he'd only said that in the heat of the moment. She had to hope so.

—◆—

Antonio led Bianca down the hall to his bedroom. It still didn't feel like his— everything in the room, the entire flat, was nice, lavish, but that wasn't him. He was used to spartan furnishings, never owning more than a few sets of clothing, a handful of personal items, never more than he could throw in a rucksack and carry. Now he had a whole flat's worth of things. It had been considerate of Don Enrico to furnish the place, but the impersonal possessions made the space feel alien, temporary. Like a hotel room. Not permanent. Not his.

Bianca raised a brow when she saw the gorgeous four-poster bed that dominated the master bedroom. "It's like something out of a movie," she said. She released his hand, and he shut the door while she walked over to the bed and slid a hand along the dark, heavily carved wood of the nearest post. A sudden flash of her holding on to that post while he took her from behind made his cock throb. But he wanted something else this time. Something slower, a little more leisurely, now that he'd worked off some of his pent-up sexual frustration. Something to take his mind off what he'd said to her on the balcony. Had he really said that she was his?

And did he mean it? Some part of him did, obviously, but it had to be some primitive lizard-brain part of him. Because those words, those feelings, certainly weren't governed by anything rational.

The two of them, together? Not possible, not with her family, their past, the uncertainty between them...

Fuck all that. He needed to shake those thoughts off and focus. He had Bianca in his room, and who knew how much time he'd get with her? Better make the best of it.

He dropped his leather jacket on a chair and kicked off his boots, watching her all the while to see if she'd follow his lead. She wrapped her hand around the post and watched him, unmoving, as she worried her bottom lip with her teeth. Had he been too rough on the balcony?

He started to unbutton his shirt, and her gaze followed his movements, but still she didn't move. So he was going to have to take charge again. Fine by him. He dropped his hands to his sides. "Come here."

She said nothing, just stared at him for a moment, then she let go of the post and came toward him. "Undress me," he said. Her eyes widened, as if she hadn't expected them to be getting naked, but she moved to comply, her fingers fumbling with the tiny buttons of his dark blue shirt. She was shaking. Okay, so she was really shy. She'd been shy the first time too. But certainly— "Bee, you've done this before, haven't you?"

Her eyes darted to his. "Of course." She quickly refocused on her task. Too quickly.

He grabbed her wrist. "The truth this time."

She wouldn't look at him. "You're the only one."

"The only one what?"

She met his gaze then. "The only one I've been with."

Was she serious? Looking the way she did, she must've had men dropping at her feet every day. "Those Swiss bastards must have thin blood."

Her lips curved up and a blush rose to her cheeks. He leaned down and kissed one of them, her honeyed skin soft and warm beneath his lips. "You were meant to be adored."

She snorted. "Does all this flowery crap work for you?"

"Usually." Her pulse beat fast beneath his fingertips. "And I think it's working now too." Another quickening of her pulse. He kissed the inside of one of her wrists, then released her and motioned to his clothes. "Continue."

"Women just let you order them around?"

"You weren't complaining earlier."

"That was—that was—"

"Hot. Wasn't it?"

Her chest rose and fell, drawing his eyes to the deep V of her scandalously unbuttoned top and how her breasts threatened to spill out of it. "If you didn't want this, Bee, why are you dressed for it?" He stepped in closer, reached between her legs, and cupped her *figa*. "These aren't the sort of panties a nice girl wears."

"How would *you* know what a nice girl wears?"

"Because I remember. I remember everything about our first time. And you weren't dressed anything like this." He fanned his fingers over that thin bit of fabric, then squeezed lightly, making her gasp. "Though I'm not complaining."

"Why the inquisition?" she asked.

"Because I want you to admit the truth." She stiffened and he placed a hand at her neck, cradling it. "Admit what you want. What we both want." She relaxed the barest bit, and he kissed her neck. "Admit it."

"Yes."

"Yes what?"

"I want you." She breathed the words, her voice catching on "want," and he was harder than steel in an instant. How long had he waited to hear her say those words? He wanted to toss her on the bed and go at her fast and furious again, but she seemed fragile, on edge. They both needed something else.

"Finish undressing me then." He let his smile fill his voice, and she sighed, her hands finishing the task easily, and soon he was bare before her. Her eyes moved over him slowly, lingering below his waist, and he grinned, making her blush. He'd have loved nothing more than to order her on her knees, but that might be pushing her too far, too fast. "Now it's your turn."

She raised her hands to her blouse, but he stopped her. "Allow me."

He couldn't help kissing every centimeter of her flesh that he revealed. Ah, she was a marvel. She'd been beautiful back then, but she was a woman now, with a woman's curves. Her breasts were large, the tips turning up, her hips and ass plush enough to drive him wild. She even had that slight rounding of the belly that he loved. She was a girl—a woman—he could really hold on to, all softness, all lushness. He'd never be happy with a girl built like a beanpole, and he told her so. She moved her hands over her belly. "Don't say that because you think it's what I want to hear."

"I said it because it's true."

She pinched her stomach. "I need to lose this."

He shook his head. She was crazy. "You're perfect."

"*Davvero?*" She stared at him for a long moment.

"Truly."

"I thought you'd want a skinny girl."

"I can't believe I'm going to mention this, but remember that girl you saw me with at Barfly? She wasn't a stick, was she?" When Bianca made a face, he laughed and led her to the bed, then lay beside her, placing a hand on her belly. "You are just right the way you are." He kissed her. "And stop reading fashion magazines."

Bianca giggled and the sound made his heart feel lighter. How long had it been since he'd heard her laugh?

Dio, he wished they hadn't made so many mistakes. He couldn't fix the past, but maybe he could fix their future. Starting this instant.

He ran a hand over her cheek. "I'm sorry, Bee. For getting you pregnant. I know I'd said I would pull out, but I was so overwhelmed."

Her eyes glistened. "I know it wasn't on purpose. It was an accident."

"Forgive me?"

She rolled onto her side and cupped his face in her hands, her palms soft on his cheeks, her eyes flooding with tears. She pressed her lips to his, the kiss shaky and sweet, and he pulled her flush against him and held her tight, chest to chest, as she continued to kiss him. Her tongue slipped into his mouth. She let out a little moan and clutched him harder to her and that was the end of the sweetness. Something more primal took over between them. He rolled her onto her back, his lips leaving her full mouth and traveling down her neck. He couldn't help biting her a little bit hard, and she arched and moaned, sending him higher.

She pulled him closer, but he wanted her to lie back, to let him do the work. To worship her the way she was meant to be worshiped. He grabbed both her wrists in one hand and held them over her head.

"Don't move. No matter what."

She nodded and he let go and slid down to her breasts. Her nipples were large and dark, the color of milk chocolate, and he couldn't wait to get them in his mouth. He rolled one between his lips and tongue and tweaked the other with his fingers, delighted when she shivered and moaned beneath him. She started to reach for him, but he stilled her with a look, before going back to his task.

She tasted like honey, vanilla, something sweet, her scent intoxicating, the feel of her under his mouth—her skin like heated silk—making his pulse pound in his cock. What was it about Bianca Lucchesi that drove him so crazy?

Now that he had a second chance with her, he was determined to find out.

He kissed down her belly to the juncture of her closed thighs. Still shy. That wasn't going to last, not if he had anything to do with it. He tapped her knee. "Open up."

Her face flushed crimson, but she didn't move.

"Show me. Or I'll stop." He put an edge of command in his words and held her eyes. When he started to move away, she relaxed and let her legs open a little. *Grazie a Dio.*

"More." She parted them farther, and he could see a hint of her treasures, but not nearly enough. "Bee, there's nothing to be ashamed about."

She huffed in protest, but her knees spread wider, baring more of her glistening pussy to his gaze. He pressed her legs apart until the sides of her knees rested on the mattress.

"Tonio." She tried to wriggle away.

He held her flat to the bed. "Do I need to call Raffaele in here to hold you down?"

Her eyes widened. "You'd do that?"

He grinned. "Idle threat. Of course."

She crossed her arms under her breasts and gave him an exaggerated pout.

"So you *do* want me to call him?"

She laughed this time, even though she tried again to close her legs. He pressed down harder. "You're going to like this. I promise."

"Will not," she said, sounding almost breathless.

This was going to be fun. He'd have her panting and begging in no time. "You asked for it," he said. "Remember that."

He blew on her curls and she gasped and wriggled, trying again to close her legs, but he held them open. She was so beautiful. Why did women never see that? All they saw were flaws. And she didn't have any.

Letting go of her left leg, he stuck a finger in his mouth to wet it, then ran it down the center of her *figa*, slipping it between the lips and inside her, then dragged her moisture back up to her swollen *grilletto*, which was just begging for his tongue. He circled the stiff little nub, making her gasp, but didn't touch it more than in passing. Again and again he circled it, until her hips started gyrating, trying to force better contact. He smiled to himself. She was shy, but not as shy as she'd like to think.

He leaned forward, using his elbows to hold her legs outspread and sucked her clit into his mouth, swirling his tongue over it and making her cry out. She wasn't quite there, but she would be soon. He repeated the action a few more times, then added his fingers to the mix, inserting them inside her and stroking the front wall, searching for that spot... He knew he'd hit it when she let out a deep moan and writhed underneath him.

Now for the fun part. He took her up and up until he was sure she was about to come. Then he sat back and waited. Her reaction was immediate. "Tonio, *per favore*," she groaned.

"*Per favore*, what?"

"Don't make me beg."

He laughed and kissed her inner thigh, his fingers circling so close to her *figa* that they brushed its fine curling hairs. "But the begging is the best part."

She threw her arms over her face and hissed in frustration.

"It's only a few words." He blew on her *figa* and she inhaled sharply.

"*Per favore*," she said again, then gave in. "Make me come, Tonio."

"Why didn't you just say so?" He resumed the rhythm he'd built up before, loving her every whimper and wiggle, the trembling of her thighs beneath his arms, the way she pumped her hips up at him, the way she strained for more. But most of all the sweet rasp of her voice when she called his name and clutched the sheets in her fingers. That was a sound he'd never tire of. A sound he wanted to hear from her again and again.

CHAPTER 9

Bianca was still trembling from her climax when Antonio grabbed a condom from the drawer in the bedside table. How did he have so much power over her? A few kisses, a few touches—*Dio*, that tongue of his!—and she was potter's clay in his hands, his to do with as he wanted. She'd been in his flat what—not quite an hour?—and already he had her acting like a *troia*. She wanted to be angry with him, but how could she be? She'd wanted it, all of it, all of him. He'd only made her admit it.

And then when he'd apologized and asked her to forgive him—it was almost too much. She'd almost stopped him there, almost run out, but she'd wanted to forgive him, to kiss him. To make everything right between them. If only for a little while.

He turned back to her and held up the condom. "Don't let me forget again," he said lightly, then kissed her, so soft, so sweet. So Antonio. He was so much more confident now as an adult, but that gentle, tender side of him was still there.

He rolled over her, holding her gaze, his stiff *cazzo* pressing into her thigh. "*Bellissima*. Every bit of you."

"You are too," she heard herself say. And he was *molto bello*. He had the hard body of a man who'd spent hours in the gym—broad shoulders, big biceps, strong forearms, and a narrow tapered waist, the muscles of it forming a V that pointed to his very impressive *cazzo*. Had it grown since they were kids? The rest of him sure had. His thighs and calves bulged with power, and his ass was as tight as any professional soccer player's. She reached down and squeezed it, making him laugh and surge into her. The feel of him inside her again, the feel of him filling her up, tore a moan from her. *Dio*, the things Raffaele was hearing! But she didn't care anymore. Couldn't care. All she wanted was a few more moments of bliss, of being in Antonio's arms, of having him inside her.

He swiveled his hips, eliciting another gasp from her as he touched every bit of her inside. He did it again and again until he was panting as fast as she. Pleasure coiled tight inside her. One more time he swiveled, and then she was soaring.

He didn't let her come back down. With a guttural cry, he pistoned into her, pulling her knees up and pushing them to her chest, bending her almost double as he worked himself into a frenzy. He came with a suppressed roar, the sound making her shiver and clench around him, milking him dry.

With a long, satisfied groan, he collapsed on the bed, tugging her into his arms. He pressed kisses into her hair, onto her cheeks, her lips. Telling her silently how he felt, and she returned his every caress, his every kiss, forgetting for just a moment that she was there for any other reason. She was in his bed, in his arms, and for once she felt content. Safe. Happy.

They lay together in silence for quite a while, their breathing and their hearts slowing, going back to normal.

But would she ever be able to say the same about herself? What would normal be for her after this?

"It's funny," he said, breaking into her thoughts. "For all these years, when I thought about that night we spent together, I only thought of it as my first time." He squeezed her. "*Our* first time. But now I realize that it was also the night our son was conceived. And that makes it even more special than I'd believed."

Her eyes welled up and her throat grew tight. He'd said it like they were a couple, a team, in this situation together. But they weren't. And they couldn't be, not with the doubts lingering in her heart. Not with the mission she had to complete.

He noticed her tears and stroked her cheeks. "Hey, what's wrong?"

She shook her head. "Nothing. I'm just thinking about him."

"We'll get him back, Bee. We will."

She wished she could believe that. She wished she could confide in him.

After a while, he dropped into a light sleep, one arm still wrapped around her. She rolled over, out of Antonio's grasp. He made a little sound of protest, but didn't try to stop her before sinking deeper into sleep.

Bianca watched him for several minutes. He looked so innocent, and she wished with all her being that it were so. But was he? Maybe now was the perfect time to ask. She shook him awake.

He came alert in an instant. "Is something wrong?" He reached for the nightstand drawer. No doubt it contained a gun.

"No. But I want to know something. The night Papà was killed, Sandro said you were the last one seen with him."

He glanced away from her. "Probably. I don't know for sure what happened after he refused my protection."

"Why would he do that?"

Antonio shrugged, his eyes and face going cold. "He didn't explain himself to me." He hesitated, then added, "I'm sorry. I wish I'd insisted."

Alarm bells went off in her head. His whole demeanor had gone from relaxed to on edge the minute she'd brought that night up. He was hiding something.

She took a deep breath, trying to loosen up lungs that had gone tight. What if she'd just had sex with her father's killer? What if he was guilty?

There had to be a special place in hell for women like her.

"Why are you asking?" Antonio said. "Did you think you'd get me to *confess* to something?"

She swallowed hard at the anger in his eyes, in his voice. "I just had to be sure, Tonio." She dropped her gaze to the sheets.

He placed two fingers under her chin and coaxed her to look at him. "That brother of yours—he's nothing but trouble. Always throwing fire on the straw."

"That's true," she said. And it was.

But maybe this time, Sandro was right. She lay back down and snuggled against Antonio, although it was a long time before he fell asleep again, and longer still before she could creep out of bed.

There wasn't a computer in Antonio's bedroom, but they'd passed a few rooms on the way. Perhaps one of them was a home office.

Bianca dressed quickly, her gaze darting over to Antonio asleep on the bed. Part of her just wanted to stay there, safe in his embrace, and forget about everything else. But she couldn't forget the coldness on Sandro's face. She couldn't allow him to get anywhere near her child. She had to be brave; she had to be strong.

Cracking the door open, she peered down the hallway. No sign of Raffaele. Good. She slipped out and eased the door closed. Carrying her shoes in one hand so they wouldn't click on the marble and give her away, she sneaked down the hall and hoped Raffaele was out on the balcony smoking, or whatever it was he did when Antonio had a girl over. A vision of Antonio with that *troia* from Barfly flashed through her mind. The hot, dark, way he'd held Bianca's eyes as he'd kissed that girl's neck sent a shudder through her. She knew what he could do with that mouth, knew how he could drive a girl insane.

How many other girls had there been?

Stop it, Bianca. Focus. She reached the first door. A bedroom—probably Raffaele's. The next door was a small bathroom. Which left only one more—yes, this was what she'd been searching for. She crept inside, leaving the door slightly ajar, and didn't dare turn on the lights. Sitting down at the desk, she wiggled the mouse, and the screen sprang to life. Fortunately, Antonio had one of those laptops with a lighted keyboard, and she rested her fingers on the keys.

What on earth would Antonio use as his password? His nickname in secondary school had been "Casanova." She tried that, but it didn't work. Biting the inside of her lip, she tried his birth date. Nothing.

Damn it. This was impossible. Did Sandro expect her to just ask for it? How could she ever do such a thing?

She sat back in the chair and crossed her arms. *Think, Bianca. What else can it be?*

If she'd ever known anything about Antonio, it was that his life seemed to be filled with women, thus the "Casanova" nickname. What if he had a new nickname? She tried "heartbreaker," "Romeo," "Don Juan," and "lady-killer," in variation combinations of capital and lowercase letters. None of them worked.

Bianca wanted to bang her head on the keyboard. It had to be something to do with sex or women. She was sure of it.

Then it hit her. What he'd said about their first time. That it was even more important than he'd thought. Could he have used that date? It would make sense. Because it had been *his* first time. And he certainly hadn't forgotten.

She punched in that date, first spelling it out, then putting it into numbers.

Neither one worked. Then she thought to include all four numbers of the year. Suddenly, the Windows desktop appeared. She was in!

Hopefully, he was like her and most of the people she knew and had only one password for everything. She couldn't keep track of more than one—she'd tried, but had only succeeded in confusing herself and getting locked out of several accounts when she'd kept typing the wrong one.

She heard footsteps in the hall and quickly relocked the computer. A tap on the door made her jump in her seat. Heart pounding, she whirled around and saw Raffaele silhouetted in the light streaming through the open doorway. "Can I help you with something?" He flipped the lights on, his query polite on its face, but edged with suspicion.

"I just wanted to check my email. But the computer is locked."

"Don't you have a smartphone?" he asked.

Bianca ducked her head. "I do. But I can't figure out how to set up the email."

"It's easy. I could show you."

"I don't want to bother you."

He grinned. "It wouldn't bother me at all."

"I really ought to be going. If I'm late for midnight mass, Mamma will kill me. You'd better wake Antonio so he can get ready." She rose and headed toward him. For a second, she thought he wasn't going to give way, but he stepped aside and let her pass.

"He hadn't mentioned wanting to go," Raffaele said.

Obviously, they'd had no plans for Christmas Eve. It was just another day to the two of them. And wasn't that sad.

Not that she had much to smile about either. But at least she had a family to go home to. Such as it was.

She walked into the living room and grabbed her handbag. She was about to go when Raffaele spoke. "Don't you need these?" he asked, holding up her heels by their straps.

Blushing, she took them, then slipped them on. "Evil creations," she said. "They kill my feet."

His eyes followed her fingers as they buckled up the straps. "But they look fantastic."

"*Grazie.*"

"You know, you should have asked him for the password."

She froze, then forced a smile. "I didn't want to wake him."

"You sure you don't want me to help with your phone?"

"Next time. I'd better get to the church."

"*Ciao*, then."

She returned the goodbye, then left, letting out a sigh of relief once she was outside. What if Raffaele mentioned what he'd seen to Antonio? What if Antonio changed the password before Sandro could use it? What if it wasn't the right password for Antonio's work account?

One worry at a time, she reminded herself as she headed to her car and buttoned up her blouse to a level that looked respectable. Her son was going to be okay. The only thing that mattered was keeping Luca safe.

———◆———

Despite all her mother's fussing over Christmas breakfast, Bianca had barely been able to choke down a few bites. She'd done it, she'd given Sandro the password during midnight mass. Her son was safe. But she didn't feel any relief. Instead she felt worse than ever, her stomach threatening to spew up the small amount of food she'd managed to get down.

No matter what happened, someone was going to lose. Someone she cared about. She did care about Antonio—she'd never stopped, no matter how she'd tried to convince herself otherwise. She just wished she knew the truth: What had happened the night her father had been killed? And what was Antonio's role in his death?

If he'd killed her father, if it was like Sandro had said, she'd never be able to forgive Antonio. She could forgive him many other things, but not that.

With a huge yawn, Matteo came into the kitchen and sat down across from her, where she was still nursing a cappuccino. "Sandro told me about the password," he said. "He's at the bank now."

Her gut cramped. She wasn't sure what to hope for—that the password worked, or that it didn't.

When she said nothing, Matteo leaned closer. "Did you have to sleep with Legato?"

"What do you think?" she snapped.

He scrubbed a hand over his face and through his dark hair. "I'm sorry, Bee. I don't like what Sandro's been doing."

She shrugged. "You know how he is."

Matteo shook his head. "He's obsessed this time. *Possessed*, even. He's taking risks—" He looked away.

"Like poking at Zio Enrico?"

"Yes, but…" He hesitated and his eyes dropped to the floor.

"What are you worried about?"

"He's made a deal with someone he shouldn't have."

"A deal? What kind of deal?"

"I don't know all the details."

She wanted to strangle her little brother. "Who's the deal with, then?"

"Sandro's going to kill me."

"Then you shouldn't have brought it up." When he didn't respond, she pushed. "Who? You obviously want to tell me."

His gaze bounced around the room before coming to rest on her. "Lorenzo Andretti."

An icy blast swept down her back. "Tell me you're joking."

His face grim, he shook his head. "It's no joke."

"But why? Sandro hates the Andrettis."

"He hates Antonio Legato more."

"But Lorenzo Andretti? What the hell is Sandro up to?"

"I believe he intends to unseat Zio Enrico."

"Is he insane? And he thinks Lorenzo will help him?"

"I think Lorenzo wants the same thing."

"But the bank—"

"Exactly. The bank is critical to the 'Ndrangheta. And Zio Enrico controls it. Don't you think that sticks in Lorenzo's craw?"

"And what? Sandro thinks Lorenzo will put him in charge of it?"

Matteo nodded. "Something like that."

"We need to tell Zio Enrico."

Matteo's eyes widened. "No."

"Why not?"

"I hate to say this, but I don't trust him. Not after what's happened."

"You think Zio Enrico has sold us out?"

"I don't know what else to think. First he makes Legato *capo di società*, then he doesn't avenge Fedele, then he marries his son to an Andretti and takes another one into the bank."

"Tell me honestly—was Fedele plotting with Dario Andretti against Zio Enrico?"

He knotted his fingers together. "Honestly? I think he was."

"But you don't know?"

"I'm not sure."

She smacked the flat of her hand on the table. "*Cristo*! What is wrong with all of you? You claim to hate the Andrettis, yet the first thing you do is try to use them to undermine our own *cosca*!" She blew out hard. "I never realized what spoiled children my brothers are."

"Papà and Zio Enrico had been fighting before he died. Papà didn't like what Zio Enrico had done—how he'd put the *cosca* in danger over Kate."

"So he was just supposed to stand by and let her husband kill her?"

"It wasn't Lucchesi business."

"Since when does 'Ndrangheta law condone the abuse of women?"

"By intervening, he restarted the feud." How easily her brother said those words. As if nothing else mattered. As if Kate didn't matter.

"Carlo Andretti was just searching for an excuse."

"That's probably true. But it doesn't change the facts. Our uncle didn't act in the best interests of the *cosca*."

She couldn't argue there, but still… Her uncle had done something admirable. Something her own father wouldn't have done. Tears pricked at her eyes. No, Papà would have let Kate die. Look at how he'd treated his own daughter. Look at how he'd discarded his own grandson, sweeping him out the door like so much dirt. "Papà wasn't perfect either."

Both of them fell silent. Finally Matteo said, "Sandro won't listen to me."

"You think *I'll* change his mind?"

He spread his hands. "I can't tell Mamma about this."

"No. You can't. She doesn't need any more stress." She took a deep breath. "I'll handle it."

Dio, *please let Sandro listen to me. Just once.*

———◆———

He'd just given the knife in Antonio Legato's gut the first twist. *Buon Natale, Legato.*

Sandro grinned and gunned the engine as he rounded a curve. Almost home. He'd had a very productive morning in Milan. By the time Legato and Zio Enrico figured out what had happened, the damage would be too far gone to overcome. Gianluca d'Imperio would be baying for Zio Enrico's blood, and so would Lorenzo Andretti—at least for show.

Odd though, how the account for La Provincia had been nearly empty already. Lorenzo must have moved the bulk of the money for safekeeping. Wise. Much better than losing it, even if it would have been for the greater good.

It was just a matter of weeks—maybe even days—before Sandro would finally get his due. No, better than that. He'd be *capo. Capo* of the Lucchesi *cosca.* He and Matteo would lead the Lucchesis forward, to a more prosperous future, one unconstrained by their uncle's old-fashioned ideas. They'd keep the bank, of course, but they'd expand into drugs, prostitution, and pornography—and would reap the profits of all those ventures. *Finally.* Theirs was one of the few *cosche* that had clung to the old ways. Well, that was about to end. Like a lot of other things.

Such as Antonio Legato's miserable little life.

Sandro pulled into the drive leading to his home. He'd need to marry soon. It was well past time. He'd wasted years at university at his uncle's insistence. He should have had at least a couple children by now.

An 'Ndranghetista needed to build his legacy young—this wasn't a life that let you be an adolescent well into your thirties. This wasn't a life that let you take your time. You had to seize opportunities, take risks, and mow down anyone in your way. *That* was the *malavita.* Not some pseudo-legitimate, pseudo-respectable life that his uncle seemed to think they could have.

The man was a fool—at the least, he was fooling himself. But no one else. Certainly not Sandro. *He* knew the score. He knew how to win. Even if he had to work with the enemy. But that was only temporary.

Sandro shut off the car and bounded up the front steps and inside. He couldn't wait to tell Matteo the good news.

He called for his brother when he entered. No answer. The house seemed empty. Where was everyone?

Maybe they'd gone over to his uncle's for the day. Mamma had tried to talk to him after the fight with Legato, and he seemed to recall her suggesting they spend Natale at Zio Enrico's, but he'd been only half-listening.

He headed into the kitchen and opened the refrigerator. Maybe there was still some of Mamma's *cannoli* left. If Matteo hadn't eaten all of it first. He scanned the shelves and spotted what he'd been hunting for. *Perfetto!* He was just reaching for the pan when a voice startled him.

"Sandro, we need to talk." He bumped his head on the top shelf of the fridge. Bianca.

Rubbing his head, he turned around with the pan in hand. "Damn, Bee. You surprised me."

She crossed her arms. "I knew you were upset, but I didn't think you were foolish."

He took the pan to the table and uncovered it, grabbing a *cannolo* and taking a bite. Pure heaven. No one made them like Mamma. He'd have to have her give his future wife the recipe. "What are you talking about?" he asked around a mouthful of ricotta cheese, chocolate, and candied fruit.

"Lorenzo Andretti. What the hell are you thinking?"

"I'm planning for the future. *Our* future."

"Of all the stupid things you've done, this is the worst."

He took another bite. Why did she have to shit all over his perfect day? He pointed a finger at her. "If we're going to talk stupid, you win the prize. Getting yourself knocked up with an orphan's kid. Brilliant. You couldn't have picked Leandro d'Imperio? At least then you'd have snagged a rich husband."

Her face reddened, and her hand twitched as if she were thinking of slapping him. But she didn't. Instead she took a deep breath. "You honestly think Lorenzo Andretti will give you whatever he's promised?"

"He's not *giving* me anything. I'm taking it. My birthright."

"He'll kill you the minute he no longer needs you."

"He's an old man. I'm using him. Means to an end."

"Oh, I see. So he's *not* using you to destroy our *cosca*?"

"I'm not stupid."

She snorted. "Did Fedele think that he was *using* Dario Andretti?"

The *cannolo* in his mouth tasted like chalk. Lorenzo hadn't been happy during their last phone call. He'd even mentioned that he'd been the one to suggest Zio Enrico bring Cris Andretti into the bank, as a gesture of goodwill between Zio Enrico and Dario. But Sandro had known what Lorenzo really meant. Cris was there to watch over Sandro, to protect Lorenzo's interests. Maybe even to take over and finish executing their plan if Sandro failed to get the job done quickly. That was why Sandro had had to push Bianca so hard. But it had worked. He'd done it. Lorenzo couldn't fault him now.

Unless he'd never intended to keep his end of the bargain.

———— ◆ ————

Bianca watched Sandro closely as he finished swallowing the *cannolo* he'd stuffed into his mouth. Was that finally uneasiness she saw on his face?

"You know nothing about the business, Bee. Leave it to me and Matteo." He licked his fingers, his eyes skittering away from hers.

She put her hands on her hips. "You don't seem too sure of that."

His gaze locked with Bianca's. "I know what I'm doing."

Her stomach tightened. Sandro *was* afraid; she could see it. If even he recognized the danger, he must be in deep. But he'd never do what he should: confess all to their uncle.

Which meant she had to fix this. Enrico and Antonio needed to know what was going on, and she didn't have a minute to waste.

CHAPTER 10

Antonio had woken up alone, surprised Bianca hadn't stayed. But it was Christmas morning. And maybe she was trying to avoid a confrontation with Sandro.

Or maybe she was still angry with Antonio. Those questions she'd asked last night—clearly Sandro had planted plenty of doubt in her mind.

And unfortunately, it was a doubt he couldn't counter. He'd been the one who'd delivered Don Domenico to his death. He hadn't pulled the trigger, but he might as well have. Hell, he'd even asked Don Enrico if he could. He was just as responsible for her father's death as Enrico. Maybe even more so. Enrico had almost granted Domenico exile, and he might have done so had Antonio not argued against it.

A pit grew in his stomach, a yawning chasm. If Bianca ever found out, she'd never forgive him.

And yet, how could he ever have a future with her if such a secret lurked between them? He'd always know what he'd done. He'd always know that he'd lied to her, that he'd caused her a great and terrible grief.

He'd give anything to have his parents back, and here he'd ripped one of Bianca's away.

Even so... the execution had been justified. Domenico had betrayed the *cosca*, and he'd almost gotten Enrico and Kate killed. And he'd done it all out of greed.

He'd left them no choice.

But as much as Antonio wanted to confess all to her, he had no other choice either. He absolutely couldn't take that risk. Enrico had forbidden him to speak of it. Telling the truth would only cause Bianca more grief—Sandro and Matteo would attack Don Enrico, and they'd die for it.

There was no winning this, was there? All he could do was help get his and Bianca's child back. Perhaps that would make up in some way for the blow he'd inflicted on her family.

He raked a hand through his hair, then leaned on the balcony railing with both elbows. He couldn't stop thinking about Bianca—how she looked, how she smelled, how she felt. He hardened again and inhaled deeply.

He'd have thought having her twice last night would dampen his lust; if anything, that taste of her had only whetted it to a fine edge. He wanted her again and again, in every way, in every place, in every position his fevered brain could conjure up.

What the hell had he been thinking? This wasn't going to end well for anyone. He had to break it off—now—before any more damage was done. The way he felt already, he'd suffer again over her for months, if not years. But the way he'd feel in a few days, a few weeks? That would be so much worse.

Best to end it, do what they could to withdraw and lick their wounds. He'd help her with their son, but that was all. That was all the comfort he could have with her.

Anything else—no matter how desperately they both wanted it—was out of the question.

The glazed doors to the balcony opened and Raffaele stepped outside. "Need anything, Don Legato?"

Antonio shook his head, then realized why Raffaele was asking. He *was* hungry; he hadn't eaten breakfast, and a glance at his watch confirmed it was nearing eleven.

"You sure? I was going to heat up some of that food Signora Lucchesi sent over."

Antonio grinned. Raffaele could be such a mother hen. "Okay then."

"*Bene.*" The guard nodded and left.

They really ought to learn to cook. They couldn't eat every meal from restaurants, yet that's what they'd done since they'd moved in. The food Kate had sent over for Natale would be the first homemade meal they'd be eating in the flat. *Dio*, what would Kate think if she knew? Maybe he could ask her or their cook, Nonna Drina, to give them some lessons.

He'd just turned back to the courtyard when he heard Raffaele approach. "Is there a problem?" Antonio asked.

Raffaele shook his head and handed him a brightly wrapped package. "This was in the box with the food. It has your name on it."

His stomach tight, Antonio took the package. It was a present, and a card was attached. He set the package down and opened the card, immediately recognizing the handwriting.

"Tonio,

I know you didn't want to exchange presents, but I wanted to do something for you. Nonna Drina has been teaching me to knit, and I made you something. It's my first try and I know it's awful. Enrico couldn't stop laughing, but I thought *you* still might appreciate it.

Buon Natale,
Kate"

Raffaele watched him open the package. Inside was a soft, navy blue scarf—if one could call it that. The stitches weren't even, and the width was all over the place, tapering down and then widened back out several times. The whole thing looked like it might unravel at any minute. Antonio grinned, even though his throat had gone tight. He hadn't received a present at Natale in years. "Is that supposed to be a scarf?" Raffaele asked.

Laughing, Antonio nodded, and wrapped it around his neck. "She cooks a lot better than she knits."

His expression skeptical, Raffaele patted his stomach. "Let's hope so." He disappeared back into the kitchen, and Antonio went back outside. He took out his phone and texted Kate. *Mille grazie. It may not be the most beautiful scarf, but it's beautifully warm. I love it. Buon Natale.*

The glazed door opened again. *Dio mio, she didn't hide another present in the box, did she?* Raffaele motioned behind him. "You have a visitor." He stepped aside, and Antonio saw the last person he'd expected, and the one he most wanted to see: Bianca.

She walked out onto the balcony, and he wanted nothing more than to touch her, his mind flashing back to last night again. Had that really happened? Seeing her now, seeing the worry on her face, it was hard to believe anything had happened between them.

"Sandro?" he asked.

The crease between her brows deepened and she hugged herself, her shoulders hunching, her lips compressing tightly.

That bastard. He scanned her for injuries, but found none he could see. "I'll kill him if he hit you."

Her face crumpled and her lower lip started to tremble. "It's not that," she choked out.

"Then what?"

She looked up at him, her eyes filling with tears. "I'm the one you should be angry with."

"Why would I be?"

Her gaze left his and she pressed a hand to her mouth. "I helped him."

He took her by the shoulders. "Helped him how?"

"He wanted your password. He was going to hurt our son…" Her voice trailed off, and she sobbed, then suppressed her tears.

Antonio shook her slightly. "Bee, what happened?" And then he knew. Raffaele had mentioned finding her in his office. Checking her email, she'd said. He'd thought nothing of it, but now… "You gave him my password."

She nodded. "He went to the bank this morning."

Porco Dio. His fingers started to tighten on her arms, then he released her abruptly and stepped away, taking a deep breath. She'd betrayed him. Again. Just what had Sandro done at the bank? He had to call Don Enrico. He reached for his phone, but she grabbed his arm.

"*Per favore—*"

"You *lied* to me, Bianca. You used me. And now you *want* something from me?"

"Our boy. Sandro will hurt him once he knows I've turned on him. You have to protect our son."

"Of course." He tried to dial Don Enrico, but again she stopped him.

"*What?*" he snapped.

"Sandro is working with Lorenzo Andretti."

Fuck. "This just keeps getting better."

"Lorenzo will kill my brother if he finds out he's no longer useful."

"*That* is not my problem." He tried again to place the call, but she tugged on his arm.

"*Per favore!* You have to help me. I can't lose Sandro too." She sniffed hard. "Not after Papà and Fedele."

Heat flooded his face and chest. "Why should I care? Your family has done nothing but betray Don Enrico."

"Fedele and Sandro, yes, but Papà—"

"You don't know what he did—" He slammed his mouth shut. *Cristo.* He'd almost told her.

Her brow furrowed. "What are you talking about?"

He wanted to blurt it out, to see the expression on her face when she realized her precious Papà was a traitor. But there'd be no recovering from that. Not that there was much hope anyway. Not if Sandro had done something foolish…

He needed to think. He needed to talk to Enrico.

"Answer me," she said, her voice shaking.

"I misspoke."

"*No.* You said my father had done something."

"It was nothing."

"Then why are you so angry?"

"Your brothers keep plotting against me. Against the *cosca.*"

"Don't try to confuse the issue. You were talking about Papà."

"I meant Fedele."

"I'm not stupid."

He crossed his arms. If he didn't go on the offensive, he was doomed. "You come here, you tell me your brother betrayed this family—that *you* betrayed this family—and now you think you can interrogate me? You forget who I am. You forget *yourself.* We may have fucked, but that doesn't make you special."

It hurt him to say it, it hurt to see her shock, but he had to stop her. And he had to break this bond between them. Now, and for good.

"So last night was just a 'fuck'?" she asked. "It meant nothing?"

"You're the one who came to me with an ulterior motive. Obviously, it meant *nothing* to you."

She paled and shook her head. "I had to. Our son—"

"*We* don't have any idea where he is. How could Sandro know?"

She spread her hands. "I'm not sure, but he seemed awfully confident."

Antonio shook his head. "He's *bluffing.*"

"I don't think so. He has a plan."

"He joined up with Lorenzo Andretti. If he has a plan, it can't be that good. Only an idiot would take on that vulture as a partner."

"Sandro's arrogant, but he's not stupid."

"He's not? He's fighting his own *capo.* He's taken a partner who will stab him in the back without a second's thought. Your brother is hardly clever."

"Are you willing to gamble our son's life on that? I'm not."

Was he? What if Sandro knew something they didn't? An idea occurred to him, a possible way of discovering where their child was. Had Sandro thought of it too? There was one way to find out.

He raised the phone. When she tried to stop him, he gave her a stern look. "I'm calling the orphanage. I want to see if Sandro's been there."

He dialed the main number and explained to the weekend matron in charge that he had an urgent need to speak with Gina, Dottor Laurio's secretary. The woman gave him a difficult time, but she eventually looked up Gina's home number. He dialed it and waited impatiently for her to pick up. She finally answered, her throaty voice so familiar from his childhood that he always found it comforting. "Gina, it's Antonio Legato. Has Sandro Lucchesi been at the orphanage recently?"

"A few days ago."

His stomach tightened. *Merda*. "What did he want?"

"He said a friend of his and his wife couldn't have children, but they weren't sure about adopting, and he wanted to get them some information."

"At any point did you leave him alone with your computer?"

She hesitated. "He stayed to read the brochures. I went for an espresso."

"Was your computer secured?"

Silence. "No. I didn't see the need. He's family." She paused. "Did I do something wrong?"

He didn't want to ruin her Natale. "No, Gina. Everything's fine."

She hesitated, then said, "*Buon Natale*."

He wished her the same then ended the call, his stomach in a knot. "He knows where our son is," he said, and Bianca sank to her knees.

"What are we going to do?" she whispered, her arms wrapped around her waist.

Could he go to Enrico with this? Would the don put their child ahead of the *cosca*? Maybe. But Enrico had his own child to consider. Depending on what Sandro had done, the damage to the *cosca* could be severe. And what if Sandro had told Lorenzo Andretti where to find their son?

There were too many questions, and he needed some answers. He dialed Ruggero, who was supposed to be returning from Calabria sometime today. "Where are you?" he asked.

"On my way back."

"And you have your nephew?"

"*Sì*. Why?"

"I need his help. How far are you from Milan?"

"About two hours south."

"Meet me at the bank in two hours, and bring Orlando."

"What's going on?"

"Not sure yet. He'll help me find out."

He ended the call and helped Bianca up, then headed to his office with her at his heels. He logged in to work and changed his password to something no one could guess. Not even her.

"What are you going to do?" she asked.

"Find out what the damage is. And then I'll decide my next move."

"What about our baby?"

"I'm going to see Kate."

"She won't tell you."

"She will now."

"I'll go with you."

"No. You're going home and you're going to do nothing. Not *one* thing. If only you'd been honest with me, if only you'd trusted me—"

"The way you trust me?" she snapped. "You're hiding something, I know it. I *feel* it."

"Don't push me, Bianca. I don't answer to you."

"You expect me to just shut up and wait for you to decide what's going to happen?"

"You're the one who lied. About our child. About how you felt last night. About why you were here. So yes, you're going to do what I say. You're going to let me handle it."

She stared at him, her eyes blazing, then filling with tears. "I told you why I did that. I didn't have any choice."

"You could have shown some faith in me."

"I want to. I want to, but you won't make that possible." When he said nothing, she cleared her throat, yet her soft voice remained hoarse. "Tell me what happened to my father."

"I can't. You have to trust me. For once."

She wiped at her tears and straightened the handbag strap on her shoulder. "That's all you have to say?"

He nodded, and she turned and left. He watched her go, his stomach sinking. He wanted to tell her. But he'd sworn to his *capo* that he'd keep the secret. An 'Ndranghetista wasn't worth anything if he couldn't obey one basic rule: *omertà*. Silence.

———◆———

Bianca wanted to trust Antonio, but how could she? He'd admitted he knew more than he was saying, that her father had done something—but was it something bad enough to turn Zio Enrico against him? Was that why her uncle had chosen Antonio over her brothers?

She hurried down the street, away from Antonio's flat, careful not to trip on a section of cobblestones. Maybe she should call Gio. Gio had told her she didn't know anything about her father's death, but was that really true? Someone had to know. Perhaps if Gio didn't, her boyfriend Cris Andretti did.

Bianca took a sunny outdoor table at a sidewalk café and dialed her friend. "Can you meet me?" she asked, struggling to keep her voice even.

"What's wrong, Bee?"

Crap. She was no actress. "I had a fight with Antonio."

"Where are you? I'll be right there."

"I'm sorry to pull you away from your family on Natale."

"You're doing me a favor; Leandro's been drinking and Papà is about to have a fit."

Twenty minutes later, Gio arrived in a flurry of concern and jangling bracelets. "Sweetie, you look awful."

"You always know the right thing to say," Bianca joked.

With a shrug, Gio flipped her blonde-streaked hair over her shoulder. "It's true. So what's going on?"

Bianca rapidly explained what had happened between her and Antonio and how Sandro and her son were involved. Gio's eyes were wide by the end of her tale. She took Bianca's hand across the table and lightly squeezed it. "Oh sweetheart, I wish I could help."

"You can. I need to know what happened to my father."

Gio threw out her hands, palms up. "I have no idea. My family wasn't involved."

"But Cris must know something."

Picking at her cuticles, Gio shrugged again. "He might. But I never ask him about business."

"Could you?"

She shifted in her chair and took a sip of the hot chocolate she'd ordered. "It's not a good idea."

"*Per favore*. For me."

This time Gio gave her a hard stare. "Maybe there's a reason you shouldn't go digging."

"I need to know."

Gio leaned forward, her many bracelets clanking against the table. "You haven't exactly endeared yourself to Cris." She clicked a long, beautifully manicured nail against the ceramic tabletop. "Leave it be. You don't want to stir up that mess."

Bianca studied her friend. Gio knew something. Or she suspected something. "I'm not giving up."

Her face an angry mask, Gio raked both hands through the mass of her hair and shook it out over her shoulders. "Bee, you are bloody frustrating sometimes, you know?"

"If you were me, what would you do?"

"I'd leave it up to the men to sort out."

Bianca's face grew hot. "*Davvero*, Gio? You'd leave your child alone in this mess?"

"Tonio's a good guy. He'll take care of your son." Gio took another sip of her drink. "You have told him he's the dad, right?"

"Yes. He was so angry with me."

"Can you blame him? You kept it a secret for six years. It was so hard for me not to say something about it."

"I thought Antonio knew." Bianca looked down at her cup. "Right before I left for Switzerland, Papà made me tell him who the father was so he could ask him to do the right thing. But now I know he never spoke to Antonio."

"Your father didn't want you with Tonio. True?"

Bianca nodded. It was so obvious now. But she'd never have thought Papà would lie to her like that. Not about something of such consequence.

Then again, he'd treated the whole incident as something shameful. Something best forgotten. He'd discarded her son without hesitation.

What else might he have done?

"Gio, please. I need to speak to Cris. No one will be honest with me. And it's time I knew the truth."

"You aren't going to listen to me, are you?"

"I can't, Gio. I can't let this go."

"Fine. But if you don't like what you hear, it's not my fault." She dug out her phone and called Cris. They spoke briefly, Gio saying that she wanted to see him. She didn't mention Bianca. After Gio hung up, she settled back in her chair. "This isn't going to make you happy."

"I just want the truth."

"I don't think you do."

Cris Andretti drove up a short time later. Once again, his size and his looks struck Bianca. If she hadn't known him, she'd have wanted to. But he only had eyes for Gio. The way he lit up when he saw her friend made something in Bianca's chest twist. She wanted that. She wanted that from Antonio. But they could never be. Not after what she'd done, and not after what he'd said. They were through.

Cris kissed Gio, then sprawled out on the chair next to her, one arm around her shoulders. "*Buon Natale*. This is a welcome surprise. I hadn't expected to see you today." He rubbed his nose against hers before kissing her again. "I missed you." When Gio smiled at him, he laughed, and the happiness in the sound pierced Bianca. How long had it been since she'd felt like that?

After a few more kisses, Cris turned to Bianca, his hands cradling one of Gio's in his lap. "I didn't realize you had company," he said to Gio, but he focused on Bianca as he spoke.

"I asked her to call you," Bianca said.

His brow wrinkled. "Why?"

"I need your help."

"With what?"

"I need to know what happened to my father." She paused. "If your family was responsible."

He smirked. "So suddenly you're not sure?"

She shook her head. "I'm not sure of anything, except that I've been lied to."

He scrubbed a hand over his face and sat back in his chair. "I really can't say."

"Just tell me if it was your family that did it."

"That's the rumor."

She wanted to scream in frustration. "But is it true?"

He raised a dark brow. "You do realize that I shouldn't answer that question."

"So it *is* true."

"I didn't say that."

"Yes or no."

"What does it matter? He's dead either way." His tone had hardened. This wasn't going well.

"It matters." Her voice shook with all the emotion she was holding back.

"I can't help you."

"You *know*. Please. Just one word."

Cris leaned forward. His face went utterly still, his eyes flat as a reptile's. "You grew up in this life. You know there are doors you shouldn't open, conversations you shouldn't hear, things you shouldn't know. What happened that night is one of those things."

"Damn it. Tell me!"

He rose from the table. "Stay out of the business, Bianca Lucchesi. You'll live longer that way." He touched Gio's cheek and smiled. "We'll talk later, *dolcezza*," he said to her, then left.

Bianca started to rise, to follow him, but Gio grabbed her wrist. "Don't."

"But he knows!"

"And he won't tell you. Trust me. You've pissed him off. He's not going to budge."

Bianca's stomach went hollow and her insides shook. No one would help her. No one would tell her the truth.

She was alone.

CHAPTER 11

As Antonio turned onto the drive to the Lucchesi Home for Children, the memory of the first time he'd seen the place flashed into his mind. That day, the day he'd met Don Enrico, had changed everything.

Antonio had been twelve, and he'd just been returned to the orphanage in Rome again by Zio Gino after running away. He'd spent the prior two weeks on the streets, begging for money and food, and fending off the advances of pimps and johns. Some of the boys he'd fallen in with had urged him to do it, to become a rent boy. But he couldn't stomach the thought. That was something he wouldn't do, no matter how hungry.

When he'd finally had enough and had gone to his uncle for help, hoping that this time, Zio Gino would take pity on him and take him in, Antonio was gaunt, dirty, ridden with lice, and thoroughly exhausted.

Zio Gino regarded him somberly from the doorway to his home, his frown deepening when Antonio started scratching his head, but he said nothing, and a lump rose in Antonio's throat. Why wouldn't his uncle bend? Were they truly so very poor? "*Per favore*, Zio. I won't eat much. I promise. I can't go back there."

Violetta came racing down the hallway, her face lighting up when she saw him. "Tonio!" She'd grown since he'd last seen her, her blonde ringlets longer and pulled back from her face. She was eight now, and she was starting to lose the chubbiness of early childhood. She tried to scramble past their uncle, to run to Antonio, and his heart ached to hug her, the sister he missed, the only part of his family he had left.

Zio Gino caught her up by the waist. "No, Violetta. He has lice."

"I don't care!"

Antonio smiled at that and blinked away the tears that threatened to flood his vision. "Zio Gino is right. If you get them, they might have to cut off all your hair."

She looked horror-struck for a second, then she giggled. "Zia Sylvana wouldn't like that. She's always brushing my hair and telling me how pretty it is."

"It's beautiful." His voice wavered, and he stepped closer. He wanted to touch

89

her cheek, but his hands were filthy.

She wrinkled her nose. "You need a bath!" She laughed. "Zia Sylvana says boys hate baths."

Antonio smiled. "It's true." He made a silly face at her. "Boys like being dirty."

"Well, you smell like a goat." She gazed up at her uncle. "You'll make him take a bath, won't you?"

He nodded and set her down. "Go inside, *dolcezza*."

She flashed another smile at Antonio, then raced back into the ground-floor apartment, yelling, "Tonio is here!"

"I have to take you back, you know," his uncle said, the words low and soft.

This time Antonio couldn't stop the tears. "I hate it there. The bigger boys are always hitting me and pushing me around and the food is awful and I miss Violetta."

"I know. But there's no place for you here."

His uncle ushered him around back, to the table under the vine-laden pergola. "We'll feed you, but that's all I can offer."

When his uncle went back inside, Antonio broke down in sobs. Why wouldn't his uncle take him in? What had he done? He let himself cry for a few minutes, but when the family cat rubbed up against his leg, purring madly, he sniffed back the rest of his tears. He wasn't a baby.

He was wiping his eyes when his uncle came out with a tray of meats, cheeses, olives, and pickled vegetables. Violetta carried a pitcher of ice water and a stack of plastic glasses. His uncle set the tray in front of Antonio, then took the glasses and pitcher from Violetta and poured, careful to keep himself and Violetta on the other side of the table.

They watched him eat, Violetta burbling on about her classes at school and her friends and how she'd dressed the cat up like a baby—she showed him a long scratch she'd received for her trouble—and he nodded and laughed and asked her questions, trying not to reveal the ache in his heart.

"How long are you staying?" she finally asked.

He glanced at his uncle before answering. "I can't. I have to go back. I just wanted to see you."

"But you just got here." Her lower lip trembled.

"I know. But I have school tomorrow."

She pouted for a second, then she sighed. "Zia Sylvana says school is very important."

"It is," he said, even though he hadn't taken any interest in it for the last two years. His grades had suffered as a result.

"You'll come back?" she asked. "For a whole weekend?"

"Of course." But that was a lie. At best it would be a few hours, maybe a night if his uncle was feeling generous.

Zio Gino consulted his watch. "I'd better get you back."

Antonio nodded, his throat squeezing shut. He followed his uncle to the car, not objecting when he pulled an old blanket out of the trunk and put it over the front passenger seat and head rest. He waved goodbye to Violetta, unable to speak. Zio Gino drove them to the outskirts of Rome.

"You must stop this," his uncle said as they drew near the orphanage. "Every time you come, Violetta cries for you in her sleep for at least a week. It's not fair to her. Or your aunt."

It's not fair to me, Antonio wanted to shout, but what was the use? Nothing was going to change. His aunt hadn't even come out to see him. She always cried when she did, and that made Violetta cry, and so he supposed his uncle had told her to stay away. If his aunt had come out, she'd have insisted he stay the night. She'd have washed his clothes and fussed over him, the way Mamma used to do. And that always made leaving that much harder.

He was glad he hadn't seen her. He was glad he hadn't hugged his sister. That made their parting a little easier.

"Are you listening to me?" his uncle asked.

"I heard you."

"Did you? Because I've said this before."

"I heard you," Antonio repeated, his voice harder.

"*Bene.*" Zio Gino escorted Antonio inside and handed him over to Dottor Rocca, the director of the orphanage, and left without another word.

After Antonio had bathed and changed clothes, Dottor Rocca summoned him to his office. The nurse had shaved Antonio's head and covered him with a delousing solution. The acrid smell still clung to him, despite the shower, and his eyes were red-rimmed from it as well. He still bore the traces of a black eye from a fight with an older boy over a half-eaten sandwich he'd found outside a restaurant a few days before. But at least he was clean now, and his stomach was pleasantly full.

Dottor Rocca, a plump, balding man with tiny square-rimmed glasses, stared at him over the top of his desk, his hands clasped together. "Signor Legato, I despair of you. The constant fighting and running away, your foul mouth, your disrespectful attitude. You are turning into a ruffian, boy, and I don't see how we will ever keep you from the gutter. You seem to enjoy it there."

Bile, hot and caustic, rose up Antonio's throat. He'd just seen what that future was like, and he wanted no part of it. And yet, wasn't that where he was headed? He ignored his studies and spent all his spare time thinking of escape. But there was nowhere for him to go.

And deep down, he knew that had he spent just a few more days on the streets, he would have caved in, would have gladly sold himself for a meal and a warm bed to sleep in. That wasn't the future he wanted. But what else was he fit for?

"Have you nothing to say for yourself?"

Antonio shook his head. What was there to say? He agreed with Dottor Rocca. Perhaps he might follow the lead of the boy who'd hung himself in the shower a few months ago. That would save him a lot of pain, wouldn't it? Even if it damned his soul to hell.

Dottor Rocca sighed and shook his head. Then he said, "Come with me. There is someone who wants to meet you."

He ushered Antonio into a small office. A handsome, dark-haired man in his early thirties sat in one of the chairs in front of the desk. His legs were crossed, his left ankle sitting on his right knee. The man was elegantly dressed in a dark blue pinstriped suit, and a beautiful gold watch peeked out of his left cuff. He extended his hand for Antonio to shake. "*Ciao*, Antonio. I'm Enrico Lucchesi."

Antonio shook the man's hand, noting its strength and lack of calluses. Signor Lucchesi's smile seemed genuine, but a shark could hide behind a grin. And something about this man made him wary. There was an ease, a sense of power, emanating from him. He had the air of a man who was used to getting what he wanted. And what did he want with Antonio?

The man looked at Dottor Rocca. "You may leave us." The words were clearly a dismissal, yet his voice wasn't unkind, merely firm.

"As you wish, *signore*."

Signor Lucchesi motioned for Antonio to take the seat across from him. "Do you know why you're here?"

Antonio shook his head. He'd learned early it was best to say little and see what the other person assumed.

"Dottor Rocca tells me you are incapable of reform. That you are beyond hope." He waited for Antonio to say something, and when he got only a shrug in return, he continued. "I think he's wrong. You are a smart boy—at least your school record prior to coming here indicates that."

Again, Antonio shrugged. He had enjoyed school at one point. But that was before.

"I sponsor an orphanage up north. Near where your family was from. The orphanage is small and much more comfortable than this one. However, I expect every child there to study hard. The children in my care will not end up on the streets." He paused. "Would you be interested?"

Antonio rolled the idea around in his head. He hated this place, hated the bullying of the older boys, hated the dismissive attitude of Dottor Rocca. But going north meant he'd never see Violetta again.

"Is something troubling you?"

"If I leave, how will I see my sister?"

Signor Lucchesi studied him. "That's why you run away so often."

"It's part of it. I hate it here."

"I am frequently in Rome on business, and it would be no trouble to make a detour occasionally, say three or four times a year."

The man was being too accommodating. He wanted something. "Why would you do this? Why would you take me out of here?"

"Because I think you have potential. My orphanage specializes in handling difficult cases where the children show promise, but aren't thriving in their current environment. Dottor Rocca suggested we consider you."

There was more behind this than the man was saying. There had to be. "That's not the whole truth."

Signor Lucchesi appraised him for a moment, then he nodded. "You are very astute." Sadness crossed his face. "My wife and I are unable to have children. But she refuses to adopt. So I suppose this is my way of having children of my own."

There was an ache in the man's voice that rang of honesty. Antonio had feared the man had some dark agenda. But the simple, straightforward words, spoken so unhesitatingly and sincerely, swayed him. "You promise I will see Violetta?"

"I promise."

"Then I will hold you to it."

The man grinned. "You are quite fearless."

Antonio held his gaze. "Should I fear you, *signore?*"

A glint appeared in the man's eyes. Some secret. Perhaps it was related to that sense of power Antonio had detected earlier. "No, Antonio. You will never have anything to fear from me."

Don Lucchesi had been true to his word, and more, and as Antonio sat in his car staring at the orphanage that had been his home, he felt again the keen bite of loneliness, of abandonment, that he'd felt at Sandro and Matteo's *comparaggio* ceremony. What had he done to make Don Enrico push him away? Was it because of Nick, because Enrico had finally gotten his son back? Or was it because Antonio had pushed Enrico to kill Don Domenico for his betrayal? Did he hold that against Antonio now? Was that why everything between them had become so brittle?

Or was it really just Antonio's closeness with Kate? A closeness he planned to lean on?

He'd called the don's house before he'd left and was surprised to hear that Kate was at the orphanage. Apparently she was supervising the kids at some activity before they headed over to Enrico's villa for the afternoon.

He left the car and went inside, nodding to the guard posted at the front. His pulse quickened. Kate wouldn't refuse him this time, not now that his son was in danger. Would she?

He walked down the marble corridor, following the sound of excited voices into the large parlor that acted as an entertainment room for the children. He turned the corner and came to an abrupt stop.

A huge, bushy evergreen—it must have been over twelve feet tall—had been set up in the corner by the fireplace, and the scent of fresh-cut pine filled the room. Twenty or so children were swarming all over, digging decorations out of boxes. Kate's bodyguard was on a step ladder, putting decorations on the upper branches at the children's excited—and often contradictory—direction.

Kate sat to the side on a sofa, one of the youngest girls perched beside her, looking on eagerly while Kate read to her. A lump filled Antonio's throat. There hadn't been a tree, or much of a Natale, for these children the last two years, ever since Antonella, Don Enrico's first wife, had fallen ill and died. But Kate had changed that.

She looked up from her reading and saw him. "Tonio!" she called over the noise, and he coughed to clear his throat before he went to her. When he approached, she smiled, as lovely as always, but for some reason he didn't feel the same jolt of attraction he'd always felt before. Was that because of Bianca?

Kate motioned to the scarf around his neck. "You're wearing it! I'll have to tell Enrico. He bet me you wouldn't. The color is perfect, just like I thought. It brings out your eyes."

He gave her a grin. "I don't think you should mention that part." She sighed, and then he added, "It's a lovely gift. Thank you."

"You already sent me a text. You didn't have to come over here to thank me."

"Actually, that's not why I'm here. Can we speak in private? It's urgent, or I wouldn't have bothered you."

"Sure. Give me a moment." She found an older girl to finish reading the book, then led Antonio to her office. She took her seat behind the desk and gazed up at him. "What's going on?"

He sat on the edge of her desk. "Sandro was here a few days ago. I'm certain he accessed my son's file on Gina's computer."

"How?"

He repeated what Gina had told him. "There's no other reason for him to have come here. He knows where my son is, and he's threatened to do him harm."

Kate blanched. "He wouldn't."

"You have more faith in him than I do."

"But why?"

Antonio raised a brow. "Think about it. I have a son who's half Lucchesi. An heir. I am part of this family, whether he likes it or not. I have a tie to his sister, to the Lucchesi name. And he hates that idea."

"But his own nephew?"

Antonio leaned toward her. "You know this family's history. His father and his brother both betrayed this family and went after Don Enrico. And Sandro is following in their footsteps. He wants to head this *cosca*, and he doesn't care how he does it." He almost mentioned Sandro's involvement with Lorenzo Andretti, but until he had proof, he didn't want to say anything.

"And you want me to tell you where your son is."

He nodded. "I won't contact him or the people who adopted him." He couldn't bring himself to call them his son's parents. "I only want to set up surveillance, to make sure Sandro doesn't go near them."

"Enrico could handle that for you."

"You don't trust me, Kate?"

"I do. It's just—" She caressed the slight bump in her belly. "I know how strongly you feel. How your emotions trample all over your reason."

"And so you know why I want to take charge of this. Why I *must* do this myself. He's my son," he said, his voice cracking on the word. "I must keep him safe."

Kate's eyes filled with tears. "You have to promise me you'll behave."

"This place was my home. It saved my life. I promise they'll never see or hear from me, unless Sandro makes a move."

She studied him for several moments before turning to her computer and typing a few words. Then she printed a sheet with the names of a couple and their address. Nothing on the sheet indicated who they were. "Don't tell Enrico. He'll be furious."

"I won't." He rose and pressed a kiss to her cheek. "*Mille grazie*, Kate, from the bottom of my heart."

"I'm trusting you, Tonio. Don't make me regret it."

"You won't."

He turned to go, but she stopped him. "I wish you'd come by the house today and spend the holiday with us. Nick and Delfi arrived this morning. I know they'd like to see you. I'm sure we can keep Sandro in line."

Should he tell her truth? He hesitated, then decided she didn't deserve a lie. "Natale doesn't have a lot of good memories for me. I just don't want to be there, Sandro or not. It's hard for me being around the children—I used to be one of them, going to 'Zio Enrico's' for Natale."

"I'm sorry, Tonio. I'm sorry for everything you went through." She paused, then softly said, "I read your file."

His stomach clenched. He couldn't do this today. Not on top of everything else. "Kate, *per favore*. I don't want to talk about it."

"You should. You should talk to someone."

Anger flared up in him, but he tamped it down. She wasn't trying to hurt him. He took a deep breath and tried to push out the feeling as he exhaled. "I'm fine. Really. I've got to go."

He went out into the hall, closing the door behind him, then stared at the paper in his hands, his belly fluttering. He finally knew where his son was. Milan. All these years he'd had a child. All these years he'd been a father, and he'd never known. How had Bianca managed it—the longing, the ache to see him? He had to tell her, to reassure her, that he could keep their son safe.

He pulled out his phone and called Bianca as he headed to his car. Oh, he was still furious with her. But they needed to talk, after he saw Orlando and tried to figure out what Sandro had done at the bank.

He'd told Kate he wasn't going to jeopardize the orphanage, and he meant it. But he was going to see his son with his own eyes. Nothing would stop him.

Bianca deserved the same, no matter what she'd done. Antonio understood now. He understood the madness, the turmoil, of loving one's child. And the complete and abject terror that consumed a parent when that child was in danger.

———◆———

Antonio checked his watch as he parked his car down the street from the Banca di Falcone. He'd had to push hard to hit Milan on time. Given Ruggero's lead foot, it was entirely possible they'd beaten him. He scanned the cars lining the street and grinned when he saw it: Ruggero's shiny new blood-red Maserati convertible.

He waved at the occupants and the doors opened, Ruggero stepping out the driver's side, and a younger man in his early twenties arising from the passenger side. Like his uncle Ruggero, Orlando Farnese was dark-haired and relatively tall, but there the resemblance ended. Where Ruggero was all muscle and intimidation, Orlando was lanky and seemed unsure of himself, glancing around them as if searching for enemy spies, before giving Antonio a tentative smile. He had a long thin nose, dark eyes, and his uncle's squint. But on Orlando that squint looked like concentration, instead of his uncle's air of assessing the object of contemplation and searching it for weakness.

"*Buon Natale*," Antonio said to them. "I still can't believe you came back."

"Told you there'd be trouble," Ruggero said.

They headed inside, Orlando continuing to eye everything as if he expected it to bite him. "Relax," Antonio said.

Orlando nodded, but his demeanor didn't change. They went up to Antonio's office on the third floor. The corridors were silent, as expected for Natale. Not that anyone came in on the weekend unless they had to, and the bank didn't have commercial hours on Saturdays and Sundays. One of Don Enrico's rules. Besides, their clients weren't the sort who needed to do their banking outside the work week.

When they entered Antonio's office, he noted with a sickening jolt that his chair hadn't been pushed in, the way he'd left it on Friday, the way he left it every day. If he hadn't known Sandro had done something, would he have chalked the placement of his chair up to the custodial staff moving it? Probably. But he knew otherwise.

He took his seat, and Orlando and Ruggero pulled up chairs on either side of him. "What are you concerned about?" Ruggero asked.

"I have reason to believe that Sandro has accessed my user account, and I'm sure if he has, he's been up to no good."

"You've told Don Lucchesi," Ruggero said.

"Not yet. I wanted to know how bad it was first. Besides, it's Natale."

Ruggero crossed his arms. "He should know."

"And he will." He shot Ruggero a stern look. "It's my mess, and I'll handle it."

He logged in and accessed the transaction record for his user account. His stomach clenched when he saw the list of client accounts Sandro had accessed: La Provincia, Gianluca d'Imperio, Dario Andretti, Lorenzo Andretti. His adrenaline spiked when he saw who else was on the list: Enrico Lucchesi, Sandro Lucchesi. And last of all, Antonio's own personal account.

Porca miseria.

He opened the records on his own account and his jaw dropped open: It was flooded with money. Money that shouldn't be there.

"Is all that yours?" Orlando asked.

"Hell no." Antonio swallowed. "Sandro transferred it from somewhere. And I'm pretty sure I know where."

He started opening the other accounts on the list, and sure enough, most of them were drained considerably. La Provincia had not a euro left. His heart pounded as he stared at the 0.00 balance. *That fucker.*

Orlando squinted at the screen. "Something's not right."

"You don't say," Antonio said.

"No, I mean these figures don't add up. I've been keeping a rough tally of the transfers in my head, and they far surpass what's in your account. So where did the rest go?"

There was one account Antonio hadn't opened yet. Don Enrico's. It felt as if he were overstepping his bounds to do so, but he had to know.

When he opened it, he could hardly register what he was seeing. His *capo*'s balance had grown by over two billion euros, from one day to the next. Antonio's mouth went dry. Sandro wasn't after only Antonio, and now Antonio had proof. Sandro was out to ruin Don Enrico as well.

"Does it add up now?" Antonio asked.

Orlando frowned again. "No. It's still off. By maybe another two billion euros, give or take."

Antonio gaped at him, and Ruggero grinned. "I told you he was a genius with numbers."

"No argument." Antonio turned to Orlando. "He must have transferred money to outside accounts. There's a lot of data to sift through, and the transfers between banks are a bitch to sort out. Can you help me?"

"Show me how to get into the wire transfers and where to look up the IBAN and SWIFT codes, and I'll sort through it."

Antonio set Orlando up in Sandro's office and logged him in to the network. "Don't try to fix anything. Just document where it all went."

He returned to his office and Ruggero rose and shut the door. "You didn't say how you knew Sandro had been in your account."

For a moment, Antonio considered lying. If he told the truth, Bianca could be in danger. But he had to trust in Don Enrico's love of his family. Her actions hadn't been malicious. "Bianca gave Sandro my password. He was threatening her son. *Our* son."

"You have a child together?"

"When we were teenagers, I got her pregnant. It's why she went to Switzerland."

"*Porco Dio,*" Ruggero muttered and shook his head. "You have to call Don Lucchesi."

"I will. As soon as I know what's happened."

"You *do* know. And he needs to know, right this minute."

"We have the weekend to fix it."

Ruggero pinned him with a hard stare. "What if you don't?"

"What do you mean? The customers won't know anything until Monday."

"You think Sandro hasn't placed an anonymous call to the authorities? You think he hasn't alleged wrongdoing?"

Ice slid down Antonio's back. Sandro had finished his work early this morning. It was now a little past one. However, it was also a holiday weekend, and the Financial Intelligence Unit (FIU) at Banca d'Italia, Italy's central bank and financial regulatory authority, would need time to investigate before they'd call in the Guardia di Finanza, the Italian finance police, but no doubt some hungry bureaucrat eager to make his name could be found to expedite matters—or was already in Lorenzo Andretti's pocket.

Fuck. Antonio couldn't have felt worse if a bomb had detonated in his chest. Of course. Lorenzo would have thought this all through, would have had it all planned out. He'd have set the trap with precision.

Antonio had allowed himself to get sidetracked with protecting his son, and no doubt that part had been planned out as well to distract him. He'd lost precious hours because of it.

He grabbed his phone and dialed Don Enrico. They needed to act now, or both of them could be behind bars before nightfall.

CHAPTER 12

By the time Don Enrico arrived at the bank, Antonio was ready to tear his hair out. Sandro must've been working on this for days, planning where to stash the money. No doubt he'd had help from Lorenzo. It would take hours to reverse the transactions, provided he could even get someone on the phone at the other banks. This was a disaster, through and through.

And it was all his fault. He should have stepped aside, walked away when he'd wanted to. He should've done the right thing.

Instead he'd been selfish.

Enrico strode into Antonio's office, his mouth grim, his brow furrowed. "What's the situation?"

Antonio recounted everything he and Orlando had discovered. Enrico fiddled with his watch as he paced. Then he stopped. "You did shut off ATM and Internet access, yes?"

Cristo. He hadn't been thinking. He shook his head, feeling about four years old.

"Bloody hell, Antonio!" Don Enrico hadn't yelled at him in what, at least five years?

"I'm sorry. I'll get on it."

"Do you even know who to call?" Enrico asked.

"IT?"

Enrico sighed. "You'll just get the tech on holiday duty. And he doesn't know anything about us. Who we really are. We need people who do."

He pulled out his phone and tapped the screen several times, then spoke rapidly and firmly to the bank's head of IT. "I need you to get down here, right now. We have an emergency."

He placed another two calls and summoned his security expert and his lawyer to the office. When he was finished, he hung up and stared at Antonio. "Why didn't you call me the minute you knew there was a problem?"

Antonio glanced at Ruggero, who had the grace to merely nod instead of saying, "I told you." Then he focused on the don again. "It's Natale. I didn't want to bother you until I knew."

"No, I mean why didn't you call me as soon as you knew your user account had been compromised."

"My son was in danger."

"You couldn't spare five minutes to call me?"

Antonio spread his hands helplessly. "I wasn't thinking."

"No, you weren't. You did exactly what Sandro expected. You let him run the game."

"I'm sorry. I—"

"And why the hell didn't you tell me you suspected there was a problem with La Provincia's account!"

"You'd just kicked me out of the house, and the *comparaggio* was coming up—"

"So you were feeling sorry for yourself?"

"No. I was just distracted—"

"You aren't a bloody child anymore, Antonio. I gave you this job because I thought I could trust you. I thought I could rely on you. It looks like I was wrong."

The words hurt like blows. "I would never betray you."

Don Enrico shook his head and scrubbed a hand over his face. "I know that. But this"—he gestured around them—"*this* is catastrophic. You didn't handle it well. Not at all."

Antonio swallowed hard, his cheeks burning. "I know. I let myself get sidetracked by my personal problems."

"*Dio mio!* You're not *listening*. I need you to use your head. All. The. Time. If you see a threat, or even a hint of a threat, you have to tell me. That bloody minute, and not a second later. We can't give Lorenzo—or anyone else—time to plot out the next move."

Enrico stopped pacing and grabbed the back of a chair in front of Antonio's desk. "Do you know why Lorenzo Andretti has lived so long? The man must have a list of enemies from here to Calabria. But nobody goes after him. Why?"

"Because he's smart."

"Because he's always planning. He never stops. He never rests. He never relents. He is merciless. And when he sets his sights on something, he gets it. And he wants this bank."

"I'm sorry." Antonio could barely choke out the words. He would not cry, not in front of Don Enrico and never in front of Ruggero. But he wanted to crawl into a dark hole and never come out.

"This isn't the time to be sorry. It's time to think, to act. If we're lucky, a number of the wire transfers haven't gone through yet, so we can recall them without any real damage. The rest..." He paused. "It's going to take a while."

Enrico pulled out his phone again, and this time, his voice was all smiles. When he hung up, he said to Antonio, "That was Demetrio Ricci, the director of the FIU. He's a friend of mine."

Antonio raised a brow. "Can he help?"

Enrico inclined his head. "He may not be able to stop the investigation entirely. At the least, he can slow it down, buy us some time."

A stir in the hallway alerted them to new arrivals. Two men, one dressed in an impeccable suit and carrying a leather briefcase and the other in a pressed shirt and jeans, arrived. Shortly after, another man, in a black windbreaker and turtleneck, also carrying a briefcase, steel this time rather than leather, strolled in. Antonio had met him only once before, but he recognized Max Strasser from the time he'd upgraded the security system at Enrico's estate after Kate's estranged husband had broken in. Enrico introduced the others as Agostino Trapani, his lawyer, and Gavino Idoni, the bank's head of IT. "Max will check into the physical security issues, and Gavino will investigate the database changes. If the transaction record from La Provincia has been tampered with, he'll find out who's responsible."

"But it has been." Antonio dug through the papers on his desk and found the wrinkled stack that he'd sat on just over a week ago. When he'd failed to tell Enrico because he'd been too rattled by Bianca and her brother. When he'd been determined to prove he could handle this on his own. That he could confront Lorenzo Andretti and win.

What an idiot.

He handed the printout to Enrico, who studied it quickly, his frown deepening. His eyes lingered on the bottom corner, which showed the date. "If you'd come to me with this back then, we could've stopped him."

"I did. It was the day Bianca came to the office—"

"So it's all because of Bianca?" Enrico stared at Antonio for a moment, and Antonio decided silence was the best response. "I'm reminded of something. That night when Vincenzo Andretti almost killed Kate and me, you were off with some girl then, too."

Ruggero cut in. "I gave him permission to go that night."

Enrico waved him off. "True." He turned to address Antonio. "But this is the second time you've allowed a girl to get in the way of doing your duty."

"It wasn't Bianca's fault—"

"No. It was yours."

The words hung in the air, frosted with ice. Antonio had no rebuttal. "I know."

Ruggero cleared his throat. "What if Bianca isn't so innocent?" Antonio and Enrico both turned to look at him. Ruggero continued, unfazed. "What if she's working with her brother?"

No one spoke, then Enrico shook his head. "As angry as I am with her, I can't believe it. If she truly was working with him, she'd have never told us and given us the opportunity to undo the damage."

Antonio wished he could say the same. Wished he could banish the doubt that lingered in his heart. Was Bianca telling the truth, or merely playing a game he was only now beginning to understand?

———— • ————

Antonio, Orlando, Enrico, and Gavino worked feverishly all afternoon and well into the night to reverse the damage that Sandro had wreaked in mere hours.

Don Enrico and Agostino Trapani charmed one bank president after another into allowing them to reverse the interbank transfers, calling in favors and promising others. Enrico had his jeweler, Giacomo Parini, on the other line, making a list and sending out his and hers watches from the likes of Cartier, Rolex, and Patek Philippe to everyone who cooperated.

However, the head of the bank in Liechtenstein—the same bank Lorenzo Andretti had made all those troubling transfers to—stonewalled them, demanding a written request and five days to investigate. "He's in Lorenzo's pocket," Enrico said after he hung up. "We'll have to write that off. I'll cover the loss. Take it from my account."

"But it's a half-billion euros!" Antonio said.

"And I'm sure Lorenzo was counting on me having to do that. But if I let them investigate, he and the clients affected will be contacted, and we know Lorenzo will trumpet our problem far and wide. Even though he engineered it."

"You can't absorb that loss."

"I will manage." Don Enrico's voice was soft.

"I don't see—"

"I will manage." The words were much firmer this time.

Gavino came in, followed by Strasser. "I've finished analyzing the transaction records, and I found the culprit—at least one of them." Gavino paused, his hands on his hips, his head hanging down. Then he looked up. "I feel responsible. It was one of my own hires, Narciso Acerbi. I trained him myself." Gavino's face darkened. "Narciso's quite clever, but he forgot that one of the mirrors lags a day behind the others so that we can restore the database in the event of a major user mistake. He could have manually updated that mirror, but he forgot. So we've got a record of how things were yesterday before all the chaos."

"Mirrors?" Ruggero asked.

"Copies of the database. For redundancy," Orlando added.

Gavino nodded at Orlando. "I've cleaned everything up in the primary server and initiated overwrites of the mirrors. And I've made copies of the transaction records before and after this mess. If we hadn't caught it today, and if Narciso hadn't screwed up, we'd have been fucked."

"So we're in the clear?" Antonio asked.

Enrico sighed. "Once we finish the transfers from my account."

Gavino rubbed a hand over his face. "And only as long as the FIU believes our explanation for all the updates."

"We could use some insurance on that point," Ruggero said. "Shall I go see Narciso Acerbi?"

Enrico nodded. "Find out who paid him."

"And then?" Ruggero asked.

"Keep him under surveillance. And make sure he knows we're watching. We may need him if we can't stop the FIU's investigation."

"You know how the FIU is," Gavino said. "They'll go over and over the transactions. We're going to have to answer for all the changes. We've moved a huge amount of cash around in the last twenty-four hours."

"I invited Demetrio Ricci, the director of the FIU, to meet with us after we've finished our investigation," Agostino said. "Along with his team."

"So what's our story?" Antonio asked.

The attorney tilted his head to the side. "The most rudimentary version of the truth. A rogue employee who'd been fired and had a grudge against us."

Antonio had to smile at the irony. "Not far from the truth."

"We'll be instituting biometric passwords this week," Strasser said.

"I'm not sure that's a good idea," Ruggero said. "Having our fingerprints on record."

"I'm one step ahead of you. We'll use iris scans only."

"*Bene,*" Ruggero said.

"When are you dealing with Sandro?" Antonio asked.

A look passed between Strasser and Don Enrico before Strasser answered. "There's a problem."

"Problem?"

"Your keycard was used to access the building. Not Sandro's."

"But I have mine. It's been with me the whole time." Antonio dug the card out of his pocket and held it up.

"May I see it?" Strasser took the card and left the room.

Antonio gazed at Enrico. "You don't think *I* did this?"

"No."

"Then what?"

"Max will get to the bottom of it."

Antonio's stomach tightened. He didn't like the expression on Don Enrico's face, the sense of disappointment that radiated from him. Antonio hadn't done anything wrong, and yet there were so many things he hadn't done right.

Strasser returned a few minutes later. "I compared the card's signature to the one that was used earlier today. They differ, but both cards are registered to Don Legato."

Antonio frowned. "That's not possible."

"You've checked the security records?" Enrico asked Strasser.

He nodded. "A new card was issued to Don Legato last week through the interoffice mail. The note says that he lost his card and called to request a new one."

"But I didn't. Sandro must have done it." Antonio thought for a moment, then he said, "The security cameras—we need to check the footage."

"I've got some bad news about that," Strasser said. The group of them followed Strasser into the security center, where he pulled up the day's recordings. Everything was fine until around five-twenty AM. Then the screens went dark. Someone had turned off all the cameras. They went on again around nine AM.

"You think Sandro could have done this?" Enrico asked Strasser.

"Maybe, if he knew how to hack into the system remotely. I think a better bet is our culprit in IT."

"I'll find him," Ruggero said. He asked Gavino for Narciso Acerbi's address, then he left.

"How do we handle Sandro?" Antonio asked again.

"That *stronzo* was at my house, eating my *panettone*, all afternoon." Enrico shook his head. "I take him as my son, and he spits in my eye."

"So we confront him today?"

Enrico crossed his arms. "All we have to go on is Bianca's word."

"And that's not enough?"

"To fire him? No."

"This is your bank. You can do what you want."

Enrico sighed. "The FIU will have us under a microscope now. You think Sandro won't take advantage of that and allege that we've wrongfully terminated him? You think he won't say we tried to pin all this on him with no proof?"

"Fuck," Antonio muttered. Sandro had certainly done his part to destroy them. And yet the feeling lingered: This was all Antonio's fault. He'd failed to act when he should have. He'd failed to see the trap that he'd blundered into.

He'd failed his don, his *cosca*, and everyone who depended on him. And now they all were going to suffer because of his poor judgment.

———◆———

By the time Antonio returned to his flat, he was exhausted. It was nearly two in the morning, and he felt like he hadn't slept in days. But more draining than the physical and mental exhaustion was the knowledge that he'd let Enrico down. If Enrico wanted to demote him—or worse—he wouldn't protest. He couldn't, not in good conscience.

Before Antonio could put his key in the lock, Raffaele opened the door with a finger to his lips, signaling Antonio to be quiet. What was going on?

Raffaele stepped out and pulled the door shut behind him. "She's here."

"Bianca?" *Merda*. He hadn't answered any of her calls or texts. He'd just turned his phone to silent.

Raffaele nodded. "She was… distraught. A real mess. I didn't know what else to do—I couldn't get you on the phone—so I let her in. She's been asleep on the couch for a couple of hours."

"Asleep?"

"I might've helped with that." Raffaele made a drinking motion. "You know women and liquor."

Great. Bianca was drunk *and* upset. Hopefully she wouldn't wake up.

They crept inside, and Raffaele headed to his bedroom, leaving Antonio alone with Bianca. She was curled up on the sofa, her arms wrapped around herself, a throw covering her body. Light snoring betrayed her inebriated state.

He gazed at Bianca, his emotions in a tangle. A part of him wanted to wake her, to reassure her, and another part of him wanted to wake her and interrogate her. And then there was the part he didn't want to examine too closely—the part that wanted to hold her close, to make love to her. To forgive her for what she'd done. If only she'd told him. If only she'd trusted him.

But really, why should she have? Had he done anything to merit her trust? Even one thing?

She shifted on the couch, her arms flailing, and then she cried out and came awake. "Luca!"

When she saw Antonio, she started and screamed, then she placed a hand on her chest, as if to slow her heart. "You scared me."

He sat down on the low occasional table by her head and reached out, stroking a few strands of toffee-colored hair off her face. "Who's Luca?"

She colored and glanced away. "No one."

"So you just scream the names of unknown men at random?"

"He's not a man. He's a boy." She met his eyes. "Our son." She pressed her lips together for a moment. "At least that's what I put on the birth certificate. I have no idea what they call him."

They. The people raising their child. His mouth twisted as a peculiar pain lodged in his chest. Luca. It was a good name.

How had she managed to suffer alone with this all these years? He'd known for only two days, and it felt like someone had ripped his heart from his chest.

"Is he okay?" she asked.

"Yes. Ruggero has a man watching him."

"Just one?"

"One is enough. We don't know that Sandro will do anything."

"He will. I know it." She sat up and smoothed her hair back behind her ears. "As soon as he knows I told you, he'll do something."

"Don't worry."

She pounded a fist against the cushions she sat on. "How can you be so calm? I thought you cared."

"I do. And I'm not calm."

"You look it."

He balled his hands into fists and clenched them, then slowly stretched his fingers out, feeling the tension ebb from his upper body. "Well, I'm not." He scrubbed his hands over his face. "I've spent all day worrying. But mostly I've been fighting to stay out of jail. Do you have any idea what your brother has done? And with *your* help?"

Bursting into tears, she covered her eyes with her hands. "I'm so sorry. I can't think straight anymore. I worry about Luca, night and day. And what Sandro is going to do and what he's already done—"

Antonio leaned forward and gathered her into his arms, tugging her onto his lap. "Shh." He rocked her as she sobbed. "I wish you'd told me," he whispered. "But I understand why you didn't." She sobbed harder and said something incoherent. "What was that?"

"I let Sandro get to me. I let him plant doubts about you in my mind."

Guilt stabbed at him. She had every right to those doubts, as did Sandro. If they ever knew the truth... "Never mind."

Bianca shook her head. "You're too forgiving."

"Everyone makes mistakes. Especially me."

"The only mistake you made was trusting me."

The only mistake I made was not running the other way when I saw you again.

Dio, he wanted to tell her everything. He wanted to confess. He wanted this horrible secret between them to be exposed to the light of day. He wanted her to know him, every millimeter of his being, the good parts and the bad.

He wanted her forgiveness.

He wanted her love.

But he could never have any of that.

He felt like he had at twelve, sitting out back at his uncle's house. The boy who couldn't have what he wanted most in the world: a normal life.

Bianca quieted in his arms, then looked up at him, wiping away her tears. "What's wrong?" she asked.

How could he possibly answer that question with any shred of honesty? He said the one thing that was truthful, the one thing that they could both embrace. "I want to see our son. I promised Kate I wouldn't. But I have to."

"Can I go with you?" Her voice was so soft, so small, his heart broke a little.

"Of course." She threw her arms around his neck and peppered his face with kisses, making him laugh. Catching his laughter, she made a game of kissing him everywhere—his eyelids, his forehead, his nose, his ears. Everywhere but his mouth. She studiously avoided it, even when he tried to capture hers. He finally took hold of her chin and held her still. "Kiss me."

She met his gaze for a long, hushed beat, the moment dragging out until Antonio's mouth went dry and his heart thundered in his chest. Had everything between them these last few days been a lie?

Slowly, hesitantly, she smiled. "You truly want me to kiss you?"

"Very much."

Her smile spread, lighting up her face. "I want that too."

Antonio made no move to close the gap, even though every fiber of his being urged him to plunder her mouth, to push her back on the cushions and take her, every bit of her.

Ever so slowly, her right hand descended on his cheek, her fingers shaking, and she leaned in and pressed her lips to his. A shudder coursed through her and into him, and he let his desire loose.

Thrusting both hands into her hair, he took hold of her skull, angling her head for his kiss. A whimper burst from her lips, exploding into his mouth, and he couldn't stop his answering groan as he deepened the kiss, pouring all his wants, all his desires, all his feelings into that connection. He wanted this, he wanted her, and for at least one night, he was going to pretend he could have what he wanted. That somehow it would all work out.

Bianca kissed him back, greedily, fervently, as if she'd been waiting for this, for him. As if she wanted him as desperately as he wanted her. One of her hands slipped inside his shirt, brushing across his pecs, then she pulled at his buttons almost angrily, and that was all the prompting he needed. He gathered her up in his arms and carried her down the hallway into the bedroom, kicking the door shut behind them.

This time, she needed no prompting. Tearing at his clothes, she pressed kisses to his flesh, as if she'd starved for him the way he had for her, during all those long years they'd been apart. Oh, he'd filled his bed with other women, but they'd all been poor substitutes for her. Bianca.

She'd owned him all this time. Heart and soul. He'd never stopped caring for her. He'd never stopped longing for her.

When she had him stripped bare, Antonio grinned. He'd hardly moved a muscle during her frenzy. She was still fully clothed, but that was about to change. "Your turn." He walked her over to the bed. Time to make one of his fantasies come true. "Grab that post," he said, motioning to the nearest corner.

Her hands wrapped around the carved wood and her eyes darkened. Moving behind her, he ran a hand from the nape of her neck to the base of her spine, his fingers trailing along the zipper that ran down the back of her dress. She shivered, and the sight made him smile. She was just as keyed up as he was.

He took hold of the zipper tab and pulled downward, the two halves of the dress moving apart and baring her delicious honey-colored skin to his gaze. He pressed kisses the entire length of her spine, and she writhed and trembled beneath his touch. He sank to his knees behind her.

"Step out of the dress," he said, his voice hoarse. She released the post and complied. He didn't have to tell her to grab hold of it again.

She stood before him in just her lacy white bra and boy-short panties and a pair of black heels with straps that buckled around the ankles. He loved those and couldn't help circling his hands around the straps as he nudged her legs apart with his shoulders, until she stood splayed in front of him, breathing fast.

He trailed his hands up the backs of her legs, toward the high, round curves of her ass. He nipped at that lovely flesh through the thin cloth of her panties, and she yelped. "Are you going to eat me or make love to me?" she asked.

"I'm going to eat you, *then* I'm going to make love to you." He nuzzled her ass through the cloth, then blew between her legs and made her shiver. When she widened her stance a little more and arched her back, he had to grin. She'd lost her shyness.

He took hold of her panties at the waistband and tore them in two, letting the shredded halves fall away.

"Hey!" she said. "Those were expensive."

"I'll buy you more." He dove between her legs, his tongue sweeping over her pink folds and then delving inside. Moaning, she bent forward at the waist and pushed out, giving him better access, and he found her clit this time. When he circled it with his tongue, she cried out and thrashed against him. He circled it again and again, then stuck his fingers in his mouth to wet them before sinking two of them inside her. She gasped out her pleasure at the invasion and rocked her hips back in response.

His cock was so hard he could feel his pulse pounding through its length. He couldn't wait any longer. Planting a kiss at the base of her spine, he rose. "Stay right there," he said, pressing the small of her back with his hand.

He grabbed a condom from the nightstand and ripped it open, rolling it on as quickly as his impatient fingers could manage.

"Hurry," she whispered, her face flushed, her eyes darkened with desire, her breasts heaving against the confines of her brassiere. He'd get to those treasures later.

He gave her a light smack on a well-rounded buttock. "So demanding."

"It's your fault." She looked at him over her shoulder. "Making me stand like this. Waiting. It's driving me crazy."

"That's what I wanted." He took hold of her hips and rubbed his *cazzo* across her firm buttocks. "I wanted you as crazy for me as I am for you." He plunged inside her, and anything she might've said was lost in a raw moan that amped up his desire.

Dio, there was nothing better than this—her hot, tight walls clamping around him, practically making him come already. He pulled out and plunged back in, watching his cock disappear inside her, and the sight was very nearly too much.

He closed his eyes and folded himself over her, reaching forward with his right hand, seeking her engorged *grilletto*. He rolled it between his fingers and she practically screamed in his ear. His hips thrust forward of their own accord, and he was lost, utterly lost in her.

"Tonio," she groaned and pressed back against him. His fingers slipped in her juices, and he worked them frantically across her clit, hoping she'd come soon, because he couldn't last much longer, the way she kept clenching around him with each thrust. It was maddening and heavenly, and he never, ever wanted it to stop.

Suddenly she bore down on him and shuddered, calling his name again, and his orgasm erupted from him, the pleasure so intense it was nearly painful. His legs shook, and he clutched her hips for support, praying that she could hold on. She staggered beneath him, and he pulled out, letting her catch her balance. He swung over to the wooden chest at the foot of the bed and collapsed onto it, pulling her down beside him.

"*Cristo*," she whispered. "You about killed me."

"Sorry. I lost my balance."

She laughed. "Not that. The orgasm. I thought I was going to have a heart attack, it was so intense." She took his hand and placed it on her heaving chest. "Can you feel my heart?"

It beat fast beneath his palm. "It's your fault, Bee. You kept squeezing me."

She blushed. "It felt so good."

"I'm not complaining."

"Good." She reached behind herself and unhooked her bra. "Because I'm not done with you yet."

CHAPTER 13

Making love with Antonio this time was so different from the last. Bianca wasn't lying to him, she wasn't there because Sandro had made her, and she couldn't fool herself that what she was feeling was anything but real. She wanted to be with Antonio, and his forgiveness of her lies, of her helping Sandro, seemed like a minor miracle.

She dropped her bra to the floor and was pleased to see Antonio's eyes laser in on her breasts. She cupped them in her hands, as if offering them to him, and he smiled, then leaned forward and took her left nipple in his mouth, his lips closing over it, his tongue working against the tightened peak. The sensation sparked through her and shot straight between her legs. He tweaked the other nipple with his fingers, pinching and tugging until she cried out.

"You like that," he whispered against her skin.

She wrapped her arms around his neck, pulling him closer, and planted a kiss on his bent head. "I love everything you do to me."

"And I love doing things to you." He looked up at her as he bit down lightly on the nipple in his mouth.

I love you. She almost blurted it out, but she stopped herself. Not yet. Not until she knew they had a chance.

Suddenly he sat up straight and ran a hand through his hair, alarm on his face. "What is it?" she asked.

"I just realized—you're not still drunk, are you? Because if you are, I'm sorry. I didn't mean—"

She placed a finger on his lips. "I may still be a little tipsy, but I'm not drunk. I know what I'm doing."

"Unlike our very first time," he said, his tone rueful.

"You didn't take advantage of me back then, either. I wanted it as much as you did."

He shook his head. "I had such a crush on you."

"And now?" she asked, holding her breath for his response.

He gave her that lopsided half-grin she knew so well. "We're beyond crushes these days, aren't we?"

"So you're saying you feel more than that."

His grin widened. "I'm not a boy anymore, Bee. What I feel… is more than a crush."

"Me too." Her cheeks grew hot under his intense gaze.

"Putting all your cards on the table."

"I don't want to play games anymore. I never did." Her pulse was skipping like an alarmed rabbit's.

"*Bene.* Neither do I." He touched her cheek, his fingers feather-light on her skin.

"Make love to me, Tonio," she whispered.

He rose and took her hand, urging her up onto the magnificent four-poster bed. She stared at the silken canopy and then focused on him. He was studying her, his face so reverent that her throat closed up. Could they have a future together? Somehow? Despite Sandro, despite everything?

He bent down and kissed her, and tears threatened to rise up. She loved him. She loved him so much. Would she ever get to tell him?

His hands roamed her body, their caresses teasing, gentle, but not focused on a goal. It was as if he were discovering her, getting to know her by touch alone. She wanted to do the same. She took his hand and stilled it.

"Lie back," she whispered. "I want to explore you."

His face lit up and he grinned, stretching out on the mattress.

Starting at his head, she pressed kisses to his temples, his jaw, his chin, all the while marveling at the intensity in his blue eyes. Something, some shadow, flickered across his face and she paused. "What's wrong?"

The corner of his mouth curved up, but the look in his eyes spoke of pain. "Nothing's wrong. In fact, it's very, very right."

Had no one paid him this kind of attention before? If all his women had been short-term, then perhaps not. Something tightened in her chest. Tonio deserved more than he'd been getting.

She kissed him lightly on the lips, not lingering long, before moving to his throat. She licked the skin below his Adam's apple, and his breath hitched. So he was sensitive there. Good to know. She trailed kisses to his pecs and ran the flat of her tongue over his nipples, gratified to hear him hiss in pleasure. She hadn't been sure if he'd like that.

He was all muscle, all hard planes of perfection—from the sturdy, well-developed muscles of his chest and arms, to the tightness of his abs, to the cords of his obliques and the V they made as they pointed south to his impressive cock.

Kissing across his belly, she edged toward her goal, her anticipation and her anxiety climbing. She'd never taken a man in her mouth before. What if he laughed at her? Or grew impatient?

His *cazzo* bobbed before her, twitching as if it expected her touch, and she couldn't help glancing up at him as she reached it. "Go ahead," he said. "It won't break. Just be careful with your teeth. If you're going to—"

"I am."

He gave her a dazzling grin. "Then I'll shut up." He shifted beneath her, his powerful thighs and abs flexing as he moved. *Dio mio*, he was more perfect than Michelangelo's David. She cupped her hand over the head of his *cazzo*. His shiver of pleasure made her grin.

Clasping him loosely, she pumped up and down the shaft, and he seemed to thicken even more under her fingers. "Spit on your hand," Tonio said. "Makes it feel even better." She did as he asked, then experimented with different speeds and pressures, thrilled by each sigh of pleasure she wrung from him.

The size and shape of his *cazzo* fascinated her. This was the first time she'd truly studied it, and its earlier transformation from flaccid to hard seemed even more miraculous. No wonder men liked sex so much. They got to show off how amazing their bodies were. She lay down beside him, resting her head on one of his thick, muscular thighs. "Having fun?" he asked with amusement.

"Very much. I've never really had a chance to see it like this before."

He laughed. "I've been remiss."

"You've just been too generous," she said, and raised her eyes to meet his.

He held hers for a moment, then he grinned. "One can never be too generous in bed."

She smiled. "I beg to differ." Then she took a deep breath to steel herself and licked the tip of his cock. She ran her tongue around it, as if it were a treat she couldn't get enough of, which wasn't far from the truth. She loved the feel of him, the velvety skin sliding over the hardness below.

Then she opened her mouth wide and slid him between her lips, careful not to graze him with her teeth. As she swirled her tongue around the head, he groaned deeply, and all she wanted was to hear him make that noise again. And again. She pushed downward, taking him in as far as she could, humbled to find his size exceeded her capabilities.

She raised her head and met his avid gaze. "Am I doing it right?"

He chuckled. "Oh yes. Keep that up, and I'll finish in a few minutes."

"In my mouth?" she asked.

"If you want."

"You'd like that?"

"I'd love it."

"Then I'd love that too."

He started to speak, then hesitated. Finally he said, "You'll have to either spit or swallow continuously when I come, or you might gag. I don't want you to be surprised."

"Thanks for the tip." Bending her head again, she wrapped her lips around him and clamped her right hand around his shaft. She found that if she got her mouth and her hand working on him at the same time, he twitched and grunted and bucked as if he could barely handle what she was doing. She pressed her body into his thighs, using her weight to hold him still.

"A little harder," he rasped. "I promise it won't break."

She complied, and his soft little groans, the way his powerful hands clenched the sheets, the way the cords of his neck stood out, all told her that he was getting close.

Speeding up her movements, she tried to engulf as much of him as she could on each downstroke, and suddenly he stiffened and cried out. His *cazzo* pulsed and twitched as he found his release, and a great sense of power and pride flooded her. She'd done that. She'd given her Tonio the ultimate pleasure.

Enjoying his every shudder, his every groan, she continued working him until he told her to stop, that she was going to kill him. Sitting up, she grinned at the sight of him panting before her, as if he'd just run a marathon.

After a moment, he opened his eyes and gave her a wide smile that lit her up inside. "*Cristo*, Bee. That was amazing."

She blushed at his admiration. "I'm so happy I could do that for you."

"I think *I'm* happier." He laughed and blew out hard.

She crawled up beside him, and he put an arm around her, then pressed a kiss to her temple. "Wasn't I the one who was supposed to make love to you?"

She traced the ridges of his chiseled chest and belly. "Aren't we supposed to share in this?"

His arm tightened around her, but he said nothing. After a moment, he spoke, his voice a little thick. "I don't feel that I have a whole lot more to offer."

Her throat clogged with emotion. At least part of that was her fault. "Tonio, I want you to know how sorry I am. I never, ever should have made you feel that you weren't worthy of me—or anyone else. I was trying to protect you. But I shouldn't have let you think it had anything to do with who you were or where you came from. I used that because it was something you'd believe, and I knew it. I knew it would hurt you, that it would keep you away from me." She paused. "I suppose in a way, what I said was true. If you'd been from a family in the 'Ndrangheta, maybe things would have been different. But it had nothing to do with you being an orphan."

When he said nothing, she tilted her head to look at him. Were those tears? He rubbed his eyes and shook his head. "If I'd had a family, things could have been different. For all three of us."

"That isn't your fault," she said. "My father didn't have to handle it the way he did."

Antonio was silent for a long time, then he sighed. "I'm not sure I would've done anything differently if I'd been in his position."

She couldn't believe her ears. "You agree with what he did?"

"No. But I understand it."

"*I* never will."

"He was trying to protect you. The way I should have." He dropped to a whisper. "I should've looked out for you better."

"It was a mistake. That's all."

"It was careless." He paused. "I will never be careless with you again."

She kept her tone light. "You've been good with the condoms."

"That's not what I mean, Bee, and you know it."

Oh. He wanted to be serious still. "When can we see Luca?" she asked.

"He's in Milan. We could go tomorrow."

Her stomach tightened. She was going to see her son again. After all this time.

Biting her lip, she nestled close to Antonio. She'd get to see her son, but where would it lead? Did she dare hope she'd be able to get him back?

111

———— ♦ ————

A hand on her shoulder shook Bianca awake. "Get up and get out," Sandro said in a harsh whisper.

Sandro was here? In Antonio's bedroom? Every hair on Bianca's body stood up. *No.* Wide-eyed, she tried to see Sandro, but could make out only the outline of his body hovering beside her. The door to the hallway was open, and a pale shaft of moonlight shone inside.

"Move." Sandro shifted, and the blade in his hand caught the light from the hallway.

She didn't want Antonio to fight with Sandro, but she couldn't let Sandro stab him either. Opening her mouth and filling her lungs, she shrieked Raffaele's name, and Antonio started up beside her. "Bee, what the hell?" he asked, then he must've seen Sandro because he lunged for his nightstand and ripped the drawer open.

Sandro tried to throw himself across the bed, but Bianca got in his way and he snarled at her. "What are you doing?"

She didn't have time to answer. The racking of a gun made them both freeze. "Get the fuck off her. Now," Antonio said, his voice like ice.

Sandro scrambled off the bed and out the door. Antonio made no move to go after him. Instead he turned to her. "Are you hurt?"

She shook her head. "I'll have some bruises, but I'm okay."

He slid off the bed, gun in hand, and went out into the hallway, calling for Raffaele. She followed, wrapping a sheet around her body.

Sandro was gone, but he hadn't left without a warning. Raffaele lay still on the marble tiles near the open front door, his throat slit. A huge pool of blood spread around him, and Antonio dropped to his knees in it, checking for a pulse. He finally broke the hush that had fallen over them. "He's dead."

Bianca's knees buckled and she grabbed the hallway table to steady herself before she sank to the floor. Her brother had killed Raffaele. And he'd wanted to kill Antonio too. What about her son?

"Luca!" she cried, and Antonio rose and grabbed the phone on the table beside her. He switched on the table lamp and shut the front door, then came and sat beside her, cradling her in his arms as he punched in a number.

"Ruggero," he said. "Sandro tried to kill me. He got Raffaele, and he could be going after my son." He listened for a few moments, then hung up. "Ruggero's on it. He'll send reinforcements to Milan, and he'll be here soon."

He placed another call, to the *polizia*, then urged her up. "We'd better dress before they get here."

"I knew he was capable of this, but seeing it…" She trailed off as they reached the bedroom.

"I wish you hadn't."

She clutched his arm. "Sandro's going to die, isn't he?"

Antonio wouldn't look at her, but a muscle worked in his jaw. "If not by my hand, then someone else's." His eyes rose to hers. "This is war. And your brother is on the wrong side."

———— ♦ ————

Ruggero, Tommaso, Don Enrico, and several guards waited patiently on the balcony while the officers took statements from Antonio and Bianca, but all Antonio could think about was the hard, tight expression on Enrico's face when he'd walked in. Was he planning to demote Antonio? Did Enrico blame him for sending Sandro over the edge?

Or was Enrico angry that Antonio had taken up with Bianca? She was Don Enrico's charge, and of course he'd want her to make a good marriage—one that wouldn't anger her brothers. Antonio shouldn't have been with Bianca. He might as well have thrown a lit match into a pool of petrol.

Yet another thing he'd screwed up royally.

Finally the *polizia* left, and Enrico and the guards stepped inside. Enrico still looked angry, and Antonio's pulse jumped. The don's eyes traveled from Antonio to Bianca and back. "I hadn't realized I'd given you permission to *court* Bianca," he said.

Oh fuck. "Forgive me, Don Enrico. I have no excuse."

"You do realize this is just about the worst thing you could do." He didn't wait for an answer. "I thought you were trying to help me resolve the situation with Sandro."

Antonio said nothing. What *could* he say?

The don crossed his arms. "I want you to move back into the house."

What? "That is not necessary."

"You were right. It's not safe for you here."

So now, suddenly, Antonio was right? Out of nowhere, his anger erupted. "I don't want to cause any more trouble between you and your *wife*."

Ruggero gave him a look loaded with disapproval. Enrico passed a hand over his face, then stared down at the tiles, his eyes straying to the pool of blood that marked where Raffaele had lost his life. "I want you safe, Tonio, whatever it takes." His voice was unexpectedly soft.

Antonio wasn't willing to let go of his bitterness just yet. "Give me two guards then."

"I'd really like you back in the house."

"So you can police who I sleep with?"

"Tonio."

"I'll be fine with two guards."

Enrico focused on the guards and Bianca. "We need a moment." As soon as they'd all gone out to the balcony, Enrico sighed. "I thought you had grown up some. That you'd stopped acting like a boy."

"This is about Bianca."

"Among other things."

"She's an adult."

"She's also my goddaughter."

"And you want her to do better than a damn orphan."

Enrico scrubbed a hand through his hair, the gesture impatient. "That is not the issue. If she were Giovanna d'Imperio, would you have taken her to bed?"

"Of course not."

"And why not?"

"Her father would skin me alive." His cheeks heated at the admission.

"And I should do any different?"

Antonio studied the marble floor. "Bianca and I—there's something there. Something we can't resist."

"You should have spoken to me about it."

"I know."

Enrico was silent for several moments, probably waiting for an apology Antonio wasn't going to make. Finally he spoke. "Because you're my second, I'll let this pass."

"Do we have your blessing?"

"For what? Is this headed toward marriage?"

What a question. "I don't know."

"Do you love her?"

Antonio remembered Enrico's desperation after Kate left him. Would Antonio be that way if he lost Bianca? The answer came from the flip of his stomach: yes. "I think so."

Enrico shook his head. "You had better know, Tonio. I had hoped to arrange a marriage for you—if not Giovanna d'Imperio, then maybe one of the girls in Lorenzo Andretti's family. Something to strengthen our alliances. If we're going to throw that chance away and lose Sandro and Matteo over it, you had better know."

"We've barely reunited."

"Which is one of the reasons why you shouldn't be sleeping with her."

This was just too much. "And you and Kate?"

Enrico gave him a tight smile. "I knew."

"She didn't."

"She knew soon enough."

Antonio had to smile at that. "I think we remember that differently."

"It doesn't matter."

"It does. You're asking me to make a very serious decision here. Right now."

Enrico clapped his hands together in frustration. "You're telling me you're still a boy then?"

"I'm telling you this situation is fucking impossible."

"Then stay away from her until you know."

Cristo. He wanted to punch something. "Doesn't she have a say in this?"

"I'm asking you to be a man here."

"And I'm asking you to let me figure this out."

"Tonio."

"You're not my father." The words flew out of his mouth before he could recall them. Heat flashed across his cheeks. He was acting like a child.

The don said nothing, but a look passed over his face that Antonio couldn't read. Finally he spoke. "I wish I were."

Antonio blinked in surprise and his belly gave a foolish flutter. "What?"

The don didn't answer. "I'm leaving you Ruggero and Tommaso."

"I can't take your most senior guards."

"Ruggero and Beppe then."

"I'd rather have someone who won't lecture me."

Enrico smiled. "Maybe Ruggero will get through to you." He crossed over to the balcony and let the others in. "Ruggero, you and Beppe are taking over for Raffaele." He addressed Bianca. "And you're coming with me."

She gazed at Antonio, then back to the don. "I can't go home, not with Sandro there."

"You'll come to my home then."

"I'd rather stay here." Then she tacked on, "Please."

Enrico pinched the bridge of his nose and sighed. "You are coming with me. I have many questions for you."

"You can ask them here," Bianca said. Antonio raised an eyebrow at that. She was much more ballsy than he gave her credit for.

"Fine, then," the don snapped. "Why didn't you come to me when all this started?"

Her eyes dropped to the floor. "I wasn't sure I could trust you. Sandro said—"

"Sandro has said a great many things that aren't true."

She raised her eyes. "You didn't choose my brothers to help you lead this *cosca*. Why?"

Enrico crossed his arms. "You have betrayed this family. You have betrayed *me*. If you were anyone else, Bianca, you'd be dead."

She reddened, but she held the don's eyes. "That's why I didn't go to you. You won't answer the question."

"I don't *have* to answer that question. Or any other. I am your *capo* and your *padrino*. Are you telling me you're going to follow in Sandro's footsteps?"

"No. I realized that I'd made a mistake. I didn't want to help him. And I wouldn't have, except for Luca."

"Then stop questioning me. I have reasons for everything I do. And I think Sandro's behavior has proved me right."

"He wouldn't have acted against you if he didn't feel justified."

"I refuse to take responsibility for Sandro's lack of honor. He's sworn vows to this *cosca* and to me. His role is to trust me. Not fight me or question me. And that's not your place either."

Bianca nodded. "*Mi dispiace, padrino.* I swear my loyalty to you."

"Do you?"

She came to him and knelt, then kissed the signet ring on his hand, the one with the Lucchesi crest. "I swear it."

"*Bene,*" the don said, and Antonio let out the breath he'd been holding.

After a moment, she asked, "May I stay here, with Antonio, please?"

With a laugh, Enrico shook his head, then threw his hands in the air. He looked at Antonio. "You will have your hands full with this one." Finally he nodded, then left with the other guards.

They'd barely been gone a minute before Ruggero motioned Antonio out to the balcony. They stepped outside, and Antonio's gut tensed. *Here it comes.*

"You could have been killed." The slight catch in Ruggero's voice was a shock.

He rarely showed even a hint of emotion.

"I know."

"I don't think you do." Ruggero stepped up into his personal space, and Antonio resisted the urge to give ground. "Did I teach you nothing?" Ruggero shook his head, disgust on his face. "You couldn't have been stupider. I finally found Narciso Acerbi. In the morgue. Any guesses who killed him?"

Heat rushed to Antonio's face again. "Okay, maybe I shouldn't have refused a second guard when I moved in here."

"Not just that. *Her*. She's Sandro's sister. She compromised you."

"She didn't have much choice—"

"And aside from that, she's Don Lucchesi's goddaughter. You're lucky her father isn't still alive."

"I just got a lecture from Enrico. I don't need this from you."

"Yes, you do. Your *cazzo* is still doing your thinking. Something you should have fucking outgrown."

"Sandro already hated me; my involvement with Bianca doesn't really change anything."

Ruggero crossed his arms and narrowed his eyes. "You break her heart, and who do you think Don Lucchesi will side with?"

Family. It always came down to that.

"I don't intend to break her heart."

"Intentions mean nothing. Actions are everything. You've put your *capo* in a bad position. You've put *yourself* in a bad position. You had better not be fucking around here." Ruggero pinned him with a hard stare before going back inside.

Antonio turned and gazed down into the courtyard below. Everyone else seemed to know what he should do.

So why didn't he?

CHAPTER 14

Dario was probably a lost cause, but his great-grandson Cristoforo could still be useful, even potentially Lorenzo's heir. But Lorenzo had to tread carefully. He sat back against the plush leather seat as the driver took him through the gates of Dario's estate on the shores of Lake Como.

Cristoforo was loyal to the family, which was good, but not if he remained blindly loyal to his useless father. Lorenzo needed Cristoforo on his side. And there were a few ways to ensure that.

Now that Sandro Lucchesi had done his part—albeit somewhat botched, since Enrico had gotten wind of it almost immediately and had mitigated most of the damage—Lorenzo needed to work on Cristoforo's part in the plan.

When the car pulled up at the front entrance, Lorenzo waited for the driver to come around and open the door, mentally steeling himself to climb all those bloody stairs to the door.

He was still too proud to carry a cane, but he'd soon have to reconsider, judging by the way his knee crunched as he headed up the steps. The driver hovered on his left, and Lorenzo paused in his ascent. "I don't need a fucking nursemaid. Go back to the car."

The man blanched and tipped his cap at Lorenzo. Where the fuck did his grandson find these idiots? If he needed help, he'd ask for it. Did Dario think him a doddering old man?

Finally he reached the top stair, keeping his face stony for the maid who held the door open and bowed her head as he passed. "Don Andretti," she murmured, just loud enough for him to hear.

He gave her a nod, but all he could really think about was his throbbing knee. Bloody doctors said he needed an operation and a pharmacy of drugs for his arthritis. He couldn't afford the downtime of surgery, and drugs only muddled one's mind. The pain didn't allow him much rest sometimes, but that was life. A man who couldn't take a little pain was not a man.

Besides, the pain gave him focus. Urgency. He was in the sunset of his life, the eternal dark fast approaching. If he were going to secure his legacy, he had to act now. He'd been too reliant on Benedetto always being there. And he'd made the mistake of counting on Benedetto's loyalty—a loyalty that had existed only to a point.

Unlike Dario's, which didn't exist at all.

Lorenzo finally reached Dario's study and found his grandson at his desk. Holding back a sigh of relief, he sank onto one of the leather chairs across from Dario.

"May I offer you an espresso?" Dario asked. "Anything to eat?"

"Espresso. I ate on the plane."

Dario picked up the phone and called the kitchen, then set the receiver back in its cradle. "So what brings you here, Nonno?"

Lorenzo almost smiled at the endearment, which Dario somehow made into an expletive. Of course, when Carlo was still alive, "Papà" had also sounded like a curse coming from Dario's mouth.

"I thought we should discuss what happened at the meeting in San Luca."

"You could have called for that."

"This way I can see you lying to me."

Dario gave him a half-smile. "You always assume the worst of me."

Ah, they were going to play this game. So be it. "I could say the same." He shifted in his seat, trying not to wince at the pain that shot up his leg. "Let me make this easy. Your alliance with Lucchesi is shaky at best."

"I wouldn't say that. Aside from the marriage between Niccolò and Delfi, I have ten percent of the bank, and Cris is working there."

"Those are mere tokens. Not a true partnership. Or you wouldn't have challenged Lucchesi for head of Lombardy."

Beneath his palm, his grandson rolled a pen back and forth across the felt blotter on his desk. A muscle worked in his jaw. "What business is this of yours?"

Lorenzo leaned forward, forcing his face to remain still instead of breaking into a smile. "It's *all* my business now."

"We put you in charge of La Provincia. Not us."

Was his grandson really so naïve? "It's my job to make sure the families are at peace and united. And I see cracks in your alliance."

"The alliance is strong. I challenged Lucchesi for Lombardy because… well, someone had to."

"Gianluca spoke up first."

"Someone who isn't an arrogant prick."

Lorenzo laughed. "And here I thought you wanted an alliance with Gianluca too."

"I do. That doesn't change the fact that he's an arrogant prick."

"And what about Lucchesi? Don't tell me you're such good friends that all is forgiven."

"We are better friends now than we've ever been."

"And what if I told you he was working on a plan behind all of our backs?"

Dario sat up straight and stilled the pen. "I have Lucchesi under control."

"Forgive me, but I don't see how."

"You don't know everything, Nonno."

"Please enlighten me."

Breaking eye contact, Dario started rolling the pen again. "I have everything I need to keep Lucchesi in line." He met Lorenzo's gaze. "And that is all I have to say about that."

His grandson seemed awfully confident. Perhaps he wasn't bluffing. Lorenzo would have to see if he could pry the details out of Cristoforo.

The maid who'd answered the door brought in Lorenzo's espresso and he took a sip. Superb, as always. He studied Dario over the rim. "I actually came up here to talk to Cristoforo about the bank. I had an interesting phone call yesterday."

One of Dario's brows went up. "Oh?"

"Apparently a large transfer was made from La Provincia's account." He set down his cup. "Without permission from me."

"You *are* joking."

"No. A bank manager in Liechtenstein called me. Said Lucchesi called him personally about it, tried to talk him into reversing it."

"And?"

"I checked today. The account has been reimbursed. No sign of the transaction, as far as I can tell."

Dario frowned. "You've talked to Lucchesi?"

"Not yet. I wanted to talk to Cristoforo first. Have him do a little digging. If there's something going on, I want to know the extent of it. For example, if any other accounts were affected."

"Could just be a computer glitch."

"Could be."

His grandson seemed lost in thought, no doubt wondering how he could use this information to his advantage. Good. The first seed was planted. Now to sow the rest. And figure out what leverage Dario seemed to think he had over Lucchesi.

"Let me call Cris for you," Dario said. He dialed Cristoforo and spoke to him. "He'll be down in a minute."

When Cristoforo walked in a few minutes later, his features seemed sharper than they had just a few weeks ago, the layer of baby fat almost entirely chiseled away. Lorenzo's great-grandson was turning into a man.

"*Buongiorno,* Bisnonno." Cristoforo embraced him with a hug and a kiss on both cheeks. "You wanted to see me?"

Lorenzo rose. "Let's take a walk. I want to stretch my legs after being on that plane." Not at all true, but he didn't want Dario party to this conversation.

They left through the rear doors of the house, which mercifully entailed just a single step down to the terrace. Lorenzo's knee clicked loudly when he descended, and Cristoforo took his elbow. After a moment's hesitation, Lorenzo allowed it. Having Cristoforo think him feeble would help allay any suspicions he might harbor.

"A serious matter has come to my attention," Lorenzo began, as they headed for the path through the now mostly bare garden. "I need your help to determine how serious it is, and if I need to take action." He detailed what he'd learned from the bank manager.

A deep furrow set up camp between Cristoforo's eyebrows. "I'm sure it's nothing to worry about. Have you spoken to Don Lucchesi?"

"I wanted to have my facts straight before saying anything. Just in case."

"Don Lucchesi is an honorable man."

"Which is why I am so surprised. However, his relations with this family have been... fraught, to say the least. I merely want to ensure that he is still my friend. And still a friend to all the 'Ndrangheta."

"I understand your concerns, but I believe they are unwarranted."

"I would like to know what happened, and if any other accounts were affected." He paused. "And I am, of course, giving Don Lucchesi a chance to contact me himself, though that has not happened. Yet."

"He could be waiting until Monday. It is Santo Stefano's Day today, and after all Sunday *is* a day of rest."

Lorenzo snorted with amusement. "Only for some, my boy." They continued down the path, their shoes crunching on the gravel, each little slip of the stones underfoot sending twinges of pain radiating up and down his leg. "There is another matter I wish to discuss."

"Oh?"

"I am concerned about your father, and his stewardship of this family's interests in the north." Before Cristoforo could say a word, Lorenzo raised a hand in a placating gesture. "I am not trying to stir up trouble. I am trying to prevent it."

"What are your concerns?"

"When the family heads gathered in San Luca, I noticed a great deal of tension between your father, Don Lucchesi, and Don d'Imperio. It was unexpected, to say the least."

Cristoforo flipped his jacket collar up against the cold. "I hadn't expected it either. Then again, I think your proposal took many in that room by surprise, and no doubt it set everyone on edge."

"No doubt. Still, it concerns me. I do not like to see your father fighting with our allies in the north. Not to mention the friction between him and me."

"I don't like it either."

"A family divided is weak. And we are in a time of war. The Russians will make another move soon."

Cristoforo sighed. "I still feel somewhat responsible for that."

"I do believe it is Don Lucchesi's son, Niccolò, who deserves much of the blame. Had he not killed the Vilanoviches—"

"I involved him, Bisnonno, and had he not killed them, I would be dead. What happened is my responsibility. Besides, I believe the Russians had planned to double-cross us."

"They call themselves *Mafiya*, but they don't know what it means to have honor."

"No. When Ilya Vilanovich had that knife pressed to Delfina's throat—" Cristoforo's hands balled into fists, and he stopped talking for a moment. "I am glad they are dead."

"The ones who came are dead. There are still other Vilanoviches."

"We will kill them too, if they come."

"*When* they come. Which is why I must ensure La Provincia's account is in good hands. I need to buy arms and supply the families and coordinate our efforts. I cannot one day discover that our funds have gone missing."

"I will look into it."

Lorenzo paused before saying more, thinking hard about how best to phrase it. He had to be very, very careful. "In case Don Lucchesi is not our friend, I want to be ready. Your father seems very confident of the cards he holds in that regard."

Cristoforo nodded. "Lucchesi wants those recordings badly."

How could he ask the question without tipping Cristoforo off to his bluff? "Are they really so damaging?"

"Of course. Don Domenico and Nonno Carlo were planning—" Cristoforo abruptly stopped speaking, and Lorenzo realized he must have let his surprise show. "You didn't know this already?"

Lorenzo shrugged. "I knew enough." He paused, decided to ask directly. "You've heard these recordings? They show Domenico's betrayal?"

Cristoforo's shoulders visibly tightened. Here was the test. Would his great-grandson lie? "We believe they exist."

"So you aren't sure if you have them?"

"There are many, many hours of recordings to sift through. Nonno Carlo was fanatical about recording his calls." Another surprise. "But he was terrible at cataloguing them."

"If there were such recordings, they would be quite valuable."

Cristoforo stopped and leaned up against a bare-branched tree. "To Don Lucchesi, yes."

"And to me. If Don Lucchesi is hiding something, those recordings could be the key I need to discover the truth."

"They could also be used to unseat Don Lucchesi and destroy his *cosca*." His great-grandson said the words so calmly, so coolly, that Lorenzo wasn't sure what Cristoforo was thinking.

"They could. But I do believe—as long as he remains loyal—that Don Lucchesi is useful to all of us in his current role." He paused. "I am not sure your father agrees, however."

"I'm not sure either."

"I think your father would be happy to see Don Lucchesi gone."

"Perhaps, though he is now linked to us through Delfina's marriage."

"There is no child yet, no blood, to cement the bond."

Cristoforo appeared troubled. "No."

"Let me be frank. Your father may very well torpedo his own ship. He may sink our major ally—Enrico Lucchesi—at the same time he pushes me away. Things are already strained with Gianluca d'Imperio. Where exactly, does that leave you, as Dario's heir? You may very well inherit nothing but problems."

"I can resolve the problems with the d'Imperios. If Papà will let me."

"How?" Lorenzo played dumb, but he'd seen how Cristoforo had looked at Giovanna d'Imperio at Niccolò and Delfina's engagement party.

"I wish to marry Giovanna."

Lorenzo smiled as if he were genuinely happy. "And you have spoken to Gianluca?"

"No. Well, sort of. But he turned it down. It was right when Delfina and Leandro fell apart, so Don d'Imperio was not in the best of moods."

"I am sure your father could persuade him."

"Papà is still embarrassed by Delfi's behavior."

"These are modern times. These things happen."

Cristoforo shrugged. "I like Nick, so I'm glad it happened. And it gives me a chance with Gio, which I wouldn't have had if Delfi had married her brother."

"You love this girl?"

Cristoforo flushed. "I do."

"And she loves you?"

"I believe so. We haven't spoken about it, since there's no point yet."

"I may be able to help with this matter."

Cristoforo held his gaze. "And in exchange?"

Lorenzo almost smiled. Cristoforo was learning. "Just help me help your father, your branch of the family. Help me ensure our alliance with the Lucchesis is strong, and help me forge you a new one with the d'Imperios. Those recordings should not be in your father's hands. I know how to handle this. I am not the slave to anger that he is."

"True." Cristoforo straightened up and stepped away from the tree. "I will find those recordings. And I will get to the bottom of what's happening at the bank."

"*Bene.*" Lorenzo clapped Cristoforo on the back and took a deep breath of the damp lake air. Every bone in his body was aching from the cold, but the trip had been worth it. His plan was unfolding, and soon he'd have all the players firmly in his grasp.

———— ◆ ————

Antonio had been awake for at least half an hour, devising and discarding plans for how best to ditch Ruggero and Beppe so he and Bianca could go to Milan and see their son. He'd finally come up with something that seemed foolproof.

He rolled over and studied Bianca, still asleep, her toffee-colored hair draped over her pillow, her long lashes fanning over her cheeks, her lush mouth beckoning for his kiss. What would it be like to wake up to her every day? Was that even a possibility?

Leaning forward, he pressed his lips to hers, and her eyes popped open. She started, and he regretted his impulsiveness. He'd forgotten that Sandro had awakened her much more roughly last night. "Sorry," he said, abashed.

She gave him a shy smile. "Don't be. It was nice—once I knew what was happening."

"With Ruggero and Beppe here, we shouldn't have any more surprise visitors."

She frowned. "I feel terrible about Raffaele."

"So do I. But he knew what he was getting into. We all do, when we take the vows." He paused. "I do wish I'd taken on a second guard though. He might not have been killed if I had." And that was another thing that would have to go on his list of failures.

"You can't know that." She sighed. "He was so young though. Our age."

"Which is why"—he pulled her into his arms and planted another kiss on her lips—"we shouldn't waste time." He kissed her neck, enjoying her gasps of pleasure as he journeyed southward. He wanted to keep going, but they had a lot to do today. "I have a plan for going to see Luca."

"A plan?"

"Ruggero won't let us near him."

"Oh."

"So we have to lose them."

"How?"

"I'll go into the bank to check on things, and you'll go with me to Milan to do some shopping. Then you'll bring something to me at the bank for lunch. We'll pretend to eat, but we'll really slip out the back. I'll have a car waiting for us."

She smiled. "I feel so James Bond right now."

He pulled her into his arms and dipped a hand between her legs. "No. I'm James Bond. And you"—he stroked his fingers over her *figa*—"are Pussy Galore."

"I never saw that one. Did she even like James Bond?"

"No woman can resist Bond." He dipped a finger inside her, then spread the moisture over her *grilletto*, enjoying the gasps he elicited from her. His cock jumped to attention, and he glanced at the clock. "We have just enough time, if we take this into the shower."

She nodded and scrambled off the bed. He gave her beautiful ass a light smack as they entered the bathroom. "Hey!" she said, whirling on him.

"We haven't got all day," he teased, and backed her into the shower enclosure. He directed the shower head away from them, then turned it on to warm up. She smiled at him and something in his chest tightened. He wanted this, all of it— waking up with her, showering with her, making love with her—every day, for the rest of his life. Somehow he'd figure out a way to make that happen.

Picking up the soap, he gave her a wink before handing it to her. "Be sure to drop it at some point."

She laughed and let it slip from her fingers. "Oops." With a wink, she bent over at the waist to retrieve it, and he took his cue.

CHAPTER 15

Everything had gone according to plan, and now Antonio and Bianca sat in the car outside the apartment building their son lived in. The lights seemed to be on in all the ground-floor flats, so most likely they were at home. Antonio's stomach was in knots, and he was gripping the steering wheel too tightly.

"Do you think we could go up and buzz them?" Bianca asked.

"And say what?"

"Maybe that we're looking for someone, and we can't find them?"

"Too risky. Ruggero has a man watching this place." He tugged on the hat he was wearing to hide his hair. "Even with this, he might recognize me."

"Well, then?"

"We wait."

"What if they don't go anywhere? It is Santo Stefano's Day today."

"Then we come back."

"Ruggero doesn't seem stupid."

"He's not."

"Yet you think we'll get away with this twice."

Antonio shrugged. "We'll figure something out."

They sat in silence for several minutes, then Bianca spoke. "You know, you've never said much about your family."

"Because it's not a happy subject."

"Well, neither is mine."

He shrugged and said nothing, and she tried again. "Tell me what happened. All you've ever said is that there was a car crash."

He nodded, his eyes glued to the house. Why was she asking him about this? "And?" she prompted.

"My parents and my brother Aldo were killed."

"You had no other family?"

"My aunt and uncle took my sister, Violetta."

"But not you."

124

"No." His gut turned to stone.

"Why not?"

"They were poor."

"They were that poor?"

"I don't know."

"Didn't that seem strange?"

He turned to her. "No. It seemed cruel, if you want the truth." He spat the words at her. Why was she digging at him?

She pressed her lips together, but her gaze never left his. "It seems that way to me too."

"Then please stop talking about it." He turned away from her.

They were silent for several moments, then she spoke again. "When was the last time you saw Violetta?"

"I was fourteen and she was ten."

"Why didn't you see her again?"

"Because she, like you, couldn't leave it alone. She got hysterical, and so did my aunt. Uncle Gino got upset with them, and I couldn't stand to be the cause of their fighting. It wasn't worth it."

"You mean *you* weren't worth it."

He didn't answer. When she touched his shoulder, he jerked away. "I don't need your pity, Bee."

"It's not pity."

He scoffed and rubbed a hand over his face. "*Per favore*, let the past stay where it is. I don't need it dredged up."

"I just want to understand you. Get to know you better."

"Well, now you know what there is to know."

"I hardly think so."

"I'm not that deep."

She fell silent, then she said, "I think you would like everyone to think that. But I see through you, Antonio Legato."

"You've got me all figured out."

"I doubt it."

He turned to her again. "You know what's worth knowing."

"*You* are worth knowing."

A flicker of unease gripped his belly. How easily she read him. How would he ever keep the truth about her father's death from her?

Suddenly she grabbed his arm and pointed toward the apartment building. "The front door is opening!"

He turned to see a couple come out, both tall brunettes, the man carrying a picnic basket. Could they be Fabrizio and Marilena Lamberti? Before the door closed, a heavily bundled up boy around five or six years old raced out past the couple and barreled down the walk, sunlight glinting off his blond hair, his breath visible in little puffs. The woman shouted "Luca!" and the boy pulled up short at the end of the walkway and waited for her to reach him. Then they all crossed the street toward what looked to be the family's Fiat.

"It's him. They kept his name." Bianca choked out the words, and Antonio's throat closed up. Their son. He wanted to get out of the car and grab him, steal him away, but he resisted the impulse. He'd promised Kate. And the future of the Lucchesi Home for Children rested on what he did today.

The family got in the car and Antonio started his engine. He waited until they'd gone about half a block, then he pulled out behind them.

Bianca sniffed beside him. She was crying. He squeezed her knee briefly. "We'll get him back," he said.

"How?"

The thought formed as he spoke. "I can contest the adoption. I never signed away my rights to him."

"So the adoption isn't legal?"

"I'm no lawyer, but I think I have a case."

"Oh *Dio, per favore*," she whispered.

They followed the family to a large park, where they stopped and took the basket from the back of the car. Luca ran circles around the couple, his laughter high and bright, and the sound made Antonio smile and want to cry at the same time.

Following the family on foot, Antonio and Bianca kept their distance, walking hand in hand, as if they were just a happy couple out for a stroll.

When the family set up a meal at a picnic table, Antonio and Bianca stopped a short distance away and sat on a park bench where they could observe the Lambertis without being too obvious. Bianca surreptitiously snapped a few photos of Luca with her phone.

After the family ate, Luca and Fabrizio kicked a soccer ball around. At one point, Luca fell, and Bianca's hand tightened on Antonio's. She let out a little gasp, but Luca bounced up and started laughing. "You made me fall, Papà!" he teased.

Papà. The word tore at Antonio. *He* was Luca's Papà, not that man.

"Luca, I did no such thing," Fabrizio teased back, and Bianca made a small noise.

"It hurts to watch them." Her hushed words were filled with tears.

Antonio put an arm around her. "I know."

A golden-brown puppy raced up to Luca, and he dropped to the ground to wrestle with it, throwing his arms around the dog. After a few minutes of furious play, he hefted the puppy up and carried it over to Marilena. "Mamma! Mamma! Can we keep him?"

She scanned the area. "I'm sure he belongs to someone here. You should let him go so that he can get back home."

Looking doubtful, Luca set the puppy down, and Antonio got an idea. He slapped his hands on his knees, and the pup ran straight to him, Luca following close behind. Bianca clutched Antonio's knee painfully hard, and his heart pounded in his chest as his son drew near.

Luca stopped when he saw them. He pointed to Antonio. "Is he your dog?"

Antonio rose from the bench and crouched down so the puppy could jump into his lap. He petted the dog for a moment, its warm tongue bathing his fingers, but his gaze was on Luca, not the pup. Luca's eyes, so big and blue, were glued to the dog, and a smile lit up his face, until Bianca sniffed and drew his attention. A frown creased his brow. "Why are you crying?" Luca asked.

She wiped at her tears. "It's just so beautiful," she said, her emotions strangling the words.

"I know!" Luca agreed. "I want to take him home."

Antonio's throat closed up with longing. His son, his child, was right in front of him. Close enough to touch, to embrace.

He heard someone yelling for a dog. "Pippo! Where are you?" Antonio opened his hands and let the wriggling pup loose. It bounded away in the direction of its owner.

"You let him go!" Luca complained.

"He doesn't belong to us," Antonio said, straining to keep his voice even.

Luca stared up at Antonio for a moment, then he heard Fabrizio and Marilena calling for him.

"You'd better get back," Antonio said.

"*Ciao ciao!*" Luca called, then he raced back to his parents.

Bianca wiped furiously at her tears, and Antonio urged her up from the bench before Luca's parents noticed her odd reaction. He put an arm around her as they walked, hugging her close, and steered her toward the park's restrooms. "We're just strangers to him," Bianca sobbed.

"I know." Antonio was fighting tears himself. "I know."

She detached herself from him and went into the women's restroom to compose herself. Antonio leaned up against the brick wall outside and rubbed his eyes. What were they going to do?

A sharp ping and a piece of brick breaking beside his ear had him diving for cover, his heart lurching in his chest. Someone was shooting at him. He dashed inside the women's restroom, and using the steel door as a shield, he drew his gun and scanned the area. He could see no one in the vicinity.

He didn't want to return fire in such a public place. Whoever had shot at him had used a suppressor—and possibly a rifle with a scope.

Bianca came out of one of the stalls, and he turned at the noise. "What are you doing in here?" she asked, then she saw the gun. "Luca!" she cried, and Antonio's heart kicked into overdrive. He had to draw—and keep—the shooter's attention. Who else could it be but Sandro?

"I'm going to head for the south entrance to the park. You run to the car and then circle around and meet me there." She nodded, her gaze glued to his. "Wait thirty seconds after I leave." He eased the door open, then slipped outside and scanned the area. Nothing. Had Sandro given up?

Antonio started toward the other end of the park, almost believing he was safe until a bullet thunked into the trunk of a tree just ahead of him. The shooter was still after him. Antonio broke into a run, and another shot whizzed by. Fuck! His Glock felt entirely useless in his hand.

He stopped behind a large oak and searched for movement. Finally he saw something: a large, well-built man crashing through the trees some distance away. Taking aim, Antonio fired twice in rapid succession. The first shot missed, but the man stumbled after the second one and went down. Was he dead? Antonio hoped so, but he didn't dare check. There were too many people in the vicinity, and no doubt his unsilenced shots had drawn attention.

He sprinted away and reached the far side of the park soon after. His heart pounding madly, he dashed through the wrought-iron gate and into the rented Alfa idling at the curb.

"Drive," he ordered Bianca while searching behind them for any sign of Sandro.

She peeled away from the curb, and he put a hand on her wrist. "Don't speed. It attracts the police."

When she eased off the gas, he buckled his belt. How the hell had Sandro known they were in the park? "Did you tell anyone where we were going today?"

"No. Why would I?"

"I can't figure out how he found us."

"*Merda!*" she said. "My phone. We have that family-tracking app on it." She banged a hand against the wheel. "I forgot about it. I didn't think. I'm so stupid!"

"Stop it." He reached for her bag, grabbed her phone and swiped through the list of apps. "Found it." He deleted it, then turned her phone off. "Maybe we should get you a new one."

"*Porca miseria.*" She smacked her hand against the wheel again. "We almost got Luca killed."

He had to tell her. "I hit Sandro. I don't know how badly, but he fell."

She slapped a hand over her mouth and muffled a sob.

"I'm sorry," he said. "But only because it hurts you."

She nodded and sniffed back tears, before taking a deep breath. They drove in silence for a time, then she said, "Where are we going?"

"I think it would be safest if we didn't go back to the bank or my apartment. We should get a room somewhere here in town."

"What about Ruggero and Beppe?"

Antonio sighed. He'd shut his phone off shortly before they'd left the bank. No doubt it was full of furious messages from Ruggero.

"I'll call Ruggero later, let him know we're safe."

Not that they would be, until he knew for certain that Sandro was dead.

———◆———

The hotel clerk had given them quite the smirk when they'd checked in without luggage. Bianca wanted to smack that knowing look off his face. Though, if she were honest, that was mostly because she was trying to distract herself. Anything to avoid focusing on the painful facts of that afternoon: Her son already had other parents he loved, her brother had tried again to kill Antonio, and worst of all, her brother might be dead.

She curled up on the enormous bed in the center of their hotel room and hugged her knees to her chest. All she wanted to do was cry. Why couldn't *Dio* take pity on her? Must He compound the tragedy of losing her son with the tragedy of losing her brother? Even if Sandro wasn't already dead, he soon would be. And so soon after losing Papà and Fedele too.

She couldn't take anymore.

Antonio stood at the window, staring out through the curtains, his shoulders rigid, his jaw working. He wasn't angry at her, but he was still a formidable sight, and so not what she needed. She just wanted him to hold her, but she didn't dare ask. Her throat clamped shut, and tears squeezed out from under her closed eyelids. She had to get a grip on herself without his help.

He pulled out his phone and called Ruggero, telling him in clipped tones what had happened at the park and where they were. He listened intently for a few minutes, then said, "I am your *capo*. I know you didn't like it, but that was my decision to make. Not yours." He listened again for a bit, then said, "If you wish." He pocketed his phone and rubbed his forehead. Then without turning, he said, "Ruggero and Beppe are coming here. They'll take a room on this floor and keep watch."

She wanted to say that Sandro couldn't find them there, but she didn't trust herself to talk without bawling. *If he's even alive.* A fresh wave of tears leaked out.

The mattress dipped beside her and Antonio laid a hand on her cheek. "*Dolcezza*, please, please stop crying. All these tears won't change anything."

"You're right," she sobbed, the words so choked they were half unintelligible. "But I can't stop."

He pulled her head and shoulders onto his lap and stroked her hair. "I want to cry too," he said. "But what's done is done." She gazed up at him, saw the glimmer of tears in his eyes, the redness at the tip of his nose. Somehow the sight gave her strength. Antonio was in this with her. He understood—and felt—her pain. And that made it a fraction easier to bear.

She wiped her face and sniffed. "Luca loves them," she said, all her misery packed into those three words.

"I know." He pressed his lips together, as if against a great pain. "We can't have him back. We never could."

Breathing in deep against the ache in her chest, she nodded. "He'd hate us if we tried to take him away."

"I can't do that to him. Can you?"

Her vision clouded with tears again, and she shook her head, unable to speak.

Antonio stroked a few strands of hair off her cheek. "Ever since you told me about him, I've wanted to see him, hold him, call him mine. I got to do the first, but the rest..." His voice cracked and he sighed. "Oh Bee, we've been so foolish, getting our hopes up. But I'm thankful he's happy."

"Me too," she managed. She took hold of his hand and kissed his fingers.

They were silent for a long time, and gradually the pain in her chest eased. At least she knew Luca was well-loved. She knew what he looked like. And that he still bore the name she'd given him. Even though it seemed so little, it was much more than she'd had mere hours ago. It wasn't enough, would never be enough. But it would have to suffice. She wouldn't put her child through hell—wouldn't rip him from the arms of the only parents he'd ever known—just to try to make herself feel whole.

Her son was happy and healthy. She had to be grateful for that. And somehow, she had to let him go. She had to focus on his future, on what was best for him. And keeping him out of the mess that was her life seemed like a good idea.

"The only thing I'm happy about is that he won't grow up in the 'Ndrangheta,"

Antonio said, echoing her thoughts.

"But Sandro—if he's alive—"

Antonio put a finger to her mouth. "Ruggero put two more men on Luca and his family. He'll be safe." After a moment, he caressed her lips. "The question now is how to keep *you* safe."

"I'm safe here, with you."

"Perhaps. But if Sandro isn't dead, he'll come for me, sooner or later. You shouldn't be anywhere near me."

"He didn't try to harm me last night or today."

"Accidents happen."

"I'm not leaving you, Antonio Legato." She said the words with a fierceness that surprised her.

"You should."

"I made that mistake once. Never again." She took a deep breath and said the words she'd longed to say. "I love you, Tonio."

He stared at her, astonished, then he nodded, his face solemn. "I've loved you forever, Bee. I've never loved anyone else."

Something eased in her chest, a great ache she'd had so long she'd grown used to it. "I've been waiting for you this entire time. I never forgot you." She sat up and leaned forward, pressing her lips to his in a sweet, soft kiss. "I am so sorry I ever didn't believe in you and trust you."

"You had good reason." Emotion thickened his words. He cupped her cheeks and studied her for several long moments. "Do you trust me? Truly? That whatever I've done, whatever I do, I have only ever acted in the best interests of your family?"

He was still worried about shooting Sandro. "I do. I trust you with all my heart."

"You're certain?"

She remembered how he'd reacted when she'd questioned him about the night her father had died. Of course he'd been wary, tense—Sandro had accused him of something, and he'd had no idea how she'd felt back then. It was time to reassure him. "I have no doubts about you. None."

He grinned and pressed his lips to hers, rapidly turning the kiss carnal. Desire rose in her, swift and rampant. She craved the same closeness, the same connection he did. "Make love to me," she whispered.

Antonio smiled against her mouth. "I'm already doing my best to keep up with your outrageous demands, woman."

She laughed, and though she still ached for Luca, it wasn't the same, wasn't as sharp. Her son was okay, and she had a future now with Antonio, a great gift she hadn't had before.

Dio had taken pity on her. At last.

Putting her hands on his shoulders, she gave Antonio a sly look. "You haven't seen demanding yet."

He raised a brow. "Is that so?"

She leaned in, whispering in his ear, "I want to erase every other woman from your mind. I want you exhausted. I want to ride you so hard and so long you'll beg for mercy."

"You don't know what you're asking for." He nipped at her lower lip.

"I'm pretty sure I do." She started unbuttoning his shirt, baring his firm pecs to her gaze. "And you're not keeping up," she teased.

"We've got all night."

"You can go that long?"

He growled. "You really *are* asking for it."

"I hope so."

He flipped her over on the bed and shoved up her skirt, planting kisses on her buttocks as he pulled off her panties. "I love your ass," he said, and she blushed. She'd always thought it big, but if he liked it, shouldn't she?

"Up on your knees," he said, tapping her on the hip. She rose up as directed, and he slipped two fingers inside her, the invasion making her moan. His thumb brushed against that sensitive spot between her cheeks and she blushed at the groan that stole from her.

He pumped his fingers in and out of her, taking care to press the pad of his thumb against that spot again and again until she pushed back into his touch. That particular caress was driving her wild.

"Do you want more than this?" He flicked his thumb over that spot. "Among your other outrageous demands?"

"No. But what you're doing..." She let herself trail off, suddenly breathless.

"Feels good, doesn't it?"

She nodded against the mattress, unable to say more.

"Which one of us is going to be begging for mercy?" he asked.

She grinned. "Probably me."

He laughed and rolled her onto her back. He stared at her below the waist, his eyes darkening. How she must look to him—legs splayed open, completely bare, face flushed. "I feel like such a bad girl."

"Bad girls are the best." He stripped off his shirt and opened the fly of his trousers, freeing his erect *cazzo*. When her gaze went to it, he grinned and stroked a hand along its length. "You want this inside you?"

"I do." Her mouth had gone dry, and her *figa* felt swollen, wet, achy.

"I think he needs a little more encouragement." He stood up and moved to the head of the bed, his cock just centimeters from her face. He took it in hand, as if offering it to her. "What do you think?"

Grinning, she rolled onto her side so she could reach him. Stroking him softly, she wrapped a hand around the shaft and guided him into her mouth. He let out a low groan. "*Perfetto*," he moaned.

She sucked hard at the tip and he shuddered, then she took more of him in, imagining he was taking her below, filling her. Swirling her tongue around him, she slowly withdrew. "Fuck," he panted.

She leaned back, holding him at the base, and looked up. "Does he still need more encouragement?"

His eyes dancing, he took a condom from his pocket and swiftly rolled it on. "Not at the moment. Maybe later."

He pushed her back on the bed and rolled on top of her. Reaching between her legs, he circled her clit with his fingertips, making her cry out, then replaced them

131

with his stiff *cazzo*. The feel of that thick blunt tip against her, sliding between her lips, sliding in her wetness, was almost overwhelming. "Now," she whispered. "Please."

Lifting up her legs, he plunged into her, seating himself to the hilt, and making them both groan.

"Oh *Dio*, more," she cried.

He rose up on his knees, pulling her legs up over his shoulders, his hands biting into her ass and hips as he pistoned into her, his breathing growing harsh. "Touch yourself," he demanded through clenched teeth.

Heat flooded her cheeks and neck. She couldn't. She shook her head, her eyes closed. She was disappointing him, but how could he ask her to do that in front of him?

He shifted position slightly, then one of his thumbs was touching her swollen *grilletto*, just like she needed. She blushed again, imagining what he was seeing, what he was thinking, but she writhed into his hand nevertheless while he watched, while he pounded into her, and she came with a scream. He drove into her, saying, "You belong to me, *dolcezza*," before his back arched and he shuddered. He sank back on his heels, still inside her.

She was sweating in her blouse, her cheeks hot, her breath coming in pants, when he smiled at her. "You look so sexy," he said.

"You too." His chest was glistening, the chiseled muscles of his torso rippling with his breathing. This man, this magnificent golden god, was hers. Had all her suffering been for this, to take her to this one shining, perfect moment?

A knock came at the door. "*Signore*." Ruggero's gruff rumble penetrated the thick wood.

They scrambled apart and she ducked into the bathroom, her cheeks flaming. Had he heard them?

The outer door opened and she heard the murmur of voices, which grew louder after a few seconds. Ruggero must have come into the room. She slapped a hand over her mouth. Oh *Dio*, her panties! Where had Antonio put them? She'd never be able to look at Ruggero again.

After what seemed like forever, the room grew silent and Antonio tapped on the bathroom door. "You can come out now." He sounded amused.

She stepped out, her gaze zeroing in on her crumpled pink panties beside the bed. She snatched them up, crushing them in her hand. "I've never been so mortified."

He laughed and caressed her cheek. "Don't be."

"What if he heard us?"

Antonio shrugged. "I told you. It comes with the job."

She frowned. "I wish he was deaf."

"No, you don't." He threaded his hands through her hair. "What we did is beautiful. It's not something to be ashamed of."

"But we're not married."

He pulled her down to the bed, sitting beside her and holding her hands. "Do you want that? A future with me?"

She grinned. "I do."

"And children?"

Her throat tightened, and her voice came out hoarse. "I know we can't have Luca, but I'd like to have other children with you."

He pressed his forehead against hers, his warm breath caressing her lips. "Perhaps, someday, we'll get to know him. Maybe we can ask for that much."

"I'd like that."

"I'll need to ask Enrico for his blessing—for both things."

She squeezed his hands. "And then we can be happy."

He was silent for a moment, then he nodded. "I should tell you. Ruggero and Beppe went to the park. They found the *carabinieri* there, searching for clues. There was blood, but no body."

Her heart leapt into her throat. "Sandro's still out there."

"And so is Lorenzo Andretti."

Antonio looked so serious, so grim. Would their lives always be like this? Would the *malavita* never let them find peace?

CHAPTER 16

They'd made love again—this time in the shower, at Bianca's insistence so that the guards couldn't hear them—before Don Enrico called Antonio. "What the devil have you been doing?" Enrico demanded before Antonio could get out a word.

"What I had to do. I had to see my son."

The don let out a sigh. "You've just made a rotten situation worse. You shot at Sandro in a public park. You'd better pray no one can identify you."

"What was I supposed to do? Go my whole life without ever seeing my child?"

"You were supposed to do what I did. Walk away. For his own good."

"If you had it to do all over again, is that still what you would do?"

There was a long silence. "Yes. It was the best thing for Nico, the safest thing."

"But it was difficult."

"Unbelievably."

"Luca seems quite happy. With them." The words hurt to say, but they were true.

"They're his parents." Enrico paused, then added, "Your son has a family; he doesn't know anything else. Give him that happiness, give him that chance to grow up whole. Let him grow up safe from your enemies."

Enrico was right, but that didn't make the decision any easier. "We've talked it out, and we've come to the same conclusion. It just feels..." Antonio had to stop for a second; the words were sticking in his throat. "It feels like we're giving up."

Enrico sighed again. "Tonio, I'm sorry. But you're making the right choice for Luca, and you have to focus on that, as painful as it is."

Antonio rubbed at his watery eyes. Time to change the subject. "What do we do about Sandro?"

"You're positive it was him?"

"Who else would it be?"

"Lorenzo could have sent someone."

Blood rushed in his ears. "It was Sandro in my flat. I heard his voice. The man I saw today looked like him."

134

"We have to be sure."

"I am." It *had* to be Sandro. The other possibility... he didn't want to think about.

Enrico said nothing for several moments before finally speaking. "Okay then."

"What about Matteo?"

"I'll need to speak to him. He helped Bianca, so I think there's a chance there." Enrico was silent for a long time, then he said in a defeated tone, "I never wanted to be forced to do this."

"And it's because of me."

"No, it's because of Dom. It all stems from his decisions, his actions. It's not your fault, Tonio."

Then why did it feel that way?

"So what's the emergency?" Antonio asked. Cris had called him the night before and said they needed to talk right away. After driving up from Milan and dropping Bianca off at the apartment, Antonio had met up with him for a late breakfast at the *pasticceria* near Antonio's flat. They'd taken an outdoor table, both of them hunkered down in their coats against the cold, each with a steaming cappuccino and a pastry. Beppe sat at a nearby table, his eyes scanning the street and every car and passerby.

Cris took a flash drive out of his pocket and slid it across the table to Antonio. "My great-grandfather wants this. So does my father. But I got to it first, and I think you and Don Lucchesi should have it."

Antonio's gut clenched. It could be only one thing. "This is the proof against Don Domenico?"

Cris nodded. "Good thing Nick and Delfi came to stay for the holidays. He had some software that we used to quickly analyze the recordings yesterday. We found what we were hunting for, and I made a copy. I erased the originals."

Antonio closed his fingers around the flash drive, barely able to breathe. "You're certain your father has no copies?"

"Fairly certain. He seems frustrated that he hasn't found them yet. But that could be an act. Something big like this—Papà might be hiding what he knows, even from me." Antonio started to reply, but Cris held up a hand. "You should know something."

"What?"

"Bianca asked me what happened the night her father was killed. I've told her nothing. It's not my place. But I thought you should know she asked. Maybe these recordings can help."

The lump in Antonio's stomach grew. Had she been truthful yesterday, when she'd said she had no doubts, or had she lied? He took a deep breath, then focused on Cris. What an amazing friend. "*Mille grazie.* How can I ever repay you?"

"Delfina told me what happened in the library with Ilya Vilanovich. You were willing to die for my sister. This is the least I can do to repay you." Cris stared at his cappuccino. "But you could tell me one thing."

"About what?"

"What happened at the bank Saturday?"

Merda. How much did Cris already know? And how much was safe to say? "We had a data breach."

Cris wrapped his scarf around his neck and took a sip from his cup. His eyes were flat and hard. "I asked for the truth."

Fuck, fuck, fuck. Sweat broke out on Antonio's back despite the chill. "It was Sandro. He messed with several client accounts. It's all been corrected."

"I did some searching Sunday. It was a little difficult to find, but the transaction logs show a great deal of activity by your user account."

"He got hold of my password."

"It doesn't look good."

"You know I wouldn't do anything to jeopardize the bank."

Cris nodded. "I believe you. But others might not."

"Which is why we need to keep this to ourselves."

"It's too late. A bank manager in Liechtenstein has alerted Lorenzo to the problem."

Antonio's lungs felt ten times too small. "Have you told him anything?"

"Yes. I had to, since I've given you the recordings he asked for. I couldn't fail him twice, or he'd get suspicious. I'm giving you a warning so you aren't caught out."

Antonio was going to be sick. "Has he told you what he's planning to do?"

Cris shook his head. "But I can guess."

Antonio could too. He scrambled for his phone. Don Enrico needed to know that Lorenzo's noose was tightening.

———◆———

Bianca was sitting in the kitchen of Antonio's flat, looking at the pictures she'd taken of Luca at the park. They were so painful to look at, she ought to delete them from her phone. But they made her smile too.

Ruggero stepped inside and headed for the fridge. Setting the phone down, she hurried to wipe away her tears before he noticed. He grabbed a bottle of Pellegrino water, then held one up and turned to her. "Want one?" he asked, the offer surprising her. He rarely even acknowledged her presence.

"Yes, please." When she accepted the bottle, he glanced down at the picture on her phone.

"So that must be him. He looks just like Antonio."

She zoomed in the photo a little, then looked up at Ruggero, noting the faint smile on his face. "Do you have any kids?"

He shook his head. "This isn't the life for them."

"That's not true. Lots of us grow up in the *malavita.*"

He gave her a skeptical look. "You saw what happened to Raffaele."

"And you think that'll happen to you?"

His gray eyes held her gaze, the look in them hard to read. "I've got one purpose in this life. And it's not having a family."

She thought she detected a hint of regret in his tone. "You're sure about that?"

He didn't answer at first. Then he said, "You and Don Legato will always have guards to die for you. Even so, accidents happen. None of us get any guarantees."

"No, we don't. But that doesn't mean we can't try to have lives."

He drained his bottle, then set it on the table. "Answer me this: If you could have your boy back, would you want this life for him?"

She'd never really considered the idea. You didn't leave the 'Ndrangheta, not ever. There was no point to speculating about anything else. She was silent for so long that Ruggero gave her a curt nod. "I thought so." Then he turned and left.

She watched him walk away. He was right; was this the life she wanted for Luca? No. They'd made the right decision in letting him go. And she needed to stop dreaming about any other possible outcome. She found the app where she could delete the photos of Luca on her phone. Her finger hovered over the screen.

She needed to say goodbye to Luca, forever.

A tear rolled down her cheek and splashed onto the table. She couldn't do it. Not completely. She closed the app, then kissed the screen. She'd keep this little piece of Luca. Even if it was all she ever had of her boy, it was something worth holding on to.

It was something worth dreaming about. Another world, another life. Another future.

———— ◆ ————

After consulting with Don Enrico over Cris's warning, Antonio returned to his flat, Cris's other revelation—the one about Bianca—still troubling him. So much had happened since she'd spoken to Cris; it was possible her doubts were truly gone.

But Antonio knew the truth. And as long as she didn't, there was the possibility that it would blow up in his face someday.

He *had* to tell her.

But how, without damaging Don Enrico as well?

Bianca must have read the disquiet on his face, because she greeted him with a frown. "What's wrong? Is it Sandro?"

After determining that Ruggero and Beppe were out on the balcony, he sat beside her on the sofa and took her hands. "It's not that."

"What, then?"

"I'm not sure how to say this, but there's something we need to discuss."

"Whatever it is, we'll handle it."

I hope that's true. "It's about the night your father died."

Her lips compressed together, but she said nothing, her attention riveted on his face.

"Your father betrayed the *cosca*."

She shook her head. "That's not true. He would never do such a thing."

"He was angry with Don Enrico over Kate. Your father blamed him for restarting the feud. So he plotted with Carlo Andretti to eliminate Don Enrico."

Bianca's eyes blazed. "You're lying!"

His gut cramped. This wasn't going well. Should he play her the recordings? "I have proof."

"Whatever you have, it's false. Papà would never, ever betray his *cosca*." She wiped at her tears. "How could Zio Enrico believe such lies?"

"Because they weren't lies. And he didn't want to believe them himself. He was going to exile your father."

"So why is he dead?"

He didn't want her to hate her uncle too. So he told her what he wished he'd done. "I spared Don Enrico from having to make the decision. He loved your father like a brother. I took care of it for him."

She exploded. "That was not your decision to make! You were just a bodyguard." She gaped at him, horror-struck. "Sandro was right. You wanted Papà out of the way. You wanted his place. You wanted what wasn't *yours*."

That's really what she thought of him? His heart sank to the floor. "I have recordings of your father talking to Carlo Andretti. Let me play them for you."

"They're fakes. Just like you." She grabbed her handbag and stomped out of his flat, slamming the door behind her.

He didn't know whether he was more angry or more stunned. He smacked a fist into the back of the sofa. How could she act that way? After everything they'd shared. After he'd said he loved her. After she'd said the same.

Had anything between them been real?

———— ◆ ————

Bianca could hardly believe what Antonio had told her, but it all made sense now. His evasiveness about the night her father had died. His questions for her the other night, how he'd wanted her to affirm that she believed he'd always acted in the best interests of the family.

Lies, half-truths, and blatant hypocrisy. He'd probably lied about not knowing about Luca too. He might have held Papà's decision not to let her marry Antonio against him. Maybe he'd waited all these years for the perfect opportunity to get rid of Papà.

And if Sandro had been right all along... then she'd betrayed her brother for a clever con man. A con man who'd wanted to marry into the Lucchesi family. He'd already taken her brother's position—now all he needed was to marry her to cement his place in the *cosca*. His children would carry on his legacy.

Cristo, had any of it been real between them? He'd seemed so heartbroken about Luca, about his missed opportunities with her. But he'd also lied to her. And he'd done something that wasn't his to do, without his *capo*'s orders.

Bianca halted in her tracks. Something didn't add up. She'd been blindly charging down the street, with no idea where she was going. She needed to stop, to think.

She walked into a nearby café and ordered a hot chocolate. Huddled over her cup beside a steamed-over window, she tried to puzzle it out. If Antonio had acted without Zio Enrico's knowledge—or against his orders—there was no way Enrico would have made Antonio *capo di società*. So if Antonio had shot her father, Enrico had ordered it.

And he wouldn't have done so without proof.

But if Enrico believed that her father had betrayed him, her father should have died a traitor's death, and his family—at the very least, his sons—should have joined him.

Instead, Enrico had taken her brothers as his sons, had become their *compare*. Why?

Nothing made sense, no matter how she looked at it.

Her uncle had always been a kind man, but he knew 'Ndrangheta law—a traitor's family died with him. Any *capo* who wouldn't enforce that law would be seen as weak, and his *cosca*—or La Provincia—would eliminate him.

And there was still the curious choice of Antonio as *capo di società*. Fedele should have been the one, and after him, Sandro. But Zio Enrico had chosen neither of her brothers. He'd chosen a mere guard.

Again, why?

Maybe she should have listened to those recordings Antonio claimed to have. She'd said they were fakes, but what if they weren't? She ought to be able to tell if they were genuine.

She wanted to believe Antonio. But she wanted to believe Sandro too. Yes, he'd been ruthless in pushing her into Antonio's bed, and he'd tried to kill Antonio. But looking at it from his side, if Antonio had schemed against Papà, what other choice did Sandro have? Zio Enrico seemed either blind to what Antonio had done—or worse, complicit in it—and the don had made clear he wasn't changing his mind about Antonio. So everything Sandro had done—every cruel, merciless thing—had been what he'd felt he had to do.

And so far, Sandro hadn't tried to hurt her or Luca. He'd threatened Luca, yes, but he hadn't acted on it. Had that just been a ruse to get her compliance? And maybe to distract Antonio?

She took another sip of the thick, almost pudding-like hot chocolate, but it brought her little comfort.

Which did she choose? Family, or Antonio?

And did she dare trust Zio Enrico?

———— ◆ ————

Enrico was at his desk at the Banca di Falcone, in the midst of composing a carefully worded client letter regarding what Sandro had done at the bank Saturday, when the man in question showed up, demanding an audience with him.

Enrico called in two guards before authorizing Security to send Sandro up to his office. What would Sandro have to say in his defense? Enrico couldn't think of anything that would change his mind, but despite his anger, he owed his godson the opportunity to say his piece.

The guards thoroughly searched Sandro before letting him in. All they found was a flash drive and a few printouts in his pockets. "He's clean," Tommaso said.

"You two may wait outside." Enrico gestured for Sandro to take a seat.

Sandro looked pale. He was unshaven, and a sheen of sweat filmed his skin. His clothes were rumpled, as if they'd been slept in. But most disturbing of all: A dark blotch stained the right side of his black jacket. Enrico searched for a bullet hole, but saw nothing. That didn't mean there wasn't one.

Heat flashed through his chest—there were no coincidences in this life, especially not in the *malavita*. Had Sandro been a better shot, Antonio would be dead. Enrico's hands almost shook with the urge to rip Sandro's head off, but until he knew his godson's purpose, he'd keep his temper under check.

"Are you unwell?" Enrico asked, forcing his tone to remain neutral.

Sandro shifted in his seat and grimaced. "I'll be fine."

"You don't look it."

"I'll be *fine*, as soon as someone listens to me."

"I'm listening." Enrico folded his hands on the desk and studied Sandro. What was he thinking, coming here, after what he'd done?

Sandro placed the printouts and the flash drive on the desk. "Antonio Legato has been stealing from this bank, and I have proof." He shoved the items toward Enrico. "These are records of the accounts he altered on Saturday. He transferred funds from several accounts to his own. He even transferred some money to yours, I guess to make you appear guilty as well if he were caught. He also transferred money to several unmarked accounts in Liechtenstein."

Did Sandro think he was stupid? "I already know all this. But you're the one responsible."

"And you believe that why?"

"Because someone ordered a new keycard for Antonio and told Security his card had been lost. That new card was used on Saturday."

"He's trying to make it seem like he's being framed."

"He is."

Sandro smacked a fist on the desk. "No!"

"Your own sister said she stole the password for you."

"That slut is in love with him. She'd say anything to make him happy."

"She'd accuse her own brother of being a traitor?"

"We haven't seen eye to eye over Legato, ever." Sandro stood up and leaned over the desk. "He killed my father. Are you telling me you'll side with an outsider, an orphan, over your own blood? You are my *padrino*, my *compare*. I am your son. Or did those vows mean nothing?"

"Those vows are the only reason you aren't already dead."

"So you believe Legato over me."

"I believe him *and* your sister over you."

Sandro reddened, his eyes on fire. "Where's the proof against me, besides the lies they've told? Who saw *me* enter this building Saturday? Who can prove *I* made those changes?"

Enrico sat back. Sandro did have a point. Not that Enrico doubted Antonio or Bianca, but should La Provincia get involved—and that seemed likely, given Cris's warning—the case against Sandro looked quite murky. And Lorenzo would be sure to use that to his advantage.

Enrico needed to bring Sandro back to his side. He needed Sandro to come clean about Lorenzo's involvement.

And that meant he needed to come clean to Sandro about his father. He had to have those recordings of Dom. Perhaps if Sandro heard them, he'd understand what Enrico had done, and Enrico could make Sandro an underboss to assuage his wounded pride. If Sandro could just understand, they could mend this rift between them.

Enrico had tried hiding what Dom had done. He'd tried hiding the decision he'd made out of sentiment and caution, a decision that would make him appear weak in the eyes of La Provincia. But if it didn't seem weak to Sandro, if it looked compassionate instead, if he could win Sandro to his side, he stood a chance to get back his godsons.

And a chance to expose Lorenzo Andretti for the viper he was.

He gazed at his godson. "You have a point. I must investigate further." He motioned to Sandro's right side, to the stain on his jacket. "Tell me how that happened."

"You know damn well what happened."

"You went after Antonio in Milan. In a public park. You put the whole *cosca* at risk. Not to mention that you tried to kill my *capo di società*. What do you have to say for yourself?"

"I'm only sorry I missed."

Taking a deep breath, Enrico forced his anger down. He needed Sandro. Sandro was his only path to exposing Lorenzo. Enrico didn't speak until he could keep his voice even, steady. "You *will* be sorry about something if you don't calm down and trust in me."

Sandro gave him a mulish look, and Enrico finally allowed his anger to show. "I am your *capo*, first and foremost. You will go home and you will do nothing. Not one thing. If you go anywhere near Antonio, I will not hesitate to end your life."

His godson wrapped the drawstring of his tracksuit jacket around his fingers but said nothing.

"You hear me?"

"I do."

"And?"

Sandro eventually nodded. "I will do nothing."

"*Bene.* Tommaso will take you home and a doctor will meet you there." Sandro started to rise, but Enrico took his wrist. Sandro's skin felt feverish, clammy. "You are my blood, my son. Your father was like a brother to me. We are kin." He remembered Fedele, Sandro, and Matteo as boys, remembered how painfully they'd reminded him of Nico, the child he'd had to give up. Remembered how he'd played with them as if they were his own. "I do not want us to be enemies."

Sandro's eyes glistened. "Then why am I not your *capo di società*? Why wasn't Fedele? What did we do wrong?"

Enrico squeezed Sandro's wrist, then let go. "I will explain everything, very soon. After the doctor has seen to you."

"*Sì, compare.*"

He waited until Sandro and Tommaso had left. Then he picked up the phone. It was time to test his alliance with Dario, to see whether they could stand united as they'd pledged, or whether they'd tear each other apart, and Lorenzo would feed on their carcasses.

CHAPTER 17

Enrico hadn't been in Dario's study since their last conversation there, when Dario had claimed that his sister Antonella had never loved Enrico. That she'd been an Andretti to the core. He'd mulled over Dario's words many times since then. There'd been so much love between Enrico and Toni, but there had been secrets, too. And now it was impossible to know the truth.

If Dario had been trying to hurt him, he'd succeeded. But he wasn't about to admit that to Dario.

Right now, he needed Dario's cooperation, his help, or they'd both be mowed down by Dario's grandfather. Enrico had to have those recordings of Dom, and he wasn't taking "no" for an answer.

The maid who answered the front door showed him directly to the study, where Dario had two steaming cups of espresso waiting. He offered one to Enrico, then took a sip of his own. "You said you needed to see me."

Enrico explained what had happened at the bank and the coming threat from La Provincia. When he mentioned Cris's involvement, Dario's eyes narrowed. Interesting. Did he not know?

"If we're to stand together against Lorenzo, I need Sandro to testify against him. Otherwise, I will lose the bank, and we'll both be easy targets." He didn't mention the financial hit he'd taken; Dario didn't need to know just how vulnerable he was. He'd make back the money eventually, and of course he had some stashed away here and there under various aliases, but he lacked the resources to take on Lorenzo alone.

"And how can I help?" Dario asked.

"I need those recordings of Dom and your father. Now. And don't tell me you still haven't found them."

"What do I get in exchange?"

Enrico wanted to explode. "You get to live without your grandfather's boot on your throat."

"I want thirty percent of the bank. Not just the measly ten I've got."

Dario Andretti would be the death of him. "Fifteen."

"Forty-five."

Enrico almost laughed. "We are both dead then." When he started to rise, Dario motioned for him to sit.

"You can't blame me for trying."

Enrico sighed. "Eighteen."

Dario nodded. He turned to his laptop and started typing. "Give me a moment."

Enrico sipped at his espresso, thankful that Dario was being more or less reasonable. Losing another eight percent would hurt, but he'd manage.

After a few moments, Dario frowned.

"What is it?" Enrico asked.

"I thought they were the ones in this folder. But it's empty." He clicked around, the frown deepening. "I know Cris was looking into them." He called Cris, and they both waited for his arrival.

Cris seemed taller, thinner, when he walked in. *He must still be growing.* Sometimes Enrico forgot Cris was barely what, twenty? "Yes, Papà?" Cris asked.

"I need those recordings of Domenico Lucchesi."

Cris dropped his eyes. "They're gone."

A frisson of alarm skittered down Enrico's back.

"Gone?" Dario asked.

"Bisnonno asked for them."

Enrico's blood turned to ice. "*Dio mio.* You gave them to *him?*"

Cris shook his head. "With respect, Don Lucchesi, I am not stupid. I gave them to Antonio. Bianca had been asking me about how her father died. It's not my place to tell her. I thought they could help him explain it."

"*Porca miseria!*" Dario said. "You couldn't have asked me?"

"I know what you would have said."

"You are not *capo* yet. Remember that."

"I have. We need to keep this alliance strong. That is why I have protected Don Lucchesi."

"What *else* did Lorenzo ask you for?" Dario demanded.

Cris focused on Enrico, as if asking for permission. Enrico raised a hand to stay him. "Antonio said you gave the bank records from Saturday to Lorenzo. Correct?"

Dario stared at his son in astonishment. "You did what?"

"We need Bisnonno to think he has me in his pocket, do we not?"

"You could have informed me."

"I thought it best that you be genuinely surprised when he told you."

"*Cristo.* You're going to give me a heart attack."

Cris shrugged. "I'm a man now, Papà. Not a boy."

"Yes. But we need to work together. Not separately."

With a smile, Cris clasped his hands behind his back. "We do, all three of us. But you don't always remember that." He pointed to Enrico. "Don Lucchesi is supposed to be our ally. But you don't treat him like one. And you've done nothing to repair the rift with Gianluca d'Imperio."

Dario held his son's eyes for a long moment. "I hear my grandfather talking."

"Is he wrong?"

Without answering the question, Dario showed Cris out of the study. A muscle worked in his jaw. Perhaps now Enrico could get a straight answer about Toni. "You still want that eighteen percent?"

Dario just glared at him in response.

"What you said about Toni. Was it true?"

With a sigh, Dario picked up a pen, rolling it back and forth between his fingers. He gazed out the window, the silence heavy between them.

"Will you go to your grave hating me?" Enrico asked, making his voice soft. "I cannot fix your hand," he said, referring to the missing pinky on Dario's right hand. "I cannot undo what my father did to you. I wish I could. I've wished a thousand times that our fathers hadn't hated each other. We have a chance to end that. It seems that Cris and Antonio are ahead of us there."

"My sister always wanted us to be friends. You don't know how I suffered when she left, when she became your wife."

"I can imagine." Enrico took care to remove any trace of pity from his words.

"I will never call you friend."

"Ally, then. As we swore. A marriage binds us, and soon blood will as well."

Dario nodded, then he met Enrico's eyes. "My sister never betrayed you."

Relief flooded him, soothing the ache he'd carried since Nico and Delfina's engagement party. He hadn't given up his son for nothing. *Grazie a Dio.* "Thank you."

Dario nodded. "It seems we both need to talk to our seconds. I wonder why Antonio did not tell you he had the recordings?"

It was an excellent question. A niggling unease settled in Enrico's gut. Tonio knew how critical those recordings were, how much not having them worried Enrico. And here he'd had them for some time, and he'd neglected to mention it.

Certainly things had been tense between them for a while, but not so much that there was cause for worry.

Or was there?

Sandro claimed to have been framed. So did Antonio.

Only one man could be telling the truth. And *Dio* help him, it had better be Antonio.

———————◆———————

The crispness in Don Enrico's tone when he'd summoned Antonio to his home made Antonio more than a little uneasy. His discomfort only increased upon his arrival. He'd expected to go to the don's study, as usual, but instead Tommaso told him to go to the dock and to take Ruggero with him.

As they walked down the wooden dock, their shoes thudding on the boards, Antonio's heart sped up and his scalp prickled. Something was wrong. Very wrong.

Don Enrico stood at the wheel of the beautifully preserved Riva Aquarama that had been in his family for decades. The sleek speedboat bobbed on the gunmetal gray water, reflecting the dark bank of clouds overhead.

Antonio paused beside the boat. "You sure you want to go out today?" He made a show of glancing at the sky. "Looks like rain."

"Get in. We have something to discuss that I don't want to talk about at the house."

Antonio's blood froze. *Because he doesn't want Kate to get wind of what's going to happen.* Ruggero gave him a nudge on the shoulder, his face like granite. Swallowing hard, his insides gone to jelly, Antonio clambered into the boat, his limbs stiff and uncooperative.

The don nodded at Ruggero, who frisked Antonio and removed his Glock from its shoulder holster. So that's what that phone call Ruggero had received on the way there had been about.

"What's going on?" Antonio asked, his voice sounding thin. He wished now that he hadn't told Bianca, that she hadn't stormed out. He didn't want their last conversation to have been a fight.

The don didn't answer, just turned away and started the boat. He steered them out to the center of the lake, far enough from view of the shoreline that no one could be sure what was happening.

After a few minutes, the don cut the motor and let the boat drift. He turned to Antonio and crossed his arms. Ruggero stood behind Antonio within reach, his limbs loose, his stance indicating a readiness to act on his don's orders.

There was no question who was boss here. Ruggero was Antonio's friend, but Don Lucchesi was his *capo*.

Antonio felt dizzy. "What have I done?" he asked.

"That's the question." The don's face was hard, his eyes piercing. "I had to find out from Cris Andretti that you have something that could destroy me."

What? It took Antonio a moment, then he realized what the don meant. "The recordings. Yes, Cris gave them to me this morning."

"And you neglected to tell me."

"It's not what it seems."

"Enlighten me then."

"Cris didn't want his father to have them. Or Lorenzo. He thought they might help me with Bianca."

"That matches what Cris said." Enrico paused, the words soft, menacing. "But why didn't you tell *me*? You've had ample opportunity."

"I wasn't sure what to do."

Ruggero stepped closer behind him, and every muscle in Antonio's body went rigid. He hadn't seen a signal pass between the don and Ruggero, yet clearly the guard was ready to act. How many times had the two of them played out a similar scenario?

"In this matter, you shouldn't be making decisions on your own." The don leaned against the leather seat beside him. Waves lapped against the boat's hull, and a freezing gust of wind sliced through Antonio's jacket and whipped his hair about. "Just like you shouldn't be ordering Ruggero to watch over your boy. Or ditching your guards to see him either."

"I did what I felt I had to do."

"So you're making a habit of defying orders."

"No, I—"

"What are you planning, Tonio?"

"Nothing. I swear it."

"Are you so impatient to be *capo*?"

"No. Nothing like that. Never."

The boat rocked again, the Italian flag mounted on the stern flapping wildly in the wind. No one spoke. Despite the chill, sweat snaked down Antonio's back.

"I want to believe you," the don said, his statement barely audible.

"You can. I swear it."

"This business at the bank. Sandro claims you framed him."

"*Merda*! You have Bianca's word as well."

"Ever since she came back, you haven't been yourself."

It was true. But... "I haven't been disloyal. I never would be. You *know* this. That's why you chose me."

"I never thought Dom would betray me either."

Antonio's face heated. "I am not him. I am no traitor."

"Haven't I given you cause?"

Antonio froze. Here was the true test. How he answered would determine everything. "You have angered me, yes. But nothing could make me betray you." He thought back to the day they'd met. His voice thickened. "You saved my life, Don Lucchesi. I owe you a debt I can never repay."

The don closed his eyes and pinched the bridge of his nose. "*Madonna*," he muttered, as if to himself. Then he beckoned Antonio forward. Antonio stumbled across the boat, uncertain. The don folded him into a tight embrace, kissing him on both cheeks, before stepping back and regarding him at arm's length. He lightly squeezed Antonio's shoulders. "You are the son of my heart, Tonio," he said, his gaze glimmering with emotion. "You scared me half to death."

Relief and warmth flooded him and tears pricked at the back of his own eyes. "How could you think I would ever wrong you?"

"After Dom, anything is possible."

"It's not," Antonio rasped. "Never that. I would never betray you, Don Enrico."

Enrico chuckled. "You have to stop that."

"Stop what?"

"Calling me 'Don Enrico.' Dom never did."

"But he was family."

"And what are you?"

Antonio stared at the don for a long moment, unsure what to say, and Enrico didn't clarify. With a clap on the shoulder, the don released him.

Antonio took a deep breath. He had to tell Enrico what he'd done. "I did do something you won't be happy about, however."

"What?"

"I told Bianca her father was a traitor."

"*Porca vacca*!" the don snapped. "And you think telling her is any less a betrayal?"

Antonio tensed, but he held his ground. "Remember how she questioned you about why you didn't choose Fedele or Sandro? She's not stupid. Neither is Sandro. They've both guessed that something was wrong. Our plan was never going to work."

"That was for me to decide."

"I told her that I shot Don Domenico. I didn't want her to hate you."

The don seemed confused. "How does that help?"

"I implied that you didn't order it. That you were going to exile him."

"So now I look even weaker."

"I may as well have done it. I pushed you."

Enrico's eyes blazed. "Yes, you did. But do you think it wasn't my decision?"

Antonio shook his head. "I know it was. I just—"

"*I* made the decision. It was the only decision I could make. And I don't need you taking it from me."

"I'm sorry. I—"

The don touched his shoulder. "*Basta.* What's done is done. I know you meant well." He paused. "And you're right. It's time we came clean."

———— ✦ ————

They assembled late the next morning in Francesca Lucchesi's kitchen—Antonio, Bianca, Enrico, Kate, Sandro, Matteo, Francesca, and Ruggero. Antonio nervously fingered the flash drive that contained the recordings. What if this didn't work? What if Sandro didn't come around?

What if Bianca hated Antonio afterward?

Enrico took control of the family meeting. He held out his hand to Antonio, who placed the flash drive in it. Enrico held it up for all of them to see before plugging it into the laptop they'd brought with them. "I never wanted to speak of this. Ever," Enrico said. "But the time has come for there to be no secrets between us."

They were all seated around the well-worn wooden kitchen table, except for Ruggero, who leaned against the far wall, his hands clasped behind him. While not a member of the family, he'd been party to what had happened that night, and he'd be useful if Sandro or Matteo erupted. He'd already frisked both Sandro and Matteo for weapons, to their annoyance but to Antonio's relief. He didn't want any bloodshed, not in this house, not in front of the women.

Enrico looked at Francesca, then Bianca, Matteo, and Sandro in turn. "These are recordings Carlo Andretti made of phone calls he had with your father." He clicked the mouse a few times, then Carlo's and Don Domenico's voices filled the room.

At the sound of Domenico's voice, Bianca pressed a hand to her mouth, and Francesca's eyes filled with tears. Domenico and Carlo were setting up their final trap—Kate's abduction. Kate pressed her lips together, and Antonio took her right hand at the same time Enrico took her left. After a moment, she let go of Antonio and cradled the slight bump at her belly. The child that had been nearly killed—twice—by Carlo Andretti.

Sandro and Matteo were frowning, Sandro with his arms crossed and his head shaking. As soon as Enrico ended the recording, Sandro leaned forward, stabbing at the table with a thick forefinger. "This is a clever fabrication."

Francesca, surprisingly dry-eyed now, jumped in. "It's not, and you know it. Your father—my husband—said those words. He was a traitor"—she crossed herself and spat—"to this *cosca*."

Sandro's chair scraped across the tiles as he rose. "How can you say that, Mamma? Even if it is true, he had every reason for what he did. He was trying to save this *cosca*. From him." He pointed to Enrico, and Bianca and Francesca both let out little gasps.

Antonio felt the slightest bit sick. There was some truth in Sandro's words, but it was blasphemous to say them. To accuse Don Enrico of wrongdoing.

The room went silent. Finally Antonio spoke. "Your *capo* protected a woman from an abusive husband. He was following our laws when he intervened."

"Was he following them when he fucked another 'Ndranghetista's wife?" Sandro asked. Francesca jumped up and slapped him across the cheek, but he barely registered the blow. "And how, exactly, did restarting the feud with the Andrettis help this *cosca*?"

When Enrico said nothing again, Antonio jumped in. "It was the right thing to do." The don would never defend his actions, but someone should.

"And our *cosca* suffered as a result. We lost men, good men, and money, and for a while our only alliance. And all because *he* wanted *her* in his bed." Sandro's finger pointed from Enrico to Kate, and Antonio felt every jab of that finger. Because he'd thought the same thing; he just hadn't said it.

"It was more than that," Kate said. "He cared when no one else did. He intervened when no one else would. And he had no reason to, no promise from me."

Sandro turned to her. "Your problem was one for Carlo Andretti to resolve. It was not our *cosca*'s business."

Francesca broke in. "We can argue this all night." She sat back down and clasped her hands together on the table. "Your father went to Carlo Andretti. He could have challenged Don Enrico by calling for a special election. He could have taken the matter to La Provincia. But he did neither of those things. He conspired to kill Don Enrico and make himself *capo*. We all know the price of a failed coup attempt."

Sandro struck the tabletop. "Then why haven't *we* paid it? Why do we still draw breath?" He turned back to Enrico. "Because you are weak. Unfit to lead. Unfit to be *capo*."

Enrico's face reddened and he rose, slapping his chest. "You think me weak? I did the hardest thing a man could ever do. I shot the one I considered a brother. *My* blood, *my* flesh. I pulled that trigger *myself*."

Antonio stared at Bianca, whose mouth was open in astonishment. Her gaze flew from Enrico to Antonio, and he nodded to confirm that the don's words were true.

"But you couldn't kill us," Sandro said. "And that makes you weak."

"I refused to destroy the remnants of this family."

"Well, it's happened anyway. Look at Papà. Look at Fedele. Both lying in their graves." Sandro tapped his own chest for emphasis. "Look at me." He paused, his eyes aflame. "I will never bow to you, *Don Lucchesi*."

Enrico set his hands on the table, leaning toward Sandro. "We took the vows of *comparaggio*. Unbreakable vows. Did they mean nothing to you?"

Sandro pointed at Antonio. "You chose him over me. Why? Because you thought I could be a traitor. You took those vows with an unclear heart. You told the men I was good enough to be your son, but not honorable enough to lead this *cosca*. How do you think that makes me feel? And how much do you think I trust your promise to me? It smells like a trap. A way to ensure I won't stab you in the back. *That's* what your vow was. Nothing more."

Enrico seemed pained. "You're wrong, Sandro."

With a smirk, Sandro crossed his arms. "If you believe that, you're lying to yourself." He turned to Matteo. "I'm leaving. Are you with me?"

Matteo looked around the table. "You're choosing Lorenzo Andretti. I can't believe he'll be our salvation any more than I can believe Zio Enrico means us harm. He spared our lives, Sandro. Can't you see what that means?"

Sandro made a cutting motion across his throat. "You are dead to me. All of you." He strode out of the room, then through the front door, slamming it with a resounding boom.

Bianca said a prayer under her breath. Antonio gazed at her. "What are you thinking, Bee?" His heart was pounding. He wasn't sure he wanted the answer.

"It's a lot to take in." Then she looked at him. "I'm glad you didn't kill Papà."

Maybe he shouldn't say it, but she needed to know. "I would have. I wanted to."

Her voice was soft. "I know. But it wasn't your place."

She rose from the table and approached Enrico. Falling to her knees, she pressed a kiss to his signet ring, the one that bore the Lucchesi crest. "I thank you for my life, Don Lucchesi."

When she rose, Matteo followed suit, then Francesca did. Three of the four had reaffirmed their allegiance to the *cosca*.

But there was still Sandro to consider. Nothing would be resolved until he came back to the fold. And Enrico wouldn't have the leverage he needed against Lorenzo Andretti without Sandro's testimony. There was only one way to fix matters with Sandro. Antonio rose. "I will step down as *capo di società*. I will no longer stand in Sandro's way. Then he will feel part of the family again."

"No." Enrico rapped the table for emphasis. "If Sandro cannot follow me, that is his choice. I will not appease him by setting you aside."

"But—"

Francesca cut in. "Sandro has chosen. His decision wounds me, but it was his choice to make."

Bianca nodded. "He has chosen." She took Antonio's hand and squeezed it. "It's not what I wanted to hear, but I'm glad I know the truth. Thank you for giving it to me."

A great sense of relief threatened to overwhelm him. Bianca knew. She knew the truth, and yet she didn't seem to hate him. Did he dare hope?

She leaned over and whispered, "I owe you an apology."

He stroked her cheek. "No, you don't." He wanted to kiss her, but not in front of the others. Not yet. Not until they'd discussed their future.

CHAPTER 18

Antonio had been reluctant to leave Bianca behind, with only her mother and Matteo. If Sandro decided to come back, they'd be in danger. Enrico had settled the matter by sending several guards to watch over them, but Antonio still didn't like having her out of his sight. He looked forward to the day when she was his, and he'd be the only one making decisions about her safety.

He sent Beppe out for food as soon as they pulled up to his building. It was just past lunchtime, and all three of them were hungry. Francesca probably would have made them something, but it didn't feel right to ask after Sandro had shattered any hope they'd had of peace.

"We should've put a bullet in him," Ruggero grumbled as he and Antonio walked up the stairs to his flat.

"I know. But that's up to Enrico. Besides, Sandro could change his mind."

Ruggero cast him a sour look while unlocking the door. "You think so?"

Antonio shook his head. "Not really." He walked into the kitchen and grabbed a bottle of Pellegrino water from the fridge and handed one to Ruggero. "But it went better than I expected."

"Looks like you'll get your woman. If you want her."

"I do."

Ruggero took a sip from his bottle. "You're lucky. Finding someone."

The somber note in Ruggero's voice surprised him. "You jealous?"

"That life isn't for me."

"Of course it is."

"I'm bodyguard to a *capo*. Just how long do you think I'll live?" Ruggero gave him a smirk. "My father made it to forty-eight. I'm three-quarters of the way there."

"Your father had a family. So can you."

"And when am I going to meet someone?"

"Enrico could arrange something for you. There are plenty of girls in Calabria who'd jump at the chance."

"To marry this?" Ruggero gestured to the scar that gave his face a sinister cast. "Besides, I don't want some silly girl."

"A young woman then."

"I'm fine the way I am." He waved his hand in the air, as if wanting to dismiss the topic.

Antonio realized something. He'd never seen Ruggero with a woman, and he'd never seen him try to pick one up on their nights off when he'd bothered to go to the clubs with Antonio, back when Antonio was still a guard. Ruggero didn't seem the type to be a monk. So if there wasn't a woman, was there a man? It wasn't accepted in the *malavita*, but Antonio didn't care one way or the other.

He cleared his throat, not sure how to say it, then he just blurted it out. "If you're, you know, gay, you can tell me."

Ruggero was in the midst of swallowing when Antonio spoke, and he spluttered water across the small kitchen. When he finished coughing, he asked, "What makes you think I like *men*?"

Antonio shrugged. "I've never seen you with anyone. You have to get laid sometime, and since you're keeping it so quiet—"

"There's a woman. A call girl. We have an arrangement."

"You don't want more than that?"

Ruggero picked at the label on his bottle. "I don't think I'd make a good husband. Or father."

"That's not true."

"And how would you know?"

"You looked out for me. You still do."

"It was my job to train you. And now it's my job to guard you."

"You've done more than that. You always have."

Ruggero kept his eyes fixed on the bottle. "Being a father, a husband—that's a lot more involved."

Antonio laughed. "I never thought I'd see you afraid of anything."

Ruggero met his gaze then. "It's not that." He took another swig from the bottle. "I just don't think it's in me."

Antonio leaned over and squeezed Ruggero's shoulder. "It *is* in you. You just need to find the right woman to bring it out."

Someone knocked on the door, and Ruggero was on his feet in an instant, gun in hand. "It's too early for Beppe. You expecting anyone?"

"No." Antonio drew his own gun, and they advanced on the door, Antonio standing to the left of the doorway, while Ruggero took point and reached for the doorknob. "Who is it?" he demanded, his voice deeper and gruffer than usual.

"Bianca."

Antonio started to lower his weapon, but Ruggero tapped the muzzle back up. "In case she's not alone," he murmured, before opening the door.

Bianca raised her brows at the sight of the guns, but she was in fact alone. "Sorry," she said. "I followed one of the neighbors in. I should have buzzed." She looked a bit drawn, her face pinched with worry, but Antonio had never been happier to see anyone. She stepped inside and said the words he'd been thinking. "I missed you."

"Me too." It was ridiculous; they'd been apart less than an hour. But it was true.

Ruggero holstered his weapon and palmed a pack of cigarettes. "I'll be on the balcony."

Antonio took Bianca's hand and led her down the hall to his bedroom. He shut the door behind them, then turned to her, the hush in the room so complete he thought he could hear their beating hearts. He stroked a finger along the side of her face, from temple to jaw, then he drew her close, into his arms, but he didn't kiss her. He just held her, her head pressed against his chest, the feel of her, warm and solid, a comfort after all the drama of the past two weeks.

He held her like that for several minutes, swaying slightly, his mind blank of anything but how much he wished he could be with her like this always. Just the two of them together, united as they faced the world. Emotion built within him, swelled in his chest until he felt he would burst. He loved her. He loved her so much it was a physical ache. He was just about to say so when she pulled back from him and met his eyes. "I'm sorry, Tonio. I'm sorry for accusing you of lying about my father. I'm sorry I ever doubted you."

He pressed a finger to her lips when she started to say more. "That's enough, Bee. You had every right to doubt me. I'd kept the truth from you for a long time."

"And now I understand why."

"You don't hate me? Even a little?"

"I heard him on that recording." She wiped her tears. "I think part of me has always known. The way he treated Luca, the way he treated me—my father hated it when things didn't go his way. He banished me, Tonio. I could have come home after Luca was born. But Papà said it would look strange if I did. I think he just couldn't stand the sight of me." She took a deep breath, then released it. "If he could stop loving me"—her voice cracked, but she pressed on—"he could stop loving Zio Enrico."

"He loved you. In his own way."

She pressed her lips together and tried to give him a smile. "It's nice of you to say so, but it's not true."

He took her hands and kissed the knuckles on each one. "I wish I could erase what happened to you."

"I don't. Because then there'd be no Luca. I can't wish him away."

"You're right. Just knowing he's out there—it makes me happy. Even if he can't be mine. He's a little piece of you and me together forever." He swallowed hard, his mouth suddenly dry. It was time to ask her. He didn't have a ring, but it didn't matter. He'd ask today and buy her one tomorrow. He sank to his knees, still holding her hands. "Bee, I already feel bound to you, joined to you through Luca. But I want more. Will you—"

A harsh knock came at the door, then Ruggero spoke. "Don Legato, it's Don Lucchesi on the phone. It's urgent. And it cannot wait."

He scrambled to his feet, his heart pounding, probably looking as distressed as Bianca did. "Sandro?" she asked.

He wondered the same and went out into the hall and took his mobile from Ruggero's hand. "What's going on?" he asked Enrico.

"It's Lorenzo. He's called a meeting. It's about the bank."

Antonio's blood turned to slush. It was happening—Lorenzo was making his move.

"When? Where?"

"He wanted it in San Luca, but I insisted on the bank. We'll be safer there. It's in three hours. He's assembling the *mandamenti* and the affected families."

"Not giving us much time for damage control."

Enrico sighed. "We had our chance, and we should have taken it. It was my decision to see if we could avoid it coming to light."

"You still have your reputation."

"It may prove of little use."

Antonio quickly explained the situation to Bianca, then he and Ruggero left her with Beppe and picked up Enrico and several guards. They had some time to strategize during the drive, and perhaps Enrico could fit in some preemptive calls to Gianluca d'Imperio and Dario Andretti before they arrived in Milan.

Whatever they did though, Lorenzo Andretti had them in his fist, and his fingers were only beginning to squeeze.

They arrived in Milan around four PM, and with the heavy clouds overhead, the early winter-time twilight was already deepening to dusk. The coming nightfall only intensified Antonio's worries.

Antonio, Enrico, Ruggero, and the guards headed up the stone stairs into the Banca di Falcone. Despite the layers he wore, Antonio shivered. Enrico had insisted the two of them dress well, so they were in suits and long overcoats, leather gloves and scarves. Antonio's Glock nestled below his left armpit, but he didn't think he could pull it easily, as bulked up as he was with clothing. He envied Ruggero the lined leather jacket he wore over his own suit. As always, Ruggero looked ready for anything.

But Enrico was right; appearances mattered. If they'd shown up hastily dressed, ready for a firefight, that would peg them as guilty in the eyes of the men who'd come to judge them.

When the rest arrived, they assembled in a large conference room on the second floor. Lorenzo Andretti sat at one end of the table, Don Battista at the other. The affected family heads and their seconds were there—Gianluca and Leandro d'Imperio, Dario and Cris Andretti, Lorenzo's second, Salvatore Ruscino. One seat remained empty, to Lorenzo's left, but Antonio was sure who'd occupy it, and his suspicions were confirmed when Sandro Lucchesi entered the room and claimed the seat.

Gianluca d'Imperio pulled out a cigar and lit it. He looked from Enrico to Lorenzo. "I'd like to know what the hell is going on. I'm hearing different things from the two of you. But both of them involve my money. So I'm understandably... concerned."

"As you should be, Gianluca," Lorenzo said. He motioned to Sandro, who handed him a stack of papers. Lorenzo slapped them down on the desk and pushed them toward Gianluca. "It's all here, in black and white. Enrico's man"—

he gestured to Antonio—"has been very busy."

Heat erupted over Antonio's face and chest, and his hands clenched into fists. It took everything he had not to bolt up and throttle Lorenzo. Beside him, Enrico didn't react, other than to place a hand on Antonio's forearm in a gesture of support—and calm.

D'Imperio pawed through the stack, the cigar clamped between his teeth, the frown on his face deepening as he studied the records.

"I am not responsible for that." Antonio gestured to Sandro. "He's trying to frame me."

Lorenzo broke in, ignoring Antonio. "You will note that someone has attempted to undo the transactions."

"Yes," Enrico said. "We spent Saturday cleaning up the damage. Everything has been restored."

"Why weren't we told about this?" Dario asked. "Why are we having to hear about it from my grandfather?"

"I was in the process of notifying all of you when Lorenzo called this meeting."

"You've had three days to contact us," Leandro said.

"We hadn't finished our investigation into the matter."

Dario cut in. "Investigation? I thought you knew the culprit."

"There are at least two players. Possibly more"—Enrico's eyes flicked to Lorenzo—"and I wanted to have something concrete to bring to you."

"What you wanted," Sandro said, rising from his seat, "is to pin this on me." He glanced from Enrico to Antonio. "But you can't."

Antonio rose as well. "Not yet."

"But you are certainly trying to fabricate evidence to make it appear that I'm guilty."

"Fabricating?" Antonio spat. "The only one fabricating anything is you. You've done your best to make me look guilty—"

"I didn't *have* to do anything. Prove, right now, that I did this."

Antonio heaved in a breath and flexed his fingers, frustration gnawing a hole in his gut. "I can't. The man who helped you is dead."

Sandro cocked his head. "Whose access card was used to enter the building?"

"Mine. But it was new. You posed as me and called Security and said I'd lost mine."

"That's a nice little story." With a smile, Sandro asked his next question. "Well, surely then the security cameras captured my face."

The burning in Antonio's gut worsened. "Someone disabled the cameras. But I *will* prove your guilt."

Sandro's smile turned into a smirk and he crossed his arms. "Will you."

Without thinking, Antonio lunged across the table, trying to snag Sandro by the tie, when Cris Andretti rose and pulled him bodily back.

"Tonio, calm yourself," Cris whispered, his fingers tightening around Antonio's biceps. "I am sure we can handle this as reasonable men." After a pause, Cris addressed the men surrounding them. "Whatever has happened, I trust that Don Lucchesi and Don Legato have acted in good faith. No one has lost anything."

"I should remain calm while my reputation is being attacked?" Sandro asked.

"He's already stolen my position from me. Should I let him take my good name too?"

"I stole nothing from you!" Antonio shouted.

Sandro's face turned red as a pepper. "You took everything!" he bellowed, and before Antonio could react, Sandro had a Beretta in his hand. Antonio threw himself in front of Don Lucchesi, pushing him to the floor, and Ruggero fell on top of Antonio as a gunshot cut through the noise and confusion. The man on top of him gasped, and that was when Antonio realized the horrible truth: It wasn't Ruggero who'd saved him. It was Cris Andretti.

Dario lifted Cris off Antonio, murmuring, "No, no, no," as he laid his son on the carpeting.

His heart pounding, his breathing harsh, Antonio ducked down behind the desk and pulled his Glock in case Sandro was still armed. He rose up and peered over the table, seeing Ruggero's back as he disappeared through the doorway, evidently pursuing Sandro. Then Antonio glanced at Enrico on the floor beside him. "I'm okay," Enrico said, rising to a crouch beside Antonio. "The guards are after him."

Antonio holstered his gun, then whipped out his phone and dialed 112, requesting an ambulance, his eyes glued to the spot on Cris's side where blood oozed out over Dario's hands. When he finished the call, Antonio pulled off his suit jacket and placed it under Cris's head. Cris was clammy, his face so pale it looked gray, and a trickle of blood ran from the corner of his mouth. He stared up at Antonio. "You okay?" Cris asked, his voice hoarse.

"Yes. But you—" Antonio's throat clamped shut on the words. He took a breath and tried again. "Why, Cris?"

"You saved Delfi."

"But I didn't. Nick did."

Cris wrapped a hand around Antonio's. "In the library. You almost died for her."

Antonio squeezed Cris's hand. "*Idiota*," he said, the word thick with emotion, his heartbeat turning frantic when Cris's grip slackened. They had to stop the bleeding. He looked around, then grabbed the red scarf he'd been wearing earlier and folded it over. He gently pushed Dario's hands out of way and pressed the scarf tightly to Cris's wound. Hot blood almost immediately soaked the woolen fabric, and Antonio pressed harder. Cris was going to die if he didn't get help soon.

Cris gave him a weak smile. "Been shot before, remember? It's going to take more than a bullet to kill me." He coughed up a gout of blood, and Dario started praying under his breath. Cris turned his attention to his father. "Papà, I love you."

Dario took Cris's hand. "You're not going to die."

Cris coughed again, another gush of blood. He took another breath, then spat on the carpet. "Tell Delfi and Mamma I love them."

No, no, no. This can't be happening. Antonio pressed harder on the wound, but Cris's breathing worsened, a gurgling rattle emerging and deepening with each inhalation.

The sing-song wail of emergency sirens grew louder. "Hang on," Antonio said. "You've got to hang on, Cris."

With a nod, Cris closed his eyes. "Tell Gio I'm sorry." His voice was weak, thready, his harsh breathing coarsening into wet and heavy gasps. His lungs had to be filling with blood. His eyes flew open and he coughed harshly, choking, and Dario rolled him onto his side. Cris spat out more blood and took another wheezing inhale, the rattle more pronounced than it had been. *Cristo.* He couldn't take much more. Hot tears pricked Antonio's eyes. Suddenly Cris went completely limp.

Dario shouted his name, but Cris didn't respond. Antonio rolled him onto his back and pressed two fingers to Cris's neck, searching for his pulse. He found a faint heartbeat. Cris had mere minutes at best.

Four officers of the *carabinieri* entered the room, guns drawn. "Nobody move!" they shouted and began lining everyone up against the walls with their hands up. Antonio and Dario were the only two who didn't comply. The officer nearest to them urged them up. "Can't you see he needs help?" Dario said. "Where is the ambulance?"

"We won't let them in until we have the room secured. Now move," the officer responded.

Antonio shook his head. "I can't." He pressed harder on the scarf, so dark now with Cris's blood that it almost looked black, then glanced up at the officer. "*Per favore.* Search me where I am. I have only the gun under my left arm, nothing else." He raised his left elbow so the officer could take the clearly visible Glock.

Another officer came up. "No. We're not breaking procedure." The first officer motioned with his gun to Dario. "Get up and step away. Now."

"He's dying!" Antonio yelled, his frustration hitting the breaking point. Why couldn't they just trust him?

"And you need to move!" the officer yelled back.

Antonio wanted to hit the man, but Cris needed help. Professional help. And there was only one way for him to get it. Antonio looked at Dario. "We have to do what they want."

"My boy," Dario whispered, staring at Cris, his voice so broken that Antonio averted his gaze to give him privacy.

Antonio let go of Cris and stepped back, putting his hands up. Cris's blood felt cool on his palms when the air hit it, and he left red handprints on the conference room wall as the officers frisked him and Dario. "Hurry, please," Antonio begged.

The officers finally gave the all clear, and a pair of emergency techs raced into the room. Antonio and Dario moved back to give them space. The men worked frantically on Cris, giving him oxygen and fluids and shocking his heart, but nothing seemed to work, and the pit in Antonio's stomach grew. "This can't be happening," he said out loud, finally voicing his disbelief. Tears filled his vision. This couldn't be happening. Cris couldn't be dead.

Finally the techs sat back. "I'm sorry," one of them said.

Dario moaned and pressed a fist to his mouth. When Antonio touched his shoulder, Dario jerked away as if he'd been burned.

The techs loaded Cris onto a stretcher and wheeled him out.

Escorted by Sottotenente Silvio Fuente, a *carabinieri* officer well-known to the Lucchesis, Ruggero entered, his cheeks red from the cold. He shook his head at the expectant looks he received. "Sandro's gone."

Silence descended on them. Finally Enrico broke it. "Dario, this is my fault, and—"

Dario wheeled on him, his face a mask of fury. "If you had done your *job*, none of this would have happened."

"He's my godson."

"I don't give a fuck. My son has paid the price for your soft heart." Dario jabbed a finger in Enrico's chest, and Antonio muscled between them.

"If anyone is to blame, it's me," Antonio said. "I should have stepped aside to make Sandro happy."

Dario grabbed Antonio's shirtfront, the blood on his hands smearing the white fabric. "I blame you both. And of course that bastard who did this. I will tear him apart with my hands if I have to." He stepped closer, his teeth gritted, his eyes burning coals, his voice low so only Enrico and Antonio could hear it. "Whatever alliance we had is dead."

"But Nick and Delfi—" Antonio said.

"They will divorce."

"You can't mean that."

"*Signori*, some decorum, please." Lorenzo cut in, motioning with his head to Fuente and the other officers, who were listening to them intently. Lorenzo had risen and was clasping with both hands the cane he'd recently started using. His dark eyes surveyed the group of them, his face betraying a strange sort of eagerness, his lips curving, almost as if he wanted to smile. Was he... *happy* about Cris's death? Antonio recoiled at the notion, but Cris's death solved a huge problem for Lorenzo—it threw the alliance between Enrico and Dario into question. Could Lorenzo have engineered this? Had he *wanted* Sandro to shoot Cris?

"What do you expect, Nonno?" Dario asked.

"I expect you to act in the best interests of our combined family."

Dario punched the wall, cracking the plaster. "As far as I'm concerned, the Lucchesis can go to hell."

Enrico raised his hands in a calming gesture. "Dario, *per favore*. Our children are united in marriage—"

"I gave you your son back," Dario said, referring to how he'd released Nick from the Andretti *cosca*. "And you took my son away with your selfishness." Dario turned to his grandfather. "So no, Nonno. I'm not going to think about this family's best interests. All I care about is making these two"—he gestured to Enrico and Antonio—"pay for what they've done."

Fuente stepped forward and raised his voice. "*Signori*, as entertaining as this is, we have jobs to do." He directed an officer to take Dario into another room for questioning. Dario stalked away without another word.

Leandro d'Imperio snickered as another officer came for him and his father. "Looks like you've landed in quite the shitstorm, Legato."

Gianluca cuffed his son on the back of the head. "A man has died. Have some respect." He turned to Enrico. "We'll talk more about this later." He gestured to Sandro's printouts, which were scattered across the table, before they left the room.

Lorenzo and Sal Ruscino said nothing, but Antonio could tell by Lorenzo's smirk that he was gloating inside. He knew it, he knew the old man was behind this, and the fury that had been mounting in him since the officers had arrived finally broke free. Antonio pointed at Lorenzo. "This is your doing."

The old man huffed with laughter. "So desperate to make this anyone's fault but yours."

"Lorenzo," Enrico said, his tone a warning.

Lorenzo's attention shifted to Enrico, and his laughter turned to a tight smile. "You and I have been playing a game of chess, Enrico, moving pieces here and there, for a long time. But I am the only one who knew this from the beginning. My trap is set, and soon you will spring it."

"You are not the only clever man in this room."

"I am the one who will win." Lorenzo gestured to Sal, who helped him on with his great coat.

Antonio opened his mouth to respond, but Enrico put a silencing hand on his shoulder.

Once Sal and Lorenzo had been escorted out of the room for questioning, Antonio felt free to speak, but kept his volume to a whisper. "What did he mean by that?"

Don Battista came over and put a hand on Antonio's other shoulder. "You must learn to keep your counsel. Accusing Lorenzo to his face..." He shook his head.

Enrico squeezed Antonio's shoulder. "We've got to be on our guard, and not just from Lorenzo." He gave a significant look at Sottotenente Silvio Fuente. The *carabinieri* officer was on the other side of the room, questioning one of their guards.

As if he knew he was the object of discussion, Fuente headed their way. The officer doffed his cap to Enrico and Don Battista, then gestured for all of them to sit at the conference table. Fuente's gaze roved from one of them to the other, as if he were taking their measure. Then he spoke. "I assume, like the others, that you agree on the shooter?" His focus settled on Enrico. "Your cousin, Sandro Lucchesi?" Enrico nodded, and Fuente continued. "And who was his intended target?"

Antonio hadn't expected the question, but Enrico answered smoothly, with no hesitation. "I believe his target was either Signor Legato or myself."

"So Cristoforo Andretti was just unfortunate?"

"No," Antonio said, the firmness in his voice surprising even himself. "He was heroic. He saved my life."

Fuente focused on Antonio, his eyes bright as a squirrel's. "You two were friends."

Were. A lump rose in Antonio's throat. His friend was dead. Cris wouldn't get to tease Antonio about his dancing or the women on his arm ever again. They wouldn't have drinks together ever again. Not trusting himself to speak, Antonio acknowledged Fuente's statement with a nod.

"What reason would Sandro Lucchesi have to shoot Cristoforo Andretti?"

Antonio could think of one, but this man wasn't the one he'd be discussing it with. He shook his head.

Fuente turned to Ruggero. "You chased him, yes?"

Ruggero shrugged. "For all the good it did."

Fuente studied each of them in turn, then said, "Aside from his mother's residence, have you any inkling where he might go?"

They all shook their heads, and on this point, Antonio knew they were telling the truth. Sandro might go to Lorenzo seeking protection, but who could say for sure? Antonio still could hardly believe Sandro had fired on them during the meeting, and in front of so many witnesses. What had he hoped to accomplish? *Had* he been acting on Lorenzo's orders?

Or was Sandro truly desperate at this point?

Antonio hoped not. A desperate man was capable of anything, no matter the risk. And that made him a formidable foe.

Fuente picked up some of the scattered printouts and started studying them. "Why were you all here today?" he asked, not lifting his gaze from the papers.

"We'd had some trouble at the bank," Enrico said. "A rogue employee."

Fuente raised a brow. "Who?"

"Sandro," Antonio said, the word seething out of him. Sandro had killed Cris. Were he in front of Antonio right now, he'd be dead in a matter of seconds.

"Ah," Fuente said, a grin spreading across his face. "Now we get to something interesting. And just what did this rogue Sandro do?"

When Antonio would have answered, Enrico put a hand on his forearm to quiet him, then he quickly explained, in a highly edited fashion, what had happened at the bank.

"And why would your... godson, yes?" Fuente asked, cocking his head to the side as if he didn't already know the answer. "Why would he do such a thing?"

Enrico stared at his hands and rubbed his fingertips on the smooth, polished wood of the table. "I gave Antonio a promotion here at the bank that Sandro felt was owed him."

Fuente furrowed his brow, his eyes narrowing to a squint. "And so, I wonder, how did Cris Andretti come to be shot?"

"I told you. He was a hero," Antonio said.

The officer sat back in his chair and smiled. "'Hero' isn't the first word I'd use to describe anyone in the Andretti family." When Antonio started to rise, about to object, Fuente held up a finger. "But I suppose there is a first time for everything." He motioned to Antonio's blood-soaked hands. "The evidence speaks for itself."

"Is there anything else?" Enrico asked Fuente.

With a smile, Fuente flipped his cap over in his hands, then settled it on his head. "Not at the moment. You will contact me if Sandro shows up." He made the words an order rather than a request.

As Fuente rose, Antonio suddenly thought of a way to prove his innocence, and Fuente would be instrumental—if he chose to help.

Antonio followed Fuente out, receiving questioning looks from Enrico and Ruggero, but there was no time to explain. He caught up to the officer in the lobby. "Sottotenente, may I have a word?"

Fuente turned with a grin and scanned him up and down. "What is it, Signor Legato?"

"There is a personal matter I could use your assistance with."

"The *carabinieri* is always here to serve."

Antonio jammed his blood-encrusted hands in his pockets. "That unauthorized transfer of funds last Saturday. We believe it was Sandro who did it, but we've had trouble proving he was the perpetrator."

The second lieutenant stroked his black mustache, his eyes twinkling. "It seems your boss left out an important detail."

Antonio didn't respond. He had to tread carefully.

Fuente chuckled and pulled on his black leather gloves. "You don't seem to understand how the game is played, *signore*."

"Game?"

"You want something, you give something. It's simple."

Pursing his lips, Antonio nodded. Of course. He shouldn't have expected to get Fuente's cooperation for free. "Yes. We aren't completely certain that Sandro is to blame."

"And let me guess again. If Sandro *isn't* the guilty party, the suspicion falls on you."

How the fuck did he know that? Antonio forced himself to remain stock still, but it was difficult not to react. Fuente's grin let him know he'd failed in his attempt to school his features.

Rubbing his chin, Fuente tried to hide his amusement. "It doesn't take a genius to sort out the reason why *you*—and not Signor Lucchesi—are here, asking me for help." He paused, then made a hurry-up motion. "I have places to be, *signore*."

His cheeks burning, Antonio made his request. "I need access to the footage from any security cameras in the neighborhood, either those controlled by businesses or the city. I need to see who entered this bank—from the front or the back—around five-thirty AM last Saturday."

"And also to prove who didn't." When Antonio said nothing, Fuente continued. "So, say I assist you in this matter. What assistance will I receive in return?"

"Name your price."

"An officer seeking advancement either needs to know the right people or needs to know about the right people. And I want to know about Lorenzo Andretti."

Antonio's pulse quickened. "I barely know the man."

The *carabiniere* lit up a cigarette. "A man in my profession hears many whispers. And many of those whispers involve Lorenzo Andretti."

"What would you like to know?" Antonio asked, the words raspy. His mouth had gone embarrassingly dry.

"You're his banker. You tell me."

"You want to know where his money goes."

Fuente tapped the side of his nose and flashed a grin at Antonio.

It all came back to that original series of La Provincia transactions from two weeks ago, didn't it? The ones Antonio had confronted Lorenzo with during the meeting in San Luca. Antonio had to figure out where La Provincia's money had gone. And perhaps if he did, he'd be able to get Enrico's money back. "I'll see what I can do."

"I'll be in touch after Capodanno." New Year's Day was coming—Antonio had almost forgotten. Fuente buttoned his jacket with a flourish, as if he'd just accomplished a difficult, albeit enjoyable, task.

Antonio's eyes followed the man out of the building. He had a lot of work to do, and little time in which to do it.

And somehow he had to find Sandro too. Blood had been shed, and blood must be shed again. Vengeance was the least Antonio owed Cris Andretti.

CHAPTER 19

Antonio still couldn't believe Cris was dead. A heavy silence filled the car as they headed back to Milan. Finally he could stand it no longer, and he brought up the subject that had been troubling him since he'd caught the look on Lorenzo's face after the shooting. "I think Lorenzo had something to do with Cris's death."

Enrico raised a brow. "Why?"

"Cris gave me those tapes. Lorenzo wanted them."

"I thought Lorenzo was grooming Cris to take over. I know Lorenzo wants the bank. Why wouldn't he want his grandson to run it someday?"

Antonio held Enrico's gaze. "We *are* talking about the man who killed his own son."

Ruggero leaned forward. "There is nothing Lorenzo won't do. We must never forget that." After a moment he asked, "Why did you go after Fuente earlier?" Antonio quickly explained his need for the security footage.

"So what did the good Sottotenente want in exchange?" Enrico asked with a smirk. "There is always a price to pay."

"He wants to know where Lorenzo's money goes."

"I'd like to know that myself," Enrico said. "But we have to proceed very carefully. That banker in Liechtenstein is on Lorenzo's payroll. We can't let him know what we want."

Antonio looked at Ruggero. "Orlando seems to know computers well."

"He's been in a little trouble over it."

"Hacking?" Antonio asked.

Ruggero shrugged. "Among other things."

"I'll need his help with this."

Ruggero pinned him with that stare of his, his face and eyes unyielding. "You get him killed, and I will have to avenge him."

"That's not going to happen. Not if he's any better at covering his tracks."

"I'm not joking. My sister will have my balls if anything happens to him. She only agreed to let him be *contabile* because he'd be behind the scenes."

"Which is where he'll be."

"Not on this. If they trace him—"

"You don't think he can do this." Antonio's gut felt heavy. He'd thought he'd worked it all out. Now...

"He can. But I'd rather not risk having my nephew in Lorenzo Andretti's crosshairs."

"This life we live, it's a risk for all of us," Antonio said. "We know it when we take the vows. Orlando isn't ignorant, yes?"

Ruggero gazed out the window at the mountainside whipping by. "He knows. My sister knows."

"When are we initiating him?" Antonio asked Enrico.

"Tomorrow morning."

"Then we start after that," Antonio said. "There's no time to waste."

No one said anything further until they reached Enrico's estate. "Tonio, I need to speak with you," Enrico said as they were exiting the car.

"Can it wait?" Antonio wanted to get back to Bianca. He needed to tell her what had happened with Sandro. And to finish the proposal he'd started.

"It cannot."

Antonio swallowed down his impatience and followed the don inside and into his study. Ruggero came with them, but stopped at the door. Enrico motioned Ruggero inside, and Antonio wondered why. Was this some security matter? But Enrico hadn't said he wanted to speak with both of them. Had he changed his mind about letting Orlando help?

Antonio and Ruggero took the chairs in front of Enrico's desk. Enrico picked up the phone and made a call. "Matteo, I need you at the house. Immediately." He hung up, and dread coiled in Antonio's gut. Of course. They had no choice, now that Sandro had openly acted against them. Matteo would have to pay the price as well.

Ruggero sat forward. "Do you wish for me to do it?" he asked, his gravelly voice soft.

Enrico shook his head, his lips pressed into a thin line. Matteo was only nineteen, and he seemed to be on their side, but his father and both his brothers had acted against the family. And with Dario's accusation, Enrico had to act, or face persecution by La Provincia.

Still, the thought of what was about to happen sickened Antonio. Yet it had to be done.

When Matteo arrived, he glanced from one grave face to another and swallowed visibly. "What has Sandro done?" Matteo asked.

"He tried to kill Antonio and me. Instead, he killed Cris Andretti," Enrico said.

Matteo sat down abruptly on the large overstuffed chair by the sofa. It was also the chair closest to the door. Ruggero rose, lithe as a panther, to take a position by the door.

The boy's gaze followed Ruggero, and Matteo shook a little, his eyes glazed with fear. Then he took a deep breath and blew it out, a nervous smile flitting across his lips. He looked directly at Enrico and nodded. "Do what you must."

Antonio shifted in his seat, the squeak of the leather the only noise in the room. What courage. Matteo would make any father proud. Antonio was glad he wasn't in Enrico's shoes.

"I am sorry, Matteo," the don said as he rose. "You must die today." He walked over and squeezed Matteo's shoulder. "But, as your *compare*, I am bound to protect you. And I will do so."

"What?" Matteo stared up at the don in confusion.

"Ruggero will take you to a house. You will stay there until he brings you a new passport. You will be Davide Bellandi, a distant cousin of mine, and you will travel to Toronto, where you will join the *cosca* started by my father's uncle Alfredo. No one there will know your birth name. You will not contact your mother, your brother, or your sister. You are dead, as far as they know. *Capisci?*"

Matteo hesitated, then he nodded.

"Disobey me, and my vengeance will be swift."

"I understand." Matteo slipped out of the chair and knelt at the don's feet. He pressed his lips to Enrico's signet ring. "*Mille grazie*, Don Lucchesi."

The don urged Matteo up, then he embraced him and pressed kisses to both of the boy's cheeks. "*Vai con Dio*," he said. Then he nodded to Ruggero, who escorted Matteo outside.

"If the Andrettis ever figure it out—" Antonio started.

"Then I will pay the price. Matteo is a good boy. Loyal." The don put his hand on the back of the chair Matteo had so recently occupied. "He's sworn his loyalty to me three times. I have to trust him."

"And you swore to Don Domenico that you'd protect him."

"Yes."

"Signora Lucchesi and Bianca will be heartbroken."

The don walked over to the sideboard and poured them each a glass of sambuca before he took his seat behind the desk. "And you will tell them nothing to change that."

"But—"

Enrico cut him off with a slice of his hand. "I will make it easier for you."

"How?" Antonio snapped. How could he keep this from Bianca?

"We must forge an alliance with Gianluca d'Imperio. If Dario is against us, we have no choice."

"What does that have to do with me?" Antonio asked, and then the answer came to him. He shook his head. "No. You cannot ask me—"

"I am not asking."

"You think Gio will want me? After Cris?"

"She will come to accept it. As will you."

Antonio opened his mouth, but nothing came out at first. Finally he said, "I love Bianca. In fact, I was in the middle of proposing to her when you called about the meeting with Lorenzo."

"But you haven't asked, and she hasn't answered?"

He could lie to the don just this once, couldn't he? But as he met Enrico's eyes, he couldn't do it. "No. I haven't asked. Yet."

"And you won't."

"I've made love to her. Many times. She's no virgin."

The don sighed. "I am well aware of that."

"Who will you marry her to, then?"

Enrico shrugged. "Orlando, perhaps. In time."

A knot formed in Antonio's stomach. He couldn't let this happen. "She could be pregnant."

The don took a sip of his drink and gave him a thin smile. "You made that mistake once, and you aren't stupid, Tonio. Foolish sometimes, but not stupid."

Antonio struck a fist against the armrest of his chair. "I can't let you do this."

"You never asked my permission in the first place, did you?" The don stared at him, unblinking.

"No. But—"

"You knew she was my goddaughter."

"Yes. But—"

"You *knew*. And you knew what could happen."

"I did. It's just—"

"*Basta*. You know how we live. We need this alliance."

How could Enrico just sit there, so calm, so uncaring? How could he do this? Anger, white hot and scalding, erupted in Antonio's chest. He rose from his seat. "And what about you and Kate? She was another 'Ndranghetista's wife. An *Andretti's* wife. Whose permission did *you* ask?"

Enrico reddened. "That was different."

"Oh yes. It was so good for our alliances." He headed to the door, his chest heaving.

The don's deep voice stopped him. "You would rather I had let Kate die?"

He refused to turn around, but he admitted the truth. "Of course not."

The don said nothing for a moment, then he spoke. "You can have tonight with her, Tonio. But then it's finished. You hear me?"

Antonio still didn't turn around, but he nodded. No doubt the don would fill Ruggero in, and Ruggero would make sure there would be no slip-ups, no stolen opportunities.

No more Bianca.

———————•◆•———————

Bianca paced the length of Antonio's balcony yet again, her hands still trembling. Sandro had sounded too strange on the phone, his words rushed, cryptic, nearly unintelligible. *I've done it, Bee. The first step toward the end of them. It won't be long now.* When she'd asked him what he was talking about, he'd laughed, the sound strangled, high-pitched. Giddy. As if he were taking drugs, but that couldn't be. Sandro never touched them. Then he'd ended the call without answering her question.

She'd tried to call him back five times, but his phone just went to voice mail. She'd tried Matteo twice, but had the same response. When she'd called Mamma, she'd been careful to sound calm as she'd asked where her brothers were. But Mamma hadn't had any idea.

What was going on? It couldn't be good. Her only comfort was that Sandro hadn't mentioned Luca, and when she'd asked Beppe if he knew anything, he'd called Ruggero and confirmed that Luca was okay. But something in the guard's face had changed during the call, and his hand had edged across his chest toward the gun in his shoulder holster. However, when she'd asked what was wrong, Beppe had said nothing, and no amount of questioning would get a word from him.

She tried Antonio, and again she got voice mail. Finally she called Kate. "Do you know what's going on?" Bianca asked. "Something is wrong, but I can't reach anyone, and Beppe won't tell me."

Kate sighed. "I haven't been able to speak to Enrico yet. He's been holed up with Antonio and Ruggero since they got back from Milan. All I can guess is that the meeting didn't go well."

"Damn," Bianca muttered. This was all her fault. If she hadn't helped Sandro—

"I'm sure Tonio will tell you as soon as he's home."

Bianca agreed and hung up, even though she had no idea if Antonio would even be speaking to her when he returned. There had to be some way she could make up to him for helping Sandro. But how?

About thirty minutes later, Antonio arrived, his face grim. But it wasn't until he removed his coat and revealed the bloodstains on his shirt that her heart started to pound. She raced over to him, blurting out, "Are you hurt?"

"I'm fine. It's not my blood."

"Then whose?"

He looked over at Beppe and Ruggero, then took her hand and led her into the bedroom, closing the door behind them.

Fear clutched at her heart. "Is it Sandro's?" she whispered, the words half strangled.

He shook his head, his face crumpling. He glanced away and rubbed a hand over his eyes and inhaled deeply.

She grabbed his forearm. "Tell me," she begged.

"Sandro shot Cris."

"Is he okay?"

Antonio shook his head, still not meeting her gaze.

"How bad is it?"

He took another breath, a hitch in it as if he were in pain. "He's dead."

The world dropped out from under her. "*Dio mio*. Gio. She's going to be devastated."

"It's my fault," he whispered. "I should have stepped down. Sandro was trying to shoot me, and Cris—" His voice thickened to the point where he had to stop talking.

She folded her arms around him, wishing she could wipe away his anguish. And Gio's... *Cristo*, what Gio must be feeling. She gave Antonio a tight squeeze, then pulled her phone from the pocket of her jeans. "I've got to call Gio."

"Wait." He put a hand over hers.

"Why?"

"I'm not sure she knows yet." He paused, then looked away. "And there are complications."

"What do you mean?"

"Dario blames Enrico and me. He says the alliance is dead."

"No. He can't—"

"There's no child yet. He says he'll make Delfi divorce Nick."

"She wouldn't do what her father asks, would she?"

Antonio pursed his lips and gave her a hard look. "I know she loves Nick. But what would you do in her shoes?"

Bianca looked away. What she *had* done, all those years ago. She'd obeyed her father. For the good of the family. "Delfina's not me."

"Let's hope not." The words stung, and his face immediately softened. "I shouldn't have said that."

She ignored the comment; he had a point. "If she defies her father, what will happen?"

Antonio shrugged. "Dario is out for blood. I'm not sure anything can change that."

"He might cool down and see reason. Dario needs this alliance."

"Not if he reconciles with Lorenzo."

That wouldn't be good for anyone. "You said there were complications. As in plural."

He averted his gaze. "We need another alliance."

It took her a moment before she grasped what he'd said, and a dread icier than any she'd ever felt coiled around her heart, making her tremble inside. "Which one of us?"

"Me."

"To whom?" She wrapped her arms around herself.

"*Dio*, I—" He pressed the heels of his hands into his eyes. "I don't want to say."

"Tell me. Please."

He dropped his hands from his face. His eyes were wet. "It's Gio," he whispered.

She opened her mouth, but no words would come. How was she going to stand it? Seeing the man she loved married to her best friend?

He tried to take her by the shoulders, to fold her in his embrace, but she pulled away. "You can't," she said, her words barely audible.

"I know. I don't want to. But..."

He wasn't going to fight for them? "So this is how it's going to be? We just give up?"

"We have to save the *cosca*."

He sounded so miserable, she felt a pang of sympathy, but her anger quickly overrode it. "Was it just my imagination, or were you about to propose to me before you left for Milan?"

He said nothing for a long time, then he beckoned her to him, and his devastated expression made her take the two steps that brought them together. He clasped her tight, burying his face in her hair, letting out a sound that tightened her already constricted throat.

"You weren't imagining anything, Bee." His voice was hoarse, raw. "I still want to. I love you. I will never love another. I—"

She hushed him as tears rolled down her cheeks. She couldn't take another word. Choking back a sob, she said, "*Ti amo tanto.*"

They clung to each other for a long time. The tears overwhelmed her, pouring out of her uncontrollably. She sounded like a heartbroken child who'd had no idea until now what grief was.

Tonio tightened his hold on her, whispering his love, his devotion, his belief that somehow they'd fix this. But she couldn't allow herself to believe that. It would be foolish, suicidal, to do so.

Finally she got the better of her emotions and managed to tamp them down. Tonio dried her cheeks with his thumbs, his hands framing her face. Inexplicably, he smiled. "What?" she asked.

"You know, maybe my being an orphan will turn out to be a good thing."

"I don't follow."

"Gianluca is puffed up with pride. I doubt he'll accept me."

She hated to say it, to crush his hope, but it was best if they both accepted the hard truth. They were never going to be together. "Tonio, Gianluca has a son who needs a wife. And even though I'm no prize, neither is Leandro."

"Don't say that." The fervor in his tone matched the ferocity in his gaze. "You are worth a thousand Leandro d'Imperios. A million. Any man would be overjoyed to have you."

Dio, she loved him for believing in her, for meaning what he'd said, however deluded it was. "You think he'll be overjoyed to realize I'm far from a virgin?" She crossed her arms. "Assuming he's sober enough to notice?"

"Any man who can't see your worth is a fool."

"We're talking about a man who's probably snorted half of South America. He hardly seems like someone who'd notice my inner worth."

"Well then, we'll have to convince Gianluca to take me. I can't stand the thought of you being married to that cokehead." He fell silent and traced a finger along her cheekbone, then he tugged her close, and his mouth descended on hers with a fire that set her every nerve ending ablaze.

Bianca kissed him back desperately, barely keeping her tears at bay. This would be their last time together, and she poured everything she felt into their kiss. She reached for him, running her hand over his *cazzo*, but he stayed her. "I want to go slow," he said. "I want us to remember every moment."

Her throat closed shut again and the tears she'd been holding back spilled down her cheeks. Why couldn't he just let her lose herself in making love to him?

Because that's who he is. That's who he's always been.

She looked into his eyes, feeling like she'd been stripped of every bit of armor, every defense she'd ever had against the world, and him. There was a hole in her chest now, one that only he could fill. And he wouldn't be able to. Somehow she'd have to figure out how to go on without him.

She wiped at her wet face and sniffed back the rest of her tears. "You know what the worst thing about this is?" she asked.

"I can think of a million things."

She had to take a breath before she could say it out loud. "I wanted to have a baby with you. One we could keep."

A dozen emotions played across his face, then a light came into his eyes, and he gave her a grin that warmed her from the inside out. "You're a genius, Bee."

"What do you mean?"

"We're going to make that baby. And then no one can separate us."

———◆———

Bianca stared up at Antonio in shock. "Tonio, you can't possibly be serious."

"I am." Nothing had ever felt so right to him before.

"Enrico will kill you."

"He'll be angry, yes. But I can handle it."

She kept her eyes steady on his. "You're crazy. And I meant that literally about him killing you."

Would he? Perhaps. But Antonio was willing to bet against that possibility. "I'm not going to lose you."

A corner of her mouth curved up. "You truly want to do this? The timing is perfect, if you do."

"More than anything."

She bit her lip, but her uncertain smile grew until it lit up her entire face, then she flung herself at him, pulling him down into a sizzling kiss. She swirled her tongue around his, making him let out a muffled groan, and he slid his hands down to her ass and cupped it, squeezing. He yanked her against him, his *cazzo* a steel rod pressing into her soft belly. "I want you," he whispered against her lips.

"Only you," she agreed between kisses.

They stripped each other naked, then he hoisted her up and carried her to the bed, making her laugh when he tossed her on it. He climbed up beside her, his body intertwining with hers in a tangle of limbs. He kissed down the side of her throat, sucking and nibbling at her soft skin, pulling back just short of marking her. Bianca was his, she belonged to him, and he was going to keep her, no matter what he had to do.

She rolled him over on his back and straddled him, her face flushed, her eyes bright. "We'd better get to work."

He took hold of her hips. "If this is work, sign me up for a double shift."

Her laughter filled him with joy. This wasn't how he'd wanted to decide to have another child with her, and it was a huge risk, but he couldn't remember being happier. And it was all because of Bianca. His beautiful, wonderful Bianca. They'd both made mistakes, but only out of love.

She was already slick against him, and he flexed his hips, rocking her *figa* along the length of his aching *cazzo*. Bianca moaned and leaned forward, lifting herself off him so she could guide him inside her.

Dio, she was tight, the wet heat of her engulfing him, calling forth the instinct to pound into her. But he wanted this to last.

She braced herself on his shoulders, then rocked slowly up and down, her pace perfect and maddening at the same time. He looked down to where they were joined; the sight of his cock disappearing inside her was mesmerizing and almost unbearably sexy. Though he had an idea how to make it even hotter. She'd denied him once, but perhaps this time she wouldn't.

"Sit up," he said. "I want you to touch yourself."

Bianca paused, uncertainty in her gaze, then she sat back and he was so deep inside her he closed his eyes for a moment to focus on the pleasure. When he opened them, she'd tentatively raised her hands to her breasts, and she rolled the nipples between her fingers. "Like this?" she asked.

Not quite, but it was a start. "Imagine it's me touching you."

She closed her eyes, then tugged on her nipples, at the same time grinding down on him with a roll of her hips that elicited a low groan from him.

"Fuck, that feels good." He practically sighed the words.

She repeated the motion, then rose up until he was nearly out of her before she slid back down, each centimeter a delicious torture.

He slipped his right thumb between her legs, seeking and finding her engorged *grilletto*. Rubbing circles around it, but not quite touching it, he listened to her frustrated moans. She ground frantically on him, chasing his thumb, desperate for relief. He gave her a brief taste, then withdrew his hand.

"More," she breathed.

"I want to see you do it," he said, his tone more challenge than request. Their eyes met, and after a moment she accepted his assault on her modesty.

Averting her gaze, she reached down between her legs, her fingers grazing his pubic bone as she sought her target. She shivered when she found it, and he watched, fascinated, as her fingers worked frenziedly.

He didn't want her to come too soon though. "Slow down, open your eyes, and look at me."

She stilled, then raised her head, blushing a furious crimson. She started to withdraw her hand, but he clamped his fingers around her wrist. "There's nothing to be ashamed of. It's just you and me, and there's nothing sexier to me than watching you please yourself."

She raised a brow and gave him a shy smile. "*Davvero?*"

"Hell yes." He took the hand he was holding and guided his fingers over hers, pressing them into the lush dampness between her legs, until they reached her most sensitive spot. "Let me see you, Bee."

A flush spread from her cheeks to her neck and chest, but she did what he asked. He released her hand and lay back, watching her face, the jiggle of her breasts, the pumping of her hand, the swivel of her hips as she ground against him.

When her thighs started to tremble and her breath came in little pants, he took pity on her. "I want to watch you come."

She moaned and her movements turned frenetic, her hand almost a blur, her hips gyrating madly until she cried out. Her internal muscles clamped around him, squeezing like a velvety fist, and he came so quickly and so hard that it was a total surprise. He shuddered beneath her, his breathing harsh and rhythmic, like a locomotive.

Bianca tumbled down beside him, then swept her hair off her face and exhaled deeply. "That was strange. And amazing."

"What was so strange about it?"

She burrowed her face in his neck, but he could feel the rush of heat to her cheeks. "That's such a private thing you made me do."

"Yes, but I still don't understand why it was strange."

She punched him lightly in the ribs. "You don't get it." She shifted to look at him. "I always thought of you whenever I did it. So it was a little... odd and overwhelming to do it in front of you. While you were in me."

"It felt like I was spying on you?"

"Kind of. But it was also very hot. Like you were making one of my fantasies come true."

He smiled. "I want to make *all* your fantasies come true."

She returned his smile, but hers was a little tremulous. "If we have this baby, if we get to be a family, *that* would make all my fantasies come true."

Slowly he ran a finger along her bottom lip before kissing her. "Mine too."

He was not going to lose Bianca again. They'd spent too many lonely years apart; they'd gone through too much together. No matter what happened, somehow he'd make her his. They both deserved whatever happiness they could claw from this world, whatever happiness they could find to sustain their little raft, bobbing up and down in a sea both vast and heartless.

CHAPTER 20

The morning of Cris Andretti's funeral dawned cold and wet, the gray sky spitting down a freezing rain. The gloomy, somber day fit the occasion and Antonio's own mood. Cris hadn't lived to enjoy all the frenzy of San Silvestro and Capodanno, all the fireworks and festivities of New Year's Eve and New Year's Day.

How all that celebration over the last two days must have grated on Cris's family. Nick and Delfi had stopped by a few days ago, but neither was much in the mood to talk, and though they'd asked him to tell them what had happened when Cris had been shot, the two of them could hardly speak his name without tearing up. According to them, Dario had been locked in his study most of the time since Cris's death and refused to speak about it, and Ilaria had hardly said a word either. Neither of them had any insight into Dario's plans, what he was thinking.

There was only one bright spot about today: He'd finally get to see Bianca. It had been five days since he'd seen her, five endless days where she'd been cooped up at Enrico's estate. They'd called and sent texts, but nothing compared to the feel of her in his arms, her delicious scent enveloping him, her lush curves cradled against him.

She'd told him it would be at least two more weeks before she'd know if their plan had worked. He wasn't looking forward to the wait, the uncertainty. They'd made love twice more that night, but there were no guarantees.

Given Dario's threats, Ruggero had strongly suggested that Antonio and Enrico stay away from the funeral, but they overrode him, though they did take two extra guards besides Ruggero and Tommaso.

Antonio hadn't spoken to Enrico since their fight over Bianca, and a heavy silence had reigned over Antonio, Kate, Enrico, and Bianca as they drove to the large cathedral in the center of Como. But Antonio was only half-focused on the tension. His main concern was the woman next to him. Was Bianca carrying his child even now?

Kate was the one who broke the impasse. She took Enrico's hand, then leaned forward and took Antonio's where he sat across from them. "You two have to talk sometime," she said. "Now seems as good as any."

Antonio squeezed her hand lightly. "I have nothing to say."

"Bullshit," Kate said. She nudged Enrico. "What about you?"

"*Cara*, you're right. We do need to talk. But I'd rather not walk inside that church ready to strangle someone."

"Neither would I," Antonio said.

"Isn't that how you already feel, the both of you?" Kate asked.

Antonio released her hand and crossed his arms, careful not to touch Bianca as he shifted, though he fancied he could feel the heat of her thigh, only millimeters from his own. He stared out the window. A stiff breeze whipped the bare branches of the trees that lined the lake shore.

Bianca leaned forward and addressed Enrico. "Zio, after what you went through with Kate, how can you do this to us?"

It was an excellent question. Antonio's eyes snapped to the don's, curious what he would see there, but the don's face betrayed nothing. "If there was another way, I'd take it," Enrico said.

"What if Tonio and I weren't available? What would you do then?"

"I'd figure out some other arrangement."

Without looking, Bianca took Antonio's hand and pulled it to her lap, cradling it in both of hers. "Could you figure something else out anyway?"

As amazed at Bianca's persistence as he was, Antonio couldn't help his astonishment at the don's reply. "I'll try. But it may not be possible. Gianluca's trust in me has waned, and I'm not sure anything short of a marriage can repair the damage."

That was more of a concession than all of Antonio's bluster had accomplished. He squeezed her hand and smiled, trying to convey his admiration without speaking. And here he'd thought he was the strong one.

"See?" Kate said, directing her comment at Antonio.

He shrugged. "*Grazie*, Don Lucchesi."

Enrico sighed. "Tonio. Please. I'm only doing what I must to save this family."

Antonio crossed his arms again. "I know that. I want to save the *cosca* too. But not at my own expense."

"Sacrifices are often required of any leader. A *capo* is no different."

Antonio gave a pointed glance at Kate, then turned back to Enrico. "So you would ask me to do what you wouldn't do yourself?"

"I gave up a son. I married a woman I hadn't chosen for myself. I've made my sacrifices." The don's tone conveyed his frustration. "Besides, this situation is different. After the fiasco at the bank, we are in a precarious financial position."

"You mean you are," Antonio said. "And I am sorry about that."

"No, I mean the *cosca*." The don's voice was soft. "I have been shoring up our funds with my own for some time."

Antonio clenched his jaw. Damn it. Why hadn't Enrico said anything before? This wasn't good. At all. And now perhaps Antonio and Bianca had jeopardized everything. "I wish you'd told me earlier."

"You already felt bad enough about the bank."

"I am your second. I should have known."

"Now you do."

"We've got to recover that money from Lorenzo Andretti."

"Orlando hasn't had any luck so far," Enrico said.

"Give him time."

"We don't have forever. We will need to act soon."

"How soon?"

"A week. Maybe two."

Antonio's gut tightened. It wasn't enough time. He made one last appeal. "You know what a shit Leandro d'Imperio is."

"Yes. Which is why I suggested you and Giovanna."

"What about Matteo and Giovanna?" Bianca asked.

Antonio froze, his eyes darting to Enrico's. She didn't know?

Enrico stared at the carpeting beneath their feet, the purr of the limousine's engine and the smooth hiss of its tires the only noise. "What's wrong?" Bianca asked.

"Your father and your brothers betrayed this family," Enrico said.

Bianca's voice rose. "Matteo's done nothing."

"He supported Sandro for a time."

"But not now."

"You know our laws." The don met her gaze.

"You didn't." Her words were thick with emotion.

Kate stared at Enrico. "He's just a boy."

Enrico said nothing, and Bianca started to sob softly, the sound gutting Antonio.

Tears streaming down her face, Kate slapped Enrico, the crack of her hand against his cheek loud in the confines of the car. "How could you?" She moved to strike him again, and he grabbed her wrist.

"*Cara, per favore—*"

"You told me no innocents ever died by your hand. Was that a lie?"

Antonio leaned forward. "Tell them. Or I will."

Enrico pressed his lips into a firm line. "It's safest not to."

"We trust them with so much. Why not this?"

The don raked his hands through his hair, then he looked from Kate to Bianca. "You must never repeat this." He sighed. "I've exiled Matteo to Toronto. He will live under a new identity and be part of our *cosca* there. But he must never see any of you again or set foot on Italian soil."

"Why?" Bianca asked.

"Dario Andretti must believe that Matteo is dead. As Sandro soon will be. That's our only hope of repairing the rift."

"We have to tell Mamma," Bianca said.

"No."

"This will kill her." Bianca's brow wrinkled. "She must be worried by now. Why hasn't she called?"

"I allowed Matteo to tell her he was traveling on business for me. He wanted her to get used to him being gone before she heard."

"She must know the truth," Bianca said. "She can't lose so much."

"It might be easier for her this way. There can never be any contact."

"I beg you, Zio."

Kate clutched his hand. "*Caro*, you must tell her. It would be cruel not to."

"I need her to react naturally at Matteo's 'funeral.' The casket will have to be closed. That will raise suspicion right there, so I need her not to know."

"I'm not sure she'll be able to take it," Bianca said.

"Your mother is strong. It will be a blow, but we will soften it—afterward." He paused for a moment. "You have heard me?"

Bianca nodded. "I will obey your wishes."

Kate stroked the don's cheek where she'd slapped it. "*Mi dispiace*," she murmured.

"Your faith in me was not misplaced," Enrico said.

"I was just so shocked."

He took her hand and kissed the back of it. "You will have to stay that way, unless you wish to play the supportive wife."

She grinned. "Play? I *do* support you."

"And if I'd chosen to follow 'Ndrangheta law?"

"But you didn't."

"I'm within my rights. Matteo did support Sandro's claim at first. I'm taking an enormous risk on him. If Dario finds out, La Provincia won't hesitate to act against me."

Kate frowned. "I see your point." She sighed. "This business sucks."

Bianca giggled at Kate's choice of words, and the sound made Antonio chuckle. Soon they were all laughing, the sort of giddy, nervous laughter one might succumb to after narrowly avoiding a disaster.

The limo pulled up to the large Cattedrale di Santa Maria Assunta at the heart of Como, and they all sobered. This was not the time for laughter. Antonio instinctively patted the Glock under his left armpit. He met Enrico's eyes as they waited for the guards to surround the car before they got out. It wasn't likely that Dario would go after them at his son's funeral, but with tempers flying high, anything was possible. Enrico turned to Kate. "I suppose I still cannot talk you out of going inside."

She patted his cheek and kissed him. "If I survived Nick and Delfi's engagement party, I can survive this."

"Dario wants revenge for his son—"

She pressed a finger to Enrico's lips. "And he will get it when you take care of Sandro." She dropped her hand. "Dario's not a monster. He saved me from Carlo, after all."

"I hope you are right, *cara*."

Flanked by guards, they left the car and entered the centuries-old gothic cathedral. The soaring nave with its beautiful arches awed Antonio, as it was meant to do. Already the rows of wooden chairs in back were filling, and the pews in front were nearly packed. All the major *capi* and their families had arrived, everyone in sober black finery.

Cris's casket sat up front before the altar, and a fresh wave of sadness tightened Antonio's chest. Why had Cris done it?

Why had he sacrificed himself for Antonio?

Flowers filled the cathedral, their combined scent nearly overwhelming. The four of them headed up the aisle toward the front and found a place with Gianluca d'Imperio's family, which surprised Antonio. Just how far along were the negotiations? He got no indication from Gianluca or Giovanna, who had been dabbing her eyes before they arrived, and who broke into a fresh wave of tears when she saw Antonio and Bianca. Gio motioned for him to sit beside her, and he took the spot, Bianca to his left, then Kate, then Enrico on the aisle.

Antonio glanced nervously at Bianca to see her reaction, but she betrayed nothing. Gio clutched his hand, her own damp with tears. She pressed herself into his side and whispered, "Did Cris say anything about me, before—" Her voice cracked, and she stifled a sob.

"He said to tell you he was sorry." And because he knew it was true, even though Cris hadn't said it aloud, Antonio added, "And that he loved you, with all of his heart."

Gio collapsed into him, sobs racking her body, and Antonio put an arm around her. He met Gianluca's eyes over Gio's back, and her father nodded stiffly, giving his approval for the contact. *Merda.* Was Gianluca going to swallow his pride after all and accept Antonio as his son-in-law?

As Gio sobbed against him, her hands fisting in his suit jacket, he caught Leandro's gaze over Gianluca's shoulder. Leandro's lazy smirk and glazed eyes told Antonio he was high. He knew what Leandro had done to Delfi, what kind of man he was. Antonio couldn't let that happen to Bianca.

Which meant he had to accept Gio.

O Dio, there had to be another way, some other way to save the *cosca*. If Orlando couldn't trace Lorenzo's funds, Antonio had to prove his innocence. At least then, they could restore Gianluca's faith in them, and then perhaps some other solution could be worked out.

Or Antonio had to find Sandro and get him to confess to what he'd done at the bank—and to confirm whether Lorenzo had ordered Cris's death.

A wave of hisses for quiet swept through the great cathedral, and the susurration of voices died away. A few people shifted in their seats, the wood creaking beneath them, and some of the women sniffled, then all was as silent as a large gathering could be.

A row of priests filed out, followed by the bishop of the diocese. Antonio had never been much of a churchgoer, but he found the bishop's deep, sonorous voice comforting as he spoke of Cris's great fortune to be now in the kingdom of heaven.

A wail rose up from the front row, and Antonio realized it was coming from Delfi, who sat between Nick and Dario. Guilt gripped him. It should be him in the casket, not Cris.

He owed it to Cris to avenge him. He had to find Sandro, and soon. Everything depended on it: his future, Bianca's future, the Lucchesi *cosca*'s very existence.

———— • ————

His son was dead. Dario marveled that his own heart continued to beat, his lungs to draw breath, his eyes to see, his ears to hear, for all inside him was darkness, a void.

The dread he'd carried for so long, the fear for his children, had come to fruition. His son was dead. There would be no more sons to carry on his line, to bear his name. To call him Papà, to call him Nonno.

There would be no more.

Delfina let out another wail, her delicate hand clenching his to the point of pain. He should be comforting her, but what comfort was there to be had?

Ilaria sat silent on his right, her face a stone. She'd struck him and sobbed at the news five days ago, but since then, she'd been a ghost, her face pale, her eyes dark and ringed by shadow. The woman she'd been had disappeared, dead as surely as her son.

Their son. Their boy. Gone forever.

The bishop droned on about Cris being in heaven, how one day he'd be surrounded again by his loved ones, how even now he was in the embrace of his ancestors.

But it was all pretty bullshit, the lie they told themselves in the still of the night. There was nothing beyond this life, no great reward.

Certainly not for men such as they. Men who killed for what they wanted. Men who always got their way.

But none of them could defeat death. They were nothing. *He* was nothing. Powerless. All he had left was rage. Rage to fill the pit in his stomach, the hole in his chest.

If Enrico Lucchesi had done his job as *capo*, Cris would be alive.

If Antonio Legato had never been raised to *capo di società*, Cris would be alive.

If Sandro Lucchesi had never been suffered to live, Cris would be alive.

The Lucchesis had to be exterminated. Only then would Cris be avenged.

There was, of course, the problem of his daughter's marriage to Nick Clarkston, Enrico Lucchesi's son.

Cris had chosen Niccolò as his blood brother, and Dario had to honor his son's choice. He would spare Niccolò, but the tie through marriage to the Lucchesis had to be broken.

He'd already spoken to the bishop about an annulment. The bishop had assured him such a thing could be arranged, in light of Dario's generous donation to the diocese.

In time, Delfina would forgive him. She was young, and though she fancied herself in love with Niccolò, those feelings would die. Dario had already spoken to Gianluca about reviving the marriage pact they'd had. Leandro had to sober up, of course, and Dario would not tolerate any mistreatment of his daughter. He'd made that clear. He'd been wrong before, too accommodating, too worried about insulting Gianluca. He hadn't been a good father to his daughter back then.

He'd make up for that now.

Suddenly everyone around him was rising. It was time to say his final farewell to Cristoforo.

They filed up to the casket, Ilaria first, then Dario, followed by Delfina, Niccolò, Lorenzo, his wife Serafina, Sal Ruscino, and who knew who else.

Cris lay still, so very still, his eyes closed, his dark glossy curls framing a face that only recently had hardened into that of a young man. He'd never smile again, he'd never throw his arms around Dario again in that crushing bear hug he'd bestow whenever he was particularly happy.

Ilaria stroked Cris's brow, then pressed a kiss to his mouth. Tears streamed down her cheeks, yet she made no sound. Dario should do something for her, but his arms remained stiff at his sides, heavy as lead.

While she wrapped a rosary around Cris's hands, clasped together on his chest, Dario fingered Cris's knife in his pocket. The one Dario had bought him on his sixteenth birthday to celebrate his initiation into The Honored Society. Dario had thought about keeping it, but it should be with Cris.

Ilaria staggered away from the casket, and now it was his turn to say goodbye. He reached out to touch Cris's hand, grief strangling his throat. His son's skin was waxen to the touch. The last time Dario had touched him, as Cris lay dying, he'd been warm, his hot blood coating Dario's fingers, but now he was cold. Cold and stiff.

Gone.

Dario leaned over, pressed his lips to his son's frozen cheek, and slipped Cris's knife into the casket. Hot tears pricked his eyes, but he would not let them fall.

The rest of the ceremony passed in a blur—the mass, the bearing of the coffin to the waiting hearse, the drive to the cemetery. Dario had paid dearly for a permanent burial plot for Cris. He'd wanted his son in one place, forever, not disinterred and his remains crammed into a tiny box in a quarter century or so when the cemetery needed more room. Cris deserved more than that. Dario hadn't been able to protect him in life, but he'd certainly protect him in death.

At graveside, Lorenzo sidled up to him as Cris's friends and family said a few words. Dario heard none of it, beyond Niccolò saying that Cris had been a truly honorable man.

Lorenzo put a gnarled hand on Dario's shoulder. "My heart is heavy. He was a good boy."

"The best," Dario said. He hoped that would end the conversation. He didn't want to hear Lorenzo's latest scheme, didn't want to know what part Lorenzo wanted him to play. A sudden weariness overtook him.

But Lorenzo surprised him. "Have you given thought to who will replace Cristoforo?"

"No one can replace him," Dario snapped.

"Of course not. I meant your new *capo di società.*"

"No." It was true. Dario had avoided any such thoughts. He couldn't imagine having to make such a decision.

"You will need someone until you have another son who's of age."

Was he serious? "Ilaria is forty-one. I doubt we'll have another child."

"You could try. You should."

"She will have to decide that."

"Are you not master of your household?"

Dario stiffened. "A child is difficult at her age."

"Serafina gladly bore me three sons."

"Who are all dead."

"They had sons."

"Ah yes. Benedetto's boys." Dario cast hard eyes on Pietro and Severino, clustered around their mother Pia and their uncle, Sal Ruscino. "You trust them so much you chose Sal to be your second."

Lorenzo laughed. "There is Remo's son, Marcello. Or perhaps one of Concetta's."

Dario snorted. "You think I'd want another of her brood here? After Vincenzo? He'd have stabbed me in the back as soon as he felt secure in Papà's regard."

"Probably." Lorenzo squeezed Dario's shoulder, his fingers digging in with startling force. "You must have someone."

Niccolò would have been the logical choice, were he not a fucking Lucchesi.

Dario didn't like any of the options before him. He could choose one of his underbosses, but that could easily spark some level of envy and possibly lead to infighting.

"I could loan you Sal, until you've made a decision."

Did Lorenzo think him stupid, or just crippled by grief? *"Grazie*, but no."

"You must decide, and soon."

"I realize that."

"Or you could join me. Take Sal's place, and mine when I die."

What the hell was Lorenzo up to? He couldn't possibly mean that. Dario's cynicism must have shown on his face because Lorenzo let out a dry laugh.

"I know we haven't seen eye to eye. But we are Andrettis. Let this tragedy bring us together."

Dario said nothing and Lorenzo sighed. "We have both lost sons. You think me unfeeling because of Remo. And maybe I was, back then. But now, to have lost my other two…" His voice trailed off. "I've let everyone fear me, because it was helpful. But you are my blood. You have nothing to fear from me."

"As long as I do what you say and act in your best interests."

The old man gave him a wry smile. "Can you not accept the possibility of compromise?"

"I'm no fool."

"I am sincere, Dario. And we both share a common goal." Lorenzo's gaze drifted to Enrico Lucchesi.

True. But he wouldn't play lapdog to Lorenzo for any price. Perhaps there was a way to put Lorenzo in his place, a way to take the throne without submitting. The simplest strategy ever. The one Julius Caesar himself lived by.

Divide and conquer.

"What you say is true. I am not ready to make that decision, but I am willing to consider Sal, to see if he and I can work together." He paused, then dangled the carrot. "To see if the three of us can work together."

A gleam came into Lorenzo's eye. *"Bene.* I knew you'd see reason. Unlike your father."

But you don't know everything, Nonno. Far from it.

Dario would have his revenge, and so much more.

He'd be king.

Lorenzo drew Sal aside as everyone was leaving Cristoforo's graveside. They dropped back behind Pia, Serafina, and Benedetto's sons. His words were for Sal alone. "He has taken the bait."

Sal smiled, his rough features creasing. "You've made the arrangements with Concetta?"

Lorenzo nodded. If it kept Sal amenable, Lorenzo was willing to grant his wish. Prison had aged Sal, made him look older than his fifty-some years. He owed Sal for that, and he owed him a favor for remaining loyal. "Angelica will arrive in a month. You two can wed any time after that."

"*Bene*. I need sons."

"And you shall have them." *And they will be Andrettis, through and through.*

Lorenzo put a hand on Sal's shoulder and stopped, leaning heavily on his cane. He fingered the silver wolf's head, wishing he still had that creature's physical strength. "Be careful. He agreed, but he's suspicious of us."

"I know how to handle him."

"I want to know who he talks to, where he goes, where his money goes. And especially what he means to do about Lucchesi."

"It's unfortunate that Cristoforo is dead. We could have learned much more about the bank."

That was the one problem with Sal; he didn't see the long game, he was no tactician. But he was loyal and brutal, and that could be just as useful. "Soon we will own the Banca di Falcone, and we will know everything."

And the north would be Lorenzo's. Once he controlled access to every family's money, no one would dare oppose him.

CHAPTER 21

Since they hadn't been invited to the reception at the Andrettis, Antonio went back to Enrico's estate with the others. Nick and Delfina had promised to stop by that afternoon. But it was Gio who arrived first.

The four of them and Ruggero were sitting gloomily in the large drawing room at the front of the house. Antonio and Enrico had been playing a listless game of chess, both of them distracted and making poor moves, as Ruggero had pointed out more than once. Antonio was about to tell Ruggero he could play instead, when Gio walked in.

He hadn't really looked at her at the funeral—he'd been so uncomfortable sandwiched between her and Bianca—and her appearance shocked him. The blonde-streaked hair Gio had always been so proud of hung limp, and she appeared drained, lifeless, like a windup toy that had run out of power.

He wanted to do something for her, but before he could rise, Bianca had crossed the room and taken Gio in her arms. The gesture seemed too much for Gio, for she broke down in sobs again. "He's gone. He's not ever coming back," Gio choked out, and Antonio's throat closed up.

"Shh." Bianca stroked Gio's hair and steered her over to the far corner, where they sat on a large overstuffed sofa.

Antonio glanced at Kate, who shook her head slightly. Yes, he should leave them be. Gio needed her friend, and Bianca didn't need to be reminded of what was to come. Did Gio even know? Probably not.

Shortly after, Nick and Delfina arrived, the two of them ashen and stiff, especially Delfi. Nick had an arm around her waist, but something was off about the two of them.

Delfi went straight to Gio and Bianca, which set off a fresh round of crying between all three. *Cristo*. Would anyone here ever be the same? The women weren't afraid to express their grief, but the men were just as affected, no matter how they tried to suppress it. The two of them, Antonio and Enrico, had been into the liquor already. Even Ruggero had had a glass. Kate sat silent beside Enrico, touching his hand or knee periodically, as if to reassure herself that he was still alive.

Nick approached their group with his hands in his pockets, his shoulders hunched. His gave Antonio a brief nod before focusing on Enrico. "Dad. Papà. We need to talk."

Enrico sat back from the chessboard. "What is it?"

Just then, a shout of "No!" rose from the girls. It was Gio. "He can't do that to you," she said.

The men all turned questioning eyes to Nick. What had he done?

Nick's lips clamped into a tight line. "Dario has asked the bishop to annul our marriage."

"*Madonna*," Enrico said. "He cannot."

"There's no child," Nick said.

"Even so. On what grounds?" Enrico asked.

Nick shrugged. "We didn't get that far before Delfi stormed out."

"He cannot force you."

Nick's gaze dropped to the carpet. "He's threatened to report me to Interpol."

"Fuck," Kate said, and Antonio almost smiled. She had the worst vocabulary, though you'd never guess it to look at her.

"Then quit Interpol," Antonio said.

"It's not that easy, mate." Nick rubbed a hand over his face. "They'd have me up on charges. Delacourt—my boss—can protect me only so much if they start asking questions."

"*Figlio di puttana*," Ruggero muttered.

"That's about it," Nick agreed. "By the way, our luggage is in the car. Delfi doesn't want to leave her mum just yet, but we can't stay there."

Delfi came over, tears streaming down her cheeks, and wrapped her arms around Nick, burying her face in his chest for a moment. Then she straightened and sniffed her tears back and wiped at her eyes. She took hold of Nick's tie. "You and I have a job to do."

Nick raised an eyebrow. "A job?"

"Bianca gave me an idea. We'd better make a baby. Cris..." She paused, her voice breaking. "He would have wanted us to do this. To try." She turned to the rest of them. "My apologies for being so frank, but these are the facts. We need this baby. All of us."

Enrico rose and touched her cheek, tears in his eyes. "Delfina, I cannot beg your forgiveness enough. I feel responsible for Cris's death." Enrico's voice thickened. "He was a good boy, and he should have lived a long and happy life. He did not deserve this."

Delfina let out a sob and shook her head. "It's not your fault. You never could have predicted this would happen."

Enrico pressed a kiss to her forehead. "You are far too kind." Then he wiped his eyes and took Nick by the shoulders. "Baby or not, we will fix this. Do not worry. Once we have taken care of Sandro, Dario will see reason."

Jealousy swamped Antonio. Enrico would "fix" things for Nick, but there were no guarantees when it came to Antonio. Again. Because Nick was his son, and Antonio was... not.

He needed fresh air. He left the table, irritated anew when no one tried to stop him. He stalked out to the back terrace, suddenly annoyed with himself instead. When had he started expecting any different? Enrico had given him plenty, despite the difficulties that doing so had caused. Antonio should be grateful. None of them had it easy. And compared to Nick, who'd grown up thinking both his parents had abandoned him, Antonio's path had been much easier. Wasn't it natural for Enrico to do what he could for the son he'd been forced to ignore all those years?

I'm acting like a damn child. But still the ache in his chest remained.

A soft cough behind him made him turn. Bianca stood in the doorway. "Want some company?"

He nodded, a surge of gratitude welling up inside him. He wasn't alone. At least not for now.

She crossed the flagstones and put her arms around him, nestling into his embrace, chest to chest, hip to hip. "Are you okay?" she asked.

"Not really. I feel like this is all my fault."

"It's not."

"I knew I should have stepped down. Or if I'd just taken the shot when Sandro was in the bedroom with us—"

"Could you see him? Could you see where I was?"

"No, but—"

"You could have shot me. That's why you didn't do it. If anyone's to blame here, it's me for helping him."

He shook his head. "I wish we'd been able to talk back then. I wish I hadn't been so angry with you."

"If wishes were horses, beggars would ride."

She was right; he was being foolish, wishing for things, dreaming of a different past or future, instead of doing something concrete.

It was time to stop wallowing and fix things himself.

He stroked Bianca's cheek and kissed her, the touch tender and reverent, full of everything he didn't know how to say. She was his rock, and he needed to be hers. "I will fix this. All of it."

She smiled and kissed him back. "I know you will."

And he would. Or he'd die trying.

———— ✦ ————

Killing Cris had been a tactical mistake on Lorenzo's part, and Antonio would make sure he'd regret it. If all went well today, he'd have the evidence in hand to exonerate himself and prove Sandro guilty. Then all he'd have to do was tie Sandro to Lorenzo. Unfortunately, that would be no easy task.

He pushed his Alfa Romeo Spider hard, making the trip from the lake to Milan in well under forty-five minutes. He bounded up the steps to the bank and into his office, where he found Orlando hunched over his laptop, his brow furrowed in concentration. He barely glanced up at Antonio. "Tell me that espresso in your hand is for me," he said.

"Of course." Antonio deposited the cup on the desk and sat down on the edge so he could see over Orlando's shoulder. "Any progress?" Orlando had done nothing for the last four days other than try to hack into the bank in Liechtenstein.

"Sort of. I haven't been able to gain full network access, so I haven't been able to see everything that's been happening with those accounts, but I have been able to research some of those La Provincia transactions from before all this started."

"And?"

Orlando sat back and smiled. "I think we've got him."

A tingle started in Antonio's gut. He'd known something wasn't right.

"Half of those transactions went to various accounts that have been accessed through a bank in Russia. The account holders are dummy corporations, as far as I can tell. And you know what that means."

"*Mafiya*," Antonio said, pronouncing it the way the Russians did. "I'd bet good money those accounts have some tie to the Vilanoviches." The family of the *figlio di puttana* who'd nearly killed him.

"But we need to prove it."

Antonio pulled out his phone. "There might be someone who can help."

Orlando held up a hand. "Before you make that call, I found something else interesting. There are a lot of payments to another account that seems to be owned by someone here in Italy. But again, it's a maze of dummy corps that I haven't been able to crack. So we need to get to the bottom of that too. Lorenzo wouldn't give that kind of money to just anybody."

Orlando was right. Lorenzo wouldn't pay someone he thought he could control by other means. So whoever it was, that person most likely wasn't in the 'Ndrangheta and no doubt had a high level of power and influence.

Antonio dialed Nick. "Can you access the Interpol databases from here? I need you to look up the owners of some companies for me." He explained the situation to Nick as cryptically as possible.

"No worries. I'll call as soon as I have something," Nick assured him before getting off the line.

"Anything else?" Antonio said to Orlando. He tried not to fidget while he waited.

"There's been some activity on Sandro's account."

Antonio raised a brow. "What?"

Orlando turned the laptop so Antonio could get a better view, then cued up a video of a scruffy Sandro withdrawing money from an ATM.

"Where and when was this?"

"This morning. The Crescenzago district in Milan."

"He has to know we're watching."

"I'm sure he does. I doubt he'll go back to the same one." Orlando took a long pull on his cup of espresso.

"At least we know where he is." Though it wasn't much comfort. If Sandro was in Milan, it meant he probably had some plan up his sleeve.

Antonio's phone rang. Nick. "I got a hit." His excitement matched Antonio's own. "The Russian stuff is going to take a while, but I've got something on the Italian company. It belongs to Italo Baldassare. He's been on Interpol's radar for a while, so someone had already researched it and logged the details." He sighed. "If only we'd obtained this information through legal means, we could finally prove a Mafia connection."

Minchia! The Prime Minister of Italy was on Lorenzo's payroll, and that could only mean that Lorenzo was making a major play. A surge of triumph rocketed through Antonio. "Can you email me the details?"

"You'll have them in a minute."

They said their goodbyes, then Antonio turned to Orlando. "Keep working on the rest of those transactions. I want to know who else Lorenzo is paying off." He checked his watch and rose.

"Where are you going?" Orlando asked.

"To prove I wasn't here Natale morning."

————◆————

Antonio was late. He'd had trouble finding parking anywhere near the church of Santa Maria delle Grazie, home of *The Last Supper*. Why Fuente had chosen this place, probably the largest tourist attraction in Milan, he had no idea. It wasn't exactly private.

Antonio filed inside, going through the double airlocks with a large contingent of Japanese tourists, who chatted enthusiastically among themselves. Their chatter died down when they stepped inside and beheld da Vinci's masterpiece. Antonio had seen it before, but he still took a glance before searching for Fuente.

He spotted the *carabiniere* lounging at the far end of the railing that separated the viewers from the fresco. Fuente was out of uniform, instead sporting a stylish brown leather jacket and gloves over a pair of navy trousers. His characteristic cap was missing, but his black hair was still slicked back, not a strand out of place.

Antonio took the open spot at the railing beside Fuente, acting as if he didn't know the man. "Did you get the footage?" he asked, keeping his gaze trained on *The Last Supper*.

Fuente motioned to the painting. He obviously wasn't going to pretend he didn't know Antonio. "Don Lucchesi has another Judas in his family."

Antonio's pulse quickened. "Sandro? He's on the tapes?"

The officer stroked his mustache. "Do you have something for me?"

So that's how he wanted to play it. Fine. "Perhaps."

"You show me yours, I'll show you mine?" A teasing smile turned up a corner of Fuente's mouth.

Antonio almost rolled his eyes. "Outside." He took a last look at the painting, his gaze zeroing in on the figure of Judas, clutching his bag of silver. Except in Sandro's case, more than mere money had been at stake. His pride, his position, his future.

If only Sandro had been like Matteo, instead of like his father and his brother Fedele.

But what would Antonio have done differently if he'd been in Sandro's place? He'd like to think he'd have been loyal and trusting, but would he have? Or would he have allowed jealousy and mistrust to eat him up?

He led Fuente around the corner and down the block to his car. They got inside and both pulled out their phones. "The footage first," Antonio said.

"As you wish." Fuente started playing a video. In grainy black and white, Sandro appeared and walked up the front stairs to the bank. "Taken from the jewelers next door." Fuente pointed to the time signature in the corner. "Five thirty-five AM, December twenty-fifth."

Perfetto. "And the back entrance? Did you get any footage of that?"

"The restaurant behind the bank had a recording. No one went in or out that way all day."

"Send them both to me." He gave Fuente his email address at the bank.

Fuente typed a few words on his phone, then looked up. "Done. And the information I wanted?"

"Lorenzo Andretti is in bed with Italo Baldassare."

A sly expression passed over Fuente's face. "Anything else?"

"There's a possible connection to the Russians, but nothing definite."

"You will keep me informed."

"Of course." He started the car, signaling Fuente that the conversation was over.

The *carabiniere* laughed. "Young men are always so eager, so to the point."

Was that some kind of insult? Or was the man hitting on him? Antonio studied him, and Fuente burst out laughing. "You are safe with me. I only have eyes for my wife."

"What else do you want then?"

Fuente tapped the side of his nose. "Be on your toes. Lorenzo may be old, but he's not dead."

"I should be giving you the same warning."

"But I don't need it." Fuente winked, opened the car door, and stepped out, then poked his head back in. "*Ciao*," he said, giving Antonio a mocking little salute.

Antonio had what he needed, but Fuente's warning and his irritating salute bounced around in his head.

Lorenzo Andretti had been at least two steps ahead of them the entire time; what else did he have planned?

Sandro's stomach rumbled as he eyed the contents of the refrigerator in the Lambertis' kitchen. They'd apparently gone out for dinner, and he had some time before they returned.

Getting inside had taken some doing, but he'd managed to sneak up on the men Zio Enrico had put in place and had taken them out. All three were rotting in dumpsters now. He pressed a hand into his right side; all that activity had aggravated his wound and made it ache. Hopefully he hadn't pulled any stitches out.

Sandro pawed through various covered dishes until he ran across some lasagna that looked fresh. He found a fork and dug in. Not bad. Mamma's was better, but this would certainly do. He'd been eating a lot of crap the last six days; it was nice to have a home-cooked meal again.

If that *idiota* Cristoforo Andretti hadn't thrown himself in the way, all his problems would have been solved. Sandro had intended to shoot Antonio first, then Cristoforo, but that damn Ruggero had been too quick when he'd wanted to try again for Antonio. Lorenzo had actually ordered Sandro to go after Enrico first, but fuck that. Antonio was the one he owed a bullet.

Sandro would have shot Enrico if he'd had the time, but his uncle hadn't been his primary target back then. Though now that Matteo was dead, Sandro couldn't wait to put a bullet in Enrico too, and he would, once Legato was out of the way. Matteo hadn't deserved to die, any more than Papà or Fedele had. This whole mess was Zio Enrico's fault, and Sandro would get justice for his family before he was through.

Lorenzo had given Sandro an earful when he'd asked for help after the shooting at the bank, though the old man had been at least somewhat mollified that one of his three targets—Cristoforo—was gone.

Sandro took another mouthful of cold lasagna, the tang of the tomatoes lively on his tongue. He almost laughed. Ironic—Cristoforo Andretti, the one he'd had no grudge against, was the only one he'd gotten. Couldn't have been Cristoforo's bastard of a father, could it? Though the agonized shout that had come out of Dario's mouth had been some comfort. Yeah, that bastard was suffering plenty. It was almost enough payback for Fedele.

A boy's gleeful yell outside alerted Sandro to the return of the Lambertis. His sister's brat seemed to matter to Antonio, and that made him invaluable to Sandro. For now. He was going to kill Antonio Legato if it was the last thing he did, and the boy would be the bait that would lure Legato to his death.

Sandro set aside the dish and fork without a sound and tightened the silencer on his Beretta. The front door lock turned noisily, Fabrizio Lamberti's keys jangling, his wife telling Luca to be patient and not get in Papà's way.

He almost felt sorry for these people. They had nothing to do with any of this mess, but they'd had the misfortune to adopt Legato's bastard. A boy who was half Lucchesi, a boy who gave Legato some legitimate claim to his place in the *cosca*. A boy who couldn't be allowed to live.

Sandro flattened himself against the wall next to the front door. It swung open, and Fabrizio Lamberti entered. Before he could do more than raise an eyebrow at Sandro, the gun was at his temple. His wife, Marilena, screamed, and Sandro yanked her inside, little Luca already clinging to her leg in confusion. "Mamma?" he asked.

"Be quiet, *bambino*," she whispered.

"Whatever you want, you can have," Fabrizio said, his voice low and urgent.

"In the kitchen." Sandro motioned the woman and boy ahead, then herded them all through the house. He'd have Fabrizio tie Marilena to a chair, then Sandro would secure the man and take the boy—

The woman cleared the kitchen doorway and darted to the right. "Fuck!" Sandro shoved Fabrizio, making the man stumble and Luca cry out. Grabbing the boy by the scruff of his neck, Sandro dug his fingers into that tiny, fragile column of bone and sinew.

"Don't hurt him!" Fabrizio shouted, his hands raised in front of him as if he could somehow shield himself and his son.

"Subdue her, or he gets a bullet." The boy whimpered and the pungent odor of urine filled the air. Luca had pissed his pants. Fantastic.

Sandro propelled him into the kitchen. The wife was clutching a huge butcher knife, her knuckles white. The husband was begging her to drop it. When she saw Sandro and the boy come through the door, she screamed her son's name.

Sandro pressed the gun to the back of the boy's head. "Drop the knife." Her hand shook, then she released the weapon. It clattered to the tiles. Sandro motioned to the husband and pulled some plastic cable ties from his pocket. "Tie her to a chair with these." He tossed the ties on the table, then stepped aside to let the man work.

"What do you want?" Fabrizio demanded as he ushered his wife to a chair. "I can give you money. Just leave us alone."

"Shut up and tie her." Couldn't anyone do as they were told?

Luca sobbed and the wife called his name again. The boy darted forward, heedless of Sandro's gun, and Fabrizio grabbed up the boy, his wife bounding to her feet like a gazelle. *Porco Dio.*

Sandro raised the gun and brought the husband down, then the wife, two quick shots that took them just at the doorway leading to the front hall.

Fabrizio crumpled heavily, his son still clutched in his arms. They hit the tiles hard, the boy's head bouncing. *Damn it. He'd better not be dead.* Sandro wrested the boy from his father's grip, ignoring the pool of blood spreading from the man's head.

Sandro pressed two fingers to the boy's carotid. A steady pulse drummed there. Good. He was only unconscious.

The woman stirred. "Luca," she croaked, trying to rise, but her legs weren't working. Still carrying the boy, Sandro walked over to her, placed the gun at the base of her skull, and pulled the trigger.

He put another bullet in the father's head, just to be sure.

Luca was still out cold. Sandro laid the boy on the kitchen table, righted the chair that had fallen, then washed his hands at the sink. He retrieved the lasagna and the fork. Better eat while he could. No sense doing the rest of this tired *and* hungry.

The boy didn't stir. Good. He didn't need a hysterical sobbing kid on his hands, especially not now that he was so close.

Sandro finished the lasagna, wiped his mouth on a paper napkin, then placed the dish and fork in the sink, as if he were in his own home. He touched his aching side again; blood had seeped through the bandage. He inspected his red fingers to see how much. Not a lot, but he had pulled some stitches. Damn it.

He eyed the two bodies on the floor and shook his head. If only they'd done as he'd asked. He dragged them both into the kitchen and positioned them neatly side by side, heavy smears of blood streaking the cheerful yellow tiles. Then he gathered up the boy and took him out to the living room. He patted Luca's face until he woke. When the kid yelped, Sandro slapped a hand over his mouth. "Can you be a good boy? A quiet boy?"

Luca nodded. At last, someone who fucking listened.

Sandro removed his hand and pulled out his phone and dialed his sister. Time for Bianca to again play her part.

CHAPTER 22

Bianca was taking a quick turn around her uncle's gardens after dinner. After the ordeal of Matteo's fake funeral earlier in the day, she'd wanted to be alone for a while, but maybe this hadn't been the best idea, since she was in a skirt and hadn't put on tights. A freezing wind sliced across the lake, and she pulled her winter jacket tighter. Even though Matteo wasn't really dead, it almost felt like he was. She'd never see him again. Mamma had been relieved, but heartbroken, to learn the truth about Matteo's exile. Her nerves frayed, Francesca decided to stay at Enrico's for a while instead of going back to an empty house. It had taken a sedative, but her mother was finally sleeping.

Bianca sighed; *Dio* knew if she'd be getting any sleep. She missed Antonio so damn much. Those few moments she'd spent with him after Cris's funeral hadn't been nearly enough, that last tender kiss hadn't been nearly enough. Today, they'd shared only the briefest hug and clasping of hands, nothing more.

Antonio had sworn he'd fix things, and she knew he'd do whatever it took—even if it cost him his life. And that was what worried her. There were too many ways everything could go wrong.

She pressed a hand to her belly. What if Antonio's child were growing inside her? That would allow them to be together, but what about the rest? What about Lorenzo and Sandro? Would she and Antonio survive those threats as well?

All of this waiting—it drove her crazy, made her worry. Zio Enrico kept telling her that worry was a useless emotion. He was right, and yet she couldn't stop herself. How could her uncle be so calm in the face of all the threats to their family?

Her phone buzzed in her pocket and she stopped and pulled it out. The name on the display made her stomach flip. Sandro. "Listen carefully, dear sister." The nasty edge in Sandro's voice raised the hair on the back of her neck. "I've got your brat. If you want to see him alive, you'd better bring Legato to me. The two of you, alone."

Luca! A cold sweat broke out on her face and back. Sandro had her boy.

Or did he?

"Prove it. Prove that you have him."

Sandro sighed. "You'll regret this." She heard a slap and a boy's cry, then a rustling sound as the phone was moved. The harsh, fast breathing of a scared child filled her ears, and her heart thrashed in her chest.

"Luca?" she asked.

"*Sì*," he stuttered.

"Are you all right?"

"Mamma and Papà—"

The sound abruptly cut off and she heard another slap, then another, followed by Sandro's sharp "*Basta!*" Then silence.

"Sandro?" She hated how high and thin her voice sounded.

"I told you you'd regret it. *Now* will you listen and do as I say?"

"Yes, yes. Anything."

"Don't make promises you won't keep."

"I *will* do anything. Just don't hurt him."

"*Bene.* We're at the boy's home. You and that prick Legato have an hour to get here. Alone. You bring anyone else, and that's the end of little Luca."

"You wouldn't."

"You know what they say about dead men, Bee. Nothing to lose."

The line went silent, and anything else she might have said died in her throat.

With trembling fingers, she dialed Antonio. "I have to see you; it's urgent," she said as soon as he picked up.

"That's not possible." His tone was cagey, strained. Ruggero must be with him.

"Sandro's got Luca in Milan. We have one hour to get there. And it has to be just us."

"You stay where you are. I can handle this."

"I *must* go with you. Those are his terms. You and me. We deviate from that, and he'll shoot Luca."

"How the fuck—"

"We have one hour."

Something muffled the discussion at his end, but after a few words, Antonio was back on the line.

"Can you meet me at the café by my place? The one where you told me about Luca."

"I think so. I'm in my uncle's gardens. There's a gate on the north side, but I don't have the code. Do you know it?" she asked. Antonio rattled off the passcode, told her to hurry, then ended the call.

Her heart in her throat, Bianca raced along the hedge as darkness fell, repeating the code to the gate nonstop. She found the gate, punched in the passcode, and slipped through. She was outside, but she had no transportation, and walking would take too long.

Bianca hustled down the narrow alleyway between Enrico's estate and the one next door. Fortunately, the neighbors appeared to be having a party, and a group of smokers milled about in the rear garden, talking loudly. Maybe she could sneak inside, pretend to be a guest, and ask someone for a lift? But only if there was no perimeter fence inside the tall hedge surrounding the property.

She stuck a hand into the hedge and waved it back and forth, seeking any hint of a fence. Her knuckles struck metal and her heart sank. Damn.

Withdrawing her hand, she trotted farther down the dark alley between the homes, peering through the gloom, and a glint of something metallic in the lights from the front yard quickened her pulse. Could it be—yes! A row of Vespas lined up along the neighbor's house.

Her shoes drummed on the frozen ground as she sprinted over to them. Her hands frantic, she searched them all, hunting for someone's—anyone's—keys. Finally she was rewarded—the second to last, a beautiful, brand-new Vespa GTS 300 model, had a set dangling from the ignition. The ride was going to be freezing, but that wouldn't stop her.

She hopped on and started the Vespa with a quick crank of the keys. The engine gave a satisfying purr and she deftly maneuvered it from between the others, then shot out of the alleyway and headed to downtown Cernobbio, her hair whipping back from her face.

Bianca shivered, wishing she'd been wearing jeans and had a scarf and gloves, but nothing could have removed the chill from her heart. Sandro meant business. At least one person she loved would die tonight. Her son, her lover, or her brother.

Tears blurred her vision. *Dio, help me.*

She was praying for her brother's death.

———— ◆ ————

How the hell was he going to give Ruggero the slip this time? And Antonio also had Beppe to contend with. He needed to split them up, distract them.

He consulted his watch. They hadn't eaten dinner yet, and Ruggero should be about to have a cigarette. There was probably enough food in the fridge to scrape something together, but he could send Beppe to get them something else. He'd done it many times before.

His pulse revving, he asked them what they'd like, then called it in at Fontana's, a restaurant on the other side of town, so that Beppe would have to leave immediately.

Once Beppe was gone, it was just a matter of waiting for Ruggero to go out to the balcony. Antonio flipped the TV on, hoping that if he could find a game show, the noise would drive Ruggero outside.

He found what he was searching for. Amid a cacophony of flashing lights and bells, a tall busty blonde clapped her hands excitedly as the show's host announced that she'd move on to the bonus round.

"How can you watch this crap?" Ruggero growled.

Antonio motioned to the blonde. "I could watch her all day."

"Her tits are fake."

"Who cares?"

Ruggero shook his head. "Hard as rocks."

"Didn't know you were that picky."

"I don't trust anyone that insecure."

Come on, go outside! Antonio turned the sound up, and after a couple more minutes, Ruggero finally shook his head and rose, extracting a pack of cigarettes from his pocket. He was nearly to the door when he stopped. "Find something else, would you?"

"I'll see." *Go!*

At last, Ruggero opened the door and stepped out onto the balcony. Antonio waited a few moments, then he slipped out of the room and down the hall. Ruggero could finish a cigarette in under a minute, but hopefully he'd linger a bit because he hated Antonio's TV selection.

Antonio grabbed his coat, keys, and gun, then hurried out the front door, gently pulling it shut behind him.

He hadn't had time for a holster, so he stuck the gun in the outer pocket of his black leather jacket. He had to hurry. Any second now, Ruggero would come back in. He might think Antonio was in the bathroom, or he might fiddle with the TV, but it wouldn't be long before he realized Antonio had left.

His heart pounding, he hit the ground floor and raced out to his car. The Alfa started with a subdued roar, and he eased out of the spot just as the outer door to the building opened and Ruggero ran outside, the look on his face murderous. Antonio gunned the engine and shot down the street. The café was just a couple blocks away, and he had only a few minutes before Ruggero either called Beppe back or alerted Enrico, who could possibly send someone else close by after him.

He didn't want to take Bianca with him, didn't want her anywhere near this business, but if he showed up alone, there was no telling how Sandro would react.

Antonio whipped the car down a side street and saw a Vespa pull up to the café. The driver, a curvy brunette in a skirt—in this weather!—hopped off the scooter just as he realized who it was: Bianca. He halted beside her and she glanced up from her phone, which she'd no doubt been about to use to call him.

"Get in!" he shouted, and she had the door open and was inside in a flash.

He didn't wait for her to fasten her seatbelt. They had to make Milan in less than forty-five minutes, or Luca was dead.

———— ◆ ————

By the time they pulled up outside the Lambertis' apartment building, a heavy snow was falling, and Bianca's stomach was one huge knot. She'd imagined dozens of scenarios, many of them ending with Luca or Antonio dead. So many things could go wrong. Including how they approached Sandro.

Antonio started to open his door, and she put a hand on his chest. "Wait."

"What for?"

"Let me go in there. I might be able to talk sense into him. He'll just go crazy as soon as he sees you."

"And what if that doesn't work?"

"Then you come in and rescue me."

"That easy?"

She swallowed hard, trying to force herself into some semblance of calm. "I have faith in you."

He opened the glove box, revealing a Glock with a silencer and four loaded clips. He pocketed the lot.

"Were you expecting an army?" she asked.

He gave her a rueful smile. "I learned the hard way that you can never have too many guns or too much ammo." He patted his other pocket, where she realized he had another gun already.

"I hope you don't need all that firepower."

"I hope so too." He motioned under her seat. "Reach down and feel around. There's a Beretta under there."

She leaned forward and searched for the gun, finally finding it. She pulled it out and tried to hand it to him, but he stopped her. "I don't want you going in there unarmed." He stroked her cheek. "You know how to use it?"

"Sort of." She rested her cheek on his palm, the warmth of his hand going some distance toward thawing the block of ice inside her.

"Give it to me." He held out his hand. He took the gun from her and racked the slide. "It's ready to shoot, so don't put your finger on the trigger unless you're going to pull it." He handed the gun back. "Two hands, aim for the chest or belly. Don't try any of that one-handed sideways crap you see in the movies."

The gun felt cold and heavy in her hands. So much lethal power in such a small package. A chill raced through her, and she shuddered. He placed a hand over hers. "Remember, it's you or him. He's not your brother anymore. He's working for the enemy, and he's taken our child hostage."

She nodded, not sure she could speak past the lump in her throat. Either Sandro would be dead soon or Antonio would be, and nothing would be the same.

He leaned toward her, his leather jacket creaking. Light from the streetlamps slanted through the windscreen and across his face, casting it half in shadow. He looked hard, like some tough thug she didn't know. But his scent was all Antonio, and when his lips touched hers, her heart fluttered in her chest. This could be the last time they ever kissed.

She tugged him to her and wrapped her arms around his neck, clinging to him like a drowning swimmer who'd found a rock near the shore.

This time his kiss was fierce and passionate, not sweet and tender. "I love you," he murmured when she pulled back.

"I love you too," she said, stroking his jaw.

He gazed at her for a few moments, saying nothing. Then he kissed her one last time. "You have ten minutes. Then I'm coming in after you." He dug two matchbooks out of the glove box. "Use these to prop open the doors."

She took the matches. Everything she'd feared was really happening. Someone she loved was going to die. Her eyes blurred with tears, and he reached up, wiping them away. "Listen, change of plan. I'll go," he said.

She took his hand and shook her head. "No. I'll go. I just—" She couldn't say it.

"It's normal to be scared."

"It's not that. Well, not *all* that."

"Then?"

"I never thought I'd have to choose between my son and my brother."

"*He's* the one making you choose. This isn't your fault." He smiled at her, and she felt a tiny bit better. "And when we get out of this mess, we're going to get married. I don't give a fuck what Enrico says."

She let out a nervous laugh, her stomach doing funny little flips. She inhaled and exhaled deeply, hoping to steady herself. Without another word, she stepped out of the car.

The sound of the door closing behind her seemed loud in the still night. Her breath frosted the air as she pocketed the gun and headed up the stone walkway to the apartment building. Heavy snowflakes tumbled down upon her, clumping on her eyelashes, chilling her cheeks.

The Lambertis' car was parked on the street, and the cramp in her gut worsened. She stopped at the outer door and buzzed their apartment. Sandro's voice, heavy with static, came through the intercom. "You're late."

"The snow slowed us down."

No answer, just a buzz and the click of the door unlocking. Her hand, slick with sweat, slipped on the knob, and she wiped it on her skirt before trying again. Her fingers shook, but she managed to open the door. She almost forgot to set the matchbook in the doorjamb before she closed it.

Her eyes needed a second to adjust to the well-lit interior before she hurried down the hall to the Lambertis' apartment and tried the door. It wasn't locked. Again she put the matchbook in place. She stepped inside, and what she saw made her pulse spike. A woman's handbag lay on its side to the right of the entry door. Then a coppery odor hit her nose: blood.

Every cell in her body switched to high alert. She fancied she could hear a high humming sound, but it was probably just the blood rushing in her head. She looked to her left, down a shadowy corridor that led to a kitchen. Dark streaks on the tile made her reach into her pocket and grip the gun. If that blood was Luca's, *Dio* help her. She'd shoot Sandro in a heartbeat.

She was gasping, almost hyperventilating, and she forced herself to stop. To breathe in, to breathe out. The scent of blood had catapulted her brain into alarm mode, and she fought against the urge to turn tail and run. She had to do this for Luca.

"Sandro?" she called.

"In here." His voice came from the right, where the hallway branched past a demilune table with a mirror above it and a lovely white orchid in a pot.

She cautiously stepped down the hall, walking slowly and deliberately. No matter what she did, she couldn't let Sandro see how unnerved she was. It was imperative that she appear calm, matter of fact. She needed to talk reason into Sandro, to get him to let the Lambertis—if either of them were still alive—and Luca go. And she couldn't do that if she was a quaking mess.

Bianca passed a small powder room on her right, then a hallway that must lead to the bedrooms. On her left, an archway opened into an airy living room that probably looked quite lovely in the day. But now, with the black night swallowing up the view beyond the windows and Sandro holding Luca by the neck, a gun pressed to the boy's jaw, the room seemed a sinister joke. The homey, overstuffed furniture and plush area rugs seemed out of place, the lamps throwing monstrous shadows on the walls.

A bruise on Luca's forehead seemed to be his only injury, but the crotch of his trousers looked damp, which explained the scent of urine. Sandro hadn't shaved in days, and dark circles ringed his eyes. His jacket was gaping open, and a red patch about the size of his palm marred the right side of his shirt. That must be where Antonio had shot him. If she had to get physical with Sandro, he'd be vulnerable there. "Where's Legato?" he asked.

"Outside. In the car. I asked him to let me talk to you alone."

"He's the one I want. Get him."

She put a hand up. "Wait. Just hear me out." Her right hand tightened on the Beretta. "You need to let the Lambertis and Luca go. They're not involved; they're not who you're angry with."

He laughed, bitter and short. "The Lambertis are dead. They didn't listen to me." He jabbed the gun harder against Luca. "You want him to join them?"

Adrenaline surged through her, sending her system into overload. "No. Please, *Dio*, no." She took another breath, trying to steady herself. "Please let him go. He's my son. My flesh and blood. *Your* flesh and blood. Hasn't our family lost enough already?"

"I should let Legato's bastard live?"

"He's *my* son, Sandro. Mine." Her voice grew even, to her surprise. He was frightening Luca, and the anger that called forth gave her strength. "What you really want is Antonio, and I can help you get him."

"How?"

"I'll pretend to be your hostage." Anything to free her son. Antonio would understand the game she was playing. "You can send Luca outside."

Sandro shook his head and raised the gun. "No pretending."

CHAPTER 23

Dread ticked in him, like a clock counting down to the end of the world. Antonio swept his eyes over the street again, noting the various escape routes, both for a car and a person on foot. The snow could be a problem. Not only was it slippery, but it would show any footprints. Hopefully he wouldn't have to worry about that.

Drumming his fingers on the steering wheel, he checked his watch again. Damn it. He should have gone in there. He never should have let Bianca try to reason with Sandro. He pulled on a pair of thin leather gloves, then screwed the silencer on the Glock and pocketed it.

Adrenaline pulsing in his veins, he strode up to the building and eased open the door he'd seen her enter. His steps light, he walked down the hall and found the Lambertis' apartment and slipped inside, then stopped and listened. Luca whimpered softly. Bianca was speaking, her voice low, her speech rapid. "I don't want to see you die, Sandro. Why don't you leave the country? If you stay, they'll catch up to you. Even if you kill Antonio, Enrico will get you. You can't win."

Sandro laughed. "You must enjoy stating the obvious."

"I don't understand this. I know you feel wronged, but when did you turn suicidal?"

"Everything has been stolen from me. What's the point?"

"You can make another life."

Antonio crept down the hall until he reached the edge of an archway that opened into the room where the voices came from. Would Sandro just shoot him on the spot, or would he have something else in mind?

Crouching low, he peered around the edge. Fortunately, he was hidden from Sandro's view by the chair that Bianca was sitting on, Luca perched on her lap, his arms around her neck. Her right hand rested in her jacket pocket with the gun. She had Luca; why hadn't she tried to shoot Sandro?

"What other life is there for me?" Sandro asked. "I took the vows. I was raised in *this* life, *this* business. You think I can just walk away? They'll hunt me, except this time it'll be all the families, not just my own."

"Then ask Zio Enrico's forgiveness. He's your *compare*."

"He killed Matteo to appease the Andrettis. How can you not understand that it's too late?"

She sobbed. "Why did you get mixed up with Lorenzo Andretti?"

"I did what I had to do. My *capo* betrayed me."

"It was Papà who betrayed this family."

Sandro raised the gun, and Antonio stepped into the room. He had to distract Sandro from Bianca.

The gun immediately snapped to Antonio instead. "It's about time."

"Missed me? You should have called. I'd have been happy to come visit."

"The Lambertis are dead," Bianca said. Luca let out a sniffle.

That was not good news. Neither was the determined look on Sandro's face. "Let them go, Sandro. It's me you want."

"Drop the gun and kick it over to me." Antonio hesitated, and Sandro fired, the bullet hitting the plaster behind Antonio's head. "Drop it now."

Antonio started to lower the gun and Bianca screamed. "No!"

Jumping to his feet, Sandro trained the gun on her. "You always were a lying bitch, always out for yourself. You never cared about this family. You proved that when you opened your legs for this damn orphan instead of behaving yourself."

Two things happened almost simultaneously. Bianca lurched out of the chair and jammed Luca into Antonio's arms as Sandro raced forward and shoved his gun in her face. "Go!" she screamed as she elbowed Sandro in his injured right side. "Go, or I'll never forgive you!"

He didn't want to leave her, but he had to make sure Luca was safe. That was what they both wanted, the whole reason they'd come, the reason they were risking their lives.

Cradling Luca to his chest, Antonio bolted out of the room. Sandro yelled obscenities and fired at them. Bullets smashed into the wall behind him, and his gut clenched. He had to hope Sandro wouldn't shoot Bianca, or that she'd shoot him first. She had the Beretta. Was she too afraid to use it, even with Luca gone?

Antonio raced down the front walk and across the street into a dark alley he'd made note of earlier. He needed to hide Luca somewhere safe. Then he could go back for Bianca.

He spotted a dumpster halfway down the alley. Even in this cold, it reeked of garbage, but it was the best choice. He opened the lid and came face to face with one of the men Ruggero had posted at the Lambertis, his throat gaping open in a red gash. Thankfully Luca was still curled into his chest. He dropped the lid and took Luca to the other side of the bin and pushed it away from the wall far enough for the boy to crawl behind it. Fortunately, Luca was wearing a thick coat with a hood, and mittens were clipped to the ends of his sleeves. His pants were damp, but the ground beneath the dumpster was dry, and Antonio had worn the scarf Kate had made him; if he spread it on the ground, it would help keep Luca warm.

Antonio pried Luca's hands from around his neck and held them, looking into the boy's eyes. "Do you remember me, from the park? The day with the puppy?" Luca nodded, his face solemn. "Okay. Then you know I'd never hurt you, right?"

The boy nodded again. "I need you to crawl behind this dumpster and make yourself very small and very quiet. Can you do that?" After another nod, Antonio touched Luca's cheek. He took out his smartphone and set a timer for one hour. "You stay here until I get you, or until the phone starts beeping. If I don't come for you by then, you go to your apartment building and hit everyone's buzzer until someone answers. Okay?"

Luca nodded stiffly, then he finally spoke. "Mamma and Papà are hurt, aren't they?"

"We'll see. But stay here; don't go inside. I have to stop him."

"The bad man."

"Yes." He set Luca on the ground, zipped his jacket, pulled up the hood, and shoved the mittens over his hands, then used Kate's scarf to make a little nest for his son to sit on. He wished he could do more, but this would have to be enough. He waited until Luca crawled behind the dumpster. "You'll be a good boy for me, yes?" Luca nodded, his big blue eyes staring up at Antonio. *Per favore, Dio, don't let this be the last time I see my son.*

Antonio spun away before he caved in to the urge to pick up Luca and kiss him, then headed back to the open mouth of the alley. He'd heard no gunshots or anything else, and the silence frightened him. Had Sandro killed Bianca and slipped away?

He was about to leave the alley when he remembered his footprints. They made a clear path for Sandro to follow. Antonio grabbed fistfuls of snow, the cold and the wet soaking through the thin gloves. By strewing snow around the mouth of the alley, he obscured his tracks there, but it didn't do anything for the footprints that led straight to it. He kicked snow over some of them, but there wasn't much point. If they ended up outside, Antonio would have to do his best to distract Sandro from Luca.

Antonio dried his gloves on his jeans, then gripped the Glock and stalked up to the building, his heart thudding in his chest, his breathing shallow. Bianca had to be okay. He'd never forgive himself if she wasn't.

He crept inside the apartment, listening for the slightest whisper. Nothing. No sound. Silently, he glided down the hall, his back to the wall, the gun in both hands aimed in front of him. Where the fuck were they?

He eased up to the archway and crouched down, peering in on a scene that made his heart lurch into his throat. Bianca lay motionless on the floor, blood streaking her forehead, Sandro standing above her, staring at her body, his face contorted, as if he were in pain. Was he crying? Suddenly Bianca stirred, and Antonio must have made a noise, because Sandro's head shot up and he whipped the gun forward and fired it so quickly that all Antonio could do was duck around the corner.

"Legato!" Sandro roared, and the rush of his footsteps forced Antonio to his feet. He had to get Sandro away from Bianca. He turned and ran.

His throat tightened and his eyes burned as he raced through the apartment and out to the street. She had to be okay. She had to be. They were going to get married and have children and a life together. His beautiful Bianca had to be okay.

Another shot pinged off the passenger door of Antonio's Alfa, and he raced to the left, leading Sandro away from Bianca, away from Luca.

He ducked into a narrow alcove at the doorway to a business and took aim at Sandro from there. The bullet hit Sandro in the left shoulder, but that didn't seem to slow him down. Crouching behind a nearby car, Sandro fired again, then paused, possibly to reload, possibly to inspect his shoulder, and Antonio took off again, looking for a better vantage point.

Trains thundered somewhere nearby, their wheels screeching. He must be close to a railway station or train yard. There'd be plentiful places to hide and wait for Sandro.

Following the sounds, Antonio headed east, Sandro behind him, cursing him and firing off an occasional shot. Antonio stumbled into a rail yard and took shelter behind a nearby train car standing off on a siding. He had to find a way to hide his damn tracks; Sandro was right behind him. He tested the door on the empty car. It wasn't locked. He hefted himself inside, then raced to the other end and jumped out. The gap in his tracks wouldn't confuse Sandro for long, but it was something. He hit the ground, then rolled under the end of the car and pulled out the switchblade he had in his inside pocket. He flicked the knife open and waited, trying to still his breathing. If he could disable Sandro, he might be able to question him. To get the truth about Lorenzo, to avenge Cris.

The crunch of footsteps in snow wasn't loud, but it was enough to let Antonio know someone was coming. Sandro's voice echoed in the space between the cars. "What a fucking coward you are. Come out and face me!"

Poised to slit Sandro's Achilles tendon, Antonio waited until Sandro reached the end of the train car. But the bastard was wearing thick heavy boots like Antonio's. Still, he could do something. He stabbed the knife down, into the top of the boot closest to him. Despite his howl of pain, Sandro grabbed Antonio's forearm and dragged him halfway out into the snow. His legs still under the train, Antonio scrambled awkwardly to his feet, Sandro fighting him for the knife the entire time.

With his left hand, Antonio grabbed Sandro's throat, his fingers trying to crush the man's windpipe, but Sandro gave a grunt and headbutted him, their skulls knocking together hard. Antonio lost his grip, and Sandro squeezed Antonio's right wrist until the bones ground together. It was all Antonio could do to keep his hold on the switchblade.

Sandro kicked him in the shin and when Antonio's leg buckled, Antonio pulled Sandro down with him, the two of them grappling in the snow. Antonio pounded the bastard's face, but it wasn't until his fist mashed into the cartilage and bone of Sandro's nose that Sandro finally gave way. Antonio tossed Sandro onto his back and stabbed him in the thigh, twisting the knife until Sandro yelled. Panting, Antonio stared into Sandro's swollen, blood-streaked face. "This is for Cris Andretti."

"That *figlio di puttana* deserved to die."

"He was a better man than you. Much, much better." Antonio twisted the knife again. "This is for Raffaele."

Sandro gritted his teeth, his words seething out between his lips. "I can do this all day."

With a yank, Antonio pulled the knife out and plunged it in again, this time higher up, the tip striking bone, the shock of it traveling up his arm. "This is for Bianca." He gave the switchblade a vicious twist. Sandro's eyes slammed shut and he screamed. Antonio let up on the knife. "Did Lorenzo order you to kill Cris?"

Panting, Sandro looked up at him, then laughed, and Antonio pulled out the knife and struck again. Grunting with pain, Sandro swung wildly, slapping a flat palm over Antonio's right ear and producing a hollow pop. Pain seared through Antonio's eardrum, and all he could hear was a high-pitched ringing. His head spun, and his gorge rose into his throat. He jerked the knife out of Sandro's leg just before he vomited.

With a roar, Sandro threw him off and staggered up. He'd tossed his gun when Antonio had stabbed him, and now he hobbled to where it lay half-buried in the snow. Antonio dropped the knife and clawed in his pocket for the Glock, trying to stop retching, his eyes watering, his throat burning. He was going to die. He was going to die any moment if he couldn't get to his gun. He pulled it and tried to aim, but his head reeled and he couldn't focus. He shut his eyes, then forced them open, making another attempt. Sandro wavered in his vision and Antonio gagged again.

He was going to die. Sandro stood over him, gun pointed. As Sandro squeezed the trigger, Antonio threw up his gun hand to shield his face. The bullet tore into his right forearm, shattering the bones. His hand went limp, nerveless, and he dropped the Glock. It lay useless at his feet.

The death he'd momentarily warded off was coming for him, and this time it was inevitable. He saw it in Sandro's sneer of triumph. Sandro raised the gun again and sighted on Antonio. Antonio closed his eyes. It was over. He'd never see Bianca and Luca again. He'd failed Cris. He'd failed Enrico.

A shot rang out, but it wasn't from Sandro's gun. Sandro staggered and took a step forward, putting a hand to his upper belly, before falling to the ground. Bianca raced over to them, tears streaming down her face, the Beretta in her hand.

Sandro moaned and raised his gun, and Antonio threw himself on top of him, pinning Sandro's gun hand. Antonio looked up at Bianca. She spun crazily in his vision, and all he wanted to do was close his eyes. "You've got to finish him."

She raised the gun. It shook in her hands. Shook and finally fell back to her side. "I can't."

Sandro thrashed beneath him. "I'll kill you, I'll kill you," he growled and wrapped a hand around Antonio's injured forearm and yanked. White-hot agony enveloped him. Bile rose up Antonio's throat, and his vision went gray. If Sandro did that again, he'd pass out.

There wasn't any other choice. Sandro wouldn't stop. Antonio put out his left hand. "Give me the gun, Bee. Let me do this for you."

Bianca released a great wail, but she surrendered the gun. It was awkward to hold with his left hand, but he managed to shove it against Sandro's temple. He was about to pull the trigger, then he remembered. "Did Lorenzo order you to kill Cris? Or me, or Enrico?"

"*Vaffanculo.*"

"Did he?" Betting on Sandro's overdeveloped sense of justice, Antonio made one last appeal. "You want Lorenzo to skate away from this? You want him to get away with what he's done?" Sandro stared up at him, his whole face hardened with rage. "Please," Antonio added.

For a second, Sandro tensed, as if he'd received a blow, then he slumped back on the ground. Must have been from the gunshot wound. His eyes closed, and Antonio almost panicked. Was Sandro going to die without saying anything? "Sandro?"

His eyes popped back open, as stony as ever. "Lorenzo ordered it. All of you. Enrico first. Then Cris. You if I could."

A chill ran down Antonio's spine. He'd been right. And that meant there was still a target on his back. "If you're willing to say this in front of La Provincia, all can be forgiven. I'll step down from *capo di società*, and it'll be yours." Anything to save the bank, to save them all.

Sandro hawked a glob of spit into Antonio's face. "Fuck you and your leavings."

He'd tried. He'd tried. Bianca would have to remember that. "Don't look," he said to her, then he turned his own face away and pulled the trigger. Sandro jerked and shuddered beneath him, and the thick, coppery scent of blood flooded Antonio's nostrils.

It was finished. Sandro was dead. Bianca cried out, then muffled her sobs with her hands. Antonio exhaled long and hard. He wanted nothing more than to lie still, to wait for the spinning in his head to stop, but he had so much more to do. Bianca's tears came to an abrupt end. "Where's Luca?" she asked.

"Behind a dumpster. Not far from the apartment." Antonio tried to get to his feet and failed when the motion jerked his right arm, the pain instant and overwhelming. Both ears buzzed and the world spun. He looked at his right forearm, at the blood spurting out with every pump of his heart. Sandro must have hit an artery.

Bianca's gaze followed his, and she dropped to her knees beside him in the snow. She fumbled at his belt buckle and a funny thought hit him, making him laugh. "Now isn't the time, *dolcezza*."

"*Idiota*," she muttered. "I'm trying to save your life." She got his belt off and wrapped it around his arm, just below the elbow, cinching it tight. She tore a strip off her skirt, turning it from a modest just-above-the-knee length to a flirting-with-scandal one. He patted one of her bare thighs with his left hand. "You *are* trying to tempt me. Don't deny it." He wanted to keep her distracted; he didn't want her to focus on what he'd done to her brother.

She bound up his arm, ignoring his groans and hisses of pain, but she released a nervous laugh. "You're incorrigible."

"Kate calls me that too."

"Well, she's right."

"Can't help it," he mumbled. He felt so damn exhausted. He took a deep breath, closed his eyes, and wished his head would go still. The ringing abated slightly and the dizziness seemed to be receding. He still couldn't hear much out of that ear though.

Bianca patted his pockets. "Where's your phone? I can't find mine."

"It's with Luca. I set a timer for him, for one hour. I didn't think he could stay outside longer than that in this cold." He started to rise.

"Wait. Your face. There's some blood. Luca can't see that." She gathered up a couple handfuls of snow and washed them over his skin. Her breath hitched, then she let out a sob, and her eyes flicked in Sandro's direction.

Antonio touched one of her hands. "I'm sorry, Bee."

She sniffed back her tears and gulped down some air, then finished washing his face. Freezing water dripped down his neck and under his shirt collar, making him shiver. The only good thing was that it seemed to clear his head a little. She cleaned her hands in the snow beside him. "Can you walk?" she asked, her voice not quite steady.

"He shot my arm, not my leg. Just give me a hand up. I'll be okay."

Navigating him away from Sandro's body, she helped him to his feet, and he swayed a bit and gagged, then caught himself. Okay, so maybe he wasn't doing that well. But he'd make it to Luca.

"You should stay here. You need an ambulance."

"I'm not sitting down until I know he's safe."

"Tonio—"

"The sooner we get there, the sooner you can call."

She huffed with irritation, then put his good arm around her shoulders. He was surprised by how tempted he was to lean on her. Not good.

They walked as quickly as they could, trying to avoid the stares of the people who'd come out onto the street to see what the source of the gunshots had been, Antonio fighting the temptation to sit down again and again. His breathing was too fast, and his skin felt clammy. Could he be going into shock? A deep shiver almost drove him to his feet. Okay, that was a pretty clear answer. Despite Bianca's ministrations, he was still losing blood.

But they were close to the alley now. He pushed himself to keep going, even though the world kept threatening to spin away from him. "There," he said, pointing to the dumpster. Bianca shrugged out from under him and left him propped against a wall. He sank down on his haunches, then sat, his breath coming in harsh little gasps.

Bianca walked around to the far side of the dumpster. "Luca?" she called. There was a rustle of clothing, then Luca scrambled out and into her arms. She brought him over to Antonio and set him down.

His hands and knees covered in filth, the now-dirty blue scarf wrapped around him, Luca eyed Antonio with trepidation, his gaze glued to the bloody mess of Antonio's right arm. "It'll be okay," Antonio said.

Bianca took the phone from Luca and dialed Enrico, explaining where they were and what had happened. She ended the call, then said, "He's sending us his lawyer here in Milan." She then placed a call to emergency services, but Antonio was only dimly aware of what she said. He couldn't stop looking at Luca. They'd saved him. Their boy was still alive. That was all that mattered.

Luca's bottom lip started to quiver, and Antonio motioned him closer. The boy hesitated for a moment, then he was in Antonio's lap, his face buried in his chest. A lump formed in Antonio's throat as he curled his left arm around Luca. He was holding his son. Hopefully not for the last time.

He thought back to the dark smears of blood leading into the Lambertis' kitchen. Though there was joy in this moment, it had come at a terrible cost, and Luca would forever bear the scars.

CHAPTER 24

Antonio woke up in the hospital to find Kate, Enrico, and Ruggero at his bedside. But not Bianca.

An IV ran into his left arm and his right arm was sheathed in a cast. His head felt fuzzy, his mouth parched. His right ear still rang a little, but the world was no longer tilting at odd angles. "Where's Bianca?" he managed to croak.

Kate placed a hand on his good arm. "She's okay, but she's upset."

"Sandro."

She nodded. "And Luca."

A frisson of alarm ran down his back. "Was he hurt?"

"He's fine," Kate said. "But he's had a terrible shock. He'll need time."

She looked away, and he said the word that hung in the air. "But?"

After a moment she met his eyes. "Bianca wanted to take him, but of course, she couldn't. He's with his grandparents."

Merda. "What can we do?"

"What *should* we do?" Kate asked. "Luca knows them, not the two of you."

"But we're his blood."

Enrico interrupted. "You'd already decided he belonged to the Lambertis."

"Yes. But that was when his parents were still alive. Now..." He allowed the words to trail off. "He came to me. He climbed in my lap." His voice had thickened to an embarrassing degree. "He feels safe with me."

"He was in shock," Kate said gently. "He might not remember you."

"I never signed away my rights to him. The adoption was never legal." His words shook with vehemence.

"You're sure you want to fight this?" Enrico asked.

"Of course! We risked our lives to save him."

"You're the reason he was in danger," Ruggero said, his tone matter of fact, but not unkind.

"And he'll *stay* in danger, no matter what we do. Lorenzo Andretti could go after him at any time. I'd rather have him close and protected. Besides, his grandparents are in danger if they keep him."

Enrico crossed his arms and frowned. "You do have a point. Perhaps we can handle this privately."

"You'll speak to them, explain the situation?"

"No. You will."

"Me?"

"Let's see how Luca reacts to you. Maybe that will persuade them by itself."

"And if he doesn't react favorably?"

Enrico said nothing for a time. "Then you'll have to decide what you're willing to do."

It was time to say it. "I do know this: I'm marrying Bianca, no matter what you say."

The don took a deep breath and let it out through his nose. "All right, Tonio. I will not fight you on this."

"So we'll figure something else out?"

"We will. Somehow."

He would have smiled, but he hadn't won yet. What if Bianca no longer felt the same way? "I need to see Bianca."

Kate squeezed his hand. "Let her come to you. Trust me."

He clenched his teeth together. Had he fought so hard, only to lose everything?

———— ◆ ————

All Bianca could see was the bullet wound in Sandro's skull, the pool of blood beneath his head. For the last two days, the sight had haunted her dreams, haunted her waking thoughts. Shouldn't she have been able to do something different, something more, to fix things?

Shouldn't she have stayed away from Antonio? Or at least not taken up with him? Had she done so, maybe Sandro would have listened to her, taken her seriously.

She'd ruined everything. And now her brother was dead.

Mamma could barely speak to her—not out of anger, but out of grief. Her husband was dead, two of her sons were dead, and one might as well have been. Her house was nearly empty; only she and Bianca were left. Mamma's devastation weighed on Bianca, a millstone around her neck.

She ought to go see Antonio in the hospital, but she was afraid of how she'd react. Would she even be able to look at him without seeing him pull that trigger?

And then the loss of Luca again—it all seemed too much to bear.

Kate had called, told her Antonio was asking for her. But it was too soon; she had to be strong for him, not the other way around. She was more likely to break down than be of any comfort.

She'd needed a distraction, so she had come to the orphanage today to let the comfort of work, of routine, numb her to the horrors of the other night.

And then maybe afterward she could face Antonio with something other than sobs.

Kate wasn't in the office, which was a relief. She was probably at Antonio's bedside, but Bianca forced herself not to think of that. Instead, she typed away for a couple hours, transcribing files, but her mind kept wandering back to Antonio, to his childhood spent in this orphanage. How had Antonio felt, living in this building, roaming its halls? He'd said the Lucchesi Home for Children had saved his life, but had he been happy here?

Curiosity led her to look up his file. It was still on paper, in the Inactive drawers in Kate's office.

Bianca opened the thick manila folder. It featured photos taken of Antonio each year he'd been at the Lucchesi Home, along with reports from the social workers, his school transcripts, vaccination records, and a small stack of unopened letters rubber banded together under a piece of paper that said "Refused" in large black block letters.

The old rubber band broke when she tried to remove it. All four letters had been addressed to Antonio in a young girl's hand, and the postmarks indicated the letters were nearly eight years old. The return address on the backs said "V. Legato" and gave an address in Rome.

These letters must be from Violetta. Why hadn't Antonio opened them?

She tapped the first letter against her lips. Should she take them to Antonio? Would they help, or hurt?

Maybe she should open them first. It was prying, yes, but Antonio clearly harbored a lot of hurt about the past. Too much for him to willingly dig into it, to reconnect with his sister. But wouldn't it be good for him to do so?

Bianca couldn't fix everything, and she couldn't give Antonio Luca back. She couldn't give her mother her family back. But maybe she could return his sister to Antonio. Maybe she could do that much to make things right.

Picking up a long steel letter opener from Kate's desk, she slit the oldest letter open.

"Dear Tonio,

I miss you. I'm sorry I made Zio Gino angry and Zia Sylvana and you upset. I won't do it again. Will you please come back?"

The letter was embellished along the edges with stickers of kittens, puppies, and butterflies, interspersed with hand-drawn hearts and stars.

Her eyes filling with tears, Bianca traced her fingers over the stickers. How Antonio must have hurt over this, to turn his back on his sister, his family. She opened the other three letters, and the message in each one was roughly the same, only the pleading grew more intense.

A sudden anger shook her, making her shiver inside. How dare Antonio's uncle treat him so shabbily? How dare he turn his back on a boy who needed him? How dare he keep a brother and sister apart?

She studied the return address. The odds were good they still lived there. She grabbed her handbag and car keys.

She was going to pay Antonio's uncle a visit. And she was going to find Violetta. It was time Antonio had a family again.

———◆———

It was late afternoon when Bianca pulled up outside the address on Violetta's letter. The small apartment building seemed well-kept and neat, just like the others on its street. If Antonio's uncle had truly been so poor, it didn't show in the neighborhood.

The long drive south had given her plenty of time to think. Though she was still angry, she'd calmed somewhat. Part of her anger—a large part—was self-directed. She'd screwed up so many things, and right now she was probably making Antonio worry. But hopefully she'd make it up to him in the end. Family was too precious to lose.

Tears pricked at her eyes again as she remembered telling Mamma about Sandro. The only child her mother had left was Bianca. And Bianca couldn't even give her mother the joy of a grandchild. Because the *carabinieri* had taken Luca from her as soon as Antonio had been packed into an ambulance.

That was another reason she hadn't wanted to see Antonio yet. After everything they'd been through to save Luca, she'd lost him. She'd given him up to strangers again, just like that. She'd known it was hopeless to fight, known it would have only made things worse. Acting like a crazy woman wouldn't have helped their cause. This way, perhaps, she and Antonio might eventually be able to make some arrangement to see Luca again.

But letting Luca go a second time… it had been like ripping a limb from her. The depth of her attachment was frightening. How could she feel so strongly in such a short time?

Then again, she'd nurtured Luca inside her for nine long months. Almost a year she'd fretted over him, crooned to him, speculated about him. And then to finally meet him after all those years of separation, to finally hold him again…

Bianca moaned, unable to suppress her sobbing completely. She needed Luca back. Antonio needed him back. They needed to be the family they always should have been. But would the government see it the same way?

She wiped at her wet cheeks. She needed to pull herself together, or she was in danger of Antonio's family reporting her as a crazy woman indeed. Checking her makeup in the rearview mirror, she wetted a fingertip and wiped off her smudged mascara, then took a deep breath. She could do this. She *had* to do this. For Antonio.

Bianca opened the front gate and headed up the short walkway to the entrance, her heart fluttering in her chest, and pressed the intercom beside "Legato" in the list of tenants. A woman answered, and Bianca asked for Violetta. The outer door buzzed to let her in, and Bianca stepped inside, quickly finding their ground-floor apartment. She knocked on the door and tried to quell her nerves. What if Gino was there? What would she say?

After a few moments, she heard someone approach—someone female, to judge from the click of heels on tile. A middle-aged woman with lightly graying hair opened the door. She gave Bianca a polite, but quizzical look. For a second, Bianca wasn't sure how to start. Then she said the simple truth. "I'm a friend of Antonio Legato's. And I'm looking for his sister, Violetta."

The woman raised a hand to her chest, placing it in a protective gesture over her heart. "Has something happened to him?"

Oh dear. "No, he's fine. Well, he's in the hospital at the moment, but he'll be fine."

"Goodness. You gave me a fright."

"I'm so sorry." Bianca extended her hand. "I'm Bianca Lucchesi."

The woman took her hand and gave it a light shake. "I'm Antonio's aunt, Sylvana. But then you probably already knew that." She stepped away from the door and motioned Bianca inside. "Won't you come in?"

The apartment was neat and clean, and while not extravagant, it was nicely furnished. Again she wondered. Had they had a reversal of fortune in recent years, or had their so-called poverty been a lie?

"Is Violetta here?" Bianca asked.

"*Sì.* I'll call for her." Sylvana showed her into a cozy sitting room that was picking up the last of the day's weak sun. After asking Bianca if she'd like something to drink, Sylvana left the room and called down the hall for Violetta.

The slap of bare feet on tile preceded a tall, beautiful blonde girl with long hair. Bianca studied her, seeing traces of Antonio's looks reflected in Violetta's face. "Who are you?" Violetta asked, her words direct, but not a challenge.

Bianca was just introducing herself when Sylvana returned with espresso and a few slices of *panettone* for them to share. "It was our cake for Natale. But it's still good."

So maybe they weren't so well-off. Maybe they were just good at hiding it.

"What brings you here?" Sylvana asked.

Bianca focused on Violetta as she spoke. "Antonio will never do this, so I'm doing it for him. I think he needs his family in his life."

A look passed between Violetta and Sylvana, one that Bianca couldn't interpret. What was going on?

Violetta set down her piece of *panettone* and folded her hands together. "I'm not sure it's a good idea."

"I read your letters to him. The ones he didn't answer."

Violetta's eyes glittered with tears. "He showed them to you?"

"Not exactly." She waited a moment for Violetta to say something more, but she didn't. Sylvana wore a worried expression, but she wasn't any more forthcoming. Finally Bianca broke the silence. "Why wouldn't it be a good idea?"

Violetta fidgeted in her chair, staring at her hands. "It might be too painful for him."

"I'm sure he'd be happy to have his sister back."

In a soft voice, Violetta said, "His half sister, you mean."

Bianca wasn't sure she'd heard correctly. "Half sister?"

Violetta nodded, then glanced at her aunt. "We didn't have the same father."

Bianca's stomach tightened. *Merda.* What had she stepped into? "Does Antonio know?"

Again Violetta looked at Sylvana, who jumped in this time. "No. My husband didn't want anyone to know that his brother had been shamed."

"That's why he wouldn't take Antonio in?"

Sylvana dabbed at her tears with a napkin. "*Sì.* I wanted to take him, but Gino refused. He said..." She trailed off and shook her head.

"What did he say?"

"I won't repeat it."

"If you're trying to spare me, there's no need," Violetta said. "I heard you two fighting. I heard him call Mamma a *puttana*."

Sylvana closed her eyes and shook her head. "You shouldn't have heard that."

"But I did."

"Well, it's not true. A lot of marriages have rough patches. Your mother loved your father."

Violetta shrugged. "It doesn't matter now."

"It *does* matter," Bianca said. "I know it does. Antonio thinks he did something wrong. He's never understood why your uncle wouldn't take him. He needs to know."

Violetta grew still. "You think this news will make him happy?"

"Maybe not happy. But at least he'll know it wasn't his fault." Bianca sipped at her espresso, just to have something to do with her hands. "Don't you miss him?"

"All the time," Violetta said, and Bianca saw how very young Violetta still was at eighteen.

"Would you like to go back with me to Como? I think he could use some cheering up right about now."

"Where will I stay? It'll be too late to come back home today."

"You can stay with me. We have plenty of room." She somehow managed to keep the quaver out of her voice when she pictured those three empty rooms at the end of the hall. She turned to Sylvana. "Is that all right with you?"

Sylvana nodded. "Gino won't like it, but then I never liked what he did to Antonio. It wasn't right."

"No. It wasn't." Bianca left the bite in her words.

Violetta gave her a tentative smile. "I agree."

Sylvana reddened and ducked her head. "I should have pushed Gino more. This is my fault." She took a shuddering breath.

"Zia, no." Violetta rose and put an arm around her aunt. "Zio Gino is a difficult man."

"I'd like to show him difficult," Bianca said.

"I'd love to see that." Violetta giggled.

Sylvana leaned over and took Bianca's hand. "Tell me. How is Antonio? I've worried about him often."

"He's fine. Sort of. His job is… challenging. And my family hasn't always treated him well either."

"Are you two close?" Sylvana asked.

"Yes. He wants to marry me."

Sylvana smiled. "And you've said yes?"

"I want to. My family though…" She looked down at the floor, letting them draw their own conclusions.

"Is there any hope?" Sylvana asked.

"I'm not giving up on it."

Sylvana touched her knee. "Fight for him. I should have, and I will always regret my cowardice."

Bianca couldn't meet Sylvana's eyes. Was that who Bianca was: a coward who couldn't face the man she loved? She turned to Violetta. "Pack an overnight bag. We'd better get on the road."

They were getting in the car when a tired-looking, thick-waisted man in his late forties arrived, and Bianca quickly realized it was Gino. He grabbed Violetta by the shoulder. "What's going on?" he demanded. When Violetta explained, he turned to Bianca with a frown. "You have no right to interfere in this family."

All of the anger Bianca thought she'd let go came rushing back to the surface. She stabbed a finger in his chest. "You are a petty, small-minded man, and I don't take orders from your kind." She stopped for a moment and took a breath, trying to rein in her emotions. "Antonio was a child who needed protection and love, not scorn. Only a monster could turn his back on family."

"He's no family of mine."

"He's your niece's brother. That makes him family."

Gino stepped into Bianca's space, trying to force her to back down, but she held her ground. "I didn't need another mouth to feed. Especially not some bastard son of the slut who shamed my brother."

"Is that what I was to you?" Violetta asked. "Another mouth to feed?"

His features softened. "No. I've always loved you like my own."

She shook her head, her eyes glistening. "No, you haven't. You denied me my brother. I needed him, and you kept us apart."

Gino looked down at the wet ground. "You had your aunt and me."

"It wasn't enough. I wanted Tonio with me too. How could I be happy when he wasn't?"

"I was within my rights to refuse him."

"You're a horrible, horrible man." Bianca crossed her arms, staring at him with all the disdain she could muster.

After a moment he glanced away, then he opened the front gate. He stepped inside before turning back to them. "I loved my brother."

"And he loved Tonio." Violetta's voice was on the verge of breaking. "Why couldn't you see that?"

Gino said nothing, just shook his head and closed the gate behind him. Violetta wrapped her arms around herself, and Bianca pulled her into a hug, stroking Violetta's hair while she cried.

"You're going to see Tonio again," Bianca whispered. "It's going to be okay." When Violetta finally stepped away and wiped at her tears, Bianca picked up Violetta's bag and stowed it in the trunk. Maybe she hadn't won the fight with Gino, but she was glad she'd come.

She'd taken a stand, taken charge.

She was done running. She was done letting her family make decisions for her. She was done letting Antonio down.

CHAPTER 25

Antonio's arm throbbed in its cast and his head ached, but he didn't want to take any more painkillers. Not until he knew where Bianca was, that she was okay. That they had a future together.

He'd tried her mobile phone several times but there'd been no answer. Kate had wanted him to stay with her and Enrico after his release, but his pride made him say no, even when Enrico insisted.

He wasn't in the mood to see anyone. Not until he knew where he stood with Bianca. Could she ever forgive him for Sandro's death? He'd thought she had, but now... There had to be a reason she was staying away. A reason she hadn't called, a reason she wasn't answering the phone.

She hated him, after all.

And who could blame her? He'd killed her brother and urged Enrico to kill her father.

Yes, they all knew the rules. She'd even grown up with them. But knowing something and accepting it, believing in it, were two very different things. And clearly she was having a tough time coming to terms with what he'd done. Who he was. Who he was always going to be.

An 'Ndranghetista. A killer.

Ruggero stepped inside from the balcony. "There's some ziti in the fridge. Beppe picked it up yesterday."

Antonio shook his head. He couldn't think about food.

"Well, you can't drink." Ruggero motioned to the painkillers on the living room table.

"I'm fine," he snapped. No he wasn't. Not if he was yelling at Ruggero. He raised his good hand and shook his head. "I'm sorry."

Ruggero shrugged. "Food, booze, or fucking. Pick a distraction. You need one."

Fucking. Yeah, that isn't going to be happening any time soon.

He needed to get out of this flat. He needed to do... something. Anything but pace and worry.

212

Why hadn't she called?

The intercom for the front entrance buzzed, and then Antonio heard the voice he'd longed to hear: Bianca's.

His heart thumped hard. If she was here, she must at least want to talk to him. But that didn't mean she wanted to be with him. She could just have come to say goodbye face to face.

A few minutes later, Bianca knocked at the door and he let her in. She was followed by the shock of his life: Violetta. His sister gave him a tentative smile, and he couldn't stop his grin in response. Before he knew it, she had him wrapped in a tight hug. She reached up and patted his hair, her eyes filled with tears. "I've missed you so much," she choked out.

"Me too." A sudden warmth filled him. This must mean… He turned to Bianca. "Thank you."

She nodded. "It was the least I could do."

"The least?" He was lost.

"After Luca." She gazed away. "I lost him."

"That wasn't your fault. Kate and Enrico told me what happened."

She still wouldn't look at him. "I should—I should have taken him and run."

"Where would you have gone?"

"Somewhere," she said, emotion strangling the word. "Now I don't know what's going to happen."

"We'll get him back." He put a hand on the nape of her neck, his fingers gently stroking her skin.

She turned wet eyes to him. "I wish I had your faith."

"I can't believe, after all we've been through, that we'll lose him."

"Bad things happen all the time." Bianca's gaze slid between him and Violetta, and he realized with a chill that she was right. He and Violetta had lost their parents and their brother.

And he and Bianca could lose Luca.

He touched her cheek. "Whatever happens, we'll have each other."

She placed her hand over his. "You're sure?"

"I told Enrico I'm marrying you."

Her slow smile lit him up like a ray of sunshine. "And he said yes?"

Antonio grinned. "I've been told I'm irresistible when I really want something."

Violetta giggled and nodded. "Mamma always used to say that."

He hugged his sister to his side. "So what brings you here?"

She gave Bianca a glance, then looked at Ruggero and Beppe. "There's something I need to tell you, but it's private." She hesitated. "Bianca already knows."

"Ruggero knows everything about me."

"You might not want him to know this," Violetta said.

"Seriously, Vee, just say it."

She sighed and crossed her arms. "There's a reason why Zio Gino didn't take you in."

He wasn't going to like this. "And?"

"Papà wasn't your father."

Antonio's gut cramped. "That's not true. Zio Gino's full of—"

"Your eyes, Tonio. They're blue. Mine aren't. Aldo's weren't. Papà's weren't. Only Mamma's."

"That's not conclusive."

"She had an affair. Papà knew. He told Zio Gino. He forgave her and took her back. But she was already pregnant with you."

The room seemed to spin around him. Who the hell was he, then? He didn't even know his last name.

"Do you know who my father is?"

She shook her head. "I asked Zio Gino. He doesn't know."

He felt like he was going to be sick. So much of what he thought he knew about himself—how he'd shared Papà's irreverence, how they'd both been good at sports—he'd just wanted to see those things. But they hadn't really been there, had they?

Bianca touched his cheek. "*Caro*, are you okay?"

Antonio's face flushed hot and he felt a little dizzy. He looked at Ruggero, who had the grace to meet his eyes with a little shrug. "I could use that drink."

Ruggero laughed. "I'll warm up the ziti."

"Let's sit down," Bianca suggested.

The three of them sat on the sofa side by side, Violetta to his left, Bianca to his right. Both of them took one of his hands. "I'm sorry," Violetta said. "Maybe I shouldn't have told you."

He shook his head. "I'm glad you did, actually. It answers some questions."

Violetta squeezed his hand. "I'm still your sister."

He leaned over and kissed her cheek. "Can you forgive me for how I acted? I should have answered your letters. It was… it wasn't right of me not to."

Her eyes filled with tears. "You had every right to be hurt. Zia Sylvana felt horrible about it."

"But *he* doesn't."

"I think he does now, a little. After what Bianca said to him."

Bianca cut in. "After what *you* said, you mean."

"What did you say?" Antonio asked his sister.

Violetta stared down at her hand in Antonio's. "It doesn't matter. He doesn't control me anymore. I'll be done with school soon, and then I could move up here. To be near you."

"I'd like that. Very much."

They caught up on Violetta's life—what she wanted to study at university, who she was dating, her plans for the future—until Ruggero called them in to the kitchen. Antonio smiled to see Ruggero in an apron, then he noticed the butt of Ruggero's Glock lying half behind a loaf of bread. He motioned to the gun with his eyes, and Ruggero concealed it, but not before Violetta saw the quick movement. Her gaze traveled from Antonio to Ruggero, then back again. Then she looked around the beautifully appointed kitchen.

Antonio waited for the questions, tried to decide what lies to tell her. But when she finally turned to him, she said, "You're a man of honor." There was no question in her voice.

He nodded slowly, waiting for her reaction. She picked up her fork and took a bite of the ziti, studying the scar that ran down one side of Ruggero's face. Then she said, "I wondered why you had two guards. And how you could afford all this." She gestured around with the fork.

"And?"

She gave him a level gaze. "It's not like Zio Gino left you with a lot of options." She took another bite of ziti. "Mamma always did say you were like a cat, always landing on your feet."

Antonio didn't know how to respond. He'd expected hysterics, or at least disapproval. Not his sister's cool assessment of the facts.

She addressed Bianca. "And your family is too, I suppose?"

Bianca froze and looked at Antonio. He put a hand over Violetta's. "It's best you know as little as possible."

"I want to be part of your life, Tonio."

"I want that too, but—"

"It's dangerous, I know that. But can't I stay on the periphery? I want to be your sister still. Even if it's from Rome."

He wanted that too. "That would be safest."

She took another forkful of ziti. "So, when are you two getting married?" She grinned at him and Bianca.

"I haven't quite asked."

Bianca smiled. "You don't need to."

He shook his head. "I do." He rose and motioned for them to remain seated. "I'll be right back."

His pulse quickening, he retrieved the small velvet box from Parini's and took a breath to settle his nerves. Now was as good a time as any.

A burst of laughter came from the kitchen, and he stopped in the hallway and listened, his throat going tight. He *had* a family, no matter what had happened in the past. He had one now.

He blinked hard and swallowed, then stepped into the kitchen. When Bianca saw the box in his hand, she smiled, her lips trembling, and her eyes shone with tears. Before she could say anything, he got down on one knee beside her. "I'd planned to do this before, but then Cris was killed—"

She nodded and touched his cheek. "You don't have to explain."

He opened the box to show her the ring. "I love you, Bianca, with every bit of my heart. I can't imagine a future without you by my side. Will you do me the great honor of becoming my wife?"

She smiled as tears streamed down her cheeks. "Happily," she managed to say.

He put the ring on her finger, then kissed her, a long, lingering kiss that said everything words could not. That he'd give her his heart, his soul. That he already had.

———— ◆ ————

After conferring with Orlando, Nick, and Enrico, Antonio was finally getting his chance to confront Lorenzo with the damning evidence of his transgressions.

They'd decided to invite everyone who'd attended the deadly meeting at the

Banca di Falcone a week and a half ago, but this time the meeting would be held at Enrico's home under the tightest security. Ruggero was in charge of the guards frisking their guests—over their protests. The only one who didn't complain was Lorenzo. He submitted to the pat-down with a sly smile.

The men assembled in the dining room. Enrico took the position at the head of the table, Don Vittorio Battista at the other end. Lorenzo and Dario took the positions across from each other at the middle, with Gianluca d'Imperio, his son Leandro, Antonio, Nick, and Sal Ruscino filling in around them. Only one chair remained empty: the one to Dario's right. The one Cris would have occupied had he still been alive.

Antonio couldn't help staring at that void, a great sadness clutching at his throat and making him have to swallow hard. He avoided Dario's gaze, but when he accidentally locked eyes with Nick, the pain he saw in them was a mirror for his own. They'd both been close to Cris, but Nick's bond had been far tighter than Antonio's. He and Cris had been blood brothers, united by a near-death experience.

He tore his eyes away from Nick's. He knew Nick didn't blame him for Cris's death, and yet Antonio couldn't shake the feeling that he was responsible for it, that somehow he could have, should have, done something differently.

A stack of printouts and a tablet computer sat in front of Antonio, the things he'd use to prove his innocence. However, the thing he most wished he had was Sandro's confession on tape. Bianca waited outside in case the others wanted corroboration of his statement. Even then, Lorenzo could poke holes in what he'd say. But still the statement had to be made. The others—especially Dario—needed to know where they stood with Lorenzo. It hadn't escaped Antonio's notice that Dario had seemed almost chummy with Lorenzo and Sal when they'd arrived today, and that was not a welcome development.

Enrico rose and leaned forward, placing both his hands palms down on the table. He looked like the stalwart captain of a ship about to address his crew. Antonio couldn't help but admire the don's calm, his strength, as he faced a room almost half-full of bitter enemies and men who regarded him with suspicion. Winning the d'Imperios back wasn't just a secondary goal today; it was critical to the continued survival of the Lucchesi *cosca*. Mollifying Dario and trying to regain their alliance with him would be their third aim, as remote as the chance of success was. The don's eyes swept the table, coming to a brief rest on Antonio before he addressed the others. "I've called you all here today, not only to right a wrong, but to restore your faith in me, my *capo di società*, the Lucchesi *cosca*, and the Banca di Falcone. Today we will prove ourselves innocent of the charges leveled against us." He nodded at Antonio, then took his seat.

Antonio's stomach flipped and he cleared his throat, hoping his voice wouldn't betray his nerves. Appearances, perceptions, were as critical as actual facts today. And he needed to appear one-hundred-percent confident, one-hundred-percent calm. Matter of fact. He picked up the stack of printouts and separated it into three piles. "What I have here tells the full story of what's been happening during the last month. How La Provincia's account had been nearly drained while under Benedetto's control and then again while under Lorenzo's, how a series of manipulations by Sandro Lucchesi made it appear that the account had been

Enrico showed Gianluca and Leandro out, then he and Antonio went back to the dining room. The odds of success were slim, even worse with Sal in the room; still, they had to try.

They moved down to the far end of the table with the others. Nick and Don Battista had been speaking quietly, as had Dario and Sal, but both conversations stopped at their approach, and Dario turned eyes hard as flint to them. "So what 'family matter' did you wish to discuss?"

"You know what I mean," Enrico said, his voice soft.

"They will divorce." Dario didn't look at Nick when he spoke.

"We will not." Nick thumped the table to underline his words.

"The annulment has been arranged."

"I believe Delfi is pregnant," Nick said.

They all turned to him. How could he possibly know so soon?

Dario crossed his arms. "So this is your plan? Get her pregnant?"

Nick leaned forward. "I will not lose her." He pressed a palm against the polished wood of the table. "Cris wouldn't want this. Remember how happy he was at the wedding?"

Dario opened his mouth as if to speak. He looked down and said nothing for a moment, then blinked furiously before addressing Enrico. "Your unwillingness to follow our laws got my son killed. You *stole* him from me. That is something I can never forget, much less forgive."

He turned to Antonio, his eyes blazing. "You have even stolen my right to avenge my son. My only satisfaction is that Sandro"—he spit on the floor beside him—"had a closed casket. But that snake should have died hard, and by *my* hand."

Antonio didn't know what to say in the face of that rage, that grief. "If there had been any other way..."

Dario turned from him and rose. "If we are now bound by blood, I will bury my vendetta alongside my son. However, I will not be your friend. You are dead to me, Enrico Lucchesi. You do not exist."

Enrico opened his mouth to respond, and Dario raised a hand. "Dead men don't speak."

When Dario started to step from the table, Antonio grabbed his arm to stay him. "Your grandfather took your son from you. I am telling you the truth. I loved Cris too. We all did. But Cris gave me the recordings of Don Domenico, and Lorenzo does not like to be defied. You know this."

Dario yanked his arm from Antonio's grasp. Without another word, he left, Sal following behind, the faintest trace of a smile on his lips.

They'd won a small victory today, but had certainly lost perhaps the more crucial battle. Dario had made up his mind, and should Delfina prove not to be pregnant, there was little doubt Dario would wage all-out war against them. The four of them looked at each other. Don Battista came around the table and embraced Enrico. "We'll survive this," he said.

Antonio hoped the old man was right. Dario had gunned for them before, but he'd had a cooler head back then. Now he was liable to do anything.

Including partnering with his grandfather. They'd never faced the Andrettis united, and the prospect was more than a little daunting.

CHAPTER 26

Dario stormed out of Enrico Lucchesi's villa, careful to keep his face averted as he fought for control. He couldn't allow Sal to see how upset he was. Enrico had the nerve to try to talk to him? As if they were having nothing more than a minor spat? And then Delfina—he should have known she'd think of a way to thwart him. Of course. He'd been a fool not to separate her from Nick.

But the worst blow had been Lorenzo. As soon as Legato had said the words, Dario had known them to be true. He should have seen it himself.

Lorenzo does not like to be defied. You know this.

All those years ago, Lorenzo had killed Remo, his own son; ordering the death of a grandson? That would be nothing to him. Like killing a dog.

Before he was done, Dario would see the old man rot in hell.

Dario hadn't lied when he'd said he'd bury his vendetta. Oh yes, he would. He'd bury it beneath a placid surface, beneath a mountain of remembrance, beneath a heart of staunch, unforgiving iron. He'd let Lucchesi think he was safe enough. Let Sal and Lorenzo think he was too numb with grief to plan, too enraged at Lucchesi to hear the truth. Let them all think he was incapable of acting in his own best interests, incapable of seeking vengeance for his boy. Incapable of seeing them all in their graves.

Divide and conquer. It was time to start.

He turned to Sal as they got in the back of the car. "We need to talk. What has my grandfather promised you?"

Sal leaned back in his seat and tapped a blunt forefinger against his thin lips. "A wife. Concetta's girl. Angelica."

Dario smiled. "Only a wife? I believe we can do better than that."

———◆———

Enrico summoned Antonio and Bianca to the house the next afternoon. To Antonio's surprise, the underbosses of the *cosca* were there. So was Orlando. And

Vittorio Battista, Enrico's *padrino*. And Francesca Lucchesi. The last time they'd all been assembled at Enrico's home was for Matteo's "funeral" less than a week ago. So why were they here now?

Along with Kate, Nick, and Delfina, they all gathered in the sitting room at the front of the house, more cramped accommodations than the spacious garden in back, but a heavy snow was falling today, all the trees and shrubs blanketed in a thick white cloud.

Once everyone had settled into a loose semicircle before the fire crackling in the hearth, Don Battista walked to the front. He smiled at the crowd and smoothed a finger along one side of his mustache. Then he addressed Antonio and Enrico. "Please step forward."

What was going on? Antonio looked at Enrico, who gave him nothing but a small smile. He searched for Kate, and she beamed at him, her eyes shining with tears. He didn't dare hope, but then Vittorio started to speak.

"I have the great honor today of welcoming a new Lucchesi into the family."

Antonio locked eyes with Enrico, and this time Enrico nodded. Antonio's throat squeezed shut. He hardly heard a word Don Battista said, until he asked for Antonio's left hand. The old don made a small cut in Antonio's palm. Then he did the same to Enrico. After pressing a finger to the blood welling in their palms and mixing it together, he drew a cross in blood across Antonio's palm, then Enrico's. "This cross represents your commitment to each other, as parent and child. As father and son."

Antonio couldn't meet Enrico's gaze. He'd wanted this for so long, but what if Enrico viewed him differently now? What if he didn't want to take in a bastard son, a boy who truly had no name?

He raised his hand. "Wait." He took a breath and addressed Enrico. "There's something you should know."

Enrico took hold of his forearm. "I know. Ruggero told me. And it doesn't matter."

Antonio's vision blurred then, and Enrico pulled him into a tight embrace. He whispered in Antonio's ear. "Forgive me for not doing this sooner. I handled this all wrong."

"That's not important anymore," Antonio whispered back.

They parted, then Kate stepped forward, holding a document. She pressed it into Enrico's hand. "Tell him," she said, her voice barely containing her joy.

Enrico unfolded the paper and handed it to Antonio. "If you agree, you will be my son in name. Antonio Lucchesi."

Antonio's eyes grew hot. "What?" He scanned the paper, which said "Articles of Adoption" across the top, noting his name and Enrico's. "I'm to be your son. Legally?"

Nick clapped him on the back. "Not sure you want me as a brother?"

Antonio laughed. "No. I just—" He surveyed all the smiling faces and had to blink back tears. "I never, ever expected this."

Kate touched his arm, her tears spilling over. She laughed and wiped at them. "I'll have you know that Enrico got an earful from me about this quite a while ago."

Enrico rubbed his ear. "Still stings." Everyone laughed, and Nick called for drinks.

Antonio was barraged with well-wishes, receiving enough embraces and kisses to last a lifetime. But when Francesca Lucchesi came up, his throat tightened up again. "I don't know what to say, *signora*."

Her lips quivered, but then she smiled and patted his cheek. "My boys made their choices. So did my husband. That was none of your doing." She kissed him lightly where her hand had been. "And now I think I'm finally getting the son I should have had all along."

"You mean that?"

"I do. I'd be honored if you considered me your mother."

His eyes pricked with tears again. Before he could speak and make a complete blubbering fool of himself, Bianca came up and embraced them both. "Thank you, Mamma," she whispered.

Antonio scanned the room, his gaze finding Kate and Enrico, Nick and Delfina, Ruggero talking to Violetta, before coming to rest on Bianca and her mother.

Yes, he had a family again.

And for the first time in a long time, he was finally at home.

———— ◆ ————

Three weeks later
Milan

Bianca had never been this nervous in her entire life. Well, maybe when Sandro had a gun to her head, but she'd been so worried about Luca then that she'd barely feared for herself. But now—she reached out and took Antonio's hand as they walked up the path to the elder Lambertis' apartment building, their feet crunching in the snow.

Now she had Antonio to worry about. If Luca didn't recognize him, or her, if he wouldn't come to them, what then? His grandparents would probably continue fighting to keep him.

And maybe she and Antonio should stop.

Enrico and his lawyer followed them up the walkway, their presence meant to be a buffer.

They were buzzed in and quickly met at the doorway of the Lambertis' apartment by a white-haired couple, Luca clinging to Signora Lamberti's skirt. His thumb was jammed in his mouth, something he should have outgrown, and something she hadn't seen him do before. The blue scarf Kate had given Antonio was wrapped several times around Luca's neck and trailed on the floor behind him. Someone had cleaned it, but its fraying edges showed that it'd had some heavy wear since then.

The Lambertis showed them into the living room, no one speaking much. Signora Lamberti asked if they wanted espresso, but everyone turned it down. They wouldn't be staying long.

Her legs shaking, Bianca took a seat on a low sofa across from the Lambertis and Luca. He studied them intently, still sucking his thumb, his other hand buried in the scarf, but he said nothing. He was so different from the happy child who'd bounced up to them at the park.

And it was all her fault.

She bit her lip to keep from crying, and Antonio squeezed her hand. Then he surprised her. He slid off the sofa onto the floor, his legs extended straight in front of him and under the low occasional table. He wiggled his feet at Luca, who stood just centimeters from them.

Luca watched Antonio's feet, and the next time they jiggled, he reached out and touched the toe of Antonio's right shoe before withdrawing. Bianca's heart pounded as she took in the exchange. "Please, Luca," she murmured under her breath. "Please."

The next time Antonio moved his foot, Luca latched onto it with both hands and laughed. Bianca eased down to the tiles and stuck her legs under the table. She wiggled her feet too, and Luca grabbed at them, letting out a giggle.

They played like that for several moments, Luca trying to "catch" their feet. After a while, Antonio withdrew his legs and so did she. She waited, breathless, as Luca came around the table to them.

"Do you remember me?" Antonio asked.

The thumb went back in Luca's mouth, and Bianca's heart lodged in her throat. *Oh no.* She put a hand on Antonio's knee to stop him from saying more.

His eyes glued to Antonio's face, Luca slowly nodded.

"And me?" she whispered.

He nodded again, and when Antonio patted the floor beside him, Luca edged forward, then sat down beside Antonio and pulled the scarf around himself. After a moment during which Bianca's lungs felt locked, Antonio put an arm around Luca.

"You remember?" Antonio asked again, his voice low and soft.

"I 'member."

Signora Lamberti made a soft sound, whether of grief or happiness, Bianca couldn't be sure.

Luca seemed to be searching for something. "Where's your puppy?"

"From the park? You remember us from the park?" Antonio asked.

Luca nodded. "He was fun. I want a puppy, but Nonna and Nonno say there's no room."

Antonio nodded. "They're right. This isn't a good place for a dog."

"I know." Luca sighed with all the drama a six-year-old child could produce. "Can we visit your puppy?"

Bianca smiled. They didn't have a dog, but they were damn sure getting one.

"Maybe," Antonio said. "If your *nonno* and *nonna* say it's okay."

Luca clapped his hands together and jumped up, stumbling over the scarf in his haste to reach his grandparents. "Can I?"

They gave him stiff smiles. "We'll see," Signora Lamberti said. "Now it's time for your nap." She took his hand and led him out of the room.

Signor Lamberti spoke. "That's the first time he's smiled since he came to us."

"We know you love him—" Antonio started.

"Very much. He's all we have left." The old man shook his head. "He hasn't let go of that scarf since we got him from the hospital. You wouldn't believe what we had to go through to get it washed. He gave up his security blanket a long time ago, but this seems to be a new one."

"I gave it to him that night. To keep him warm," Antonio said. He looked at Enrico. "Kate will be pleased to know her scarf has gone to such good use."

Enrico gave them a wry smile, but Bianca couldn't return it. If she was reading Signor Lamberti correctly, he wasn't willing to give Luca up. And that meant another visit to court.

Luca's grandfather nodded. "Well, it seems to make him feel safe. But you also saw that he's started sucking his thumb again. The social workers think he'll stop soon. They say it's a temporary regression, because of the trauma."

"I'm so sorry," Bianca said. "I can never make up for what my brother did."

"We're just thankful we still have Luca."

Signora Lamberti came back into the room. She pulled a handkerchief out of her sleeve and dabbed her eyes. "We know he's your boy, but he's ours too. And after everything he's been through, we're not sure it's the right thing to put him in a new environment. He's lost so much."

Enrico broke in. "Luca does seem to have an attachment to Antonio and Bianca too. A change of scene might help him heal faster, help him put this behind him. And the DNA tests, which we will present next week in court, have confirmed their claim to him."

Signora Lamberti nodded. She took her husband's hand and they looked at each other for a moment, then Signor Lamberti spoke. "This is a difficult decision for us. We're both old. And this is no life for a child, living with us. You can give him a dog. And maybe a sibling or two." He crossed himself. "And you'll be there for him long after we're in our graves."

Antonio leaned forward. "You're his grandparents, and you always will be."

Signora Lamberti dabbed at her eyes again. "A long court battle will do no one any good. If you agree that we can come to see him and have him for the weekend from time to time, we'll stop fighting."

Bianca's belly flipped. "You mean he's ours?"

Tears welled again in Signora Lamberti's eyes as she nodded. "But you have to get him a puppy," she choked out.

Bianca burst into tears and Antonio pulled her close, stroking a hand over her hair. "I'm not dreaming, am I?" she whispered.

"If you are, then I'm having the same dream."

She had her boy back. Luca was hers again, at last.

———— ♦ ————

They drove back up to the lake, Ruggero at the wheel, Luca curled up between Antonio and Bianca in the back. Enrico and the lawyer had stayed behind to draw up an agreement with the Lambertis that they could present to the court.

Luca had barely stirred when they'd taken him. He'd probably be upset later, but hopefully he'd adjust quickly. Tomorrow they were buying him a puppy, first thing.

Antonio ran a finger across Luca's soft cheek. They had their boy back. He still could barely believe it. He looked up at Bianca, surprised to see tears in her eyes. "What's wrong?"

"Nothing. Not a single thing." She smiled, then took his hand and placed it on her belly. "I've been waiting to tell you this, in case things didn't go well today. But now there's no reason to wait."

Was she saying what he thought she was? "We're having a baby?"

She nodded, and he tapped the roof of the car with his fist and let out a whoop that startled Luca. "I love you, *bella*."

"And I love you." She wiped at her shining eyes.

His face almost hurt, his smile was so wide. "Did you hear that?" Antonio said, raising his voice and directing the question to Ruggero.

"I think all of Milan heard." Ruggero's tone was filled with amusement. "Congratulations, Papà."

Antonio leaned over Luca, who'd gone right back to sleep, and took Bianca's face in his hands. His throat tightened and his chest filled with warmth. "You've given me every dream I've ever had."

She cupped her hands over his. "And you've given me all of mine."

Their lips met in a sweet, tender kiss. *Now* he had everything: the woman he loved, the child he'd lost, the family he'd always wanted.

EPILOGUE

Lorenzo Andretti clamped his teeth around his weekly cigar and drew in a long puff of the aromatic smoke he so enjoyed. He looked around the humble den that served as his office. A fire blazed in the hearth and warmed his tired, aching bones.

He had so much to do yet, and no time to rest. Marcello was proving a challenge; he was so much like his father, Remo, but Lorenzo would prevail in the end. He always did.

He blew out a ring of blue smoke and watched it dissipate into the room. Who knew how many more of these he'd get to savor before the end? He thumped his cane on the floor. He hated the bloody thing, but he needed it. He hated any sign of infirmity, any need for assistance. It made him look frail, weak.

But he'd played that to his advantage before, and he'd do so again, as many times as necessary. If he had to sacrifice his pride to win, that was a price he was willing to pay.

Sal had given him reports on Dario for the last three weeks; so far, Dario seemed to be doing little other than stew in his grief and anger. Good. He'd given no indication of believing Legato's accusation about Cristoforo's death. Had Lorenzo gotten away with it? There was no way to tell at the moment, but sooner or later he'd know the truth. If Dario was plotting against him, he'd slip up eventually, and Sal was in place to take care of that problem.

He took another drag on the cigar and stared into the crackling fire. So Lucchesi and his blond orphan thought they'd scored a victory. Lorenzo had let them think so for a moment, but that moment was at an end. He reached over and picked up the phone, dialing a number he knew by heart.

It was time Enrico Lucchesi knew the wrath of Lorenzo Andretti, a wrath that would not rest, that would not end, until Lucchesi himself was dead.

AUTHOR'S NOTE

Due to the high level of secrecy maintained by the 'Ndrangheta (the Calabrian Mafia) and the relative scarcity of former members turned state's witnesses, there are few resources detailing the inner workings of the society. Therefore, I have used artistic license in portraying certain aspects of the 'Ndrangheta, particularly as regards La Provincia.

Until July 2010, it was widely believed that there was no overarching body in charge of the 'Ndrangheta. However, with the arrest of several prominent 'Ndranghetisti, it is now believed that there is a *capo di tutti capi* (boss of all bosses) who oversees a commission (La Provincia) with direct power over the individual families. *Redemption* deals with the formation of such a central organization; however, for dramatic purposes, I have simplified the structure somewhat and haven't enumerated all the various real-world constituents of it, such as those located in Liguria (Genoa) or Toronto, Canada.

Additionally, to make this series easier to read for American readers, I have used the term *cosca* rather than *'ndrine* to indicate an individual crime family. I have also greatly simplified the organization of individual crime families and have chosen to name crime families after their *capo's* blood family; in real life, a *cosca's* name may consist of a region or place, or a hyphenated combination of the names of the two or three primary blood families that control the *cosca*.

In Italy, women typically don't take their husband's last name; for simplicity's sake, I have chosen to reflect the traditional American practice of taking the husband's last name upon marriage.

I have also used some artistic license in portraying the workings of the Financial Intelligence Unit (FIU) at the Banca d'Italia, Italy's central bank and financial regulatory authority.

Note that all persons mentioned in this series are fictional; no resemblance to actual people, living or dead, is intended. The family names used in this series were deliberately chosen not to reflect names of actual crime families.

ABOUT THE AUTHOR

Dana Delamar is the author of erotic romance, LGBTQ romance, and the "Blood and Honor" Mafia romance series, which is set in Italy among the Calabrian Mafia. Her first book, *Revenge*, received 4 stars from *RT Book Reviews*, was a Top Pick at The Romance Reviews, and was a double-finalist for Best First Book and Best Romantic Suspense in the 2013 Booksellers Best Awards.

Her second book, *Retribution*, received 4 stars from *RT Book Reviews* and was a semi-finalist in the Kindle Book Review's 2013 Best Indie Book Awards. Her book *Malavita* was a quarter-finalist in the 2014 Amazon Breakthrough Novel Awards, and her book *Redemption* was a finalist in the 2014 Maggie Awards and a semi-finalist in the Kindle Book Review's 2014 Best Kindle Book Awards.

Dana is also an editor with over thirty years of editing experience in both fiction and nonfiction and has worked with everyone from newbie writers to experienced pros. The books she's edited have won numerous awards and critical acclaim, including two Top Picks from *RT Book Reviews*.

danadelamar.com

MORE BY THIS AUTHOR

Thank you for reading *Redemption*. I hope I have entertained you.

Writing a book is a rather crazy endeavor, similar to trying to put together a thousand-piece puzzle with no picture to guide you. When I started this series, it was going to be only one book. Then two. Then four. Now it's grown to five with more books in the "Blood and Honor" world on the way. I hope you're having as much fun as I am on this journey.

If you enjoyed *Redemption*, please consider writing a review to help others learn about the book. Every recommendation truly helps, and I appreciate anyone who takes the time to share their love of books and reading with others. (And feel free to friend me on Goodreads—I love seeing what everyone is reading!)

To hear about my new releases, you can sign up for my VIP Readers List at danadelamar.com.

Keep reading for a special preview of the next book in the series, *Reckoning*, which is about bodyguard, hitman, man of many talents—and secrets—Ruggero. As you might guess, when he finally falls, he falls hard, and for someone he really cannot have. I've waited a long time to tell his story, and I hope you enjoy reading it as much as I enjoyed writing it.

A SPECIAL PREVIEW OF *RECKONING*
(Blood and Honor, Book 4)

A brutal hitman.
A fervent anti-Mafia judge.
A far-ranging conspiracy…

Everyone thinks Ruggero Vela is just an assassin, a cold-hearted thug. But a passionate heart beats underneath his granite exterior. When he finally meets the woman of his dreams, she turns out to be Loredana Montisi, a fervent anti-Mafia judge hell-bent on prosecuting his Mafia don boss. The beautiful judge has no idea she's being used as a pawn by much darker forces with a truly frightening agenda.

With enemies closing in on every side, Ruggero walks a dangerous tightrope—can he win Loredana's heart and her help, or will he lose her and the only family he knows?

———————◆———————

Twenty years ago
Rome, Italy

Scanning the street again, Ruggero Vela leaned against one of the columns that flanked the massive double doors of the bank behind him. It was half past noon, and hot for early May. Sweat gathered beneath his leather shoulder holster, and the Beretta under his left armpit no longer felt cool. He wished he could remove his suit jacket, but that wasn't possible, not with the hardware it concealed.

His stomach rumbled, and he lit up his third cigarette of the day. Tapping the ashes on the stone steps and shifting a bit more into the shade, he turned to his father standing at the column across from him. "Papà, how much longer?"

His father took a drag on his own cigarette, squinting against the smoke rising around his face. "Don Lucchesi will be done when he's done."

The hit of nicotine should have been soothing, but it wasn't. "When do you think it will happen?" The "it" Ruggero had promised not to mention again. But it was all he could think about, what with the recent hit on the Bove family.

"Stop obsessing. You're ready."

I wish I believed you. "What's it like?"

He got the stare, the one Livio Vela was famous for among his fellow 'Ndranghetisti. "Don't be so eager."

"I'm not. Just curious." *And not sure I can do this.*

His father crossed over to him, placed a hand on his shoulder. "Listen. I'm only going to say this once. You think killing a man is like in the movies. It's not."

"I know. That's what I'm... nervous about." Ruggero wanted to tell the truth, but a *sicario*, an assassin, was never afraid. He was the sharp blade that his *capo* would send against his enemies, the shadow in the night, the man other men would fear. The one who would be the very last thing many men would ever see.

Livio's eyes narrowed again into their famous squint, as if he were taking his son's measure. Then he patted Ruggero's cheek. "I was like you once. We all were. Taking a man's life is a hard thing to do. And it's a hard thing to know about yourself. It's like a serpent coiled around your heart."

Ruggero rubbed his sternum, and Livio laughed. It was good seeing his father smile; he didn't do it often. And Ruggero knew just what to say to make him laugh again. "I hope we have lunch soon."

His father let out a dry chuckle and tousled Ruggero's hair. "You're always hungry."

With a tap to his chest, which had filled out considerably with muscle during the half-year since he'd turned sixteen, Ruggero returned the smile. "I'm a growing boy."

Motioning with his chin, his father indicated the *pasticceria* across the street. "Run over and grab yourself a pastry. Make it quick."

Ruggero tossed his cigarette and hurried through the people thronging the sidewalk, then dodged between Vespas and cars that rarely stopped for other vehicles, much less pedestrians. He made it safely to the other side before realizing he had only a few coins in his pocket—probably not enough to get anything. Turning around, he glanced over at his father, who had straightened up and ground out his cigarette, his eyes trained on their *capo* stepping through the double doors.

Damn. He needed to hustle. Ruggero started into the street, and the sharp blare of a Fiat's horn sent him back up on the curb, his heart pounding in his chest. *Cristo,* that had been close.

He flicked his eyes back to his father and the don again, and a sudden movement caught his attention—two men, dressed in dark colors, were advancing on his father and the don from opposite directions. Both men wore the intent focus of predators, and their sharp, quick movements as they dodged around obstacles marked them as professionals.

Papà! He almost screamed the word aloud, but at the last second bit down on his tongue and drew blood. Calling attention to himself and alerting the hitmen was a bad idea. Ruggero plunged into the street, his feet slipping on cobblestones slick with water from the *pasticceria* owner's efforts to keep the sidewalk clean. He flicked open the switchblade he kept in his pocket and held it pointed down, against his leg, where it wouldn't attract much notice.

He'd reached the other side just as the man on the right was coming up behind his father. This time he couldn't help shouting. Livio turned toward Ruggero's voice, and Ruggero motioned frantically, trying to make his father aware of the *sicario* that stalked him. But his father yelled "Look out!" instead of dealing with the threat that was upon him.

Pain seared across the left side of Ruggero's face, from just beside his eye and down across his cheekbone, then a massive weight slammed into him and knocked him almost off his feet. Without thinking, he stabbed upward, catching his assailant in the abdomen. As he'd been taught, he twisted the knife and dragged it hard across the man's belly, gutting him like a fish. The man gaped at him for a moment, then tried to grab for the bloody mess of intestines that bulged from the wound.

Acid rose up the back of Ruggero's throat, but he inhaled deeply and focused on his target—the man's carotid artery. With a quick slice, he severed the vessel, then shoved the man out of the way, leaving him to teeter on the sidewalk, blood spurting from his neck, as people screamed and ran.

Ruggero charged over to his father and the don. His father was bleeding heavily from a wound to the upper belly and his face looked pale. His knife was out though, and blood dripped from it as he squared off with his opponent, a young darkly tanned man with close-cropped hair. The man said something, his accent Calabrian—Ruggero couldn't hear his words over the rush of blood in his ears. Then the man lunged for the don.

"No!" Ruggero shouted, and the assailant did what he'd expected: he turned from his quarry to confront Ruggero instead. He met Ruggero's first thrust with a quick one of his own. The Calabrian's knife slashed through the light wool of Ruggero's suit coat, the tip of the knife skimming across his ribs and leaving fire in its wake.

Ruggero danced back, and his father's voice rang in his head. *Watch his eyes; they'll tell you where he's going to strike.* The man glanced up at Ruggero's neck, and Ruggero made sure he was ready to block the strike and to deliver one of his own. The attacker closed in, clearly not expecting the sudden blow to his chin when Ruggero snapped up his left elbow to block. He followed the move with a stab into the Calabrian's windpipe. Plunging the blade in, he ripped it to the right, tearing the throat open. The man let out a gurgle.

Just as Ruggero was about to relax, a flicker in his peripheral vision alerted him to another threat: a third *sicario*, who'd already reached his weakened father.

"Papà!" This time the word came out, but it was too late. The man slid up behind his father and drew his blade neatly across Livio's throat.

Ruggero pulled his Beretta, tears blurring his vision as he took aim and squeezed the trigger. He had to save his *capo*; that was their number one job. Protecting the man they served. Protecting the man who'd saved his father from a life in prison.

The bullet found its mark; the assassin stumbled, then fell. Ruggero advanced on him, his attention narrowed to one single focus: making sure the *sicario* was dead. He reached the downed man and pumped two more bullets into his head. He would have fired again, but the don laid a hand on his shoulder. "*Basta.*" Enough.

Heaving in a breath, Ruggero looked his don in the eye. Rinaldo Lucchesi stared at him, pity written in every line of his face.

Ruggero had saved his *capo*. But he'd gotten his father killed.

Falling to his knees, Ruggero took his father's hand, but the light had already left his eyes. Again, he heard his father's words. *Taking a man's life is a hard thing to do. And it's a hard thing to know about yourself. It's like a serpent coiled around your heart.*

Something squeezed in his chest, and tears flooded his eyes. The serpent was there; he could feel it. It owned him now.

———————◆———————

Present day
Como, Italy

Ruggero Vela tugged at the bow tie around his neck and grimaced. *Damn penguin suit.* Why had he ever said yes when Antonio had asked him to be best man? He surveyed the church again, all the rows of guests waiting for the appearance of the bride, then glanced at Antonio Lucchesi, the groom, standing beside him in front of the altar. Tonio looked nervous and excited in equal measure. Ruggero wished he shared Tonio's excitement.

But all Ruggero could focus on was his speech as the best man. He worried the folded-up paper in his pocket. Telling funny stories and being heartfelt in front of a crowd?

Not his thing. At all.

Maybe he should have asked Don Lucchesi for help. But he hadn't wanted to bother the don over such a small thing. Over something that any man should be able to do without blinking. Any normal man.

Ruggero knew a hundred ways to kill someone. But not much else. Not how to be a friend, for example. Or a husband or a father. Not that he ever expected to be either of the latter two, but he should know how to be a friend.

Of all the lessons his father had imparted before his death, none had included something as simple, as basic, as that. How to be someone's friend, when all you knew was how to end lives. Not how to live one.

He'd just have to muddle through and hope he hit the mark. He had known one thing though: you didn't turn down an invitation to be someone's best man. He'd never have insulted Tonio that way. Not after everything he'd been through during these last few months.

The music for the bride started up, and Bianca Lucchesi came down the aisle on the arm of Don Enrico Lucchesi, her godfather and the adopted father of the groom. She'd always been quite a stunner, but today she wasn't merely beautiful; she was radiant, like an angel. If you believed in that sort of thing. Which Ruggero didn't.

Still, he could barely look at Bianca without a lump forming in his throat. What the hell was happening to him? He coughed and glanced away, and that's when he saw it: movement in the shadows near the vestibule of the church.

The hairs prickled at the nape of his neck, and he reached across his chest for his gun… which he didn't have. *Minchia!*

Bianca and the don reached the altar, and the don embraced her and kissed her on each cheek before handing her off to Antonio.

Ruggero started to lunge forward, to get himself between the don and the unknown danger that lurked in the shadows, but the man who stepped out of the gloom brought him up short. Sottotenente Silvio Fuente, of the *carabinieri*. He was flanked by four other officers.

The don also saw the intruders. He stared at Fuente for a moment, and the man shrugged, then nodded, and the don took his seat. Ruggero tried to read his *capo*'s face, but the don seemed untroubled. Though surely he wasn't. His eyes flicked to Ruggero, then to Antonio and Bianca, and he gave Ruggero a pointed nod.

Yes. He needed to focus on the task at hand. On the ring in his pocket. He made eye contact with Tommaso, the senior guard nearest him, and shook his head slightly. They were not to interfere with the officers.

Fortunately, the bride and groom didn't seem to have noticed Fuente or his colleagues. Tonio and Bianca were holding hands and grinning at each other as the bishop spoke to those assembled. The man droned on and on about love and commitment and the special joy of two people joining as one, while Ruggero twirled Bianca's wedding ring around and around the tip of his little finger. *Come on, man, can't you see the don is going to be arrested? They won't wait forever.*

At last the bishop addressed Antonio directly, and recited the vow Tonio was to repeat. Ruggero handed the ring to Tonio, who cleared his throat, then said, the slightest tremor in his voice, "I, Antonio, take you, Bianca, as my wife and promise to be faithful to you always, in joy and in pain, in health and in sickness, and to love you and every day honor you, for the rest of my life." He slid the ring onto her finger as he said the words, and a tear spilled down Bianca's cheek.

She reached up and wiped her face, and Ruggero had to look away. It was insane to think that she and Antonio had both nearly been killed just six weeks ago, while rescuing their son, Luca. And now, here they were, on Valentine's Day, taking their vows.

Life was short, crazy, and unpredictable. None of them would ever have guessed they'd be here today, much less that the *carabinieri* would be crashing Antonio and Bianca's wedding. Fortunately, Fuente and his men hadn't advanced, presumably out of respect for the bride.

Bianca took a deep breath and blew out, then she shot a smile at Tonio that made Ruggero happier than ever for his friend. She was one hell of a woman; she'd shot her own brother to save Tonio's life. Her voice shaking, she repeated her vow after the bishop as she slid a simple gold band onto Antonio's finger. "I, Bianca, take you, Antonio, as my husband and promise to be faithful to you always, in joy and in pain, in health and in sickness, and to love you and every day honor you, for the rest of my life."

There was that lump again—right smack in Ruggero's throat. *Dio*, was he turning into a woman? He'd been to a dozen weddings, and they'd never been more to him than occasions where he'd had to watch his *capo*'s back. Even his sister's wedding hadn't meant that much to him—then again, he'd been only six at the time. He'd missed Elena terribly afterward, sure, but he hadn't registered then, or in all the time since then, what a wedding truly was: a joining of two people. The start of a family, of something new. A beginning. A chance to start over.

And if any two people had earned that chance, they were Antonio and Bianca, who'd risked everything to save the son they'd created when they were teens, a son no one other than Bianca had known existed until recently.

Six-year-old Luca Lucchesi sat in the front row snuggled up to Kate, the don's wife. He was dressed in a miniature tuxedo, and he beamed up at his parents as Kate ruffled his blond hair and whispered something to him.

Even Ruggero had to admit that Luca was a cute kid. Though Luca was still a little intimidated by him—perhaps it was the scar that sliced across Ruggero's left cheekbone—something made Ruggero want to put the boy at ease. He'd shown Luca how to teach his new puppy some tricks, and that had gone a long way toward relaxing Luca, though some lingering tentativeness remained.

But that was a problem for another day. Fuente and his men had come forward as the bishop concluded the ceremony, and now they were approaching Don Lucchesi.

This wasn't good; Fuente had belonged to them at one point. Now, he obviously belonged to another. And Ruggero didn't have to guess who that person was.

Lorenzo Andretti. The man everyone in the Lucchesi *cosca* wanted dead.

———— ♦ ————

His heart beating a little faster than normal, Enrico Lucchesi rose from his seat in the church and met the *carabinieri* officers before they'd reached him and his wife. Silvio Fuente was in the lead, of course, and his black mustache curved up as he gave Enrico a broad smile. "The day has come at last," Fuente said.

"What day is that?"

Fuente held up a pair of handcuffs. "The day when the great Enrico Lucchesi is exposed for what he truly is: a Mafioso."

It was Enrico's turn to smile, though it was the last thing he felt like doing. "Signor Fuente, you know as well as I do that an arrest does not make an allegation true." He deliberately left off the officer's title, a thing that would rankle Fuente and remind him that the title was Enrico's doing.

Fuente's lips pursed before his smile resurfaced. "You may have slipped from the law's grasp before, but you won't this time."

Enrico leaned down to whisper in Fuente's ear. "Put on a show for your colleagues all you want, but you and I both know what I can do."

Fuente huffed with laughter, but this time kept his voice low, for Enrico's ears only. "And we both know what your enemies are capable of."

So this was Lorenzo's doing. Was Fuente being paid, or threatened? "May we have a word?"

Fuente waved Enrico over to a spot several meters from his fellow officers. Enrico positioned himself so that he could see Kate, and he offered her a grin that was far more confident than he felt. Her features didn't relax, and she clutched Luca to her side. *Madonna.* He didn't want her fretting about him, not on top of the pregnancy. She'd had every possible test, checking for damage to the child after Carlo Andretti had drugged her, and she didn't need to add Enrico to her list of worries.

"What is this about?" Enrico asked.

"The Dinelli case. We have the gun."

Enrico's gut went cold. They had him at last. Fuente had hinted before that he knew where the gun was, but Enrico hadn't known whether he was bluffing until now. "And you've found Grantini?"

Fuente held his eyes. "No. But you already knew that."

"I wouldn't have asked if I'd known." Though of course he had. Sergio Grantini was nothing but bones now, somewhere in the depths of Lake Como. Sergio had betrayed Enrico; he'd gone to work for Carlo Andretti. And he'd helped Andretti frame Enrico for the murder of Judge Federico Dinelli.

Holding up the cuffs, Fuente said, "Put out your hands."

"May I have a few minutes with my wife?" When Fuente hesitated, Enrico pressed him. "She's got a lot on her mind with the pregnancy. I'd like to reassure her. I won't fight you."

Fuente sighed, then tapped the face of his fancy watch. "Five minutes. No more."

Enrico didn't thank him; he probably should have, but he couldn't bring himself to do it when what he really wanted was to punch the man. Hadn't Enrico paid him enough? Though maybe he should be feeling sorry for Fuente. If Lorenzo was applying pressure, Fuente was in an exceedingly tight spot.

Much like Enrico himself.

He quickly reached Kate's side and the knot of concerned people around her: Tonio and Bianca, Nico and Delfi, and of course Ruggero. They'd all want a word, but the one who mattered most was Kate, and he had to concentrate on her. He asked Bianca to take Luca off Kate's hands, then he escorted Kate a few meters away, his hand at her elbow.

She trembled beside him, and his stomach grew tight. This was so far from the life of comfort and ease that he'd wanted for her. Turning, he faced her and placed a hand on each of her shoulders. He held her at arm's length for a moment, then pulled her close and whispered in her ear, using his English to make sure she didn't miss a word. "*Cara,* I have to go with them. It is about the Dinelli case. They have found the missing evidence."

"The gun?"

He nodded.

"What about Grantini?" She knew as well as he did that Grantini was dead. But if anyone could hear... He suppressed a smile. She was a sharp one, his Kate.

"No. But the gun is enough to hold me. For a while." He kissed her cheek and lowered his voice so it was little more than a breath. "Call Trapani. He will know what to do. Antonio will be in charge, Ruggero his second."

She stiffened in his arms, and he tightened his grip on her. "This is only temporary. You know where the bag is?" The bag that contained their false IDs, credit cards in those names, stacks of cash, and a list of banks and account numbers. The bag that was hidden on their property.

Kate nodded. "I know."

"*Bene*. If something happens, you take it and run."

She stifled a sob. "I can't leave you."

"You may have to, *cara*. Lorenzo..."

She shifted in his arms and placed a finger on his lips. "I'm *not* leaving you."

He placed a hand on her belly and was rewarded with a kick from their son. "You have to protect him. If Lorenzo makes a move, you run."

"Where would I go?"

"Anywhere you want. The IDs will protect you."

"And who made them?"

He frowned. Of course Kate would think of the major point of vulnerability. "It is no one that Lorenzo can get to."

"You're sure?"

Enrico stroked her cheek and pressed a kiss to her lush mouth. "I would not risk your life on anything I was not certain of."

She held his eyes, her own brimming with tears. "*Ti amo*," she whispered, her voice breaking.

"*Ti amo, cara*." Somehow he kept his voice steady, firm. He kissed her once more as Fuente drew near, the heels of his neatly polished boots thudding on the cathedral's marble floor. Then Enrico turned from the woman he loved more than anything else in the world and held out his hands.

The steel cuffs snapped over his wrists, and it was done. Patches of red mottling his cheeks, Antonio tried to stop Fuente, but Enrico shook his head. "It's all right, Tonio. I won't be gone long."

Now who was bluffing? Enrico caught Ruggero's eye and motioned toward Kate with his head. Ruggero nodded once, and the determination on his face was the only thing that made Enrico relax in the slightest. Ruggero would keep her safe.

The officers escorted him outside. It was the first time in many years that Ruggero hadn't been with him, always slightly ahead, shielding him from being a direct target, gun at the ready.

Now Enrico had no one between him and death. Any one of these officers could be in Andretti's pay. If he was going to survive, Enrico would have to rely on himself alone.

The thought provided little comfort. He was on his own, without a gun or a knife. A defenseless deer among a pack of sharp-toothed wolves.

———— ◆ ————

Everyone convened at Enrico and Kate's villa for the wedding reception as planned, but no one felt like celebrating. Kate tried to get people to eat, drink, and dance, but no one was fooled by the smile plastered on her face. Don Vittorio Battista, Enrico's godfather, approached Antonio and Ruggero soon after they arrived. "We should have a family meeting," the old don suggested, and the tension in Ruggero's belly unwound ever so slightly. Yes, they needed to make a plan.

Ruggero and Antonio sent everyone who wasn't needed home. Gianluca d'Imperio and his family were the last to leave. He came over to Antonio, Ruggero, and Don Battista standing by the fireplace in the large drawing room. "You have my full support, of course," Gianluca said to them, his eyes on Antonio.

"*Mille grazie*, Don d'Imperio," Antonio said.

Gianluca laughed. "You *can* call me Gianluca, you know."

Tonio reddened. "Someday I will get used to this."

D'Imperio clapped Antonio on the back. "You weren't born to it, but you need to start acting like you've been a Lucchesi your whole life. *Capisci?*"

"I know."

Gianluca's daughter Giovanna raced up and threw her arms around Antonio in a quick hug. Then she whispered, of course loud enough for everyone to hear, "If you break the bed on your wedding night, I've heard it's good luck."

That made everyone smile and Antonio laugh, and then the d'Imperios were gone, and it was only the family left. The only problem was Tonio's sister, Violetta. She wasn't part of the business, and Tonio wanted to keep it that way. Bianca's mother, Francesca, came to the rescue. "Violetta, how about you and I take Luca and Cocco out back?"

Luca clapped his hands at the suggestion. "Cocco wants me to bring the ball!" The fluffy white pup yipped when he heard the word, his tail wagging furiously.

"Let's get you changed first," Francesca said, taking Luca's hand. She and Violetta led him upstairs where they had a bag for him. It had been a good day so far; Luca hadn't asked for Tonio's blue scarf, which he'd carried around with him nonstop since the night his adoptive parents had been killed. Ruggero hoped it remained that way; with Enrico gone, Tonio didn't need any more worries.

The rest of them headed into the spacious dining room and gathered around the long, highly polished mahogany table: Ruggero; Don Battista; Kate; Antonio and Bianca; Orlando Farnese, Ruggero's nephew and the *cosca's* treasurer; and Enrico's other son, Nick, and his wife, Delfina. The fact that Delfina was Dario Andretti's daughter made Ruggero a bit wary, even now. She'd proved again and again that she could be trusted, but still, she was an Andretti by birth. And here they were, including her in their plans.

Then again, Enrico's late wife, Antonella, had been an Andretti too. And she'd never betrayed him, as far as Ruggero knew. There was always a first time, however. But he kept his concerns to himself. The last thing they needed right now was strife within the family.

Don Battista turned to Kate and put a hand on her forearm, speaking in English for her and Nick's benefit. "Caterina, what did Rico say to you before he left?"

She put her hand over his and gave him a tight smile. Then she looked at Antonio and Ruggero. "He said that Antonio was to be *capo*. And Ruggero *capo di società*."

An icy sensation flitted through Ruggero's midsection. "That should be Orlando's job."

"He said you. And you know why." She held his gaze; did she truly know? He'd thought that had been between him and Don Lucchesi, and he wasn't about to blurt it out in front of Antonio, who was giving him a quizzical look.

Damn her for putting him on the spot, but did he really expect any less? Kate wasn't one to tiptoe around. She said what she meant, and she meant what she said. It was one of her most admirable qualities, when it wasn't making him uncomfortable. "Well"—he flicked a glance at Orlando—"yes, Orlando is quite new to this."

"As is Antonio. No offense," she said.

Tonio smiled. "It's the truth. And I do need help."

"It is settled then," Don Battista said.

Nick leaned forward. "I'll see what I can find out about the case through Interpol."

"You would do that?" Ruggero asked. Ever since Enrico had extricated his son from the mess he'd gotten into with Dario Andretti, Nick had been quite clear that he wanted nothing to do with the inner workings of the family. He'd wanted to stay in Interpol, at the London bureau, and as far out of the family business as possible. As possible as it was, considering that he was the son of one Mafia don and son-in-law to another.

"He's my dad. I have to help him. Whatever it takes." Nick looked around the table. "It's not like I'm not already compromised."

"As long as we have that clear," Ruggero said. He didn't bother to mask his irritation with Nick. The boy wanted to have it both ways, and that was impossible. But neither Nick nor his father could see that. Either you were in the 'Ndrangheta, or you were out.

But that was the story of Enrico Lucchesi, wasn't it? The man who didn't want to be a don, but was. And his firstborn was more of the same.

And yet there wasn't another man Ruggero would rather have followed. He trusted Enrico Lucchesi with his life. He'd sworn it, but it was more than a mere vow. The don had called him friend, and meant it. He'd offered to make Ruggero his right hand before, to make him *capo di società*. And Ruggero had turned it down, had insisted that Antonio was the better choice.

But that wasn't the real reason he'd refused the job.

In his heart of hearts, Ruggero knew he was unworthy. And like a coward, he hadn't wanted to admit that aloud. For the only time in his life, he hadn't been completely truthful with his don. But some things were better left unsaid.

Antonio interrupted his thoughts. "That bastard Fuente. I know why he flipped."

"Why?" Ruggero asked.

"After Cris was killed, Fuente was looking through the bank statements we'd been showing the others to prove that I hadn't stolen the money. Fuente must have pieced together how much Lorenzo and Sandro had stolen from Enrico. He must think us weak."

"Well, we're not at our strongest," Orlando said. "That infusion of cash from the d'Imperios has gone a long way toward making us less vulnerable, but we still have a huge hole in our balance sheet."

Don Battista stroked the abundant steel-gray mustache that bristled above his upper lip. "I can help in that regard. Why didn't Enrico ask?"

No one said anything. Then Kate sighed. "Pride, I'm sure."

Antonio tapped the table. "I might be thinking about this all wrong. Fuente wanted information about Lorenzo."

"What did you tell him?" Don Battista asked.

"That he had ties to Italo Baldassare. And possibly the Russians. But I didn't mention the Vilanoviches."

"Those fuckers." Nick put an arm around Delfina and hugged her close. None of them had any love for the Vilanoviches, but Nick had nearly lost his wife because of them.

"I'm sure Fuente believes he can use that information somehow," Antonio said.

Ruggero snorted. "If Fuente thinks that gives him any leverage over Lorenzo, he's an idiot."

"We ought to talk to Fuente. Find out what he knows," Antonio said.

"As if he'd be honest." Ruggero doubted anything less than a gun in the mouth would get him anywhere close to the truth with Fuente. Not that he was about to go after an officer of the law, especially the one who'd just arrested his boss. Fuente was a double-crossing prick, but an assault on an officer would rally the *carabinieri*, and the *cosca* didn't need more trouble. Certainly not with Don Lucchesi in jail.

"We've got to try." Antonio held Ruggero's gaze. "Think you can intimidate it out of him—*without* breaking anything?"

Ruggero cracked his knuckles. "I'll restrain myself." Fuente was a turncoat of the worst sort; he'd not only broken his oath to the *carabinieri*, but he'd also spit on the man he'd turned traitor for. A man had to have some principles, but apparently Fuente didn't understand the concept. There was really only one way to deal with men like that. But that way was denied Ruggero. He'd have to be creative.

"Okay then," Antonio said. He turned to Delfina. "Delfi, do you have any idea what your father is thinking? How closely is he working with Lorenzo?"

She shook her head. "I don't know. He says very little around me. He's still upset that I didn't leave Nico."

"And the baby?"

Her eyes filled with tears, and she shook her head again. "We've been trying, but it hasn't happened. I lied to Papà. I told him I was pregnant, but it has to happen soon, or he'll realize what I've done."

"We've been trying for only six weeks, honey. It'll happen," Nick said and kissed her cheek.

"And if it doesn't? That pretend baby is the only thing keeping him from attacking this family."

"Stop worrying. The stress isn't good for you."

"How can I *not* worry? At this rate, Mamma might get pregnant before I do!"

"They're really trying again?" Kate asked.

Delfina nodded. "Papà needs a new heir now that—" Her breath hitched before she said the rest. "Now that Cris is dead. Mamma's still young enough to try."

Cristoforo Andretti had been an admirable boy. The only Andretti Ruggero would ever say that about. Cris had worked hard to help strengthen the ties between the families, and he'd actually defied his father and great-grandfather to help Antonio and Don Lucchesi try to avert a crisis in their own *cosca*. But Lorenzo Andretti had made sure his great-grandson hadn't drawn breath for long afterward. Too bad they hadn't been able to prove that to Dario Andretti. He hadn't accepted the proof Antonio had offered, that Lorenzo had ordered Cris's death.

Then again, Dario had long hated Enrico, and that hatred had blinded him to the truth more than once. Now the tentative alliance forged through Nick and Delfina's marriage hung on by mere tatters. If Dario found out the truth, he'd be sure to sever the alliance altogether. As it was, he could be working against them anyway. They had to assume so.

Ruggero leaned forward. "Baby or no baby, I don't trust Dario not to attack us." He looked at Nick and Delfina. "For everyone's safety, I think we need to make some changes. Move everyone into this house. With all the security upgrades, it's the safest place to be. And we can concentrate the guards here." Not only had Enrico upgraded the security systems and electronic surveillance, he'd also had bulletproof glass installed in much of the house, though the renovations to the solarium were still underway.

"All of us?" Antonio asked. He, Bianca, and Luca had moved in with her mother rather than leave Francesca on her own in the large villa next door.

"Yes." Ruggero turned to Orlando. "Your mother too. I don't like her alone in Calabria. She's too close to Lorenzo. Between you being *contabile* and me being *capo di società*, he's bound to go after her."

"Good luck convincing her," Orlando said. "She hates it up here."

No. Elena had hated it here after their father had died. After Ruggero's mistake. With Papà gone, she hadn't seen a reason to stay around. She'd packed up her family and gone back south to be with their cousins. That's what she'd said. But Ruggero was quite certain that Elena actually hadn't wanted to see his scar every day, to be reminded that it was his carelessness that had gotten their father killed.

Well, she'd have to be reminded now. He wasn't going to lose her too. "I'll make her see that it's for the best."

"Do you need more men?" Don Battista asked.

"We could use some experienced guards for the house," Ruggero said. "We've lost quite a few these last several months, and we're behind on training replacements."

"Weapons?"

"We're well-stocked there."

Don Battista nodded. "Anything you need, you ask. Don't stand on pride. If the Lucchesis fall, I'll be Lorenzo's next target."

"Aside from you and the d'Imperios, who else can we count on?" Antonio asked, and Ruggero almost smiled. He'd been about to ask the same question. The boy was learning.

"I've been speaking to several families who have bad blood with the Andrettis. They're not happy with Lorenzo being in charge. Even though he won the vote to run La Provincia, it wasn't the landslide he'd thought."

"Can you secure their help, should it come to war?" Ruggero asked.

"I believe so. Now that Lorenzo has fired the first shot, I'll see who's willing to join forces with us."

Kate squeezed the old man's arm. "*Mille grazie*, Vittorio," she said, her voice wavering.

He leaned forward and kissed her cheek. "Caterina, do not worry. We will protect your family. I am Rico's *compare*; he is not alone. He's as much my son as any of my boys."

Tears slipped down her cheeks, and she wiped at them and took a deep breath. "I'm sorry I'm losing it. This day started out so well, and now Rico's in jail, and the wedding's been ruined—"

"No, it wasn't," Bianca said. "The wedding was fine. We'll just have a big party after Zio Enrico is back home."

Nick chuckled. "It turned out a lot better than when Delfi and I got engaged. At least no bullets were fired."

The table fell silent for a moment, then Tonio started laughing. "And I didn't end up in the hospital like I did after your engagement party. That *really* would have put a damper on the wedding."

Kate put a hand to her mouth, and for a moment Ruggero thought she was struggling not to cry. Then she let a giggle burst out before smothering it. "I shouldn't be laughing. It's not funny."

"It kind of is," Tonio said. "We're all still here, aren't we? The Andrettis have tried and tried, but they keep missing."

"Bad aim," Nick said, his voice light.

"*Really* bad aim," Tonio added.

"Colossally bad," Delfina said. "And I never thought I'd say this, but thank goodness my father is so angry he can't see straight."

Even Ruggero smiled at that. But they couldn't rely on the Andrettis to keep making mistakes. Even a blind man would eventually kill something, as long as he had enough bullets.

———◆———

After the family meeting broke up, Don Battista approached Ruggero. "Take a walk with me."

Ruggero couldn't help raising a brow, but he put on his coat and accompanied the old don outside into the barren garden. Dusk had fallen, and the air was crisp and cutting, making their breath into great clouds of smoke as they strolled along the path that led down to the lake. What business could the don have with him?

Don Battista said nothing for a while, not until they reached the edge of the dock. There he stopped and looked out across the lake, the insistent lapping of the water the only sound. Finally he turned to Ruggero. "We are at war. Make no mistake about it." Ruggero nodded, and waited for more. Don Battista put a gloved hand on Ruggero's shoulder. "Tonio is a good boy. I have no doubt he'll make a fine *capo* someday. But he is not ready for this war."

"He might surprise us."

"He might. But we can't rely on 'might' or 'maybe.' We need certainty." What was the old man saying? "*Sì.*"

"You will have to be prepared to step in. You will have to be prepared to make the difficult decisions."

"It's not my place."

Don Battista turned to him, his eyes hard. "You are *capo di società*. Rico offered you this job once before. That's what Caterina was referring to, yes?"

The don may have been old, but nothing got past him. "Yes."

"And you refused it because...?"

"Tonio is the better choice."

"Is he?"

Ruggero clasped his hands behind his back and looked away. "It is done. What does this matter?"

"It matters very much. You may think yourself a mere soldier. A guard. Rico's *sicario*. But you are capable of much more."

His throat tight, Ruggero said nothing. He shifted his weight, wanting to walk away, to not hear another word.

"I knew your father well; he was a good man. What happened to him was a tragedy."

The old anger welled in Ruggero's chest. "It was my fault."

"You were a boy."

Ruggero met his gaze. "I was a man. I'd taken the vows. I knew the consequences. I had a job to do, and I failed."

"We all make mistakes, every one of us."

"My father paid the price for mine. Don Lucchesi nearly did as well."

"You kept Rinaldo alive."

"I probably wouldn't be standing here otherwise."

The don squeezed his shoulder. "It is time to forgive yourself. It is time to be the man this family needs you to be."

Ruggero took a deep breath, the words on his tongue, nearly choking him. *What if I fail?* He opened his mouth, but didn't trust himself to speak.

He didn't have to. Don Battista clapped him on the back. "You are ready. Trust me. I am counting on you. When the time comes, you must act, even if Tonio or Rico will not. You may have to defy them. You must be ready to save this family."

"You mean killing Lorenzo Andretti."

"Exactly." Don Battista held his gaze. "While this trial hangs over Enrico, we must be careful, but when it no longer does..."

Ruggero nodded. Once a hitman, always a hitman. He'd known it, in his bones. Lorenzo Andretti must die. And it was Ruggero's job to ensure Andretti's demise.

---•◦•---

Milan, Italy

Judge Loredana Montisi surveyed the half-full courtroom before letting her gaze rest briefly on the defendant: Enrico Lucchesi, owner of the Banca di Falcone, upstanding businessman, and philanthropist. At least, that was the official story. Lucchesi was so much more than that. According to the reports from the Direzione Investigativa Antimafia (DIA), Enrico Lucchesi was a Mafia don, a tax evader, and the mastermind of a criminal enterprise with tentacles that stretched from Lake Como to Rome.

But most importantly, Lucchesi was the man responsible for the murders of Judge Federico Dinelli and his family.

Loredana's pulse quickened. She couldn't avenge her own father's death at the hands of Mafia assassins, but she could ensure that Dinelli and his family received justice at last.

The defendant stood before her, flanked by his lawyers, Agostino Trapani and Ulisse Adimari. Both men were sharp and shrewd. Lucchesi had chosen well. But she hadn't expected any less.

Lucchesi was finely dressed, not a hair out of place. If she hadn't known better, she'd have sworn he'd come from his home instead of the bowels of San Vittore prison. Lucchesi's very pretty and obviously pregnant wife sat behind him, ringed by assorted family and friends.

A handsome black-haired man to the right of Lucchesi's wife caught Loredana's eye. His dark gaze met hers, and the hostility she saw in it chilled her. The man looked as if he were thinking of shooting her where she sat, and the menacing scar that snaked down the left side of his face only added to his aura of danger.

Well, if Signor Sinister thought he could intimidate her, he was flat-out wrong. And if Enrico Lucchesi thought that bringing his poster boy for Mafia thugs was a good idea, he'd sorely miscalculated. Everyone knew Loredana Montisi didn't back down from a threat. It was in her blood, her heritage. The legacy she'd received from her parents—the judge who'd been killed, and the judge who'd been maimed in the same attack.

She'd see Lucchesi rot in jail if it was literally the last thing she did. No judge-killer was going free on her watch. And the sooner Lucchesi was locked up for good, the better.

Speaking of soon, where the hell was Corvi? Loredana checked the clock on the wall. They couldn't start until the prosecutor appeared, and the man was already ten minutes late. She was taking a sip of her espresso, the steaming liquid warm in her throat, when she nearly choked. What if Lucchesi's men—maybe led by Signor Sinister—had killed Corvi to derail the case? She picked up her mobile phone to call the prosecutor's office when it buzzed in her hand. A text from Corvi: *Almost there!* She exhaled in relief.

"Pubblico Ministero Corvi has been delayed and will be here momentarily," she announced and let her gaze rest on Signor Sinister, giving him just a trace of a smile. *Your boss is going to jail. And there's nothing you can do about it.*

The man held her stare and crossed his arms, making his shoulders look even broader and his biceps strain against his suit jacket. Like his boss, he was well-dressed, but many Mafiosi looked slick and respectable. Or tried. This one would never succeed. Nothing could mask the man's intensity, his sharp, predatory air. The wolf in the sheepfold, that's what he was.

The courtroom door burst open, and Pubblico Ministero Patrizio Corvi bustled up the aisle, his coat slung over one arm, an espresso in the same hand, his fine leather briefcase in the other. He placed his things down at his table and gave her a slight bow. "*Scusa*, Giudice Montisi. The metro stop nearest me was closed, and I had to run to the next one."

"I see you still had time to pick up espresso." She allowed a little amusement in her tone.

Corvi smiled. "Of course. An Italian doesn't run on tea."

Someone laughed, but Loredana tried not to. "Next time, give yourself an extra fifteen minutes. Everything else may be on Italian time, but not my courtroom."

Corvi cocked his head and gave her a sheepish nod. Most judges wouldn't have minded starting fifteen minutes late; she wasn't one of them. She'd always prided herself on her punctuality. Her mother said it was the German in their background coming out in her. Though it wasn't that at all. Loredana just disliked chaos and disorder. The more orderly things were, the better. And part of establishing order was keeping track of time. Couldn't people see that?

She took a breath and let it out. *Dio mio*, she was turning into Mussolini. "Pubblico Ministero Corvi, are you ready to start?"

Corvi rose. "The prosecution will show that the defendant should be indicted for the following crimes: murder, tax evasion, obstruction, and evidence tampering. And with your permission, Giudice Montisi, we'd like to look into the workings of the Banca di Falcone. Last night, we received a tip that the FIU is investigating possible money laundering."

Money laundering? So the Financial Intelligence Unit had finally caught up to Lucchesi. She shouldn't be surprised. "By all means, please consult with the FIU and bring back your findings."

"I'll have something by next Monday."

"*Bene.* Have you a recommendation regarding precautionary measures to be taken in this case?"

"Considering the severity of the charges and the means available to the defendant, we're recommending the defendant remain in custody for the duration of the preliminary hearing."

Lucchesi's wife gasped, and Lucchesi turned in his seat to comfort her. Tears streamed down her face, and Loredana felt a twinge of sympathy for the woman. Then again, Signora Lucchesi shouldn't have married a Mafioso. Loredana turned to Lucchesi's lawyers. "What is your response to these charges?"

Trapani stood up and smoothed a hand down the front of his black robe. "Firstly, we will show that there is no merit to these allegations. Our client is the victim of a well-orchestrated conspiracy, involving members of the *carabinieri* and a business rival. The recent investigation being undertaken by the FIU is merely a precaution; the Banca di Falcone suffered an internal attack by a rogue employee intent on besmirching Signor Lucchesi's good name and sabotaging his business."

Conspiracy? Rogue employees? At least Trapani was going to make this case entertaining. "Regarding the prosecution's recommendation of provisional custody, how do you answer?"

"Our client is a highly respected businessman with strong ties to the community; he's not a flight risk. He will voluntarily surrender his passport."

Corvi cut in. "The defendant stands accused of four counts of murder, not to mention evidence tampering. There is a high probability that he will resort to either or both again to avoid imprisonment."

Trapani addressed her. "Giudice Montisi, these allegations are unfounded. Our client is being accused of murder through the most tenuous of ties; no one has alleged that he himself committed these murders. He has an airtight alibi. Moreover, what the prosecution alleges to be 'evidence tampering' is more properly construed as blatant incompetence on the part of the *carabinieri*. The so-called 'evidence' against our client has been missing for nearly three years. Now it miraculously appears. The *carabinieri* cannot establish an unbroken chain of custody; therefore, this evidence is inadmissible. It would be inhumane to hold Signor Lucchesi in custody under such a flimsy pretext. The tax-evasion charges against our client have already been dismissed once before for lack of evidence, and this matter involving the Banca di Falcone has no bearing on the rest of the case."

Trapani did have an excellent point about the evidence. "We will address the chain of custody first thing. I share your concerns." Let that be a warning to Corvi; the prosecution had better have that matter thoroughly sorted. She wanted to indict Lucchesi, and she didn't want any future conviction to be overturned on appeal. She glanced at Corvi. "Your response?"

"Giudice Montisi, where there's smoke, there's fire. Would a truly upstanding businessman, as the defendant claims to be, have many encounters with the law? A few months ago, the defendant's wife killed her prior husband in the defendant's bedroom. Even more recently, a young man was killed at the Banca di Falcone by the defendant's godson. Clearly, the Lucchesis are violent people willing to murder to solve their problems."

Trapani looked like he'd swallowed a porcupine. "Objection! These matters have no bearing upon this case. And neither one involves any violent actions on our client's part."

"The defendant's associates and family members have a nasty habit of 'disappearing' or turning up dead. Or killing people who get in their way." Corvi sniffed loudly. "If it smells like the Mafia, it *is* the Mafia."

Trapani's face darkened, and Lucchesi slowly shook his head. "There is no proof of Mafia association; this is mere slander on the part of the prosecution." When Trapani seemed about to go on, Loredana raised her hand.

"Save it for the preliminary hearing. It would seem that there is enough merit for serious concern about the defendant's likelihood to resort to violence."

248

Trapani took a deep breath. "Giudice Montisi, have some compassion. As you can see, our client's wife is pregnant with her first child. She is American, alone in a foreign land, with only her husband for company. This hearing could stretch on for many months. You would deny her the only source of comfort she has during this difficult time?"

The twinge came back. On the other hand, if Lucchesi remained free, who knew what might happen, given his history? "I sympathize with Signora Lucchesi. However, I must sympathize with the interests of the citizens of this land more. The defendant shall remain in the custody of the state."

Corvi smiled and Trapani rubbed his forehead. He conferred with Lucchesi and Adimari for a moment, then turned back to her. "In that event, Giudice Montisi, we'd like to request an immediate trial."

Interesting. And risky. Both sides would have less time to prepare, since there would be no indictment phase, only the trial itself. "Pubblico Ministero Corvi, any objections?"

The prosecutor shook his head. "As long as I have a week to look into the matter with the FIU first."

"*Bene.*" She was about to dismiss them when Trapani spoke up.

"Giudice Montisi, we'd like to request that Signor Lucchesi be kept in solitary confinement. He is no hardened criminal, and considering his wealth and position, he is likely to be the target of others in the prison population."

And keeping Lucchesi separated from the general prison population would restrict his ability to communicate with any associates he might have behind bars. "Granted." She consulted her calendar. "We will reconvene next Monday."

Signor Sinister gave her another dark look before following his boss and the others out of the courtroom. She could barely restrain herself from smiling at him. *Enrico Lucchesi, upstanding businessman? My ass.*

END OF SPECIAL PREVIEW

Print and Ebook

www.danadelamar.com

Continue reading for a special preview of Kristine Cayne's second Deadly Vices novel

DEADLY ADDICTION

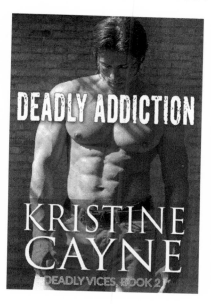

A proud people. A nation divided.

Rémi Whitedeer, police officer turned substance-abuse counselor, dreams of restoring order to his tribe. Violence and crime are rampant throughout the unpoliced Iroquois reserve, and a civil war is brewing between the Guardians, a militant traditionalist group, and other tribal factions. As the mixed-race cousin of the Guardians' leader, Rémi is caught in a no-man's land—several groups lay claim to him, but all want him to deny his white blood.

A maverick cop on an anti-drug crusade.

When she infiltrated the Vipers to take down the leader of the outlaw biker gang responsible for her brother's death, police sergeant Alyssa Morgan got her man. But her superiors think she went too far. Her disregard for protocol and her ends-justify-the-means ethics have branded her an unreliable maverick. To salvage her career, she accepts an assignment to set up a squad of native provincial officers on a reserve.

A radical sovereigntist bent on freeing a nation.

Decades of government oppression threaten the existence of the Iroquois Nation. But one man, Chaz Whitedeer, is determined to save his people no matter what the price, even if it means delving into the shadowy world of organized crime.

When Rémi and Alyssa uncover the Guardians' drug-fueled scheme to fund their fight for true autonomy—a scheme involving the Vipers—Rémi must choose between loyalty to family and tribe or his growing love for Alyssa.

Can Rémi and Alyssa leave everything behind—even their very identities—for a future together?

An excerpt from *Deadly Addiction*

Eyes closed, Alyssa pressed the glass of water to her neck. "I can do the talking if that makes you feel any better."

Although Rémi heard the words, it would have taken an act of Parliament to get him to respond.

The heat of her skin caused the condensation on the glass to liquefy. Like a tractor-beam, his gaze followed a drop of water as it slid down the long pale column of her neck, followed the curve of her right breast and slipped under the collar of her blue cotton T-shirt into the V of her cleavage. Oh fuck. He wanted to be that drop of water. He wanted to be snuggled between her warm ripe breasts. His cock swelled and lengthened, letting him know that it wanted to be there too.

He squeezed his eyes shut and willed his hard-on away. This wasn't the time and certainly not the place for Mr. Happy to make an appearance. But the more he tried not to think about where the drop had gone, the more he did. He'd thought he was a leg man, but he knew the truth now. It had slapped him in the face. He was a breast man. An "Alyssa's breasts" man, and he fucking wanted to see them, to feel them, to taste them. Right now.

Print and Ebook

www.kristinecayne.com

Made in the USA
Middletown, DE
17 September 2019